MR. KILL

Books by Martin Limón

Jade Lady Burning
Slicky Boys
Buddha's Money
The Door to Bitterness
The Wandering Ghost
G.I. Bones
Mr. Kill
The Joy Brigade
The Iron Sickle
The Ville Rat
Ping-Pong Heart

Nightmare Range

MR. KILL

MARTIN LIMÓN

SOHO
CRIME

Published by
Soho Press, Inc.
853 Broadway
New York, NY 10003

Library of Congress Cataloging-in-Publication Data

Limón, Martin, 1948–
Mr. Kill / Martin Limón.
ISBN 978-1-61695-173-3
eISBN 978-1-56947-935-3
1. United States. Army Criminal Investigation Command—Fiction.
2. Bascom, Ernie (Fictitious character)—Fiction. 3. Sueno, George
(Fictitious character)—Fiction. 4. Americans—Korea—Fiction.
5. Korea(South)—Fiction. I. Title.
PS3562.I465M7 2011
813'.54—dc22
2011024936

Printed in the United States of America

10 9 8 7 6 5 4 3 2

1

Hot metal shrieked as the Blue Train express from Pusan braked its way into the vast yard of Seoul-*yok*, the downtown Seoul Railroad Station. Someone barked an order. Two squads of khaki-clad Korean National Policemen fanned out along the cement platform, prowling like shadows through roiling clouds of vapor.

"Whoever this guy is," Ernie told me, "G.I. or not, he's about to be introduced to a whole world of butt-kick."

My name is George Sueño. I'm an investigator for the Criminal Investigation Division of the 8th United States Army in Seoul, Republic of Korea. My partner, Ernie Bascom, and I stood with our backs against brick, waiting in this overcast afternoon for the arrival of a train that, according to railroad authorities, held tragedy. The Blue Train engineer radioed ahead that a female passenger in car number three had been threatened with a knife and raped. She was found by one of the stewardesses cowering in the lavatory, too incoherent to give much information, but claiming that the perpetrator had been a *kocheingi*. A big-nose. In other words, a foreigner.

In the early seventies, what with 700,000 fire-breathing Communist soldiers on the far side of the DMZ just thirty miles north of here, there weren't many tourists in the Republic of Korea. Nor were there many European businessmen, and only a smattering of diplomats. The foreigners most likely to be using the Blue Train on this Monday morning were *Miguk*s. Americans. And those Americans were most likely to be among the 50,000 or so G.I.s who fell under the jurisdiction of the 8th United States Army. Therefore, the call had been made by the Korean National Police to us, the agents of 8th Army CID.

Exactly who this guy was, we didn't know. All we knew for sure was that the crime had been committed sometime after the Blue Train pulled out of Taejon. Between there and here, no stops. The Blue Line takes about four hours and fifty minutes, total, to travel the almost 400 kilometers from Pusan to Seoul, with only two brief layovers, the first at the East Taegu Station and the second at Taejon. At each scheduled stop, the train pauses for less than five minutes. After leaving Taejon, whoever perpetrated this crime would've had no way to get off the train. Therefore, we were assuming, as were all these Korean cops, that he was still aboard.

Lieutenant Shin, the officer in charge of the KNP detail, told me that the engineer had further explained that the victim was a young mother with two children in tow. Apparently, she'd left her son and her daughter in their seats while she used the bathroom. That's where she'd been assaulted. The rapist forced his way into the small bathroom behind her and threatened her with a knife, slicing the flesh of her throat superficially. The blood and the blade had convinced her to comply with what he demanded. Everything he demanded.

The cops in Lieutenant Shin's detail already knew that a woman with children had been assaulted by someone they assumed to be an American G.I. They weren't happy about such a non-Confucian crime being committed in broad daylight in a public place, and they allowed their anger to show when they glared at Ernie and at me, as if we were somehow responsible.

Steam puffed from the sides of the train. With a huge sigh, the big engine shut down. Usually, even before the wheels stopped rolling, people would already be hopping off metal steps, hurrying to beat the crowd filtering toward the front gate of the main station. Today, eerily, nobody moved. If I hadn't been able to make out seated silhouettes through the fog-smudged windows, I would've thought it was a train full of ghosts.

Lieutenant Shin barked more orders, and two cops took up positions at the ends of each passenger car. Other cops covered the opposite side of the train. Thus surrounded, all possibility of escape was eliminated.

Behind us, on the overhead ramparts, a crowd gathered, people waiting for other trains. Some of the civilians murmured loudly about *Miguk-nom*, base American louts. Somehow they'd gotten wind of what had happened.

Accompanied by Lieutenant Shin, Ernie and I climbed

aboard the first passenger car. The head conductor, wearing a high-collared black coat and a pillbox hat, was already waiting. He was a craggy-faced man, middle-aged, with his feet planted shoulder-width apart as if from years of pacing up and down rocking central aisles.

"She's in car three," he said in Korean. I translated for Ernie. "The children are confused," he continued. "They know something happened to their mother, something bad, but they don't know what."

"Has the perpetrator been identified?" Lieutenant Shin asked.

"No. All she told the stewardess was that he's a koche-ingi." He glanced toward Ernie and me. I nodded for him to continue. "She's in her seat, huddled with her children. So far, she refuses to move."

"Take us," Lieutenant Shin told him.

We followed the conductor down the center aisle. As we did so, row after row of Asian faces turned up to us, some of them frightened, more of them angry. I heard epithets whispered, a few familiar, a few I'd never heard before.

"Tough crowd," Ernie mumbled behind me.

As we passed from car to car, Ernie and I checked the bathrooms, just to make sure no one was hiding in them. No one was. They were small, locked from the inside, and under normal circumstances barely large enough to hold one person.

Finally we entered car three and stopped. A gaggle of grandmothers, clad in traditional Korean dresses, surrounded two of the seats. As we approached, they turned their heads and, one by one, faces soured. Wrinkled eyes evaluated me, finding me in some way disgusting, flashing disapproval—at me, and at the crime that had been perpetrated on this Blue Train from Pusan.

It wasn't me, I wanted to shout. Although I've been falsely accused before, and I know the sick feeling in the gut, I've never in my life threatened anyone with a knife—nor have I raped anyone. I stifled the urge to scream at these women: I'm a cop, not a rapist! Ernie fidgeted behind me. Americans are generally welcome in Korea. It wasn't often that we faced such hatred, but we were feeling it now—down to our bones.

Lieutenant Shin stepped forward, breaking the silence. With a rustle of silk, angry grandmothers stepped away.

The victim was a petite woman, five foot two or three, maybe just slightly over a hundred pounds. She sat huddled with her two children, the boy about four, the girl about six. She wouldn't look up. Lieutenant Shin spoke to her softly.

"Are you hurt badly?" he asked.

She didn't answer.

"Can you show me where you're cut?"

The children stared at us with wide, worried eyes. When the woman still wouldn't answer, Lieutenant Shin reached out and touched her arm. Like a startled spider, she flinched, curling herself into a tiny ball. The children clung more tightly to their mother and started to cry. That's when I saw it. Blood. On the side of her neck. The wound hadn't been completely stanched. The blood trickled slowly down the side of her small neck, staining the round collar of her dress, pooling against bone.

The grandmothers had had enough. They pushed

themselves between Lieutenant Shin and the woman, shooing him away.

He refused to back off. The authority of the elderly in a Confucian society like Korea is great, but not greater than the law. Still, the presence of two kocheingis was making his job more difficult. He motioned with his eyes for Ernie and me to continue on ahead of him toward the rear of the car. We did, passing another surly group of passengers craning their necks to see what was going on.

According to the conductor, the bathroom at the back of the car was where the crime had been committed. A nervous stewardess in a stylish blue skirt, white blouse, and matching blue cap explained in Korean that more than an hour ago she'd received complaints from other passengers that someone was in the bathroom and wouldn't come out. The stewardess investigated, pounded on the door, and finally coaxed whoever was inside to open up. She found the victim crouched on the floor, dress ripped, blood seeping from a slice on the side of her neck, covering her face with splayed fingers. The stewardess immediately reported the incident to the head conductor. Together they bandaged the wound and, after much coaxing, managed to escort the devastated woman out of the bathroom and down the aisle to her seat.

"Did you see the foreigner?" I asked the stewardess.

She shook her head.

"Did you or the conductor see an American up here in car three?"

"No. And neither did any of the passengers. They've been talking among themselves nonstop since this thing happened. Only now, because the police are here, are they quiet."

The Korean National Police are a mixed blessing. They maintain order, plenty of it. But sometimes they maintain that order at a high price, especially if you're on the receiving end of a polished wooden nightstick.

"So no one saw a foreigner in car three?" I asked.

The stewardess nodded. I explained what she'd said to Ernie. He pushed open a door, and air rushed into the car. We both studied the metal walkway leading back toward car four.

"Where are the Americans?" I asked the stewardess. At the RTO, 8th Army's Rail Transportation Office, tickets are issued free to G.I.s on official travel and sold at a discounted rate to those on leave or pass or other forms of unofficial travel. Eighth Army's policy is to try, whenever possible, to keep all the Americans in the same passenger car.

The stewardess showed us with her eyes, glancing back at car four.

Lieutenant Shin approached. While the stewardess went over the same ground with him, I crouched and studied the interior of the bathroom. There wasn't much to be seen. A little splashed water. A low toilet—porcelain embedded in the floor, Korean style, made for squatting; a small sink; and an unraveled roll of paper.

In the center aisle, men in blue smocks were trundling toward us. Stenciled on their chests, in white block hangul letters, was the word *Kyongchal.* Police. Keeping his voice low so the female victim couldn't hear, Lieutenant Shin briefed them. These were the technicians who would be searching the bathroom for traces of blood or semen or hair. I was impressed. So was Ernie. In the Itaewon bar district, loaded with business girls who catered to American G.I.s, rape wasn't taken nearly as seriously. As the technicians placed their gear on the floor and squatted down to get to work, one of them said in Korean, "First the mother of our country, and now this."

Lieutenant Shin stationed a young cop near the bathroom to make sure that no one interfered with the crime scene or with the technicians.

What we did next was what Ernie had been aching to do since we arrived at Seoul Station, ever since we'd been subjected to the hatred in the eyes of the masses of Koreans surrounding us: he reached in his pocket and pulled out a shining set of brass knuckles. Slipping them over his fingers, he clenched his fist, enjoying the fit and heft of the finely crafted metal. Satisfied, he nodded. Lieutenant Shin took the lead. Together, we entered car four.

Autumn had fallen quickly in Korea. This was not unusual in itself—seasons change rapidly on the Korean peninsula—but it had also fallen early. Gray clouds appeared, and gloomy winds started to blow. A week and a half ago, August 15, it had been the twenty-ninth anniversary of Korea's liberation from the occupying forces of the Japanese Imperial Army. The Japanese had taken over the country in 1910, stripping the Korean monarchy and the Korean legislature of any real power, and ruled the entire peninsula as a colony until 1945.

To mark this all-important day, Pak Chung-hee, the former army colonel and current authoritarian president of South Korea, had given a speech to a packed hall.

Unfortunately, a Japanese national, believed to be in the employ of North Korea, smuggled a gun into the hall and took a few potshots at the president. Pak Chung-hee crouched behind his heavily fortified podium and was not harmed. His security guards, however, pulled their own weapons and returned fire, and for a few mad seconds hot lead zinged all over the auditorium. One of the bullets struck the head of Yuk Young-soo, the wife of the president, who'd been sitting on the stage only a few feet from her husband. She was rushed to the hospital but declared dead on arrival.

Like most first ladies around the world, Yuk Young-soo was popular, much more popular than her husband. The death of such a vital woman, the mother of three young children, shocked the country, sending it into mourning. Only hours after she died, the blue skies of summer disappeared with the onset of autumn.

Does a country have a mood? Maybe. Maybe not. We only read our own moods into what we see around us. But if countries do have moods, the mood of the Republic of Korea was surly right now. Surly to the point of tipping over into rage.

As we entered car four, rows of passengers gaped at us. They were mostly Koreans, but there were a few American faces scattered among them. While Lieutenant Shin and the ranking sergeant in his detail asked for identification and briefly interviewed the Korean nationals, Ernie and I studied the Americans. The faces were confused and concerned, but nobody bolted for the door.

I pulled out my badge and held it up.

"Good morning, everyone. I'm Agent Sueño. This is Agent Bascom. We're going to be asking you some questions. First, I'd like everyone to pull out their identification and their travel orders."

"What if you don't have travel orders?" one of the G.I.s asked.

"Then your leave orders will have to do," Ernie replied.

Every American G.I. had to be able to prove that he had permission to be away from his compound. If he didn't, we'd report him to his unit and nonjudicial punishment could ensue. This was punishment short of court-martial, like restriction to the barracks or forfeiture of pay for less than thirty days.

While Ernie stayed inside the car, I took the American passengers outside onto the platform, one by one, and interviewed them. I wrote down their names, units of assignment, serial numbers, and the issuing headquarters of their temporary duty instructions. G.I.s don't travel much in Korea, unless they're under what we call TDY— temporary duty—orders. There were a total of seven G.I.s in car number four. One was a courier carrying a packet of classified documents. Another was on his way home on emergency leave orders; apparently he had a child back home who was gravely ill. Four of the G.I.s were Signal Corps technicians on their way to do some repair work at the 42nd Long Lines Battalion at Camp Coiner. The last G.I. was an officer under orders to report to 8th Army headquarters for a SOFA Conference, a joint ROK-US Status of Forces Agreement confab.

Nobody was on unauthorized travel. Nobody was absent without leave. At least, that's the way it seemed so far. The paperwork they showed me could have been forged. It was even possible that their ID cards were phony. Unlikely, but possible. Later today, Ernie and I would be checking out the validity of their stories, but for the moment I was taking what they told me at face value.

When everyone had been interviewed, Ernie and I compared notes with Lieutenant Shin. He had the passenger manifest, which had been radioed up from Pusan and Taegu and Taejon and then painstakingly transcribed by hand by the head clerk in the Seoul Station dispatch office. The manifest didn't have names, but all assigned seats were indicated, along with an annotation indicating where the passenger boarded the train: Pusan, Taegu, or Taejon. The manifest also indicated those tickets purchased by 8th Army RTO. About 80 percent of the seats were filled when the train left the Pusan Station. Pusan is a bustling international port and the second largest city in the country. Seoul is not only the capital of the country but also the largest city by far—with a population of eight million—and the home of most of the country's industrial production. As such, the majority of the passengers on the Pusan-to-Seoul Blue Train travel the entire route. Still, at Taegu twenty-two people disembarked and forty boarded. At Taejon less than a dozen disembarked and about thirty boarded the Blue Train to Seoul. At that point, every seat on the train was occupied but five.

Lieutenant Shin made another announcement, asking everyone to continue to remain in their seats, apologizing for the delay, and telling them that they would soon be released. With the conductor at our side, we walked up and down the length of the train, making sure that every seat that was supposed to be occupied was in fact occupied. They were—all but one. It was in car number four, in the back row.

Next to the empty seat a G.I. slouched, bored with the delay. I'd already interviewed him, and he'd assured me that he'd seen nothing unusual, no Americans wandering forward from car four to car three. He was a private first class, wearing a wrinkled khaki uniform, holding a big leather pouch on his lap. The courier. The nameplate pinned to his shirt pocket said Runnels. I checked my notes again to make sure I had the spelling right. His eyes popped open and he looked up at us.

"You're delaying my delivery," he told me. "This pouch is supposed to be at 8th Army J-2 by fourteen hundred hours."

"You still have time," Ernie told him.

The guy checked his watch, snorted, and gazed out the window.

"Who was sitting next to you?" I asked.

The courier turned his head and gazed down into the seat next to him as if seeing it for the first time. "Here?" he asked.

"You see any other seats next to you?" Ernie asked. He was toying now with the brass knuckles hidden in his coat pocket, aching, I knew, to pop this guy a good one. We waited.

Private First Class Runnels shrugged. "Some guy," he said finally.

"An American?"

"Yeah. Wearing civvies. He told me he was on in-country leave."

"Did he say why?"

"No, he didn't. I guess he just wanted to see Seoul."

"Where was he stationed?"

"How should I know?"

"You didn't ask?"

"What do you think I am? A bargirl?" In a singsong voice, Runnels said, "Where you *stationed*, G.I.?"

Lieutenant Shin's face tightened. I positioned my body between the two men.

"So, what did you talk about?" I asked.

"Nothing. He wanted to be quiet, and so did I."

Keeping my temper in check, I coaxed PFC Runnels into providing a detailed description of this man who had been sitting next to him. About six feet tall, dark brown hair cut short, blue jeans, sneakers, a thick pullover black sweater. Was he carrying a traveling bag? Runnels hadn't noticed. He had noticed where he'd boarded the train: in Pusan, just as Runnels had.

Then Ernie placed his hands on the armrests on either side of Private First Class Runnels and leaned in close to him, so close that Runnels winced at Ernie's breath.

"Okay, Runnels," Ernie said. "Time for the little-boy act to stop."

"What do you mean?"

"You know what I mean."

Runnels was squirming now. Ernie's green eyes shone from behind his round-lensed glasses, and his nose was pointed as if he were a woodpecker about to poke

Runnels's eyes out. These were the moments Ernie lived for. The moments when he turned the tables on criminals.

"Where is this guy?" Ernie sneered. "This invisible guy who boarded the train at the same time you did, who was supposedly going all the way to Seoul. Where is he now?"

"How in the hell should I know?"

Like a hawk swooping up toward the sky, Ernie's right hand flashed across Runnels's face. The sound of the slap filled the silent train. Everyone turned. Ernie leaned in even closer to Runnels.

"A woman has been raped, Private Runnels," Ernie told him. "A decent woman who is the mother of two children. Two children who were sitting only a few feet from her when she was assaulted. I don't give a shit about what your feelings are about MPs or law enforcement, but you're not getting off this train, at least not in one piece, until you start telling me and my partner what we want to know. You *got* that?"

Runnels held his palm at the side of his face, his mouth open in shock. "You can't *do* that," he said.

"Can't do what?"

"You can't hit me."

Ernie slapped him again.

Runnels squirmed back in his seat, leaning toward the window, trying to get as far away from Ernie as he could. Maybe it was the look on Ernie's face. Maybe it was the disapproval that flowed in waves from the passengers all around. Whatever the reason, Runnels started talking. His words came in a rush. He told us everything he knew about the silent man who had taken the seat next to him.

"The guy was complaining about the army," he said. "You know, the usual screw-the-army stuff. But then he said he was going to even the score."

"How?" Ernie asked.

"He didn't tell me. All he said was that there were a bunch of things, and people, who had to be taught a lesson. And when he rose from his seat, he glanced back at me and said something funny."

"What was that?"

"He said he was going to start now."

"Why was that funny?"

"Because he also said this would be the first check mark on a long list of what he called 'corrective actions.'"

"'Corrective actions?' You mean like after an inspection?"

"That's what the guy said."

"What's it mean?"

"How the hell should I know?"

This time, Ernie didn't slap him.

Lieutenant Shin ordered everyone off the train. Grumpily, the passengers grabbed their bags and coats and made their way onto the platform. When the technicians had completed their work and everything was done that could be done, Lieutenant Shin talked to the conductor. In a few seconds, the big train was building up steam, and we hopped off and watched it roll slowly away. We made our way back to the huge domed entrance of Seoul Station.

Inside, much to our surprise, a crowd was waiting for us behind the long metal railing. People hooted, shouting epithets. Lieutenant Shin ordered his men to pull their batons. Forming a V with Ernie and me at the center, we started to carve our way through the crowd of angry faces.

That's when we saw her, sitting in a wheelchair, surrounded by medical personnel and the same group of old women who'd been with her on the train. The victim. By now, Lieutenant Shin had told me that her name was Oh Myong-ja. As we approached, she stood shakily up from her chair. The old women patted her shoulders and tried to persuade her to sit back down. She took a tentative step toward us. The angry crowd grew quiet. We walked up to them. In Korean, Mrs. Oh Myong-ja started to speak.

"You should go home," she said.

I just stood there, wondering what she meant.

"Back to your country," she continued. "Back to America. We don't need you here any more."

The crowd was strangely silent. And then the woman's daughter was standing next to her, and then the son; and the small triumvirate put their arms around one another protectively, and all three stared at me until tears started to flow from their eyes.

I wanted to say something, I'm not sure what, but I was sure it was important that I say something at that time. Very important. Instead, I said nothing.

Finally, I felt Ernie's hand on my elbow. He told me later that as we made our way out of the station, people threw bits of wadded newspaper at us and even a couple of empty juice cans. The KNPs batted them away with their riot batons. In addition to cursing, a few people in the crowd started to chant, "Yankee go home!"

I remember none of this. What I do remember is Mrs. Oh Myong-ja, white gauze taped to her throat, knees shaking, hands clutching her children, black eyes burning with defiance. And I remember the smooth cheeks of her children's faces and the tears that flowed down them. And the fear that showed in their eyes as they clutched one another.

2

At CID headquarters, before we had a chance to take off our jackets, Staff Sergeant Riley was already complaining.

"Where in the hell you guys been? The Provost Marshal has been asking about you all afternoon."

Riley is the Administrative NCO of the 8th Army CID Detachment. His highly starched khaki uniform puffed out around him like cardboard on a scarecrow. He doesn't eat much, but he's a tireless worker and he has a habit of taking the side—in every dispute—of the honchos of the 8th United States Army, which goes a long way to explain why the Provost Marshal loves him.

Ernie ignored Riley's harangue and walked toward the big silver coffee urn on the counter in the back of the admin office. Miss Kim, the statuesque admin secretary, pecked away at her hangul typewriter. I plopped down in a gray army-issue chair.

"A woman was raped," I told Riley, "on the Blue Train, with her children sitting only a few feet away."

Riley studied me carefully. "That's why you look like somebody just placed a size-twelve combat boot up your butt."

I didn't answer. Instead, I rubbed my forehead and then the back of my neck.

Miss Kim stopped typing. Out of a plastic container, she poured some of her personal stock of barley tea into a porcelain cup. She brought it over and offered it to me. I accepted the cup with both hands and thanked her. She returned to her desk. The typing started again, more tentatively this time.

While I sipped the lukewarm tea, Riley's gruff voice grated on my molars. "She was a Korean national, wasn't she?" he asked.

"Who?"

"The victim on the Blue Train."

I nodded. "Yeah. Definitely a Korean national."

"Then why the hell did you spend all that time out there? It's a KNP case."

I sat up straighter in my seat. "We have reason to believe," I told him, "that the perpetrator was one of our brave American men in uniform."

"Did you arrest him?"

"No. He was gone before we got there."

"So how can you be sure he was an American?"

"The G.I. sitting next to him said he was."

"Was this perp wearing civvies?"

"Yeah."

"So it's just this G.I.'s opinion that the suspect was an American."

I knew what he was getting at. If 8th Army could pretend that a suspect wasn't an American G.I., they'd do it. Any way to avoid bad publicity was worth a try.

"Most of these cases," Riley continued, "nobody can pin shit on us."

Riley was correct. Rape is a hideously difficult charge to prove, especially when most of the Korean women American G.I.s hang out with are "business girls," women forced into prostitution because of economic deprivation. Still, I started to say something, but Riley waved me off and then he tossed a sheet of paper in front of me. I grabbed it on the fly.

"From the head shed," Riley said. "Chief of Staff, Eighth United States Army. The Provost Marshal wants you two on this. Immediately if not sooner. Looks like we've got the USO show from hell."

"No time," I said, tossing the paperwork back onto his desk. "We have to go to Anyang."

"Anyang? What for?"

"This rapist. That's where we think he got off the train."

Ernie shouted from the back of the room, "Where's the coffee, Riley?" He was holding up an empty tin can.

"My ration ran out," Riley yelled back.

"Your *ration* ran out? How much you been black-marketing, anyway? Can't you at least buy the coffee *before* you use your monthly ration buying stuff for your *yobo*?"

"It wasn't for my yobo," Riley replied. Riley had a thing for older women, and some of the Korean gals he hung around with were verging on the geriatric.

Ernie returned with an empty mug and clunked it down on the edge of Riley's desk. "So, if it wasn't for a yobo, what have you been using all your ration on?"

"Information," Riley said. "I've been trading coffee to get information to help jerks like you."

"Jerks like me," Ernie replied, "don't need to trade coffee for information. We get it the old-fashioned way." Ernie reached into his pocket, slipped on his brass knuckles, and jabbed a short uppercut into the air.

"Okay, Bascom," Riley said. "I'm impressed. Now convince your partner here to read that report I just handed to him. You two better get it in gear before the Provost Marshal develops a case of the big ass and takes a bite out of your respective butts."

I grabbed the report again and, after reading a few sentences, I began to understand why it had received such a high priority. It involved round-eyes. A whole bevy of them. A USO-sponsored all-female band known as the Country Western All Stars, lovely ladies who'd flown over from the States to grace us lonely 8th Army G.I.s with their presence. The United Service Organization had been around since at least World War II. Bob Hope made it famous with his star-studded appearances on battlefields all over the world, and the organization, in numerous smaller venues, was still going strong. When it comes to an all-female country-western show and review—direct from Austin, Texas—the brass can't do enough for them, and every broken fingernail shows up on the Chief of Staff's morning blotter report.

According to the band's leader, someone had been pilfering their equipment. At Camp Kitty Hawk, a microphone went missing. At the Joint Security Area, one of the girls' boots. Near Munsan, at Recreation Center Four, they thought they'd lost an electric guitar but found it behind a Quonset hut. Apparently, whoever lifted the instrument had dumped it after realizing that he wouldn't be able to make a clean getaway.

I handed the report to Ernie. He groaned.

"Babysitting," he said.

"Babysitting, my ass," Riley replied. He pointed at the report. "If you'd read the damn thing you'd see that this detail is going to involve a lot more than babysitting. There's not only been theft of equipment but also threats made against the command. If you don't get a handle on this case fast, you're going to be up kimchee creek without a paddle."

"Threats?" I asked.

"This band leader," Riley said, "one female civilian known as Marnie Orville, has declared that if she isn't assigned a full-time detective, and assigned one today, she's going to refuse to go on."

"She won't perform?"

"You got it. So Eighth Army isn't taking any chances. They're assigning two investigators to the case. Namely, Agent George Sueño and Agent Ernie Bascom."

"When's their next appearance?" I asked.

"Tonight. Nineteen hundred hours. At the DivArty O Club."

The Officers' Club of the 2nd Infantry Division Artillery headquarters, at Camp Stanley in Uijongbu.

"The Provost Marshal wants you there," Riley continued. "Standing tall and kissing some serious round-eyed butt."

I tossed the report on Riley's desk.

Ernie wandered over toward Miss Kim, who kept her eyes glued to a sheaf of paperwork and increased her typing speed to a furious rate. Ernie stood in front of her for a few seconds. They'd dated once. Until, that is, Miss Kim discovered that Ernie was involved with other romances. Ernie couldn't understand why she'd taken it so hard. When Miss Kim still didn't look up, Ernie finally shrugged and walked back across the room.

As I rose from my seat, I told Riley not to worry. We'd take care of this USO show situation.

"You'd better," he growled.

Outside, Ernie started up the jeep. He shouted over the roar of the engine, "We should go to the hotel this band's staying at. Interview them about the missing equipment. Let them know that someone's on the case."

"We should," I replied.

We were both thinking of the woman on the Blue Train, Mrs. Oh Myong-ja, and her crying children. And we were thinking of the hatred radiating out of the eyes of the people surrounding her. But mostly we were thinking of what Private First Class Runnels, the courier on the Blue Train, had told us after he'd finally opened up. In particular, we both remembered his remark about "the first check mark on a long list."

Ernie drove to Gate 5. After we were waved through the MP checkpoint, he turned left on the main supply route. Ernie plowed his way through the mid-afternoon Seoul traffic until we reached the turnoff to the Seoul-to-Pusan

Expressway. A frisson of fear entered my gut. Misappropriating a vehicle, purposely defying a superior officer's orders—these were not things to be taken lightly.

"What the hell are you doing?" I asked.

"What do you *think* I'm doing?" he replied. "That guy has to be stopped, whether Eighth Army likes it or not."

Ernie made the turn and stepped on the gas.

I didn't have any counterargument. Ernie was right. Any "checklist" that starts with a brutal rape can't be good. The little jeep rolled south. Twenty-five kilometers later, a sign with an arrow pointing off to the right said Anyang.

Compared to Seoul, Anyang is a small city. A population of about 10,000, according to my 1973 almanac. After winding our way through a few buildings over three stories tall, we reached the eastern side of the city and finally found the Anyang Train Station.

I flashed my badge to the official in charge of the station; he called the local KNPs; and in a few minutes I was being introduced to Captain Ryu, the chief of the Korean National Police, Anyang contingent. In the late afternoon sunlight, he and Ernie and I walked out onto the tracks. Captain Ryu pointed at the main rail.

"This is the track used by the Blue Train," he said. "But earlier today, for the first time in years, the Blue Train was ordered off onto that side rail." He pointed to another track on the west. I translated for Ernie. "They stopped there," Ryu continued, "for about twenty minutes." Then Ryu walked us back to the main line. "Coming from Seoul," he said, "heading south, was the special train carrying the body of our late First Lady, Madame Yuk Young-soo. It was beautiful. The entire front of the engine was covered with a wreath of white flowers. Some of my officers and I stood on the platform there and saluted." Then he pointed back to the side rail. "Most of the passengers, the ones who ventured outside when the Blue Train stopped, bowed as the First Lady's train approached." Captain Ryu stood quietly for a moment. Then he repeated, "It was a beautiful sight."

Koreans love death. It gives them a chance to practice every Confucian virtue: reverence, obedience, filial piety, loyalty. The greatest moments in Korean lives are when they travel to the grave mounds of their dearly departed, sweep away debris, burn incense, bow, and then have a picnic with the family, including ritual types of food set aside for the deceased. I can't tell you how many times Koreans have shown me photographs of themselves with their parents and their children and other family members, enjoying one another's company, sitting on the grass eating rice cakes while the death mound of their grandfather looms in the background.

When Captain Ryu recovered from his reverie, he escorted us to the Anyang Police Station. There he showed us a stack of reports from the cab drivers who had been working this morning when the First Lady's train passed. "Not one of them," he said, "picked up a foreigner."

That wasn't surprising. There were no American military bases near Anyang. If our theory was correct and the rapist, whoever he was, had taken advantage of the unscheduled stop in Anyang to make his escape, then the first thing he would've needed was transportation out of town. He couldn't stay here. A foreigner would be easy to spot. Already, Captain Ryu had checked the one tourist hotel in town and the three or four dozen Korean inns. No foreigners in any of them. We studied Captain Ryu's map of Anyang.

"Here," Ernie said. "Only a little more than a mile from the train station."

What Ernie was pointing at was the Myong Jin Bus Station.

Within a few minutes we were sitting in the back room of the ticketing office. A nervous young Korean woman, only slightly portly, twisted a white handkerchief in her lap. In hangul, her nameplate said Ju. I asked her to relax, but it didn't do much good. Then, in Korean, I asked her if she remembered selling a bus ticket to a foreigner.

"Yes," she said. "It was about eleven thirty A.M. because I hadn't yet eaten my *toshirak*." She was referring to the square metal tin most Koreans use to carry their lunch. Then Miss Ju blushed, probably embarrassed about how she remembered things in relation to food. I encouraged her to continue.

"He was a foreigner. The only one I've seen all day."

"What did he look like?" I asked.

"I don't know. I didn't see his face."

The ticketing window was made of opaque plastic with only a few holes in the middle to speak through and a horizontal slot on the counter through which to slide money.

"If you didn't see him," I asked, "how can you be sure that he was a foreigner?"

"Because of the way he spoke. The way he mispronounced Seoul."

Americans say the name of the Korean capital city as if it were one syllable, like the English word "soul." Koreans pronounce it the way it is written, with two syllables: "So-*ul*."

"That's it?" I said. "The way he talked?"

Miss Ju twisted her handkerchief even tighter, blushed a brighter shade of crimson, and said, "And his hands too."

"What about his hands?"

"So hairy," she said, crinkling her nose, "like a *won-sungi*." Like a monkey.

Then she stared at me, her eyes wide, as if she had realized her mistake, and bowed her head, twisting her handkerchief more ferociously than ever.

Ernie and I sat in a draft beer hall across the street from the Anyang Police Station.

"Seoul," Ernie said. "We'll never find him there. He'll just blend in with the crowd."

"Maybe," I said.

Captain Ryu had contacted the head of the Myong Jin Bus Line and they were attempting to locate the driver of the bus that had left Anyang at approximately 11:45 this morning, heading for Seoul. While they did so, Ernie and I decided to get some chow. What we ended up with was beer and unshelled peanuts.

Captain Ryu came over a few minutes later and told us that he'd managed to reach the bus driver by phone. He remembered the foreigner on his bus but was unable to describe him other than that he was tall and American. Where he had gotten off the bus in Seoul, the driver didn't remember, even though there were only two possible choices. The first stop was in front of the Hamilton Hotel in Itaewon in the southern reaches of the city, and the second and final stop was at the Central Bus Station in downtown Seoul, both of which were bustling locations frequented by thousands of people every day. Trying to trace a lone G.I. getting off a bus at either one of those spots would be impossible.

We thanked Captain Ryu for his help, paid for our beer, and left.

"Where the hell you guys been?" the MP said.

We were stopped in front of the big arched gate at the main entrance to DivArty headquarters, Camp Stanley. Ernie'd made good time through Seoul, skirting the downtown area by taking the road along the Han River, past Walker Hill. Still, the sun had set by the time we arrived. Floodlights glared out of the darkness. The MP leaned forward, his M-16 rifle held across his chest.

"You're the CID agents from Seoul, aren't you?"

I nodded.

"We've been expecting you for hours. And now this shit happens at the club."

"What shit?" Ernie asked.

"You'll see."

The MP motioned to his partner, and the rusted wheels of the twelve-foot-high chain-link fence began to roll open. A whistle shrilled, Ernie shoved the jeep in gear, and we drove slowly into the compound.

Camp Stanley was the home of the 2nd Division Artillery headquarters, more commonly known as DivArty. Two of the division's artillery battalions were stationed at this camp, the other in a forward position closer to the Demilitarized Zone. When Ernie parked the jeep behind the two-story edifice that was the DivArty Officers' Club, we could hear a steady pounding, like rhythmic thunder.

"What's that?" Ernie asked.

"Hell if I know."

In the long hallway leading into the main ballroom, black-and-white chain-of-command photos hung on whitewashed walls. Crew-cut men wearing pressed green uniforms glared out at the world. I stopped at the last photo, the photo of the colonel who was the current DivArty commander. There wasn't much to it: pale skin, vapid eyes, thin lips, short gray hair. Even his wire-rimmed glasses were almost invisible. Still, he was doing his best to look terrifying.

Ernie and I entered the ballroom.

A small man, hands on his hips, wheeled on us. I recognized the face, the same one I'd just been looking at in the chain-of-command photo. Instead of a green uniform, he was wearing a straw hat, an embroidered cowboy shirt, and tight blue jeans held up by a long-horned brass belt buckle.

"Where in the hell have you two been?" Spittle erupted from his tight lips.

The thunder surrounded us now, rattling the walls of the huge ballroom. Benches were filled with row after row of G.I.s in fatigue uniforms, some of them wearing cowboy hats similar to their commander's. Most of them held cold cans of beer in their hands. It was their combat boots that were causing the thunder. They were stomping them on the wooden floor, in a cadence that threatened to shake the building apart.

The thin-lipped commander approached me.

"She refuses to go on," he said, pointing at the stage. "That obstinate woman is willing to let my troops sit here cooling their heels, and she won't make a move to do her duty until the 'detectives from Seoul,' as she calls them, show up. And I'm assuming you're the detectives from Seoul."

It hadn't required great powers of deduction to figure out who we were. Ernie and I are required to wear civilian clothes while we work. That way no one will know our military rank and, theoretically, we can't be bullied by someone of higher position. But according to the 8th Army Supplement to the Department of the Army regulation, we're not allowed to wear just *any* civilian clothes: we're required to wear coats and ties. This is 1974. *No one* wears coats and ties, not unless he's forced to. With our short haircuts, Ernie and I are like blinking advertisements: "Here comes the Criminal Investigation Division."

"Yes, sir. We're the detectives from Seoul."

"Then get up there," he said, pointing once again at the stage, "and get that woman and her band off their butts and out there entertaining my troops."

I nodded to the colonel, and Ernie and I made our way past the thundering crowd, climbed up a short flight of steps, and pushed through musty velvet curtains. A naked bulb shone at the end of a short hallway. Ernie passed me and stepped first through the open doorway.

Five women looked up at us. All of them blondes. Each woman wore tight blue jeans and a tighter red-and-white-checked blouse. Straw cowboy hats had been pinned expertly to the back of their elaborate coiffures.

One of them pushed back her Stetson. "You don't look like much," she said.

"Kinda scrawny," another added, "but you'll have to do." They broke into raucous laughter.

After making us swear that we wouldn't leave before the show ended, Marnie Orville led her Country Western All Stars out on stage. One of them strapped on a guitar, and two more took up positions behind an electric bass and a steel guitar, respectively. Finally, a woman with straight long blonde hair sat behind the drum set. Marnie, the tallest and most voluptuous of the five women, fiddled with the keyboard, glanced at her fellow musicians, and nodded to the Korean man standing next to hemp ropes on pulleys. As he pulled back the curtains, spotlights were switched on out front and Marnie stomped her boot. Electric amps hummed and the band clanged to life, belting out some country tune that I'd never heard before.

The G.I.s in the audience leaped to their feet, roaring their approval. Ernie covered his ears. He stepped toward me and shouted in my ear.

"Why'd you promise all that to her?" he asked.

"I was being coerced. I had to get them out on stage," I shouted back.

"Now we're her slaves."

I shrugged. "Weren't we anyway?"

He crossed his arms and frowned at the five women gyrating before us. "Hayseed heaven," he said.

"You stay here," I told Ernie, "keep an eye on the girls and their equipment."

"What do you think I'm doing?" Ernie asked.

I worked my way backstage and then out behind the Officers' Club, where the van and the equipment truck were parked. Four Korean men—two drivers and two men to load and unload the equipment—squatted between the vehicles, smoking and murmuring among themselves. A flood lamp illuminated the scene. As I approached, they stopped smoking and stared at me above glowing embers.

"*Anyonghaseiyo*," I said. Are you at peace?

The men nodded, bemused by my use of the Korean language. As I continued using their native tongue, their eyes grew wider and then they were smiling. In a few minutes, we were old pals. The eldest driver and leader of the group was named Mr. Shin. He offered me a cigarette, which I politely refused, and then he started telling me about their adventures of the last few days, driving five white women from their hotel in Seoul to the nether regions near the heavily armed Demilitarized Zone that divides North and South Korea.

I listened, not asking any questions, taking it in.

Inside the Camp Stanley Officers' Club, guitars continued to clang, women shouted, men roared.

A half hour later, the music subsided and Ernie and I joined the band in their dressing room. I pulled out my notebook, sat on a stool, and started to ask them about the complaints they had alerted us to. Before we could finish, their break was up and they returned to the stage. G.I.s were already clapping their hands and stomping their feet again. When the curtain opened, the audience, on cue, went mad.

Ernie stayed backstage while I returned to Mr. Shin and the loading crew. After the final set, Ernie emerged from the back of the Camp Stanley Officers' Club. He pulled me aside.

"They want me to take them to a nightclub," he told me.

"Who?"

"Marnie and the other girls."

"We're calling her Marnie now? Not Miss Orville?"

Ernie ignored the remark.

"What about the time?" I asked. We had only an hour and a half until the midnight curfew, equipment to inventory and load, and a long ride back to Seoul.

"They're counting on me," Ernie said, "to work something out."

"We could get in trouble behind this," I said.

Ernie grinned. "Trouble I can handle. Especially when it's packed in tight blue jeans."

3

By the next morning, Staff Sergeant Riley had already collected much of the information I'd asked him to collect concerning the Blue Train rapist. He shoved the printouts across his desk. I sipped on my coffee and started going over them.

"Where's Ernie?" he asked.

"Last night," I replied, "he worked late on a case."

"What case?"

"The case you said the Provost Marshal was so hot on. Theft from the Country Western All Stars."

Riley squinted suspiciously. "Ernie has a lead?"

I ignored him and continued to shuffle through the paperwork.

Staff Sergeant Riley is a paper-pusher. Nothing more. Still, he likes to pretend that he's giving orders when he's only relaying them, and he pokes his nose into every case that interests him, which is most of them. Ernie and I tolerate him because he has extensive contacts throughout the 8th Army headquarters complex and he often saves us a lot of legwork.

Yesterday, before we'd left the office, I'd asked Riley to contact the American military units that are located near the route of the Blue Train. Specifically, Camp Ames in Taejon, Camps Henry and Walker in Taegu, and Hialeah Compound in Pusan. What I wanted was a list of who was on temporary duty to Seoul, who was on emergency leave, who was absent without leave, and who was on regular in-country leave. Once I had that, maybe I could start to narrow down the identity of the mystery man who'd hopped off the Blue Train in Anyang.

"You're not looking too well," Riley told me.

"I'm not feeling too well either."

"What in the hell did you two guys do last night?"

While I continued to peruse the list of names, I told him. As I spoke, Miss Kim stopped her typing.

The five women of the Country Western All Star Review were Marnie, Kristie, Prudence, Shelly, and the bass player, whose name I couldn't recall at the time. During the breaks in the show, Ernie had shown them his Criminal Investigation badge and his .45, and for some reason they took a liking to him. Maybe it wasn't so much his personality as the fact that they felt adrift in a sea of G.I.s who were fawning all over them and an ocean of Koreans they couldn't understand. Ernie listened to their problems. There were many, the pilfering of a microphone and a cowboy boot and an electric guitar being the least of them.

They complained about the food they had to eat in the hotel. They'd asked the waiter for something lighter than the greasy American breakfast that was served, and what they received instead was roast mackerel, white rice, and a bowl of clam bouillon.

"For *breakfast*," Marnie said, crinkling her nose. Marnie Orville was the voluptuous one. The one who sang most of the numbers, the one who owned the equipment, and the one who had arranged the USO tour.

The other girls chimed in, complaining about the food and how they couldn't eat the kimchee; although they realized it was made of fresh vegetables and it was good for you, but they couldn't tolerate the garlic smell on their breath.

"The boys in the front row," Marnie said, "would have to move back twenty feet."

I doubted that a hand grenade would've made the boys in the front row move back twenty feet, but Ernie let her talk. She was lonely, as were all the girls. It might seem strange, considering the rabid attention they were getting from stagestruck G.I.s, but once their show was over and they'd been driven back to their hotel, there was nothing for them to do but sleep and get up and then get ready for another show.

It was a half hour before midnight by the time we reached the Grand Hotel in Uijongbu. We could've made it back to Seoul before curfew, barely, but the Grand Hotel had a nightclub in the basement and the girls of the Country Western All Star Review couldn't wait to see what a Korean nightclub looked like. Ernie'd been there before, and he led us down carpeted steps. The joint was plush, with an orchestra of middle-aged men, a lead singer in a white dinner jacket, and three or four beautiful Korean women belting out old favorites for the mostly older crowd that sat at round tables covered in white linen.

Ernie talked our way past having to pay the cover charge, claiming that the Country Western All Star Review was in Korea on some sort of cultural exchange and therefore deserved diplomatic immunity. He never sold it, but the tuxedoed manager finally tired of arguing with him and let us in. A few minutes later, between numbers, Ernie spoke to the Korean MC, who studied our table and then nodded enthusiastically. After sipping one round of drinks, the women of the Country Western All Star Review were coaxed up on stage, and soon they were singing and dancing to some old country standards that the orchestra knew. The Korean audience clapped along, delighted.

I'd already told Mr. Shin and his crew to return to the hotel in Seoul. Marnie was worried about the safety of the equipment, but I knew better than to impugn Shin's integrity. The only problem was that once midnight came and went, we were trapped in the basement of the Uijongbu Grand Hotel until the nationwide curfew ended at four in the morning. Out on the streets, the only things that moved were military patrols with orders to shoot to kill. Still, we were cozy down there, with everything our hearts could desire.

Until about two-thirty in the morning, everything went great. Korean men kept sending bottles of locally made Oscar champagne to our table, and the American ladies danced as often as they wanted to. But by the time three in the morning rolled around, everyone was exhausted. Heads started drooping to the white linen tablecloths, and some people even spread out on the leather booths in the back. I was one of them. I'd tried not to drink too much. Ernie, however, had let himself go. He drank not only two liters of OB beer, along with plenty of glasses of Oscar, but also a straight shot or two of Suntory whiskey. Not that I was counting.

Just before four A.M., I persuaded one of the waiters to bring me a steaming hot cup of coffee. MJB instant, but it did the trick. I shook everyone awake and loaded four of the women into Ernie's jeep. That left Ernie and Marnie without a ride, so I hailed a Korean cab driver and arranged for him to transport Ernie and Marnie back to the Crown Hotel in Seoul at double the meter reading— the standard rate, since he had to leave his prescribed area of operations. The cabbie made better time than I did, and when we finally arrived at the Crown Hotel on the outskirts of Itaewon, the ladies of the Country Western All Star Review, exhausted but pleased, each gave me a hug and a kiss goodnight. Ernie, apparently, had already retired upstairs with Marnie.

He was a big boy and could take care of himself. I restarted the jeep and drove back to 8th Army compound.

"That asshole," Riley told me when I finished the story. "Always dipping it where he shouldn't."

I glanced at Miss Kim. Her face was red and she was typing furiously on her hangul typewriter. When she realized I was looking at her, she stood abruptly, snatched a tissue from a box, and marched out of the admin office, heading down the hallway toward the ladies' latrine.

"What'd they tell you about the missing equipment?" Riley asked, apparently not noticing Miss Kim's discomfort.

"They think it's a pattern," I told him. "Something goes missing after almost every performance, almost like somebody hunting souvenirs. And they believe they're being watched."

"Being watched?" Riley scoffed. "Of *course* they're being watched. Five good-looking round-eyed women. What did they expect?"

"They didn't expect Peeping Toms. Faces flash in front of windows, according to them, and then disappear."

Riley shrugged. "Just G.I.s having a little fun."

In my notebook, I made a list. From Hialeah Compound in Pusan, no one was AWOL and three G.I.s were in-country leave. I wrote down their names. At Taegu, things became more complicated. Camp Henry is a larger base than Hialeah and has a lot of Signal Corps and aviation activity. As such, I had a dozen G.I.s who'd left Taegu and were temporarily assigned to the Long Lines Signal Battalion in Seoul. Camp Ames in Taejon is tiny, and I had a minuscule report. No one AWOL, no one on temporary duty, and only one guy on in-country leave. He had a Korean name and a very specific leave address in Seoul—31 bon-ji, 15 ho, Mugyo-dong—which meant that he was visiting family and therefore he was Korean-American, what's known in 8th Army as a "Kimchee G.I." I scratched him off my list.

The guys on temporary duty traveled in groups, doing repair or installation work on Signal Corps or aviation equipment. The likelihood that one of them would commit a rape, slip off the train in Anyang, and then not be reported AWOL was slim to none. I didn't scratch them off my list, but relegated them to the lowest priority. That meant that I would start by investigating the three guys from Hialeah Compound who were on in-country leave.

Riley logged me in for an AUTOVON call. After getting through to the 8th Army operator, I read her the authorization number and within minutes was patched through to someone named Specialist Holder, the company clerk at Headquarters and Headquarters Company, Hialeah Compound in Pusan. I identified myself, and Holder seemed impressed that the CID from Seoul would be calling all the way down to their sleepy little unit. I read the list of names to him.

"All on in-country leave," he told me. "What happened? Somebody get into some shit?"

I didn't answer but just asked him to tell me about the three men.

He knew all of them. Personally. One of the men was black, so I scratched him off my list. The other two were odd birds, according to Specialist Holder.

"In what way?" I asked.

"Both of them turned down mid-tour leave," he replied. "Didn't want to go back to the States."

I'd turned down mid-tour leave myself, but I didn't tell Holder that. Turning down your mid-tour is like admitting that you have nothing to go back to in the States. As an orphan most of my life, I fit that category, but that was nobody's business but my own. I asked, as casually as I could, "So, where are they now?"

"Weyworth is probably shacked up with his yobo, in her hooch right outside the main gate. They have their marriage paperwork in."

The process of an American G.I. marrying a Korean woman involves piles of paperwork—both on the ROK side and the US side—and usually takes six to eight months. Still, having his paperwork in didn't preclude Weyworth from taking a trip on the Blue Train.

"Do you have his address?"

"No. But it's easy to find. Down one of the alleys behind the Kit Kat Club."

"How about the other guy?"

"Pruchert? He's stranger still. No telling where he is."

"What's strange about him?"

"He likes to go to all those Buddhist temples and stuff. He's even studying the language, training himself to be some sort of monk."

"Do you have an address for him?"

"No way. He put down 'Pusan' on his leave orders, but he could be anywhere."

Holder gave me more particulars on both Weyworth and Pruchert, including when they were expected to report back to their units. Both of them had plenty of leave built up and wouldn't be returning to duty for two weeks in one case and three in the other.

Ernie still hadn't made his appearance at the CID office, so I went to the snack bar and drank more hot coffee and filled my complaining stomach with a bacon, lettuce, and tomato sandwich. I kept thinking of the frightened look on the face of Mrs. Oh when I'd first seen her cowering next to her children on the Blue Train. The cruelty that people can inflict on one another is unfathomable to me. I finished my sandwich and returned to the big silver urn on the serving line to refill my cup. I sat back down and thumbed listlessly through today's edition of the *Pacific Stars and Stripes*. International news, comics, sports, but nothing on crime. They have a policy against it. Crime in Korea involving American servicemen isn't reported unless it's something big and has already hit the Stateside wire services. There wasn't a word about the Blue Train rapist, not that I'd expected any.

On the way back to the office, I stopped in front of the PX and bought a red rose wrapped in green paper. When I reentered the CID admin office, I kept it hidden under my coat.

Ernie had arrived. Sergeant Riley was trying to cheer him up.

"You look like dog shit," Riley told him.

"Get bent," Ernie replied.

"Sueño," Riley barked as I hung up my coat, keeping the rose hidden. "The Provost Marshal wants to talk to you. Now. Along with this wasted wreck of a human being."

Too tired to lift his palm from his lap, Ernie flipped Riley a low bird.

Miss Kim wasn't at her desk; probably trying to avoid seeing Ernie.

Ernie struggled to his feet, straightened his tie and his jacket, and marched down the hallway toward the Provost Marshal's office. I held back for a second and, when Riley wasn't looking, I stuck the red rose in the celadon vase that sat on the front edge of Miss Kim's desk. It was a vase that had been empty for weeks.

"A brouhaha at the Seoul Train Station," the Provost Marshal reminded us. "The KNPs had to provide an armed escort just to get you two out of there."

"The crowd was surly, sir," Ernie replied. "A woman with children had been raped by an American. They weren't happy about it."

"An American?" The Provost Marshal raised one eyebrow.

Colonel Brace was an intelligent man, a decent man, but he was also—to his core—a military man. And a loyal one. That meant that as a full-fledged member of the 8th Army bureaucracy, he threw himself heart and soul into protecting that bureaucracy. Colonel Brace repeated the same line Staff Sergeant Riley had spouted earlier. We had no proof that the perpetrator had been an American; and even if he *had* been an American, that didn't necessarily mean he fell under our jurisdiction. He might be a civilian with no affiliation to the 8th United States Army.

The odds of the perpetrator not being an 8th Army G.I. were real but prohibitively small, especially since Private Runnels, the courier who'd sat next to the suspect on the Blue Train, had been convinced that the man was an American soldier, convinced by everything about him: his haircut, his demeanor, the language he used, even the civilian clothes he wore. They looked like they'd been purchased out of the PX, according to Runnels. Still, as long as there was a shred of doubt, Colonel Brace would continue to pretend, at least publicly, that the rape of Mrs. Oh Myong-ja in the latrine of car number three of the Pusan-to-Seoul Blue Train was not 8th Army's problem.

Instead of responding to the colonel's argument, I said, "I have some leads, sir. Movements that we have not yet accounted for coming out of Hialeah Compound. Request permission to travel down there to continue the investigation."

Colonel Brace reached across his desk and grabbed a pipe from a mahogany stand. Thoughtfully, he opened the top drawer of his desk, pulled out a pouch of tobacco, and took his time filling the pipe, patting it down, lighting it, and blowing a puff of blue smoke into the air. All the while, Ernie and I were standing at parade rest in front of his desk. The colonel was disappointed in me, of this I was sure. He had hoped that I'd take his very broad hint and just keep my mouth shut and wait for him to tell us how—or whether—to proceed on the case. Asking for permission not only to continue the investigation but to take specific action put him on the spot. If the case ever blew up in our faces and there was an after-action investigation, I would be able to say truthfully that I had requested permission to continue the search for a suspect. Colonel Brace would be in the awkward position of saying he'd specifically turned down that request.

This was part of the reason Ernie Bascom and I were not popular in the hallowed hallways of the 8th Army Criminal Investigation Division. We pursued cases, regardless of whether the honchos of 8th Army were embarrassed by that pursuit or not. Other CID agents played the bureaucratic game. They trod softly. They investigated only when and where they were told to investigate, like dumb hounds on a very short leash.

Colonel Brace knew as well as we did that the Blue Train rapist was a G.I. If he attacked again, and his US affiliation were proven, 8th Army would be blamed for not doing enough to stop him. But if he *never* attacked again—which is what Colonel Brace was counting on—and we continued the investigation, that would be tantamount to admitting publicly that the rapist was a G.I.—and, more importantly, besmirching 8th Army's reputation for no good reason. Besmirching 8th Army's reputation is something that would be frowned on by the 8th Army Chief of Staff, criticized at the 8th Army Officers' Club, something that would reflect poorly on Colonel Brace's efficiency report. If Colonel Brace ever wanted to pin the silver star of a general on his shoulder, he needed nothing but top-notch efficiency reports.

Colonel Brace snuffed out his wooden match and tossed it in an amber-colored ashtray.

"We'll hold off for now," he said. "You have enough to do with that theft investigation of the USO show."

"There was no theft, sir," Ernie told him. "The microphone that went missing was found two days later in one of the musicians' traveling bags. The cowboy boot was probably just left behind when they packed in a hurry to beat the midnight curfew back to Seoul. And, as has already been reported, the electric guitar was recovered."

Colonel Brace stared at Ernie. "Has the band retracted their complaint?"

"No," Ernie replied. "They're convinced they're being targeted."

"Targeted? By who?"

"By G.I.s peeking through the windows of their dressing rooms."

Colonel Brace pulled his pipe out of his mouth and shook his head. "Put a stop to that, will you? And until this band retracts their complaints, you stay with them." He thought about that for a second and then added, "And even if they *do* retract their complaints, stay with them anyway. I don't want any problems coming down from the Stateside headquarters of the USO."

"And the rapist?" I asked.

Colonel Brace lowered his pipe and stared at me steadily. "Like I said, Sergeant Sueño, you are to take no further action on that case. For the moment, it falls under Korean jurisdiction, not ours. Understood?"

"Understood," I replied.

We resumed the position of attention, saluted, and left.

In the admin office, Miss Kim was smiling, not looking at us but smiling nevertheless. The green paper had been unwound from the stem of the rose and water poured into the vase. Someone had delicately fluffed out the red petals. Maybe it had been a mistake to present the rose to her secretly. Apparently Miss Kim thought *Ernie* had given it to her. Ernie, for his part, didn't even notice the rose.

"During the day," Riley told us, "the Provost Marshal wants you working on the black-market detail. At night, you escort the USO show."

"When are we supposed to get any rest?" I asked.

"A soldier is on duty," Riley said, "twenty-four hours a day."

Something I'd heard since the first day I enlisted in the US Army. But only some of us were on duty twenty-four hours a day. Others seemed to be on duty hardly at all.

Ernie and I drove along a tree-lined lane to the headquarters of the Long Lines Signal Battalion North at Camp Coiner. It was less than a mile from 8th Army headquarters, on the way to Huam-dong, adjacent to the north gate of Yongsan Compound, across the street from the ROK Marine Corps headquarters.

I showed Major Rumgarde, the XO of the battalion, the list of names of the men sent to him on TDY from Camp Henry in Taegu. The names didn't mean much to him, but he conferred with his Operations NCO and came back after a few minutes to tell us that all twelve of them were working on a signal upgrade at the communications relay site atop Namsan Mountain.

We thanked him, asked him not to warn them we were coming, and hopped into the jeep.

Namsan literally means South Mountain. Its elevation is almost 900 feet at its highest point, and it is covered in lush green vegetation for most of the year. It sits just south and slightly east of the downtown area of Seoul. The city spreads out around it, some buildings running up its sides, but the main expanse of the mountain is reserved for parks and rock-paved pathways, gurgling creeks and tree-covered meadows, where the denizens of Seoul can find at least temporary refuge from the madness of the city.

Perched atop the peak is a hundred-foot antenna, surrounded by squat green Quonset huts. The United States Army, once again, marking its territory.

"I've never been up here," Ernie said, as we wound our way up the narrow road through Namsan Park. Occasionally we spotted young women, usually walking alone.

"Hookers," Ernie said.

"Nah," I said, surprised. "They're not hookers. They look so wholesome."

"That's part of the come-on."

"You're not serious?"

Ernie nodded. "I'm serious."

"Why would they be out here?"

"Rich Koreans cruise by, sometimes Japanese businessmen in their limousines. They pull over, talk to the girls, make an arrangement."

I turned in the passenger seat to take a good look at Ernie. His green eyes were glued to the road, arms reaching out straight to the steering wheel. "How do you know all this?"

He sighed. "Here. I'll show you."

With a squeal of brakes, Ernie pulled toward the side of the road. A young woman about ten yards ahead stopped walking and turned to look at us. Ernie rolled up to her slowly until I was staring out the open door of the jeep directly into her eyes.

"*Anyonghaseiyo?*" I said. Are you at peace?

"*Nei*," she replied with a bow. Yes.

She was a cute girl; round face, plump figure, wearing a demure brown skirt and a tight blue blouse. Despite the overcast gray above, she held a plastic multicolored parasol atop her head to shield her from ultraviolet rays. I continued to smile stupidly, not wanting to say anything, not wanting to corrupt her if she didn't want to be corrupted. She studied us both quizzically, rolling the handle of the parasol deftly in soft fingers. Finally, she recalled some long-ago-studied English and said, "We go?"

"*Odi*?" I replied. Where?

She pointed back down the road. "*Chogi. Yoguan isso.*" There. To an inn.

Ernie grinned at her broadly. I turned and glared at him. He was much too happy with his victory. I turned back to the girl and said in Korean, "I'm sorry. We don't have time now. We have to go to the compound on the top of the mountain."

The girl seemed disappointed but nodded, understanding the requirements of work and duty. There was a hardness to her features now that I hadn't noticed before. I said good-bye and she watched us as Ernie pulled back onto the road.

The peak of South Mountain was a flat, leveled-off area. After we flashed our identification, a khaki-clad Korean gate guard with an M-1 rifle slung over his shoulder shoved the big chain-link gate open just far enough for us to drive through. We rolled onto a dirt-covered parade field. To our left, about a hundred yards away, sat a long rectangular building with a sign that said "Namsan Mess" and, beneath that, the Korean word "*Siktang.*" Literally, food hall. In the center of the open field loomed the antenna, painted red and white, rising a hundred feet into the sky. Atop it, a red light blinked. On the opposite side of the quadrangle, beyond the antenna, sat a matrix of linked Quonset huts with a sign over the main entrance that said "Namsan Relay Site, Long Lines Battalion North."

Ernie parked next to a short line of military vehicles.

Inside, a sergeant in a neatly pressed fatigue uniform waited. Apparently, he'd already been informed of our arrival.

"Can I see your badges?" he asked.

We showed him.

"Captain Fieldjoy isn't in. He's on a supply run down in Seoul. Is there something I can help you with?"

I jotted down his name. Sergeant Ernsworth. He was a little old for a buck sergeant, maybe in his mid-thirties, and he sported a flaming red crew cut and a splash of freckles across a pug nose.

Ernie wandered over to a wall plastered with black-and-white photos of officers in uniform, shaking hands and presenting one another with plaques and awards. I showed Sergeant Ernsworth the list of names. "A dozen guys," I said, "up here from Taegu. Working on some sort of communications upgrade."

"What about 'em?"

"I want to talk to them."

"What if they're busy?"

"They'll get un-busy. At least for as long as it takes to ask them a few questions."

Ernsworth thought about it; after a few seconds, he shrugged. "Follow me."

He opened a low door for us and then led us down a long corridor, turned right, and at a new Quonset hut turned left. We entered an air-conditioned room with rows of impressive-looking equipment, like stainless-steel refrigerators embedded with the occasional blinking green light.

"All of this stuff is classified," Ernsworth said. "Don't be jotting down any nomenclatures or model numbers."

"That's not why we're here," I replied.

Finally, we reached an open area with canvas tarps spread on the floor. Toolboxes were scattered in disarray and men huddled in groups behind metal panels, peering into copper-and-rubber-wired innards that sparked and blinked and beeped. Ernsworth waited until one man who was reaching deep into a pit of complicated machinery retracted his hand and looked up at us.

"They want to talk to you and your team," Ernsworth told him. Then he swiveled on his heels and left. The man who stood to face me was a sergeant first class, balding slightly at the front of his short-cropped gray hair, holding a rubber-handled screwdriver loosely in long fingers. His mouth hung open.

Ernie and I flashed our badges.

"Just routine," I said. "We want to ask you a few questions."

I pulled out my notebook and started to ask.

On the way back down the mountain, I gazed out the side of the jeep at the magnificence of the city of Seoul. Maybe I was trying to avoid staring at the innocent-looking hookers who appeared every quarter mile or so. Maybe I was thinking about Mrs. Oh on the Blue Train and the crazed look in her eyes as her children glanced back and forth between the adults who surrounded them, wondering what had gone so terribly wrong. The city lay like a pulsating god, spread-eagled across the countryside, stretching from Tobong Mountain rising high above the mist in the north to the sinuous blue of the Han River in the fog-shrouded south. I loved this city. I wasn't sure why. It was so far from my original home, the people were so different from anyone I'd known growing up, but I'd adopted the city now. Had it adopted me? I didn't think so. The city of Seoul would always turn its back on me. I'd always be an outsider. I'd always be the stranger who, oddly, spoke a little of their sacred language. My love of the city and my love of Korea, I felt certain, would never be returned.

Ernie rounded a corner and honked at two girls walking arm in arm by the side of the road. After overcoming their shock, they both waved gaily.

"What'd you think?" Ernie asked me.

"About what?"

He turned to study me. "You okay?"

"Yeah. I'm okay."

"So what'd you think about what those Signal Corps twerps had to say?"

"I think they're telling the truth. They took the Blue Train from Taegu to Seoul two days before Mrs. Oh was raped."

"Who?"

"Mrs. Oh. The woman who was raped on the Blue Train."

"Oh, yeah."

"And everybody on their team has been present for duty every day. There's no way one of them was on that train."

"So scratch them off your list."

"Already done."

"So, now what?"

"We could work on the black-market detail like Riley told us to."

"Get serious."

Ernie hated working the black-market detail. The job consisted of lurking outside the Yongsan Compound commissary and waiting for a Korean dependent wife to come outside with a load of black-market items—Tang, instant coffee, soluble creamer, imported bananas, frozen oxtail—and follow her to the ville and bust her when she sold the duty-free goods to a black-market mama-san. A crummy job. A job that was supposedly designed to protect Korean industries from having to compete with cheap, imported tax-free American goods, but a job that was really designed to keep as many Korean yobos out of the commissary and PX as possible.

Ernie hated the black-market detail, and so did I.

"Where to, then?" Ernie asked.

"Colonel Brace said the Blue Train rapist was a Korean problem," I replied. Ernie nodded. I continued, "I agree with him. So let's go have a talk with the Koreans."

"The KNP Liaison Office?"

"The same."

When we hit the bottom of Namsan, Ernie stepped on the gas and wound his way expertly through the mid-morning Seoul traffic.

"Are you sure you want to do this?" Ernie asked. "The Provost Marshal's going to be pissed."

"Do you know any other way of finding the guy who raped that woman?"

"Maybe the KNPs will find him."

"Like hell," I said.

"Yeah," Ernie agreed. "Like hell."

The Korean police didn't have access to US Army military compounds. They wouldn't have a chance of finding him.

When we rolled up to the front gate of Yongsan Compound, an MP was waiting for us.

"You Sueño?"

After I nodded, he turned to Ernie. "You Bascom?"

"Right."

"Better get your butts out to the Crown Hotel. Like now."

"What happened?" Ernie asked.

"Something about a USO show and a bunch of hysterical round-eyes."

"Anybody hurt?"

"Hell if I know. Go find out."

The MP stood away from the jeep. Ernie performed a neat U, floored the gas pedal, and screeched off into the Seoul traffic.

4

The Crown Hotel is on the main supply route, just a half mile west of the G.I. red-light district known as Itaewon. Probably Marnie Orville and the rest of the girls of the Country Western All Stars didn't know how close to the center of action they actually were, and they wouldn't know unless somebody showed them. So far, there hadn't been time. A blue Hyundai sedan of the Korean National Police sat in front of the hotel, warning light flashing.

Ernie squealed up to the front door, turned off the engine, and we both jumped out of the jeep, showing our badges to the two young cops guarding the front door.

"Odi?" I asked. Where?

He told me the third floor.

We ran past milling hotel staff and ran up the carpeted

stairway three steps at a time. In the long hallway, a half dozen doors were open. Marnie Orville stood in front of one of them, screaming at a Korean policeman. Ernie rushed toward her, holding up both his hands.

"Marnie," he said. "We're here. What's going on?"

She swiveled on him, her blonde hair in sleep-ruffled disarray, blue eyes blazing with anger. With one hand she held a bathrobe closed over her full-figured body. With her other hand she kept pointing at the confused cop.

"This son of a biscuit keeps claiming that he doesn't understand English."

"Marnie," I said, "he probably doesn't. You're not in Austin anymore. Tell us what happened."

She took a deep breath, stopped pointing, and used the extra hand to tighten her robe. "Prudence, you okay?" she asked.

"I'm fine, Marnie."

The other woman crossed the hallway and they embraced.

Now all the women were in the hallway, in various states of undress, and the lone Korean cop seemed overwhelmed by the sheer volume of Caucasian femininity. I showed him my badge and told him that we'd take the report. He nodded enthusiastically, scurried down the hallway, and disappeared into the stairwell.

Marnie spoke first.

"I saw him standing right there." She pointed at the vase on a table that stood next to the door to Prudence's room. As she did so, her robe swung open, revealing magnificently curved white flesh. She grabbed the flap and retightened it. "He was kneeling, as if he was looking through the keyhole. But he was doing more than that. He was fiddling with the door handle in some way."

"In what way?" Ernie asked.

"As if he had some sort of tool in his hand," Marnie said. "Although I couldn't see it."

"You were looking through the peephole of your door?" I asked.

"Yes. I thought I'd heard something, like maybe a room-service cart or something, but I knew nobody had ordered anything because we were all planning on going to breakfast together."

"What did the guy look like?" Ernie asked.

"I only saw his back."

We continued to question her, about whether he'd been American or Korean, how tall he was, what type of clothing he was wearing, but all Marnie knew was that the clothing was dark and his hair was dark and when she screamed he must've taken off because when she built up the courage to look back outside, he was gone.

The Korean staff was not any more helpful. Reluctantly, the manager admitted that there'd been quite a bit of thievery lately, but such a brazen attempt at burglary was something they rarely saw. The KNPs were less tentative. The Crown Hotel, and all the lodging establishments in the Itaewon area, were meccas for thieves. American women, who were assumed to be rich, would be a tempting target.

On one thing all the staff agreed: even from down here in the lobby, they easily heard Marnie Orville's scream.

"She has a fine set of lungs," Ernie said.

Finally, the women of the Country Western All Stars calmed down. They made pledges to one another never to set foot outside their rooms unless they called one another to meet in the hallway. They also made us promise to be back as early as we could and ride with them to tonight's show. Marnie swore that she was going to contact the USO and make them move the group to a different hotel.

"One with better security," she said.

The Korean National Police Liaison Office was located on the main Yongsan Compound, not far from the 8th Army MP station. Separating the two was a circular lawn with flagstone walkways that led like spokes in a wheel to a venerable old oak tree that, it was said, had been growing on these grounds since the days of the Chosun Dynasty. Even the Japanese Imperial Army, when they'd established this headquarters some time after 1910, had never bothered the tree. Occasionally, atop the gnarled roots, I spotted gifts: knotted garlands of flowers or polished stones or elaborately crafted creatures made of colored paper, probably left by Korean workers as a wish for a loved one to get well or for good luck.

I pulled a penny out of my pocket and tossed it toward the tree.

"What the hell's that for?" Ernie asked.

"Fortune and prosperity."

"You playing poker tonight?"

"No. I'm hoping the Blue Train rapist doesn't strike again."

Ernie studied me as we walked toward the big double doors of the KNP Liaison Office. "If the rapist doesn't strike," Ernie said, "Colonel Brace is going to look pretty smart. And you're going to look pretty stupid."

"Okay by me." As long as I didn't have to look at any more confused and frightened children and violated women, I'd be happy.

As we entered the Liaison Office, a blue-uniformed police officer rose from behind a desk. He was a young Korean, and his face was sternly set.

"Lieutenant Pong," I said to him.

He asked me in Korean if I had an appointment. I told him no but it was about the Blue Train investigation. This made the young man squint and, if possible, stare at us even more sternly than he had before. He left his desk and walked down a squeaking wooden hallway. A few seconds later, he returned and told us Lieutenant Pong was waiting.

Lieutenant Pong sat behind a large desk, studying stacks of pulp fastened with brass studs. Draped attractively from a varnished pole was the white silk flag of the Republic of Korea with the red-and-blue yin–and-yang symbol in the middle. We'd worked with Lieutenant Pong before. He was a tall man, slender, and he wore round-lensed glasses and kept his black hair combed straight back on the sides. His khaki uniform was pressed so neatly that if you rubbed your thumb against one of the creases, you'd slice your skin.

"Where have you been?" he said in English.

I shrugged. "Assigned to other cases."

"Other cases?" Lieutenant Pong was flabbergasted. To him and to the other officers of the Korean National Police, no case could rate a higher priority than the rape of a virtuous woman on a public conveyance by a big-nosed foreigner. Murder, embezzlement, burglary—among Koreans, those things were routine; but when national pride was at stake, those other things could wait.

Ernie sat on one of the upholstered chairs and draped his right leg over the armrest. Gazing unconcernedly around the room, he pulled a toothpick out of his shirt pocket and used it to pry into the gaps between his teeth.

I ignored him. So did Lieutenant Pong. Pong showed me a folder containing various reports in hangul, in language too difficult for me to comprehend, but I did manage to make out that these were the forensic reports from car number three.

"Nothing more than we already knew," Lieutenant Pong told me. "Strands of hair cut short. Rich brown in color but too curly to belong to a Korean."

"Any blood samples?"

"Yes. Blood type B. Matching Mrs. Oh." Lieutenant Pong glanced sourly at Ernie. For his part, Ernie seemed totally preoccupied. He kept prying the toothpick deeper into his molars, studying the photograph on the wall of President Pak Chung-hee and, beneath that, the elegant bronze replica of the Maitreya Buddha perched on a polished pedestal.

"Anything more?"

"We did find another blood type. A-positive. Rare among Koreans."

I jotted that down in my notebook. In basic training, when a G.I. is issued his first set of dog tags, imprinted on them are his name, his service number, his religion, and his blood type. Although we couldn't be certain that this sample had been left by the rapist, an A-positive blood type would be a clue that might provide another link to a suspect, once we found one.

"So the perpetrator was cut in some way," I said, "or maybe scratched?"

"Neither, that we can be sure of. The blood type was obtained from other material."

I realized what he meant. Not blood: semen.

This was difficult for Lieutenant Pong to talk about. Despite the fact that Pong was an experienced cop, there are certain things that Koreans have trouble talking about in a formal setting, sex being one of them, poverty another. They're particularly leery of talking about such intimate subjects with a foreigner. It has to do with their 3,000-year history and their highly developed sense of national pride. By talking to an American about how Mrs. Oh had been subjected to so many indignities by this foreigner, in Lieutenant Pong's mind, all Koreans were losing face. Ernie's nonchalant attitude wasn't making it any easier. That's why I pointedly didn't bring Ernie into the conversation.

"There must've been plenty of hair and fingerprint evidence in that bathroom," I said. It was, after all, a public bathroom. "So this might help us narrow our search, but it won't do much in helping us win a conviction."

Lieutenant Pong agreed. "We'll have to rely on other evidence for that."

Now that the difficult part was over, Lieutenant Pong pulled a sheet of paper out of a folder and slid it across his desk. It was a drawing of a face.

"From Mrs. Oh?" I asked.

"Yes. It was very difficult for her to try to remember the

face of the rapist—she had her eyes closed during most of the assault—but she did her best."

Ernie slid his leg off the edge of the chair and leaned toward the drawing. He stared at it in astonishment and then barked a laugh. He continued to laugh, holding his stomach, and finally said, "You've got to be kidding me."

Lieutenant Pong's face flushed red, but he said nothing.

The drawing showed a man with devilish upturned eyes, thick eyebrows, a heavy five-o'clock shadow of a beard, and a nose so huge it was almost as big as a banana. In other words, the extreme caricature of a Westerner through Korean eyes.

Ernie held the drawing up to the light and studied it again. "This doesn't look like anybody I know," he said.

"She was frightened," Lieutenant Pong replied.

"I'll say. I would be too if something like this came at me."

"Okay, Ernie," I said. "We get the point." I took the drawing from him and slid it back to Lieutenant Pong. "I think it would be better if we didn't use this."

Lieutenant Pong shoved the drawing back into his desk. The echo of Ernie's laughter subsided and Lieutenant Pong composed himself. He straightened his shoulders and said, "Now, how about you? What have you come up with?"

I glanced away. "Not much." He stared at me quizzically. "I've eliminated a few suspects," I continued, "and identified a couple more I want to talk to."

"When will you talk to them?"

Ernie snorted. We both looked at him, and then I turned to Lieutenant Pong and said, "Maybe never. Eighth

Army is not admitting that the rapist was a G.I. They're saying this is a KNP problem."

Lieutenant Pong stared at me for a long time, as if he were having trouble deciphering my words. Ernie spoke up. "The honchos have screwed us again. They're not letting us go to Pusan to investigate."

Once again Lieutenant Pong was flabbergasted. Finally, he managed to say, "Why?"

"Because they don't want to admit," Ernie said, "that a G.I. would rape a Korean woman on a train." He splayed his fingers and spread his hands out to the side. "That's it. We're out of it. It's up to you to catch this guy."

Ernie rose to leave.

I rose with him. "I'm sorry," I said.

As we left, Lieutenant Pong remained sitting, staring after us.

Ernie and I spent the rest of the day in his jeep, parked in the back row of the lot outside the Yongsan commissary, pretending to be interested in busting someone for black-marketing. Actually what we did was buy Styrofoam cups of PX coffee from the snack stand, return to the jeep, and shoot the breeze about Marnie and the girls of the Country Western All Stars.

"You didn't take long getting into her blue jeans," I said.

Ernie shrugged. "She didn't take long getting out of them."

I sipped my black coffee. It was bitter but strong, and so hot that I could barely hold on to the cup. Women walked into the commissary and women walked out of the commissary, most of them Korean, a few of them American. Middle-aged Korean men in gray smocks pushed huge carts overflowing with groceries for them, loaded the goods into the trunks of black Ford Granada PX taxis, and then bowed as they accepted a gratuity—usually a buck—for their services. I let the silence grow until Ernie spoke.

"She wants something from me."

I swiveled my head to look at him. "Not money?"

He laughed. "You've been here too long. No, not money. She wants information."

I waited. The coffee wasn't quite as hot anymore, but it was still just as bitter.

"She wants me to find somebody for her. A G.I.—an officer, actually. One Captain Frederick Raymond Embry."

"Never heard of him."

"Neither have I. She says she met him when he was an ROTC cadet at Texas A&M. They started dating, only casually, and then she got busy with her band and they drifted apart. But later he came to visit her after he received his commission."

"Where was all this at?"

"At the time, she'd moved to Austin, Texas. Freddy Ray, as she calls him, apparently looked real attractive to her, wearing his uniform with his shiny new butter bars, and that's when it happened."

"What happened?"

"She got pregnant."

"Did she have the kid?"

"Of course. She's a good Southern girl. Goes to church every Sunday."

"So, where's the kid now?"

"Staying with Marnie's mother."

"And she wants you to find this Freddy Ray?"

"You got it."

I sipped my coffee again. "Are you going to do it?"

"He owes her child support."

Maybe, maybe not, I thought. There are ways for state agencies to apply through the Department of the Army to collect back child support directly from a soldier's pay.

"Why doesn't she use the usual channels?" I asked.

"She has. Hasn't worked. Maybe Freddy Ray has some influence with the Finance Officer."

I didn't believe it. When a mandated allotment is slapped on a soldier's pay, as far as I knew, there was no way around it. Still, Ernie seemed to be buying the story.

"So, what are you going to do?"

"Find him," he said. "Can't hurt."

"How does she know he's stationed over here?"

"Mutual acquaintances."

"Does she know what unit?"

"No idea."

"You shouldn't be doing this," I said.

"I know."

"Think about it."

Ernie tossed his empty Styrofoam cup out the jeep's window. "I just did."

"What'd you decide?"

"Screw her."

"That's what you've been doing."

"And I'll do it some more, unless she decides she doesn't like it when I tell her she can find her old boyfriend on her own."

The cannon sounded in the distance for Close of Duty Day. Metal speakers at the edge of the parking lot belted out a scratchy version of the bugle call for retreat.

"Damn," Ernie said.

We both clambered out of the jeep, stood at attention facing the main post flagpole, and saluted. I always felt like an ass doing this. So did Ernie. Normally we'd be indoors at this time of day so we didn't have to go through the ritual of standing at attention and saluting a flag being lowered somewhere off in the unseen distance. But today, what with all that was happening, we hadn't paid attention to the time.

When we returned to the CID office, Miss Kim had already gone home, but Riley was waiting for us. Frowning.

"The Provost Marshal wants to see you," he said.

"You've been talking to the KNP Liaison Officer," Colonel Brace told us. "And don't try to deny it."

"We just wanted to keep him updated on the case," I said.

"I ordered you off it."

"Yes, sir."

"So now that you told this Lieutenant Pong that 8th Army has decided not to exercise jurisdiction, he ran it up the flagpole, and somebody in the ROK government decided they didn't agree. So now the word comes down from the Chief of Staff that they want you, both of you, tomorrow morning at zero eight hundred hours to report to the SOFA meeting at the J-1 building."

Colonel Brace rubbed his eyes, as if he were extremely

tired. "When will you two guys learn to keep your mouths shut?"

We didn't answer.

"Do you know where the J-1 building is?" he asked.

I nodded my head. "Yes, sir. We know."

SOFA stands for the Status of Forces Agreement, the treaty between the US and the Republic of Korea concerning the legal standing of American forces stationed on the Korean peninsula. Whenever there's a dispute that needs to be resolved or a serious crime that comes to their attention, the SOFA Committee holds a meeting and the Korean and American representatives try to hash out a resolution. Apparently they'd been apprised of the Blue Train rape case, and now they'd also been apprised that 8th Army wasn't going to investigate. Ernie and I, by spilling the beans to Lieutenant Pong, had stirred up some serious bureaucratic waste. Not that we hadn't expected to.

Colonel Brace studied us. "When you appear before them," he said, "you answer their questions truthfully. Is that understood?"

"Yes, sir."

"But you only answer the questions they ask. You don't volunteer information. Is that understood?"

"Yes, sir," we said again.

He stared at us for a long time, seemed about to speak, but finally shook his head and then waved his hand dismissively. "Get out of here. Both of you. Out!"

We saluted, performed a neat about-face, and marched out of his office.

* * *

Marnie was all over Ernie in the van, one arm draped around his shoulders, the other hand toying with the buttons of his shirt. Shelly, the lead guitar player, slapped Marnie's hand away.

"Behave yourself," she said.

Marnie pouted, frowned, and then turned back to Ernie, cooing, "You don't mind, do you?"

Ernie ignored her. "What compound was that again, where you're playing tonight?"

Shelly, sitting stiffly and continually glancing at Marnie, checked the itinerary. "Someplace called Camp Colbern," she told us.

"That dump?" Ernie turned to me. "We should've brought the jeep, so we could get out of there early."

"You want to leave me?" Marnie asked.

Ernie shoved her hand away. For the rest of the drive, she sat alone, pouting like a little girl.

After thirty minutes of winding roads, the van finally rolled through the main gate of Camp Colbern. The narrow road between Quonset huts was lined with G.I.s, smiling, waving, blowing kisses. The van's engine churned as we climbed a short hill and came to a halt in the alley behind the Camp Colbern Enlisted Club.

Once we stopped, Mr. Shin and the other driver and their two assistants began unloading the equipment. We hustled the girls through the back door of the club. After a hallway lined with latrines, we entered a ballroom lit by dim yellow lights, with seating that would hold about a hundred people. The wall-to-wall carpet was tattered and spongy and reeked of mildew. Near the stage, beneath yellow floodlights, a reception committee waited. The post commander introduced himself, and he and his staff started fawning over the girls. Within minutes, Marnie had them rearranging the seating and running errands; soon she had appropriated the club manager's office as the band's official dressing room. MPs stationed at the front door kept the rank-and-file G.I.s at bay. The Korean staff—bartenders, cocktail waitresses, and cooks—stood back respectfully, awed by the celebrities from America who had dropped into their midst.

Everything seemed to be under control. The girls were in their dressing room getting ready. Ernie and I wandered out the back door and, after asking for directions, we found the PX snack bar. We both grabbed aluminum trays and slid along the metal railing in front of the steam table, selecting the only items on the menu: meatloaf, mashed potatoes with gravy, and yellowed green beans that had spent more time in the can than the Count of Monte Cristo.

As we ate, we sipped bitter coffee and listened to James Brown screech painfully out of a blinking jukebox.

"Did you tell her?" I asked.

"Tell her what?"

"That you're not going to find Freddy Ray for her."

"What's the rush?"

That was Ernie. Get what he wants first and ruin it later.

"What about this SOFA meeting tomorrow?" he asked. "What do they want from us?"

"They want information," I said, "to make Eighth Army admit that the Blue Train rapist is a G.I. At least that's what the ROK side wants."

"And if they get that?"

"They'll want an investigation."

Ernie shook his head. "Colonel Brace is gonna be pissed."

I jabbed my fork into a small mountain of spuds. It can't be helped, I almost said. Instead, I kept my mouth shut.

When we returned to the Camp Colbern Enlisted Club, the place was packed with G.I.s, standing room only, and the din of their howling was so loud that a pair of NCOs at the front door were handing out artillery ear plugs. I accepted a pair and twisted them into my ears. The Country Western All Stars were a massive hit, although I doubted anyone could hear their music. Marnie was shaking every quivering bit of flesh she had, and a squad of MPs lined the front of the stage, warning enamored G.I.s off with their nightsticks.

During one of their breaks, I walked out back behind the Enlisted Club to the area near the manager's office that was being used as the band's dressing room. An MP stood on duty in front of a high, painted-over window.

"Any problems?" I asked.

"None, other than I'm freezing my balls off."

"If you see anybody, give us a holler."

"Over that noise?"

"Do your best."

I continued on around the building. Everything was secure. And it continued to be secure for the next few minutes while I stood outside enjoying the fresh air, until I heard a voice scream, "Halt!" It was the MP who'd been freezing his balls off. I ran back around the building in time to see him returning from a dark lane between Quonset huts.

"What happened?"

"I took a leak," he said. "While I was back there, I heard footsteps. When I finished my business, some joker was hanging from the window ledge. He was pulling himself up so he could peek inside."

The window was mostly painted over with green paint, but from the edges, yellow light seeped out.

"How long had he been hanging like that?" I asked.

"Less than a minute. I had to piss something fierce, and when I spotted him he dropped from the window and started to run."

"Did you recognize him?"

"Naw. Too dark."

"What was he wearing?"

"Fatigues. What else?"

"Then he was a G.I., not a Korean."

"A Korean wouldn't do something like that—try to catch a peek, I mean. That's G.I. stuff."

I didn't disagree with him.

Finally, he said, "You going to report me?"

"What for? You were just taking a leak."

"Yeah. But I hadn't been properly relieved."

I let the irony of the remark pass and told him not to worry.

Later that evening, on the drive back to Seoul, Marnie kept pestering Ernie to the point that the other girls were embarrassed, and right up until we finally arrived at the Crown Hotel. Without waiting to help with the unloading, the two lovebirds ran upstairs to their room.

* * *

The next morning, I sat on an upholstered chair in the lobby of the J-1 building wearing my dress green uniform and fiddling with the collar of my poplin shirt. My low quarters were highly polished, my chin shaved, and my black tie looped into a double Windsor. I looked sharp, I was on time, I was sober, and I didn't care who knew it. I was also ready to testify, remembering Colonel Brace's instructions: answer the questions honestly but don't volunteer information.

A young lieutenant carrying a clipboard emerged from the SOFA conference room. "Where's your partner?"

"Haven't seen him yet, sir," I replied.

The lieutenant glanced impatiently at his watch. "It's fifteen after. He was supposed to be here at zero eight hundred hours."

"Probably got tied up in traffic," I said.

"Tied up in traffic? Doesn't he live on the compound?"

"Generally."

"'Generally.' What does that mean?"

Just then, Ernie shoved his way through the door. He was wearing his dress green uniform, as we'd been instructed to do, but his tie was loose and his jacket open. His brass hadn't been shined, much less his shoes.

The lieutenant glared at him. "You look like shit."

"You don't look so terrific yourself."

Red-faced, the lieutenant replied, "Listen, I could have you brought up on charges."

"For what?"

"For being late."

Ernie shook his head. "When was the last time a SOFA meeting started on time?"

The lieutenant's lips tightened, but he didn't answer. Finally, he said, "You two stay right here. You are to go nowhere, do you understand?"

Ernie tucked in his shirt.

When neither of us answered, the lieutenant said, "I'll be back. Don't go anywhere."

He swiveled and pushed through the swinging double doors into the SOFA conference room. Ernie sat in the chair next to me, straightening his tie. There was a scratch on his neck, starting just above his collar and extending below it.

"You broke the news to Marnie," I said.

Ernie shook his head. "She likes to get her way."

"I'll say. Any more damage, other than that scratch?"

"Nothing that major surgery won't fix."

The lieutenant emerged from the double doors and motioned for us to enter. We did, Ernie taking the lead, pushing through the doors and marching regally across the carpeted floor until he reached the skirted tables in front of a row of uniformed men on a dais. The lighting was bright, aimed into our eyes, as if we were going to be given the third degree.

Ernie stood for a moment; I stood next to him. When they didn't tell us to sit, Ernie reached across the table and poured himself a glass of water. I did the same. Finally, the chairman of the committee, a ROK Army colonel, told us to take our seats. Then the questioning began.

Colonel Brace wouldn't ask us for a rundown on how the SOFA meeting had gone—that would be beneath his dignity. Instead, he'd have Staff Sergeant Riley do it. As we pushed through the big double doors of the CID admin office, I fully expected to be accosted with Riley's questions. Instead, I saw Marnie.

She was smiling and laughing, sitting in a chair next to Riley's desk, leaning toward him, the top button of her blouse open, exchanging confidences as if they were two long-lost friends. They both glanced over at us, frowned, and returned to their conversation.

Ernie groaned but walked right past them, heading for the coffee urn.

Miss Kim wasn't at her desk. Her hangul typewriter was covered and her desk drawer locked. Apparently, she'd gone home for the day. The rose too was missing.

Marnie had permission to enter the compound. All USO performers were provided with not only a pass to access military compounds but also temporary ration cards, so they could purchase items out of the commissary or the post exchange. Most of them didn't use the privileges much. After all, they were only here for a few days—two or three weeks at the most—and they were put up in tourist hotels and were pretty much constantly on the go. But somehow Marnie had not only made her way from the Crown Hotel to Yongsan Compound, but she'd also managed to locate the CID office. Resourceful girl.

Ernie carried his cup of coffee back to Riley's desk and sat down in a chair opposite Marnie.

"What are you doing here?" he asked.

"None of your beeswax," she said.

Ernie continued to stare at her.

"Okay, if you must know," Marnie continued, "Staff

Sergeant Riley here is going to help me find Freddy Ray. Apparently he doesn't think it's right for my little girl not to receive the child support that is due to her."

"Bull," Ernie said.

"I beg your pardon?" Marnie said.

She was acting extremely ladylike this morning.

"I mean 'bull,'" Ernie said. "You've got a grudge against this Freddy Ray, and when you find him, you're going to do something to embarrass the hell out of him."

Marnie's face flushed red. "Well, maybe he deserves it."

Riley grabbed his hat. "Come on, Marnie," he said. "Let's go talk somewhere where we won't be interrupted."

"Yes," Marnie replied. "Let's do."

Still pouting, she stared at Ernie and then turned and walked out of the office with Staff Sergeant Riley. Ernie waited until the door closed and their footsteps faded down the hallway. Then he said wistfully, "You think he'll get any of that?"

"Not a chance," I replied.

The SOFA meeting had been an unpleasant experience. Translators were used for the ROK Army officers—most of whom could speak English but didn't want to lose face by mispronouncing words in a formal setting. The American officers kept trying to get us to admit that we had no idea, for sure, that the Blue Train rapist was a member of the United States military. This was in fact true. The ROK Army officers kept trying to get us to admit that the chances of the Blue Train rapist being anything other than an American G.I. were slim to nothing. This also was true.

When neither side could shake us from either position, Ernie and I were summarily dismissed.

It was up to the honchos now to hash it out. What came down, came down. I hoped that we'd be allowed to investigate, but after a day with no word, my hopes dimmed. After the second day, they were all but gone. It was the third day, while we were at the MP station finalizing some paperwork on a black-market bust, that the desk sergeant walked over to speak to us.

"You Sueño?" he asked.

I nodded.

"They want to see you over at the head shed."

"The Provost Marshal's office?"

He shook his head. "Chief of Staff."

"Eighth Army?"

"You know any other Chief of Staff?"

Ernie and I stuffed the unfinished paperwork in a drawer, walked out of the MP station, and climbed in the jeep. An hour later, after having our butts reamed by the 8th Army Chief of Staff, we were on a train heading south toward Pusan. A train known as the Blue Train.

Normally, I would've been happy about it. I'd played a not-so-subtle bureaucratic game, and I'd won. At least that's what I thought at first, but that's not what really happened. Actually, 8th Army never relented on their refusal to admit that the Blue Train rapist was a G.I.

Until events intervened.

Whoever he was—G.I. or not—he'd struck again.

And this time, his victim had not only been raped. She'd also been murdered.

5

The stewardess roamed the central aisle of the Blue Train, paying particular attention to elderly passengers. She was a round-faced young woman, husky but not fat, and she looked good in the blue beret, white cotton blouse, and blue skirt. I particularly admired her legs. Sturdy and smooth.

As attractive as she was, if she walked in the door of a modeling agency in New York City, they'd soon enough show her the exit. She wasn't tall and leggy, and she certainly wasn't blonde. There are many types of gorgeous women in this world, but the fashion industry's insistence that there is only one ultimate form of beauty fools many and encourages them to buy the products that Madison Avenue sells. In other words, lying pays.

One of the things I liked about Korea at the time was that advertising was kept strictly under control. No billboards were allowed to mar the serenity of the countryside, and, on Korean television, commercials were permitted only before and after programs, not during. On AFKN, the Armed Forces Korea Network, there were no commercials at all, only public-service announcements. Boring, but at least not obnoxious.

Outside my window, rice paddies rolled by, dry and yellow and already harvested. In the distance, burial mounds dotted round hills; beyond them, a red sun glowered angrily behind purple peaks. Alongside the train, straining to keep pace with us, a gaggle of Manchurian geese flapped their way south.

"You ready for a wet?" Ernie said.

He reached in his AWOL bag, pulled out two cans of Falstaff, and handed one to me. I popped mine open and enjoyed the frothing warmth of hops and barley.

Earlier this afternoon, after we'd reported to his office, the Chief of Staff hadn't been complimentary. "The only reason the Provost Marshal and I are assigning you to this case is because you're already familiar with the details."

And because I'm the only American law-enforcement official in the country who speaks Korean, I thought, but I didn't say anything.

"If you screw up, you're off the case. Is that understood?"

Ernie somehow resisted the urge to mouth off and instead replied crisply, "Yes, sir." Although he pretended he wasn't involved emotionally, Ernie didn't want to lose the opportunity to collar this rapist any more than I did.

The Chief of Staff handed us a copy of the dossier compiled by Lieutenant Pong. I thumbed through it. Most of it hadn't been translated.

"I want you on the next train south," he said. Then he responded to our surprised looks. "Okay, I know what you're thinking. If this is so important, why not a chopper? You could be down there in a couple of hours."

The Chief of Staff, Colonel Oberdorff, was a small man, wiry and tough-looking, with a short-cropped gray crew cut, and he looked lost in his highly starched khaki uniform. His voice was gruff. He spoke plainly and directly—like a plumber, the type of plumber you can trust.

"The truth is," he said, "the ROKs asked that you two be put on the case. They seem to respect you, Sueño, I suppose because you can speak their language." He looked away. "Hell of an accomplishment, that."

This was the first time I'd ever been complimented by anyone in 8th Army—officer or enlisted—for putting in the effort to learn the Korean language.

"Thank you, sir," I said.

"And your other cases," Colonel Oberdorff continued. "Word must be getting around. Goddamn it, you two ruffle a lot of feathers but you get results. People are noticing. So the KNPs want you on the case and they want you to take the five P.M. Blue Train to Pusan."

"Why the train?" Ernie asked. "If we took a chopper, we could be there before evening chow."

"I know. But the ROKs want you to take the train. Apparently, there's going to be someone else on the train, some VIP who doesn't like to fly."

Ernie and I looked at one another.

"The VIP will meet you on the train, brief you about the case. I suppose you know that all hell has broken loose in the Korean newspapers. It's even hit the radio, they tell me, and tonight the TV. The ROK government wants to put a stop to all the bad publicity, but that kind of censorship could cause more trouble than it's worth. Better to get the truth out, let the chips fall where they may. 'The G.I. Rapist,' they're calling it. And now that a woman's been murdered . . ."

Colonel Oberdorff allowed his voice to trail off.

"Murdered?" Ernie said.

"Yes. You'll be briefed on the details. No time to go into all that now. You have a train to catch."

"Who is this VIP we're supposed to meet?" I asked.

"Hell if I know. All I know is that he's some sort of inspector. Highly respected. They're putting their best on this case."

"How will we know him?" Ernie asked.

"He'll know you. I don't know who he is or what he looks like. All I know is his name." Colonel Oberdorff shuffled through a stack of paperwork on his desk.

Ernie and I waited.

"Gil," Colonel Oberdorff said. "Gilbert maybe. No, that's his last name. Damn Korean customs." In frustration, the Chief of Staff mumbled to himself. Koreans put their family name first, then their given name. When working with Americans, they sometimes switch them around to follow our customs. Confusion ensues. Finally, the colonel stopped shuffling and said, "These Korean names make no sense to me."

I leaned forward and studied the paperwork. "Mr. Gil," I said.

Colonel Oberdorff brightened. "That's right. Mr. Kill," he said, mispronouncing the name. "It says so right here."

Then he shuffled through more paperwork. "What the hell kind of name is that?"

Ernie and I knew who it was. I glanced at Ernie. He glanced at me. I realized that we were both holding our breath. Five minutes later, we were out of the Chief of Staff's office, heading for the barracks to pack our traveling bags; ten minutes after that, we were on our way to the Seoul RTO, 8th Army's Rail Transportation Office.

The stewardess walked by again and Ernie glanced at me as my eyes followed her.

"You like that, don't you?" he said.

"What's not to like?"

"You're weird, you know that, Sueño? All those gorgeous Texas women in the Country Western All Stars. Shelly the lead guitar player has even hinted that she'd like to get to know you better, and you pay her no attention."

"When we're with them," I replied, "we're on duty."

"Bull. If we were really on duty twenty-four hours a day, like the lifers say, nobody'd ever get laid."

I sipped my beer.

"But instead of a tall, gorgeous blonde," Ernie continued, "you like the kind of Korean woman who just stepped out of a rice paddy. What is it with you?"

I shrugged.

The stewardess knelt with her back to us, her knees pressed primly together. She spoke soothingly with a group of children who'd gathered around an old *halaboji*, a grandfather. Like many elderly people in Korea, the man made no bones about his age. He wore the gentleman's *hanbok*,

Korean clothing that consisted of light blue silk pantaloons, tied above white socks at the ankles, and a waistcoat of the same material that covered an outer vest the color of jade. This getup indicated that he was retired and no longer had to wear the suit and tie or other Western-style work clothes that indicated he was gainfully employed. The old man balanced a varnished wooden case on his knees. It contained an ink stone, a horsehair brush, and a small lacquered writing area. Deftly, he held the brush with his thumb and two fingers while he sketched out a Chinese character on crinkly rice paper. The children watched, fascinated by the ancient writing implements, occasionally asking questions. Then he offered the brush to the smallest girl. Shyly, she gripped the brush in her hand, dipped the tip into black ink, and traced a few lines across the paper. The halaboji complimented her, as did the stewardess, and then one of the boys insisted on his turn. After the boy had his chance, the stewardess complimented him too, rose gracefully to her feet, and continued her way down the aisle.

Ernie finished his beer, crumpled the can, and tossed it into his AWOL bag.

"Why didn't you talk to her when she was standing there?"

I shrugged again. "I didn't want to interrupt."

He shook his head. "If you've got the hots for her, you've got to do something about it."

I didn't answer.

"Okay," he said. "If that's the kind of kinky dude you are, I'll help."

He rose from his seat and started down the aisle. I tried

to call him back, but he ignored me. Instead of following, I sat for a minute wondering what he was up to. And then it dawned on me: whatever it was, it couldn't possibly end well. Already, since boarding the Blue Train, we'd received some nasty looks. The case of the Blue Train rapist was on everyone's mind, and every G.I. was a suspect. Ernie's shenanigans normally were embarrassing enough. Under these conditions, they could be dangerous.

I rose from my seat, nodding to the halaboji across the aisle, realizing that his hair was mostly black, with only a smattering of gray. He wasn't as old as he pretended to be. Instead of constantly trying to look younger, like Americans, Koreans often purposely try to appear older. I shoved the thought out of my mind and followed Ernie.

Without really intending to, I found myself stopping at the end of every car, checking into the bathrooms that weren't occupied. Nothing amiss. I passed through the dining car with its long bar and square tables covered with white linen. Only a handful of customers were sitting there, but some of the black-clad waiters glared at me suspiciously.

Near the end of the train, I found him. The stewardess had stopped in the middle of the aisle and was looking back at him, her eyes wide. From this distance, I couldn't hear what Ernie was saying; but whatever it was, most of the Korean passengers weren't pleased with his little display. His hand was on her elbow and he leaned toward her, so closely that the stewardess leaned away from him. Ernie kept talking until finally the stewardess stepped back abruptly and said in Korean, "*Na moolah.*" I don't understand.

A burly Korean man stood up from his seat, pointed at Ernie, and said, "*Ku yangnom weikurei?*" Which could be translated to "Why is this foreigner acting this way?" except that the word he used for foreigner, *yangnom*, was anything but polite. It meant something akin to foreign lout, and was a well-known insult. So well-known, in fact, that Ernie understood.

"What'd you call me?" Ernie said.

The Korean man bristled, placing both his hands on his hips, facing Ernie directly. Other men stood up.

By the time I stepped up next to Ernie, the stewardess had scurried toward the back of the passenger car and five or six more Korean men were standing in the aisle, wagging their fingers at Ernie and chattering among themselves. I knew what was causing this. The news of a rape, and now a murder, on the Blue Train had made everyone nervous. Seeing Ernie taking what the Koreans considered to be an overly aggressive stance toward the stewardess was not going to sit well.

I placed my hand on Ernie's elbow. He jerked it away.

"What did this guy call me?" he asked.

"Forget it," I said. "Let's go."

"Like hell. This son of a bitch is calling me names and waving his finger. Who the hell does he think he is?"

Two of the men stepped forward, holding their hands up, in the Korean gesture meant to placate an argument. Before I could react, Ernie stepped forward and pushed one of them. A woman screamed. Others jumped in, and soon Ernie and I were wrestling in the middle of the aisle with what seemed like a sea of angry Korean faces. But no one was hitting. That's the Korean style. When there's an altercation, they grab one another, they push, they shove—and they certainly scream—but no one hits.

Except Ernie.

He smacked the man who'd called him a yangnom full in the face.

By now the conductor had been called, and he joined in the fray. Women were screaming and children were crying and I was pushed by the crush of bodies backward across a chair and into an old woman's lap. Ernie by now had been totally overwhelmed and lay on the floor in the center of the aisle, cursing and kicking and trying to punch somebody, but his arms had been pinned down by the two men who'd originally been trying to stop the fight.

The conductor kept calling for order, but no one paid him any attention. I was still trying to struggle to my feet, apologizing to the woman I'd almost crushed, when a loud voice broke through the din of fear and confusion.

"*Ssau-jima!*" the voice said. Stop fighting!

Everyone froze and looked at the man standing at the end of the car. Everyone, that is, except Ernie, who kept kicking.

The man who had hollered was the halaboji wearing the blue pantaloons and jade vest. The man I'd seen across the aisle from us, teaching the children the ancient art of calligraphy. His hands were behind his back but his face was red, glowering with disapproval. He strode forward, barking orders in Korean. "Back to your seats! Let that man go. What is it with you? Have you no education?"

The men in the aisle faced the venerable grandfather, bowed their heads, mumbled apologies, and backed up to their original seats. Finally, the two men atop Ernie stood up, faced the halaboji, bowed, and hurried away down the aisle.

Ernie bounced to his feet, shaking his arms free, raising his fists and staring around for a target. All he saw was the much shorter halaboji staring sternly up at him.

I was still wedged between two seats and anyway too far away to reach Ernie in time. Instead, I prayed.

I could see anger cross Ernie's face. He was about to launch a straight left jab and I was about to scream for him to stop. The halaboji, calmly, stepped closer to Ernie. Ernie glared down at the man. Then the older man said in English, "You must think before you accost women."

"'Accost?'" Ernie replied. "I didn't 'accost' anyone."

"You interrupted her in the performance of her duties."

"She wasn't doing nothing."

"While she's on this train," the old man said, "she is responsible for the *kibun* of the passengers, for their sense of calmness and safety. You interrupted that."

Ernie seemed confused. He knotted his fist. His face was red, he was embarrassed, and when a young American man is embarrassed—when other people see him as a boob—his natural response is to hit somebody. Violence, in the American mind, will make you seem smarter.

The halaboji read all this in Ernie's thoughts. He continued to stare up at Ernie, but now his face wasn't stern. He was calm, waiting patiently for something. For what, I wasn't sure. I was just hoping it wasn't a right cross.

Ernie glanced back at me. Mercifully, what must have been a rational thought flitted across his visage like a skittering storm cloud. He turned back to the old grandfather, hesitated, and, at last, lowered his right fist.

I exhaled, not even realizing that I'd been holding my breath.

More mumbling broke out in the crowd; a few of the Korean men would've just as soon punched Ernie out. The halaboji motioned for Ernie to follow. He did. I followed them out of the passenger car and back toward the front of the train.

In the dining car, the old man stopped and sat at a table. He motioned for Ernie to sit, and then he stood again and greeted me with a short bow. Suddenly, he didn't seem old at all. It was because of the traditional getup that I'd assumed he was a grandfather. Now that I looked more closely, I realized that his physique was still sturdy beneath the silk vest and pantaloons, his hair gray on the edges but black on top. I revised my estimate of his age downward to about fifty. Still, he was twice the age of either Ernie or me. After the three of us were seated, a waiter approached and the man spoke.

"Have you ever tried ginseng tea before?"

"Often," I replied.

He ordered three cups of ginseng tea. We sat silently until the hot brew was served; then the older gentleman raised his handleless cup with two hands, gestured toward us, and drank. Ernie and I did the same. We continued like that, without speaking, until only the dregs of the ginseng powder remained.

The man leaned back and smiled. "My name is Gil," he said. "Gil Kwon-up. Chief Homicide Inspector of the Korean National Police."

Every American MP and law-enforcement official in Korea knew of Inspector Gil. But Americans have trouble pronouncing the first letter of Gil's name. In Korean, the sound falls somewhere between the harsh English *k* sound and the soft *g* sound. I listen carefully when Koreans pronounce the letter, and I can replicate the sound reasonably well, but most MPs and CID agents at 8th Army didn't bother. They referred to Inspector Gil Kwon-up as "Mr. Kill."

It was said that he'd made his name in law enforcement some twenty years ago, during and after the Korean War, first by hunting down Communist saboteurs who were planting bombs and blowing up trains, buses, and public buildings. Supposedly, Mr. Kill captured or killed dozens of them. After the war, he then turned his attention to the criminally insane: men—and in a few cases women—who'd been driven mad by the brutalities of the Korean War. Some of them had seen such horrific things and suffered so much that only by pain and blood and terror could they somehow continue to live. After the war, madness was common, despair rampant. People who had once been human were now inhuman, capable of the most appalling acts of violence. Inspector Kill, along with other dedicated members of the Korean National Police, had to wipe out those who were incapable of returning to a world ruled by peace.

Kill had been ruthless, we'd been told, wiping out the worst of the criminals—not even bringing them to trial, but rather bringing peace and justice back to the world out of the smoking barrel of his little pistol. And now, disguised as a calm calligrapher, Inspector Kill sat across from us, his hands resting placidly on white linen, study-ing me over the brim of a porcelain cup.

Finally, he spoke. His English was excellent, which is probably the first thing most G.I.s would notice. He'd almost certainly studied in the States, maybe trained there during the fifties and sixties when anti-Communist cadres around the world were being prepared to fight the Red demons lurking behind both the iron and bamboo curtains.

"The second rape was less daring than the first," he said, "but more brutal."

The KNP report, written in Korean, still sat in my AWOL bag back at my seat. I had yet to decipher it.

"A foreign man," Gil continued, "boarded the south-bound Blue Train, either in Seoul or Taejon or East Taegu. We're not sure which. What we're sure of is that a woman named Mrs. Hyon Mi-sook departed the train at the end of the line and then made her way through the Pusan Station, dragging two bags and three small children: the oldest, her son, aged nine, and two younger twin daugh-ters. She queued up at the taxi line and eventually caught a cab that took her to the Shindae Tourist Hotel."

Lodging establishments are divided into three catego-ries in Korea. The lowest is a *yoinsuk*, nothing more than a building, usually somebody's residence, with a traditional warm *ondol* floor heated by charcoal gas flues in the foun-dation. For a small fee, you rent a sleeping mat and you can spread it out in the communal hall and catch some shut-eye. The next step up is the *yoguan*, which again is furnished in the traditional Korean style, bedding on the ondol floor. The difference is that the room you rent is separate. The top of the line is the tourist hotel, which is a fully Westernized hotel with central heating, beds and mattresses, and indoor bathrooms with shower stalls and towels.

This Mrs. Hyon Mi-sook must have been fairly well off if she could afford to stay in a tourist hotel. Mr. Kill slid a photograph out of the inner pocket of his jade vest and laid it on the table.

"That's her?" Ernie asked.

Kill nodded.

She was a knockout. A gorgeous Korean woman with full cheeks and sparkling white teeth smiled out at us. Kill continued his story.

"As soon as Mrs. Hyon had checked in, she and her children were escorted upstairs by a bellhop. Almost immediately after her elevator doors closed, a Western man entered and approached the front desk holding a woman's handbag, saying it was hers and that she had left it on the train. The desk clerk offered to take it from him, but the man waved him off and asked which floor she was on. The startled clerk told him. The big Western man went to the stairs and climbed them two steps at a time."

"Will the clerk be able to identify this man?" Ernie asked.

"So I'm told."

We could imagine what happened next, but Kill elaborated. The Western man, lurking in the hallway of the third floor, waited until the bellhop left and then immediately knocked on her door. Whether she looked through the peephole and saw a Western man holding a purse or thought it was the bellhop returning, we'll never know.

Korea is a trusting society. Violent crime is so much more rare here than it is in the States. Whatever the reason, she opened the door.

"Are the kids still alive?" Ernie asked.

Kill nodded. "They weren't hurt," he said. "Not physically."

I studied this strange, calm man who sat in front of us. Despite his age, his body expressed the grace of someone who'd studied martial arts for years; his knuckles were callused and his waist waspish. He stared at us pleasantly, his mouth set in a half smile, black eyes absorbing everything. Waiting.

I wanted to ask more questions, about him, about the beautiful woman who'd been so cruelly raped and murdered, and about the fate of her children. But the train jerked and a blast of steam screamed out of the side of the engine. Our cups rattled atop their saucers. We were entering Pusan Station. Mr. Kill rose, spoke briefly to the waiter, who bowed, and then turned and made his way through the train back to his seat.

Ernie and I followed.

The train came to a complete stop. We grabbed our bags and waited as the elderly passengers and women with children filed off in front of us. When we reached the end of the car and were about to step off onto the cement platform, the stewardess was there waiting for us. She bowed to me and then, after I'd passed, she stepped close to Ernie. I turned in time to see her whisper something in his ear.

We walked in darkness toward the row of streetlights shining in front of the station. I asked, "What was that all about?"

Ernie held out his palm, showing me a slip of folded paper. I grabbed it and opened it, twisting it toward the light. The stewardess's name, written in English, and a phone number.

I handed the paper back to him.

"See, Sueño," he said, grinning. "Acting like an asshole pays off."

I didn't reply.

Ernie wadded up the little note and tossed it in the gutter.

The staff at the Shindae Tourist Hotel bowed so much, I almost mistook them for a flock of ducks. They weren't showing this elaborate politeness to Ernie and me, but to the revered gentleman in the blue silk hanbok—a revered gentleman who'd also flashed the badge of an inspector of the Korean National Police.

The head clerk, wearing a black suit with matching bow tie, showed us the steps the rapist had climbed to reach the room of Mrs. Hyon Mi-sook. The room had been taped off by the local Pusan contingent of the KNP, but Mr. Gil ordered the clerk to unlock the door. We stepped in.

The sink in the bathroom and the counter surrounding it were slathered in dried blood.

"He washed himself here," Gil said. "Or at least that's what we believe. The oldest son told us that he forced him and his two sisters to crouch there in the bathtub and then he jerked down the shower curtain and covered them with it. They could barely breathe."

"But he didn't actually *hurt* the children?" Ernie asked.

Gil shook his head. "No."

Not physically, at least.

"The mother was found bound and gagged with some of the towels."

We returned to the main room. There was more blood on the bed. "He tied one arm here." Gil pointed at the posts at the head of the bed. "Another arm there, and a leg each down there."

"Spread-eagled," I said.

"Yes," Gil agreed. "Spread-eagled. This rag," Gil said, pointing to a washcloth, "was found stuffed in her mouth."

Inspector Gil knew all this from the detailed KNP report that had been sent to him in Seoul by teletype. His eyes shone as he paced slowly around the room, examining everything. The bed was stained brown, as if an urn of mess-hall coffee had been spilled, but I knew it wasn't coffee. I could tell by the stench. The air reeked of the meaty odor of a butcher shop's slaughter room.

"After he raped her," Gil said, "he started cutting her. She fought. One hand was found free and there was blood and flesh under the nails."

"Good for her," Ernie said, sudden passion filling his voice.

Gil glanced at him. "It didn't do her any good. She died anyway. The boy said he heard his mother stop struggling. Then the foreign man entered the bathroom and washed himself thoroughly; and, without saying anything, he left."

"How long did the kids stay in there?" I asked.

"Until morning," Gil replied. "Until the maid found them."

Outside the Shindae Tourist Hotel, Mr. Gil ordered the doorman to call a taxi. He blew a whistle, and a small Hyundai sedan appeared almost instantly. We piled in and rode silently. The broad streets of the city of Pusan were swathed in darkness and washed with a salty mist from the sea. We swept through lonely streets until we finally reached the cement-block foundation of the building known as the Pusan Main Police Station. As we climbed the well-lit stone steps, an officer wearing a gray Western suit was waiting there for us. He bowed to Mr. Kill and then shook hands with Ernie and me. He turned and ushered us into the huge wooden building.

I paused and studied a plaque written in Chinese. A few of the characters I could read. Apparently, this building had been built in 1905 during the waning days of the Chosun Dynasty. It had originally been the Pusan area's main administrative building, but had then been converted to other purposes. Unspoken were the uses it had been put to during the Japanese occupation from 1910 to 1945. Still, the building had been in continuous use for almost seventy years.

I hurried to catch up with the other men and followed them down long wooden corridors. Inside open-doored offices, blue-clad Korean National Policemen worked at desks or interrogated prisoners, even at this late hour. There were a few Korean women in uniform, mostly typing reports or carrying paperwork. We climbed three flights of broad wooden stairs until we were ushered into an office marked with Chinese characters I couldn't decipher. As soon as I had a chance, I copied the characters into my notebook. Later I discovered they meant "Homicide Division."

We sat on hard couches surrounding a coffee table. Soon, a female officer brought a metal tray with cups and a bronze pot of barley tea. We drank. The officer in the gray suit pulled out a pack of cigarettes and offered them all around. When everyone refused, he grimaced and stuffed the pack back into his coat pocket. Then, in English, he introduced himself: Senior Inspector Han of the Pusan Korean National Police.

He pulled out a teletype report written in hangul. The ticket sellers at the train stations in Seoul, Taejon, and East Taegu had all been interviewed thoroughly. The ones at Taejon and East Taegu were certain they hadn't sold any tickets to foreigners yesterday. This made sense because there were few foreigners in Taejon and Taegu, and they were unlikely to be traveling south toward Pusan. The American military has only a small contingent in Pusan. The bulk of our forces—about 90 percent of the over 50,000 G.I.s stationed in-country—are either in Seoul or north of Seoul, on compounds in the 2nd Infantry Division area near the Demilitarized Zone.

The ticket sellers at the Seoul Station itself, however, couldn't be sure if they'd sold any tickets to foreigners or not. There are plenty of foreigners living in Seoul, and when you're a ticket seller in a busy station like Seoul's, one day blends in with another, and the customers become an undifferentiated mass.

The 8th Army RTO receives its own block of tickets and sells them to 8th Army military personnel only. That report was being created by Staff Sergeant Riley while we traveled south on the Blue Train and should be waiting for us at the MP station on Hialeah Compound.

Detective Inspector Han presented both Ernie and me with his card and we promised to call him as soon as we had any information concerning any G.I.s who'd taken the Blue Train. The time was getting on toward 2200 hours, 10:00 P.M. Ernie and I said our good-byes to Inspector Han, and Mr. Kill escorted us outside. Rather than having us take a cab, he led us to a brand-new blue Korean National Police car. A white-gloved officer sat up front. Mr. Kill opened the back door, and Ernie climbed in. Before I could follow, Kill stopped me and said, "Your report said something about a 'checklist.' What do you think it means?"

"I'm not sure," I replied. "Whatever it means, something has caused this guy to escalate his violence."

Inspector Kill stared at me, puzzled.

"Escalate means to step higher," I said. "In this case, to move up from simple rape to murder."

Kill nodded. "And 'checklist' implies a list that's longer than two."

"Yes. It implies a list that can be very long."

Inspector Kill sighed and looked away.

I folded myself into the backseat next to Ernie. The driver turned on the siren and pulled away from the Pusan police headquarters. Although his knees were scrunched up in front of him, Ernie was pleased by the plush ride. "Beats getting chased by them," he said.

After twenty minutes, we rolled up to the stone-and-concertina-wire gate of the United States Army's Hialeah Compound. Ernie and I climbed out of the sedan, thanking the driver as we did so. He saluted and roared off.

Floodlights lit wet pavement. From behind a reinforced concrete barricade, two American MPs glared at us. A heavy mist, laced with salt, was blowing in off the ocean. I shuddered, hoisted my bag, and marched toward the winding cattle chute that was the pedestrian entrance to the compound.

Behind me, Ernie muttered, "Why are those guys staring at us?" When he received no response, he raised his voice and shouted, "Mom! I'm home!"

Neither MP moved.

6

Ernie and I had met Lieutenant Messler before, on a previous case. He must've extended his tour in Korea, because that previous trip to Pusan had been almost a year ago.

"Hot one this time, eh, Sueño?" he asked. "And you brought Bascom along with you. They got tired of him in Seoul?"

"You'll get tired of me here," Ernie growled.

The lieutenant smirked. Messler was a smallish man, a fact that he tried to compensate for by keeping his chest puffed out and his posture ramrod straight, so straight that he was practically leaning backward. He was wearing his dress green uniform because he was pulling the duty tonight, and his tie was knotted tightly and his hair combed straight back. He was chomping gum.

"There's a report," I said, "should've been sent down here by now, from the Chief of Staff's office." I kept my voice as even as I could. I didn't like Lieutenant Messler any more than Ernie did, but we were going to have to work with him for as long as this thing lasted. I could at least encourage him to act professionally.

Mention of the 8th Army Chief of Staff made his eyebrows rise.

"I saw it," he said. "Not much in it." He tossed the paperwork on the counter in front of me.

"Thanks for reading it," Ernie said. "Even though it's classified and you don't have a need-to-know."

"The duty officer needs to know everything," Messler replied.

"Yeah. You're needy, all right."

I grabbed Ernie by the elbow and pulled him away from the MP desk, pretending that I needed his help in evaluating the message. What I really needed was for him to quit needling Messler. Turning the young lieutenant into a yapping Chihuahua wouldn't help us find the Blue Train rapist.

The report was from the Seoul RTO and listed the names of the G.I.s who'd been issued tickets yesterday for the Blue Train to Pusan. At the civilian ticket counters, all you needed was some hard cash, in *won*, the Korean currency, and anybody could buy a ticket. No names were recorded and no questions were asked. The military, on the other hand, issued tickets mostly to G.I.s who were on official business. And, as such, they had to present their identification and travel orders, and their names were then logged in and their train tickets were issued to them for free. A G.I. on leave orders—or even on week-end pass—could purchase a ticket at the RTO, but once again—it being the military—they would demand to see his identification and he'd be logged in with his purchase point and destination.

I studied the names.

"The courier," Ernie said, pointing at the name Runnels.

"Figures he'd be on the train returning to Pusan," I said. "It's his job to carry classified information back and forth from Seoul."

"He's the one who talked to the guy who got off the first train in Anyang, isn't he?"

"He's the one."

"So if the same guy was on this train, Runnels would've seen him."

"Maybe. Whether he did or not, we need to talk to him."

"I'll find him," Ernie said. He left me and spoke to the MP desk sergeant, who made a phone call.

While Ernie tracked down Runnels, I continued to study the list. The names were unfamiliar to me, except one. Specialist Four Weyworth, Nicholas Q. He hadn't been on the first Blue Train but he'd been one of the G.I.s I'd identified as being stationed at Hialeah Compound and on in-country leave on the day of the first Blue Train attack. I underlined his name. Ten minutes later, Ernie and I had left our travel bags in the expert care of the Hialeah Compound Military Police. We were armed with information and directions, and we were off into the Pusan night.

* * *

Ernie and I made a quick trip to the barracks on the compound and rousted Private First Class Runnels out of his bunk. The courier who transported classified documents between Pusan and Seoul was less than thrilled.

"What the hell do you want?" he asked, rubbing his eyes. "Didn't you harass me enough when you questioned me in Seoul?"

"This is the army," Ernie said. "There's never enough harassment."

I told Runnels to put his clothes on and follow us into the dayroom. I wanted him completely alert when we questioned him. He did as he was told, stopping in the latrine to splash water on his face. Finally, he joined us at the vinyl-covered chairs near the pool tables. The television was running, an old black-and-white movie that no one was watching. I knew it would be the last thing scheduled, because both the Korean stations and Armed Forces Korea Network stop broadcasting at midnight. Ernie switched the television off and returned to stand near me.

Runnels sat with his elbows on his knees. "What is it?" he asked.

"You took the five p.m. Blue Train back from Seoul yesterday."

"That's my job."

"You remember that guy you sat next to the first time we questioned you? The guy who disappeared after the train stopped in Anyang?"

"Yeah. You think he's the rapist."

"You don't?" Ernie asked.

Runnels shrugged. "How the hell would I know?"

"So, yesterday," I continued, "on the Blue Train from Seoul, did you see the same guy again? Was he on that train?"

Runnels looked away from me, scrunching his forehead. I held my breath. Ernie held his too.

"No," Runnels said finally. "Can't say I did see him."

"Were you looking?" I asked. "Did you get around the train much? Or did you just stay in your seat?"

"I've seen the train," Runnels said, exasperation in his voice, "too many times. These days I just stay in my seat. Especially when I have a good book to read. *The Last Detail*, by Darryl Ponicsan. It's about military life. *Real* military life. You ought to try it."

"Maybe I will. Did you see anybody else you know on the train? Or anything unusual?"

Runnels thought again. "No. Not that I remember."

I checked my notes. "Do you know a guy named Weyworth, Nicholas Q.? He's a Spec Four and he's stationed here on Hialeah Compound."

"What's he do?"

"Supply."

Runnels took his time thinking over the question. "No. The name doesn't ring a bell. I might recognize his face if I saw him, though."

"Did you recognize *anybody* on the train? Anybody who you thought might be stationed on Hialeah Compound?"

Runnels thought again and shook his head.

"Did you see anything strange? Anything at all unusual?"

Again he said no, he hadn't seen anything that he

thought was worth remarking on. Finally we gave up, thanked him, and told him he could return to his bunk. On the way out of the dayroom, Runnels turned and looked back at us. "That guy did it again, didn't he?"

"What guy?" Ernie asked.

"That guy. The Blue Train rapist. He did it again, didn't he?"

"What makes you think that?"

"Because you guys are here. If he hadn't done it again, you probably would've just stayed in Seoul. It's about that checklist, isn't it?"

"What do you mean?" I asked.

"I told you before. The last thing he told me before he walked away was that he had a checklist. A checklist to correct deficiencies. That's what this is about, isn't it?"

Runnels studied our faces, saw nothing, shrugged, and walked in his flip-flops down the dark corridor that led to the open bay that housed two long rows of military bunks.

The lights of the Kit Kat Club flashed brightly. The midnight curfew was less than a half hour away, but you wouldn't have known it from the relaxed atmosphere of the customers and waitresses in the G.I. bar. They looked as if they were camped out forever.

"Curfew must not be such a big deal down here," Ernie said.

In Seoul, or especially up north near the DMZ, the Korean National Police will arrest anyone out even five minutes after the midnight curfew. Down here, the G.I.s were only a hundred yards from the main gate of Hialeah

Compound. If they ran, they could make it there in a few seconds. And my guess was that down here in Pusan the local cops weren't as frantic about shutting off all lights and closing down all businesses by exactly twelve o'clock. We were a couple of hundred miles from the DMZ; a couple of hundred miles from the 700,000-man-strong North Korean Army. Life seemed more normal down here. More cosmopolitan.

Ernie and I strode into the Kit Kat Club.

Bleary eyes looked at us, some of the hostesses with interest, puffing on their cigarettes. The G.I.s stared at us with dull surprise. Two Americans they didn't know, near a small compound like Hialeah: that was an event.

Ernie stepped to the bar and ordered two beers.

"OB or Crown?" the bartender asked.

"You have draft?" The bartender shook his head. "Then OB"

The bartender popped the tops off the bottles for us. I asked for a glass. Ernie didn't bother.

"Where's Nick?" Ernie asked the G.I. sitting next to us.

"Huh?" The guy's head was about to droop to the bar.

"Nick," Ernie repeated. "Nick Weyworth."

"Hell if I know," the guy said, and allowed his nose to droop even farther toward the suds puddled on the bar.

I waved down one of the hostesses. "Weyworth *isso*?" I asked. Is Weyworth here? "Nick Weyworth."

"You buy me drink?" she asked.

I nodded. Ernie stared at me, surprised.

The bartender took his time mixing some colorful concoction and finally slapped it on the bar. "One thousand five hundred won," he said. Ernie whistled.

I reached deep into my pocket, pulled out the money, and took my time counting out two thousand-won notes, the equivalent in U.S. dollars of about four bucks. The bartender returned with my change. I pocketed it and turned back to the hostess. Through a straw, she was demurely sipping her drink.

"Show me," I said.

Her eyes widened.

"Show me Weyworth's yobo hooch." His girlfriend's house.

"I finish my drink."

"No," I said. "You don't finish your drink."

Ernie stepped next to the woman, grabbed the frothy red drink out of her hand, and set it carefully on the bar. "*Kapshida*," he said. Let's go.

She looked up at us with her heavily lined eyes, trying to make up her mind. Finally, she shrugged, stood up, and spoke to the other women seated against the wall.

"*Jokum itta dora wa*," she said. I'll be right back.

She grabbed her coat and sashayed toward the door.

The three of us wound through a couple of hundred yards of narrow pedestrian lanes. Sewage ran through open stone-lined gutters reeking of ammonia and filth. High walls made of brick and stone lined either side of the passageway, studded on top with brass spikes or shards of embedded glass. An occasional streetlamp glowed yellow at the intersection of two lanes, but mostly we were guided by the dim silvery rays of a half moon. Finally, the hostess crouched through a door in a larger wooden gate. Ernie and I followed. The hostess hollered, "Jeannie *Omma, issoyo*?" Is the mother of Jeannie here? Apparently a child was involved.

We stepped into a courtyard of swept dirt. Kimchee pots lined one wall. A *byonso*—an outhouse—behind us smelled of lime and human waste. Across the courtyard, light glowed behind a latticework door stretched with oil paper. The door slid open and a woman's face peeked out. "*Nugu-syo*?" she said. Who is it?

As soon as she saw the hostess, with Ernie and me looming behind her, she slid shut the door. A metal latch clicked into place.

Weyworth's hooch wasn't much. Just a large ondol-heated room with a cement-floored kitchen on the side.

"I'll check the back," Ernie said.

As he marched off into the darkness, the hostess who'd brought us here surreptitiously retreated toward the entranceway. I ignored her until I heard the door in the large gate shut. I stepped up to the latticework door and knocked. The wooden frame rattled.

"Weyworth," I said. "I need to talk to you."

When there was no answer, I said, "I'm Agent Sueño from Seoul. You won't be able to hide from us, might as well talk now."

Words were mumbled inside and clothes rustled.

Ernie returned at a trot.

"No way out the back," he whispered. "The only exit is through the front here and that side door off the kitchen."

We could keep an eye on both exits from where we stood.

I stepped closer to the door. "Last chance," I said, "or we're kicking the door in."

More frantic mumbling, something being dropped, a heavy object of some sort, and then a shadow appeared in front of the oil paper. I backed up, keeping my hand on my hip where my .45 would've been if I'd been armed. That's one thing that Ernie and I hadn't thought of: to check out weapons from the Pusan MP station. Suddenly it seemed like a tremendous oversight.

Ernie stepped to his right, into the darkness. I stepped to my left.

The oil-paper door slid open.

Yellow light flooded into the courtyard. Ernie and I tensed. A face peeked out, the same woman who'd peeked out earlier. This time, I caught a good look at her. She was cute, young, maybe in her early twenties, with a bemused expression and braided pigtails hanging down from either side of her round head.

Ernie stepped forward, grabbed the edge of the door, slipped off his shoes and stepped into the hooch. The woman screeched. Ernie shoved her aside.

I followed him into the hooch.

Ernie searched the kitchen and the tiny storeroom out back.

"Nobody here," he said, returning to the main room.

Nobody except a little girl who was squatting next to an inlaid mother-of-pearl armoire. She had a face and hairstyle just like her mother's, except for her coloration. She was very light-skinned and her hair was dirty blonde.

"This must be Jeannie," I said.

The little girl's eyes widened. Blue fading to green. Her mother stepped away from us and clutched her arms in front of her ample breasts. She wore only a set of PX thermal long johns, no bra underneath. The woman reached into the armoire, pulled out a winter coat, and wrapped it around herself. She squatted down next to Jeannie and placed a protective arm around her.

"Weyworth not here," she said.

"Weyworth?" Ernie said. "Don't you call him Nick?"

The woman didn't answer.

"Where'd he go?" I asked.

"He go someplace," she said, waving her free arm. "I don't know. All the time *big* deal, he gotta do. Business, he say. Where, I don't know."

"You *moolah?*" Ernie asked. *Moolah* is the Korean word for "I don't know" or "I don't understand."

"Yeah," she replied. "I moolah."

"What time does he come back?" I asked.

"Now?" she replied. "Maybe don't come back until morning time. After curfew."

"He catchy girlfriend?" Ernie asked.

The woman knotted her slender fist. "He catchy girlfriend, then most tick he catchy knuckle sandwich."

"So he's doing business?" I said, more gently.

She nodded warily, worried now that she might have revealed too much.

Ernie knelt to the warm ondol floor; I did the same. He smiled at the woman and then he smiled at Jeannie. Both of them were still nervous. I guessed from the age of the girl—about four—that Weyworth wasn't the father. G.I.s pull a one-year tour in Korea. There hadn't been time for him to sire this beautiful four-year-old child.

"Who's Jeannie's daddy?" Ernie asked.

The woman didn't get angry. "Long time ago," she said, "'nother G.I."

"Picture isso?"

I knew what Ernie was doing. He was trying, in his own way, to relax Jeannie and her mother. And showing pictures was something few Korean business girls could resist. Especially pictures of old boyfriends, and especially if those boyfriends had left them with a child.

She rummaged beneath silk-covered comforters in the bottom of the armoire and pulled out a thick photo album. She set it on the floor and flipped quickly through the pictures. Jeannie slid closer to her mother. Finally, Jeannie's mother found a photo of Jeannie on *Beikil*, her Hundredth Day celebration. In ancient times, so many infants succumbed to childhood diseases that it was thought wise to wait a hundred days, until their chances of survival looked somewhat promising, before welcoming them into the human family.

Jeannie's mother turned the photograph toward Ernie and then me. The infant Jeannie was dressed in a brightly colored silk suit, surrounded by ripe fruit and fat dumplings. Ernie and I oohed and aahed and told Jeannie what a beautiful baby she'd been. Jeannie buried her face beneath her mother's armpit, embarrassed by the attention. Then Jeannie's mother flipped the pages to a photo of herself, a few years younger, wearing a colorful *chima-chogori*, the traditional Korean dress with a high-waisted skirt and a short vest. She looked beautiful, and I told her so.

"*Ipuh-da*," I said. She beamed with happiness.

Some Koreans are trained to hide their emotions, but not all. By now, Jeannie's mother was delighted, and all thought of Weyworth had been banished from her mind. Ernie and I studied the photograph, paying particular attention to the

G.I. standing next to her. He wore a dress green uniform with three yellow stripes sewn on a well-pressed sleeve. A buck sergeant. His nameplate said Bermann.

"Did you get married?" Ernie asked.

She shook her head. "Supposed to. But he change mind. Go back States."

An old story.

Jeannie's mother filled the silence by saying, "The only thing he teach me is how to smoke, how to drink . . . " Then she hugged Jeannie, adding, "And how to make baby. *Tambei isso?*" she asked. Do you have a cigarette?

Ernie and I both shook our heads.

"Next time I'll buy some," Ernie said.

She smiled at that.

"Where is Weyworth now?" I asked.

"Somewhere," she said, reaching for a pack of cigarettes in the armoire. "Somewhere, I don't know. Maybe down on Texas Street."

Texas Street was the notorious bar-and-red-light district along the Pusan waterfront. This late, there'd be no time for him to return from Texas Street before the midnight curfew hit.

"Why is he staying on Texas Street all night?" Ernie asked.

"Business," she said.

"Business with who?"

"I don't know. Not G.I. How you say? *Shi-la.*"

"Greek," I said.

"Yeah," she said, nodding vigorously. "Greek."

"In a Greek bar?" Ernie said.

What with so many merchant marines flooding Texas

Street—many of them from Greece—there were special bars set aside for them so they wouldn't have to mingle with Americans or other English-speaking sailors.

Jeannie's mother lit her cigarette, puffed, and snuffed out the wooden match. "Yeah," she said. "Someplace he call some funny name. Mean 'makey-love' in Greek language."

"Eros," I said.

Jeannie's mother's eyes lit up. "Yeah. That's it."

An MP patrol gave us a ride to Texas Street. Ernie and I sat crouched in the back of the jeep, our knees almost touching our faces. The two MPs sat in the spacious seats in front. One of the MPs remembered me.

"Hard-to-pronounce name. Sueño, right?"

"You got it."

He'd made the ñ sound correctly, like the *ny* in canyon. "I should've thought of that before." He popped his forehead with his open palm.

"What do you mean?" I asked.

The MP's name was Norris, and he'd been on duty when Ernie and I made an arrest on that previous trip down here about a year ago.

"A guy asked about you," Norris said. "Or at least I think he was asking about you. He mispronounced your name."

Rain spattered against the windshield as we rolled over the broad, deserted Pusan roads. I leaned forward as far as the cramped space would allow. "So, who was this guy who came looking for me?" I asked.

Norris turned his face toward me slightly so I could

hear better over the sound of the swishing tires. Mist-laden wind slapped against the canvas sides of the jeep.

"A sailor," he told me. "Some sort of foreigner. I don't remember his name; I have it written down in one of my old notebooks, because he went so far as to show me his passport."

"How'd you know he was looking for me?"

"He described you. Tall. Dark hair. And an investigator. He said he had a message for you."

"Did he tell you what the message was?"

"No. He approached us one night while we were out on patrol, just sitting in the jeep smoking and shooting the shit. Not many ships in port that night. Still, he'd lurked around in an alley, watching us, and when he thought no one was paying attention, he came up and started talking."

"He could speak English?"

"Not very well. He wasn't Greek, but from somewhere in Eastern Europe. I forget what country."

Eastern Europe implied the Communist bloc. This story was getting weirder.

"Then what did he say?"

"He said he had a book he wanted to sell and you might be interested. And no, he didn't tell me what kind of book. Only that it was old, an antique, like that."

Ernie and I glanced at each other, neither of us having a clue as to what Sergeant Norris was talking about.

"Also, there's one more thing," Norris said. "He said you'd understand the book he was trying to sell."

"I'd 'understand'?"

"Yeah. You'd be able to read it."

"Was it in Korean?"

"I don't know. He didn't tell us exactly."

We reached Texas Street and rolled slowly through the narrow alleys lined on either side with dark neon signs. The bars and the eateries and the hot-bed yoguans were shuttered and locked. Wind swept through the lanes like lost souls howling for one more breath of life.

We climbed out of the jeep and thanked Norris and his comrade. Norris promised to dig out his old notebook tomorrow and provide me with more information.

As they drove off, Ernie snapped a two-fingered salute.

The MP patrol had dropped us off two blocks from the Greek bar known as Eros. We didn't want them to take us right up to the front door, because we wanted to reconnoiter the joint first. The streets of the half-mile square area known—even to Koreans—as Texas Street were empty now, almost a half hour after midnight. Plastic covers rattled in metal holders as unlit neon was being battered by a cold wind blowing in off the bay. The wind carried a salty mist. I stuck out my tongue and rubbed the salt along my lips.

"She's a cute kid," Ernie said.

"You mean Jeannie's mother?" I asked.

"Who else?"

"But she's betrothed."

Ernie guffawed.

"She *is* cute," I agreed. "I'll grant you that."

"Nice figure, too."

"Calm down, Romeo," I said. "We have work to do."

Specialist Four Nicholas Q. Weyworth had been on

leave when the first rape occurred on the Blue Train. We had no reason to believe that he'd been on the train, but he *could've* been—if he'd purchased a ticket at the Korean ticket counter and if he'd sat apart from the other Americans. When the second rape occurred, we knew for sure that he'd actually been on that train, returning from Seoul.

Still, Weyworth didn't match the description of the perpetrator that had been given by both the first victim and the front-desk clerk at the Shindae Hotel. He was shorter, smaller, not as dark. But eyewitness accounts, particularly from people under stress, are notoriously unreliable. I still didn't know what Weyworth's blood type was, but if it was A-positive, we'd have our suspect.

Gently, I tried the front door of the Eros Nightclub and Bar. Locked. I'd expected it to be. But through the thickly glazed transom above the door, a dim light glowed—and when I pressed my ear against the wood, there were murmuring voices. Maybe it was the rumbling of the sea behind me, but I didn't think so.

"Let's try the back," I told Ernie.

He nodded and led the way.

Greek sailors are notorious in Asian ports. First, there are plenty of them. The world's merchant marine is largely dominated by their country, and they greatly outnumber sailors from more-affluent countries such as Japan or the Western European nations or the United States. Lately, however, the Filipinos had been giving them a run for their money. Second, Greeks like to party. In their own way. In their own nightclubs, where the bartenders and the waitresses and, most importantly, the business girls all speak Greek; and where Greek music is played and where they can dance their famous Greek dances and break as many plates as they see fit. Americans aren't welcome in these places and seldom go in; for one thing, they can't even read the signs. The word "Eros" in the sign above the front door was written in what I assumed to be Greek letters. At least, they were shaped weird.

I'd been in Greek bars once or twice, alone, and gotten along well enough with the sailors. On one occasion, a Korean business girl had approached me, speaking Greek. I spoke to her in Korean, and soon I was speaking, through her, to some of the sailors at the bar. They spoke Greek, she translated it into Korean to me, and we went back and forth like that; not a word of English spoken during the entire conversation. Nice fellows, actually, as long as they didn't feel I was showing them a lack of respect.

Another thing Greek sailors are notorious for is fighting. Down here on Texas Street, the Korean National Police never travel alone. They travel in squads, with helmets and padded vests and lead-reinforced nightsticks. When an altercation breaks out among the Greeks, knives are usually pulled—another Mediterranean tradition—and the Korean cops don't like to take chances. They come at the problem with overwhelming force.

Usually, since international trade is so important to the Korean government, the offending sailors are treated leniently. They are locked up overnight, they're made to reimburse Korean citizens for any damages or medical bills, and they're released. That is, unless someone's murdered. Then the shipping company might have to cough up some serious reparations money.

All these things were running through my mind as I followed Ernie into the dark alley behind the Eros Nightclub and Bar. Once again, I regretted not having checked out a weapon from the armory at the Hialeah Compound MP station.

Ernie shoved me against a wall. I was startled at first but quickly realized he'd done it to hide us both in the shadows. I held my breath.

The back door of the club burst open. Two men stumbled out. Drunk. They shouted words to one another that were incomprehensible. Just as one was about to shut the door, I shoved past Ernie, saying "Wait here," and trotted the few yards to the back door. I stepped past the surprised men and grabbed the edge of the door before it closed.

"*Dikanis*," I said, waving my hand at them and keeping my head bowed. It was the only word I knew in Greek. A greeting.

"*Kala*," they replied, somewhat surprised, but by then I was already past them and inside the bar. I shut the door behind me, making sure it was locked.

I stood in a narrow hallway. The first thing I saw, and smelled, was the men's room. I used it. Then I went back to the door, opened it, peeked out, and saw that the two drunken sailors were gone. Ernie scurried up. I shut the door behind him.

"I didn't know you spoke Greek," he said.

"There's a lot of things about me you don't know."

He snorted.

We turned and walked through a dark corridor. Steps led downward to a ballroom at a split-level a few feet below us. There were two pool tables, not in use, and a long bar opposite, about a dozen cocktail tables, and a small stage. Sitting at the bar was a blond man wearing blue jeans and a cowboy shirt. Three men who looked like Greeks were huddled around him. A half-covered neon light sat low behind the bar. No bartender or waitresses or business girls in sight. All the cabinets had been locked. Small tumblers filled with a dark fluid sat in front of the men.

One of them noticed us and looked up. The rest stopped talking and stared.

Weyworth—or the man I assumed to be Weyworth—turned on his stool, gaping.

The Greek sailors reached in their back pockets. I knew, from previous experience, that that's where they kept their knives. I reached deep into my leather coat, as if reaching for a weapon—a weapon I didn't have. Ernie scurried down the steps and grabbed a pool cue.

That's him, more practical than imaginative.

The Greeks pulled their knives and stepped forward.

7

Almost in unison, they pressed buttons and the blades clicked open, gleaming in the dim yellow light. Weyworth scurried to the end of the bar. Keeping my eyes on the Greeks, I spoke to him.

"Nice company you keep, Weyworth."

"What do you want?"

I shrugged. "Just want to talk to you."

One of the Greeks stepped forward. Ernie raised his pool cue. The man stopped.

"Tell your buddies to lay off. We're not after them. We're after you."

"*You* tell 'em," Weyworth said.

Apparently, he just had. One of the Greeks waved his free hand at me and said, "Go. You go." He motioned toward the back door.

Ernie grabbed a second pool cue and tossed it to me. I grabbed it on the fly.

"How was your trip to Seoul?" I asked Weyworth.

"How do you know about that?"

"What was the purpose of the trip, Nick? Sightseeing?"

"None of your damn business."

"Or maybe picking up some contraband and selling it to these gentlemen." I studied the bar and the coats the Greeks were wearing. If Weyworth had just dropped off some contraband, it had to be small, something like jewelry. Dope was out of the question. Not only is there a small market for it in Korea but, more importantly, the punishment for trafficking in narcotics in the Republic of Korea is death. I couldn't imagine even these guys would be *that* stupid. "Maybe these guys brought something into port," I said. "Something valuable, and you transported it north to Seoul and made the sale."

Weyworth squirmed. "Get the hell out of here."

"You're coming with us, Weyworth."

Ernie stepped toward him. The Greeks started forward, but we both brandished our pool cues. They stopped. The sailors spoke enough English to understand that we weren't after them, only Weyworth. And if the transaction had already been made, if they already had their money, they wouldn't be willing to fight over keeping him here.

At least that's the way I read the situation.

I covered Ernie as he approached Specialist Four Nicholas Q. Weyworth at the end of the bar. The Greeks stood their ground. Ernie finally reached Weyworth and shoved him with his pool cue. He threw him up against the bar and turned him around, keeping a weather eye on the Greeks. He was about to handcuff the young man, who kept squealing in protest.

"I ain't done nothing."

But just as Ernie snapped shut the cuffs, a plate flew through the air. I ducked. Another plate swooped toward me, and this one connected. I shrugged it off, but by now one of the Greeks had taken advantage of the distraction and was scuttling toward me, a knife with a gleaming blade held in front of him.

I swung the pool cue. He dodged it and lunged. I sidestepped, feeling the blade slice my jacket near my elbow. I twisted the cue and slammed him flush in the gut. As he doubled over, another Greek jumped on my back and I rolled with the jarring force of his body and twisted forward and then he was upside down careering through the air.

Glassware and chairs and pool cues flew everywhere. Weyworth ran past me, heading for the front door. I lunged for him but missed. I saw Ernie punching and wrestling with two Greeks, and I ran toward them. At the same time I heard footsteps tromping in from the back and someone shouting "Halt!" The front door slammed open, and there was cursing in Greek. I shoved a guy away from Ernie, and he reeled toward the front door. I ran after him.

Just as I stepped outside, watching for knives—and just when I started to breathe the fresh tang of mist-laden air—I was hit with something heavy.

Right in the face.

* * *

When I woke up, I was lying flat on my back in a bed with crisp white sheets. My eyes focused on a weasel staring down at me. Then I realized it wasn't a weasel, but something worse: Lieutenant Messler.

"You look like shit," he said.

I tried to move my lips. They weren't working very well. Finally, I croaked out a sound. "Where's Ernie?"

"Oh, he's fine. A couple of scratches and bruises. Nothing serious. Lucky for you Sergeant Norris and his partner hung around the area."

Probably on Messler's orders, to keep an eye on the CID guys from Seoul who were messing around in their area of operations.

"Who hit me?" I asked.

"Don't know. Probably a third-country national. Try to remember, Agent Sueño, Eighth Army encourages us to make friends with our international neighbors."

I meant to say "Screw you," but I think it came out more like "Scoo you." I can't be sure, because my hearing wasn't too great either. Suddenly I felt dizzy staring at Lieutenant Messler, and a nurse came over and shooed him away. "What about Weyworth?" I managed to croak before he walked away.

"Who?" he said, stepping back to the edge of the bed.

"Spec Four Weyworth."

"Nobody else was there when Norris and his partner found you. Just you and Bascom. Knocked out. Lying on the floor." Then he grinned a weasel-like grin. "Good show, old chap."

He chortled and disappeared.

My eyes popped open. I'm not sure how long I'd been out, but it was still dark outside. A yellow-bulbed lamp glowed dimly next to my bed. A figure sat in a chair, so silently that I almost hadn't noticed he was there. He grinned and leaned into the light.

Ernie.

"They say you'll be fine," he said. "Just a mild concussion. Nothing to worry about."

"Good."

I started to get up. He held out his hands. "You should rest. At least until the morning."

"What time is it now?"

"Zero five hundred."

I groaned. "Do you know who hit me?"

"Greek sailors," he replied. "I popped a couple of them good. Would've popped more if Norris and his partner hadn't interrupted me."

"Chased them away?"

"Yeah."

"What about Weyworth?"

"One of the Greeks managed to get hold of my keys somehow."

"He escaped?"

"Yeah."

Ernie hadn't been "popping them good" like he'd claimed. He'd been overcome just as I had. Sergeant Norris and his partner had apparently saved our butts.

There was a metal guard taped to my nose. I pulled it off.

"You look *mah*-velous, dah-ling," Ernie said.

"Screw you." I climbed out of bed, found my clothes

stuffed in a bag beneath the nightstand, and started slipping them on. "Maybe we should wake up the armorer," I said.

Ernie opened his coat. The butt of a .45 peeked out of a holster.

"'Great minds' and all that," he said.

Two hours later, we were sitting at the PX cafeteria sipping coffee and perusing the morning edition of the *Pacific Stars and Stripes*. I was very conscious of my nose. It was puffed up and bright red and almost glowed, and it was very tender to the touch. While drinking, I was careful not to tilt my coffee mug back too far.

We'd already been out to Weyworth's hooch. Jeannie's mother woke up angry and remained angry while we asked about Weyworth, claiming he hadn't come home last night. We searched her hooch and its environs just to make sure. Ernie thought she was cute when she was angry.

"She's cute when she does *anything*," I replied.

We returned to the compound, and by then the cafeteria was open.

Now that the grill was heated up, I hobbled over to the serving line and ordered a bacon, lettuce, and tomato sandwich, hold the mayo. Ernie had scrambled eggs and sausage. While we ate, I gradually started to feel more human.

"So, if you were Weyworth," I asked Ernie, "where would you go?"

"Back to my hooch."

"To face your angry girlfriend?"

"Hell, yeah. She's cute."

"But eventually you'd be arrested by the likes of you and me."

"Maybe. But I wouldn't be locked up long. The Greeks don't talk—mouthing off to cops isn't in their nature—and if I kept my mouth shut and said nothing more than that I wanted to talk to a lawyer, I'd be out in a couple of hours."

"You know that because you work in law enforcement. Weyworth doesn't necessarily know that."

Ernie shrugged and continued shoveling eggs in his mouth.

"All we want to know," I continued, "is what he saw on the Blue Train."

"And if he's the killer."

"There's that."

"And if he's not the killer, who is."

"There's that too."

I walked to the serving line and pulled myself a cup of joe from the huge stainless-steel coffee urn. When I reached in my pocket for my receipt, the tired female cashier waved me past. There were so few customers, she remembered that I qualified for the free refill. I studied her face. She didn't look much like Mrs. Oh Myong-ja, the first victim, but there were similarities. They were both Korean, they were both in their early thirties, and I could tell by her ring that they were both married. Did she have children? Probably. Why else would she be working so early in the morning on a G.I. compound?

When I returned to our table, I clunked my coffee mug down and asked Ernie, "What do you think Runnels meant about the Blue Train rapist having a 'checklist'?"

Ernie looked up from the sports page. "I think the guy has a lot of people he hates."

"What makes you say that?"

Ernie shrugged. "What he did on the train was an in-your-face act. Like flipping the world the bird."

I already knew that Ernie had more brains than people gave him credit for. And more brains than he usually bothered to show.

"And what he did next," I said, "here in Pusan, is an act even more brutal than the first."

"Right."

"So the 'checklist' probably becomes progressively bloodier."

Ernie looked back at the sports page. "Unless we catch him first."

Mr. Kill was waiting for us at the Pusan Police Station.

He rose as we walked in, and within seconds we were in a police sedan being driven over to the Pusan-*yok*, the train station.

"The local police," Kill told us, "are checking with every cab driver who picked up a fare at the Pusan station yesterday. They should have a report for us some time today. Not only did Mrs. Hyon and her three children take a cab from the train station to the Shindae Hotel, so did the killer."

"So if they're checking that," Ernie asked, "why are we going to the train station?"

Mr. Kill raised a paper bag he'd been holding in his lap. "This." He pulled out a woman's purse. "This is the one the rapist showed to the desk clerk," he told us. "So he could follow Mrs. Hyon up to the third floor."

"Already dusted for prints?"

"There weren't any. He must have wiped it down."

"If the guy's so smart, why'd he leave the purse?"

"Probably thought we couldn't do anything with it," Kill said. "And he might be right."

The sedan pulled up in front of the huge flagstone expanse in front of the Pusan train station. Canvas-covered lean-tos were set up in neat rows. Some of them had wooden counters and sold hot bowls of noodles; others hawked already-packed *toshirak* with rice and kimchee and other savories inside, suitable for eating on the train. Other stands sold umbrellas or galoshes, and a few sold clothing items of various descriptions for the traveler who might've forgotten to pack something.

Mr. Kill stopped at every clothing stand, showed them the handbag, asking if they sold this type of item. Three of them did. He questioned them at length. Finally, a tall woman with a pronounced overbite admitted that she'd sold a handbag exactly like that to a foreigner. She remembered the time: it was already dark, and the Blue Train from Seoul had just pulled in.

"After that," she said, "we locked up and went home. No business after the last Blue Train."

"What did he look like?" Mr. Kill asked.

"Like them," she said, pointing to Ernie and me. She realized Mr. Kill expected more, so she said, "Big. With a big nose."

Patiently, Mr. Kill took her through all the various physical attributes a person can have. When he was finished, we had the picture we expected. A Caucasian male, about six feet tall—maybe a little more, maybe a little less—with short-cropped dark hair, but she hadn't noticed if the hair was curly or straight. His nose was big, not as pointed as Ernie's and not as puffed up as mine. He wore a dark shirt of some sort, she wasn't sure of the color, and he wore dark slacks, although they could've been blue jeans. His shoes, she didn't see.

"How about a traveling bag?" Kill asked.

She shook her head. "He wasn't carrying one. And I would've noticed. I'm in that line of work."

Mr. Kill asked about the man's hands. He'd used them to point at the handbag and he'd used them to make payment.

Yes, there was hair on the hands. She crinkled her nose at the memory. And the nails, she thought, were probably cut short, although she couldn't be sure. No rings or jewelry that she remembered.

Mr. Kill asked if he'd spoken to her in Korean or English.

"He didn't say anything," the vendor replied. "He just pointed." Her array of handbags was hanging by nails on the rafters.

"He didn't ask how much it was?"

"No. So I told him. Four thousand five hundred."

"You told him in Korean or English?"

"In English," she replied proudly. "I can speak that much."

"Isn't four thousand five hundred a little steep?" Kill asked.

The woman blushed. "All foreigners are rich," she said. "And anyway, he didn't wait for his change."

* * *

A couple of hours later, the local KNPs located the cab drivers. The one who'd driven Mrs. Hyon and her three children to the Shindae Hotel was an elderly man who sat forward on his hard wooden chair and puffed on a Kobuk-song cigarette through the entire conversation. According to him, Mrs. Hyon was having trouble with her kids, who were restless after the long train ride. When they arrived at the hotel, she paid him and thanked him, seemed all in all a very nice lady.

"*Chuggosso*?" he asked, his mouth open. She's dead?

Kill nodded gravely.

He shook his head sadly. "*Aiyu. Kullioyo.*" How pitiful.

The second driver was a younger man, with hair hanging down just slightly over his ears. He seemed nervous. "The foreigner just pointed," he said in Korean. "He didn't even wait in line. He just stepped right in front of the other customers and climbed in my cab and he pointed to the cab that had just pulled away from the curb."

"Didn't you tell him to get out of your cab and wait his turn?"

"No. He looked fierce. With those big eyes and that big nose and those big hairy knuckles. I just drove."

"When you arrived at the hotel, what happened?"

"He pointed at the side of the road. He didn't want me to follow the other cab into the driveway in front of the hotel. He wanted me to stop before that."

"But you're not supposed to stop there."

"No, I'm not. And when I did, traffic was backed up and honking behind me." The man's head had been hanging down; he raised it briefly. "I'm not going to get a ticket, am I?"

"No. No ticket," Kill said. "What happened then?"

"He thrust some money at me."

"How much?"

"At first I wasn't sure. It was wadded up. I didn't even count it right away. All I did was smile and nod my head and pray that he'd climb out of my cab. He did. Then I pulled away. Later, I counted the money. About eight hundred won, all in hundred-won notes."

"How much was the actual fare?"

"Less than four hundred."

"Easy money."

"I wouldn't say so."

"Why not?" Kill asked.

"Because he scared the piss out of me."

Kill said he was going to try for another composite sketch, using the train-station vendor and the young cab driver. Meanwhile, he had the Korean National Police put out an all-points bulletin for Specialist Four Nicholas Q. Weyworth. I told him that we suspected him of trafficking in contraband, an allegation that would be enough for the KNPs to hold him at least until the 8th Army MPs arrived.

Jurisdiction concerning the United States forces in Korea is always a delicate diplomatic dance. Under the Status of Forces Agreement, the KNPs have the right to arrest an American soldier, but immediately upon doing so they must notify the 8th United States Army. A representative is sent out to make sure that all the G.I.'s rights are respected. Despite these elaborate rules, there are always jurisdictional disputes. Sometimes one side wants to take jurisdiction, sometimes the other. Right now, we just wanted to find Weyworth, take him into custody, and question him. Then we'd go from there.

Weyworth might not be the Blue Train rapist. His description didn't match what either the train-station vendor or the cab driver had just told us, but again, eye-witness accounts are notoriously unreliable. I'd already checked, and his blood type wasn't A-positive, but his personnel records could be wrong. It happens. Or the KNP lab could've made a mistake in analyzing the sample. That happens too. Until I was sure, I had to assume that Nicholas Q. Weyworth was a very dangerous man.

In the meantime, while the KNPs searched for Weyworth, Ernie and I would continue our investigation. Corporal Robert R. Pruchert, the guy who fancied himself some sort of Buddhist monk, was next on our list. His blood type was A-positive. Very possibly just a coincidence. We promised Mr. Kill that we'd find Pruchert today and meet back at the Pusan Police Station this evening to compare notes.

When we walked into the Hialeah Compound MP station, the desk sergeant was grinning at us and the MP shift change, a whole squad of them, started hooting.

"Ernie," one of them said in a high-pitched voice, "we *miss* you."

The others guffawed, and Ernie and I strode up to the desk sergeant and asked him what the hell was going on. He slid a piece of paper across the counter. "This just came in. Your services are required."

The same MP pretended he was hugging himself and said once again, in the same sing-song voice, "Oh, Ernie!"

Ernie flipped him the bird. "What is it?" he asked. I read the message quickly and handed it to him. After staring at it for a few seconds, he crumpled it in his fist.

"Damn, Marnie," he said.

One of the MPs said, "Oh, Marnie!"

Ernie ran over and pushed him hard. The MP rebounded and raised his fists and Ernie socked him in the jaw. Other MPs surged forward, but I held as many back as I could and after a lot of yelling and shoving, the desk sergeant waded into the melee and started ordering people to back off. Gradually, cooler heads prevailed and the desk sergeant told everyone to get back to work. No one was hurt. Just a little wounded pride. The MPs filed out of the foyer, mumbling and cursing all G.I.s from Seoul.

I turned to Ernie. "Do you always have to start something?"

He straightened his jacket and examined his knuckles. A couple of them were bruised. "That's what I'm here for," he said.

8

Corporal Robert R. Pruchert worked at a commo site in a village known as Horang-ni, about twelve miles north of Pusan. In ancient times, Siberian tigers prowled these mountains. The wildlife was gone now, but what remained was a farming village that had wood huts with straw-thatched roofs, and oxen in the field, looking like something out of the Brothers Grimm. Atop a rocky hill sat a First Signal Brigade microwave relay site. A few cement-block buildings were surrounded by a chain-link fence topped with concertina wire; but the main feature, right in the center of the site, was a huge white geodesic dome, looking for all the world like a two-story-tall golf ball.

"What the hell is that?" Ernie asked.

"Science," I replied. "That class you skipped in high school."

"Why the soccer ball?"

I shrugged. I really didn't know, but I told Ernie it was to protect the equipment inside. He bought it. We were driving a puke-green army-issue four-door sedan that we'd checked out of the Hialeah Compound Consolidated Motor Pool. The engine needed work. It stuttered and puttered along but, so far, it had gotten the job done, carrying us out of the city and into this idyllic countryside on a cold, gray, overcast afternoon. We pulled up to the main gate of the signal compound. A listless Korean contract guard in a khaki uniform checked our dispatch. He called ahead. Two minutes later, a buzzer sounded, the gate opened, and we drove through. Ernie parked on a gravel lot near the largest building. We climbed out of the sedan and, before we could reach the front door, an officer burst out, asking us what we wanted. His fatigues were sloppy, as if they hadn't been pressed in a week. His name tag said Wilson, and his rank was major. I told him what we wanted.

"Pruchert's not here," he said. "He's on leave."

"Where did he go?"

"Hell if I know."

I nodded toward the inside of the signal site. "Maybe some of your men know."

"No. None of them know either." When I continued to stare at him, he started to get nervous, and suddenly he spoke. "Pruchert is an odd bird. He does his own thing. Into all this Buddhism stuff. Where he goes, nobody here has any idea."

"Then we'll want to look at his personal effects. His wall locker, things like that."

Major Wilson sighed as if it were the biggest imposition he'd ever faced. "All right. Come on."

As we walked through the orderly room and started down a long hallway, Ernie leaned toward me and whispered, "Talk about a plug in his butt."

This morning, before we left Hialeah Compound, I'd called Staff Sergeant Riley at the 8th Army CID admin office and asked him to have the Provost Marshal call ahead to the Horang-ni Signal Site to make it easier for us to get access. These signal types were fanatics for security. Not that I blamed them, but the way they kept everything—and everybody—under lock and key made me glad I didn't work for them.

Corporal Robert R. Pruchert's bunk was neatly made, and both his footlocker and his wall locker were secured. There were no personal photos tacked to the wall, only a poster of Siddhãrtha Gautama, the Buddha, perched on a flaming lotus leaf, the thumb and forefinger of his raised hand forming a circle in the air.

"What's with the circle?" Ernie asked. "Does that mean the spaghetti's done?"

Major Wilson hovered near us, looking worried.

I studied the poster too. The Buddhist idea that human beings could perfect themselves and attain nirvana was stunning, especially for those of us under the influence of a religion that asked only for grace. It was odd for an American G.I. to take up Buddhism and to spend his precious leave time—time away from this signal site—on such a demanding religious pursuit. But the United States Army is composed of many odd ducks. Chinese characters were sketched below the Buddha. In my notebook, I copied them down.

Major Wilson was watching my every move. "What're you copying that for?" he asked.

"Buddhism's a profound religion," I said. "Maybe I'll take it up some day."

He snorted in disbelief.

Ernie fidgeted, probably about to say something, either about Major Wilson's lousy attitude or about finding somebody with a crowbar or a bolt cutter so we could bust into Pruchert's wall locker. I waved him off.

"That'll do it, sir," I said, snapping shut my notebook. "That's all we need."

"That's it?"

"That's it."

I smiled, and Ernie and I walked down the long corridor. Surly G.I.s slaved over blinking equipment, occasionally glancing at us over their shoulders. Jealous, I thought, that we were able to walk out of there.

Outside, Ernie said, "Don't you want to search that wall locker?"

"No. I have all I need."

We climbed back in the sedan, Ernie behind the steering wheel. He stared sourly at the automatic transmission.

"It's just not natural," he said.

"What?"

"This," he said, pointing at the steering wheel. "No stick shift. It just doesn't seem right, not like real driving. All I'm doing here is pointing and aiming."

"That's all you do with your .45," I said.

"But that's different."

"How?"

"After I point and aim and then pull the trigger," he

said, "people start paying attention to me. With this piece of shit, they just laugh."

We backed out of the parking space, turned around, and waited until the khaki-clad guard pulled open the gate. Then we drove out into freedom.

"Where's this place again?" Ernie asked.

I had an army-issue map open on my lap. It had been printed almost twenty years ago, so some of the roads had changed: some had been paved, others had disappeared.

"Hang a left up ahead."

"Past that oxcart?"

"Yeah."

We were way out in the boonies. The Chinese characters I'd copied off Pruchert's poster were the name of a Buddhist temple. Even without being able to read all of the characters, I could understand that much because I knew the character for the word "temple." The rest was just a matter of looking them up in the dictionary. Unfortunately, out here in the countryside in the middle of Kyongsan Province, some twenty klicks north of Pusan, I didn't have a Chinese–English dictionary with me.

"So, how you going to read it?" Ernie asked.

"I'll get help."

At the first village we came to, I had Ernie pull over in front of a shack with a sign tacked to the door. The sign was a sheet of red paper with a single Chinese character printed on it, pronounced in Korean as *chom*. The word meant "divination." It was the home of a fortune-teller.

"Fortune-teller?" Ernie asked. "I thought you didn't believe in that stuff."

"I don't. But the fortune-tellers can usually read Chinese characters, because they have to look up astrological signs in the Book of Changes."

"And that has what to do with us finding Pruchert?"

"They'll be able to tell me the name of the temple that poster came from. And probably where it's located."

Ernie shook his head. "I'll wait here."

I didn't tell him how relieved I was to hear that.

I knocked on the flimsy wooden door and a few seconds later sandals shuffled across dirt. The door opened. A toothless old woman peered out. I spoke to her in Korean.

"Please help me, Grandmother," I said. "I have some Chinese characters that I can't read. Maybe you could read them for me and help me find a Buddhist temple."

The wrinkles and dark splotches on her face folded into a huge smile. She motioned to me to enter and had me follow her across a courtyard, and sat me down on a warm ondol floor. The room smelled of pungent, nameless aromas. We talked a while, and I showed her the characters and she read them immediately. Then she started pointing and giving me directions, and I tried to get her to show me on the map, but she wasn't used to that. A young woman came in with two cups of cold barley tea.

"My granddaughter," the old woman said. I nodded to the young girl, and she backed out of the room.

I listened carefully to the old woman describing directions, trying on my own to follow her on the map. But what really clinched it was when she told me that the temple was on the side of Chonhuang Mountain. *Chonhuang* meant

A Thousand Emperors, and even I could read those characters. I found Chonhuang Mountain on the map and saw nearby the reversed swastika that indicated a Buddhist temple. With my pencil, I circled the swastika.

I drank the tea, thanked the woman profusely, and offered her 5,000 won. She said that was too much and tried to turn it down, but I convinced her that she'd done me a great service. Her granddaughter smiled as I walked across the courtyard, bowing deeply. Just as I was about to duck through the small door, the old woman scurried forward, stepping halfway out after me, and grabbed my arm. She made me stand like that, completely still, while she clutched my forearm with both her gnarled hands. She lowered her head. Suddenly everything was quiet around us, as if the entire countryside had gone still. I could barely hear my own breathing, and I couldn't hear hers at all. Her grip tightened, the fingers digging deeply into flesh, cutting off circulation. The old woman's body shuddered. Then, after what seemed a long time to stand in the middle of a door, her moist eyes looked up at me.

"*Chosim haseiyo,*" she said. Please be careful.

"I'm always careful, Grandmother," I said.

"But you must be especially careful now. There is something waiting for you. Something awful and something very sick."

"What's waiting for me? A man?"

"Like a man," she said, "but different. Different here." She tapped her chest. "You must not let him drown you."

"Drown me?"

Then she let go of my forearm and stepped back. I felt blood rush back toward my fingers.

"Who is he?" I asked.

The old woman shook her head, no longer making eye contact. Finally she took a step back, pulling the wooden handle after her. Ancient hinges screeched like a thousand children screaming.

The door slammed shut.

Early that morning, at the Hialeah Compound Consolidated Motor Pool, Ernie and I had been forced to cool our heels while we waited to be issued transportation. I took advantage of the delay to fill Ernie in on what I'd learned from Riley about the previous night's message from 8th Army.

Marnie had complained to Mr. Broughton, the USO head of entertainment, that she and the other musicians were being stalked again. Things were disappearing, according to her, most recently two sets of underwear that the keyboard player had left in the dressing room at Osan Air Force Base.

"Probably one of the zoomies," Ernie said, "jealous of her wardrobe."

"There are other things missing too," I told him, "like a set of drumsticks and another microphone."

"Lost in the loading and unloading," Ernie snorted, crossing his arms.

"Maybe. And they're seeing faces again."

"In the windows?"

"Where else?"

"Just fun-loving G.I.s," Ernie explained.

"Voyeurs."

"Yeah. That too. So, why us? Why not send some guys who are doing nothing but sitting around with their thumbs up their rears?"

"Two reasons, according to Riley. Number one, the Country Western All Stars are working their way south. Tonight Waegwan, after that Camp Henry in Taegu, and, at the end of the week, Hialeah Compound in Pusan."

"So we have to drive all the way up to Waegwan just to play babysitter?"

I nodded.

"What's the second reason?" Ernie asked.

"Because they specifically said they wanted *us* and nobody else. The MPs who were assigned the last few days didn't work out, according to Marnie, and all the girls voted that they wanted you and me back."

"They own us," Ernie said.

"As long as they're here in-country entertaining the troops and as long as the Eighth Army honchos want to keep kissing their butts, you're right. They own us."

"And if the Blue Train rapist strikes again?"

I had no answer for that. Tonight, we'd drive the seventy or so kilometers to Waegwan, schmooze with the girls during their show, and then make sure they were safely tucked in for the night. After that, we'd return to Pusan as time permitted.

"You called Kill?"

"Left a message for him."

"He'll be delighted to learn that we've been pulled off the case."

"Not pulled off," I said. "We have to do both."

Ernie groaned. And groaned more when he saw the sedan we'd been issued.

The craggy peaks of Chonhuang Mountain were covered in mist. So far today, we'd been lucky because, although the sky had been gray and overcast, it hadn't rained. The roads we were traversing were mostly dirt, with plenty of ruts indicating how impassable they'd be in a storm. Ernie shifted the old sedan into low gear, and it coughed and churned its way up a winding pathway. Off to the side, sheer cliffs fell into tree-choked valleys.

"Are they sure there are no more tigers up here?" Ernie asked.

"I'm sure. The last Siberian tiger in South Korea was hunted down and shot in 1956."

"Not so long ago," Ernie said. "Less than twenty years. Who knows? Maybe a few of them survived."

"Maybe. I've heard they've been seen along the DMZ. But that could be just nervous G.I.s, exhausted after a twelve-hour shift in the cold and the rain."

"We're a long way from the DMZ here."

Almost two hundred miles. We were safe from North Korean commandos, but not safe from the occasional rockslides that washed out the road we were traveling on. Often the pathway was so narrow that we stopped so I could walk up ahead to warn off any traffic that might be coming down the hill. None ever was.

Finally, we reached a plateau that was covered with evenly spaced fruit trees, cherry and apple and a couple of others I couldn't identify. After a short drive, we came to an open area in front of a cliff. Two poles held a sign over the road. The sign was varnished red, and the Chinese characters were written in gold. I recognized them. "*Dochung Sa*," the fortune-teller had told me. Temple of the Loyal Path.

We parked in front of a large wooden gate. Men were hoeing in plots on either side of the road. They immediately put down their tools and marched up to us, tilting their straw hats back and grinning broadly. One of them, a bald one, spoke English. "Hello," he said. "Welcome."

I showed him my badge and explained why we'd come.

"Pruchert?" he asked. "The American?"

"You have other foreigners?"

He shook his head rapidly. "No. He's the only one."

"Then may we talk to him, please?"

"That would not be possible."

"Why not? It would only take a few minutes."

The monk shook his bald head again. "I'm afraid he's up there." He pointed to the cliff looming above us. "In one of those caves."

For the first time, I realized that the craggy cliff was dotted with ink-like splotches. The entrances to caves, dozens of them.

"When will he come down?"

"Impossible to say. He's meditating, even as we speak, and it could take days."

"Days? How long has he been up there?"

The monk looked to his comrades for the answer. They conversed among themselves. Finally, he turned back to me and said, "About a week. We take him water and a little food every day, leave it in front of his cave in case he needs it."

"A week?" Ernie said. "Why in the hell is he doing that?"

For the first time, the monk studied Ernie. "To better himself," the monk said.

That seemed to confuse Ernie. The monk smiled. "To become an initiate in our order, long periods of meditation are required."

"He wants to enlist with you guys?"

"So it seems." The monk smiled again.

"This is extremely important," I said. "Have you heard about the Blue Train rapist?"

The monk shook his head. "We don't read newspapers."

"Nevertheless, I must talk to Corporal Pruchert," I said. "He's a soldier and I'm under military orders."

The monk frowned, thought for a minute, and then turned and walked away. He went inside the temple. About twenty minutes later, he came out.

"If you insist," he told me, "we will send someone up to fetch him."

It took an hour. During that time, Ernie walked back into the orchard behind us to take a leak, and later I took my turn. I was starting to worry that we might not have time to make it back to the main supply route and drive north to Waegwan before the Country Western All Stars started their show.

Suddenly a young man in russet robes walked toward us. He was tall and gangly, his flesh white. On his protruding nose, he wore thick army-issue glasses. A few feet from us, he stopped.

"Cut yourself shaving?" Ernie asked.

Ernie was referring to a red slice along the side of the man's head. The man was completely bald.

"I'm Pruchert," he replied. "And I'm on leave. Officially signed out of my unit and everything. So what is it you want?"

"Just a few questions," I said.

"Like what?"

"Like, where were you on Thursday?"

"Where was I? You know the answer to that."

Pruchert looked worn, very haggard, and thin. Dirt and straw had accumulated on the rear of his robe.

"We want to hear the answer from you," Ernie said.

"I was right *here*," Pruchert said, raising his voice. "Meditating. In another few days, I could reach *chung-gun*, the middle rank, if I could just get in enough hours."

"Sort of like merit badges," Ernie said.

Pruchert swiveled on him. "It may be funny to you, but it's not funny to me. If you don't take steps toward enlightenment, you're wasting your life. Throwing away a precious opportunity."

He glared at Ernie, his implication clear. We were obstacles in his path to enlightenment.

Ernie leaned against the side of the sedan, his arms crossed. He asked, "When was the last time you had a woman, Pruchert?"

Blood flushed Pruchert's face, spreading up through the raw scalp of his shaved head.

"You come *here*," he said, pointing at the grounds of the temple, "to this holy place, and ask me a question like that?"

Ernie nodded.

I stepped between them. "When did you arrive here, Pruchert?"

Pruchert looked away. I repeated my question. Finally, he answered.

"Saturday, the day my leave started."

"And have you left these grounds since then?"

"No."

"When are you returning to your unit?"

"Next Friday."

"Have you ever been on the Blue Train to Seoul?"

"Never."

"Why not?" Ernie asked.

"Seoul's an evil place," Pruchert replied. "Full of evil people who have no sense of the crimes they're committing against the universe."

"Crimes against the universe?" Ernie asked.

"Yes. Creating evil karma. Causing people like you to come up here to this holy place."

"Get bent, Pruchert."

Pruchert started toward Ernie. Instead of stopping him, I stepped back and let him go. Ernie stood, uncrossing his arms.

Pruchert clenched a fist, his lips taut, his face turning even redder than it had been before. Finally, he threw his fist down to his side, swiveled on his leather sandals, and stormed off, mumbling—almost crying—to himself.

When he had disappeared to the far side of the temple, Ernie leaned toward me. "Frustrated guy," he said.

I didn't answer.

We took a different road down the mountain. A few splats of rain had made the gravel-and-dirt pathway slick, and when we lost traction, Ernie found himself skidding part of the way downhill. Expertly, he turned into the skids, maintaining control, and we somehow managed to avoid plunging off the edge of the rocky precipice. I held my breath all the way.

When we finally reached the bottom, I exhaled and said, "Thanks, pal."

Ernie looked at me, puzzled. "For what?"

"For not getting us killed."

"Oh, that," he said, tossing his head back toward the mountain. "If we'd been in my jeep and I'd had a proper gearshift, you could have *meditated* all the way down."

A village, large enough to be considered a small town, sat at the bottom of Chonhuang Mountain. We rolled slowly through the main street. The sun was setting now and someone had switched on a neon sign. I read it aloud: "Chonhuang Tabang."

"Chonhuang Teahouse," Ernie said. "That means teahouse girls. Maybe we should stop."

"Two reasons we can't," I told him.

"The first is we have to get to Waegwan," Ernie replied. "What's the second?"

"It might interfere with your journey toward enlightenment."

"Nothing," Ernie said, "is going to interfere with my journey toward enlightenment."

"Except for maybe Marnie Orville," I added.

"Yeah," Ernie agreed. "Except for maybe her."

From in front of the teahouse, a kimchee cab suddenly pulled out into the road, making a U-turn without even looking. Ernie slammed on his brakes and honked his horn. Sheepishly, the driver grinned at us, waved, and kept going.

"Out here," I said, "they don't even think about traffic."

"Much less worry about it."

Ernie stepped on the gas, and in less than two hours we'd reached the city of Waegwan. A few minutes after that, we were pulling up to the front gate of the huge logistics storage area known as Camp Carroll.

"Ernie!" Marnie screeched.

She ran toward him, arms upraised, and grabbed him in a bear hug around his waist.

"Settle down, girl," Ernie said. She tried to lift him but couldn't, so he lifted her instead and carried her over to a straight-backed chair and sat her down. "Sit!" he said. "And behave yourself."

Marnie stared up at him, her cowgirl hat tilted back and pinned to her blonde locks. "You can't believe what we've been through since you and George walked out on us." Then she pouted. "You didn't even say good-bye."

"Yes, I did," Ernie replied.

"Not a *real* good-bye." She smiled impishly and leaped back to her feet, the heels of her cowboy boots stomping on the wooden stage.

We were in the Camp Carroll NCO Club. The instruments were set up and Marnie and the rest of the girls were ready to start their performance. However, there was still no audience. The doors had been kept locked, by order of the base commander, because he didn't want his troops leaving work early to claim a seat near the stage. Instead, he'd instructed the club manager to set up reserved seating by unit. The tables were pushed together in various-sized clumps, and in the center of each group of tables sat a unit banner or insignia. The Headquarters Company's table was the largest, and the full-bird insignia of the base commander sat right at the head of the table, facing center stage. Rank has its privileges.

I grabbed a cup of coffee out of the kitchen. The Korean cooks studied me, some of them nodding, as did the waitresses, who were folding silverware into napkins. I greeted them all in Korean and they nodded and greeted me back. I carried an extra cup of coffee back to the stage for Ernie.

"Nothing for me?" Marnie pouted.

"You have to start work in a minute," Ernie told her.

I sat down in a straight-backed chair near Marnie and asked her about these incidents that had been happening. The musicians of the Country Western All Star Review kept tuning their instruments.

"It's been awful," she said. "Just horrid. We never have any privacy and our equipment keeps disappearing, and then, of all things, Shelly has her underwear stolen. And those MPs they assigned to help us, dumb as bricks."

Marnie's face became serious. She lost her coquettishness and suddenly I could see the intelligent woman beneath the façade of gaiety: the woman who'd organized an all-female country-western band; the woman who'd landed a contract with the USO to travel overseas to the Republic of Korea; the woman who was scouring the world looking for the father of her child.

"But there's something more important," she said, lowering her voice. "Something I really need your help on."

She reached out and touched Ernie with her left hand and grabbed my hand with her right.

"I haven't told you everything," she said.

"Somehow I thought not," Ernie replied.

She pouted at him, the scamp, for just a second, and then she returned to her serious demeanor. She squeezed my hand.

"Casey's father is not behind on his child support."

"Casey?" Ernie asked. "Who's Casey?"

"My daughter," Marnie told him. "The one who's with my mom right now."

"So Casey's father," Ernie said, "is this guy you're looking for. This Freddy Ray."

"Yes. Captain Frederick Raymond Embry."

She turned to me, as if hoping I'd jot the name down in my notebook. I didn't.

"So if he's not behind on his child support," I asked, "why are you looking for him?"

"He never sees his daughter," she said. "That's not right. Children need their daddy, even if he's a louse who walked out on us."

"Sounds like you're still carrying a torch for him," Ernie said.

"No way. Not after what he did to me. *You've* already seen it," she told Ernie. "He hasn't."

She stood up and pulled her silk cowgirl blouse out from beneath the leather belt of her tight blue jeans. Then she raised the blouse all the way up to her brassiere hook and turned to show me her back. It was a vicious scar, running from the left side of her rib cage to the center of her spine. She lowered her blouse, tucked it back in, and turned to face me.

"Thirteen stitches," she said. "And if I hadn't fought

back, Freddy Ray would've killed me. I know he's supposed to be an officer and a gentleman but, believe me, he's no gentleman."

"When this happened," I said, pointing toward her back, "didn't you file a complaint?"

"Of course I did. The cops arrested him and there was a trial, but he said that during the altercation I had attacked him, and when he'd pushed me away I'd tripped and fallen, and that's how the wound had occurred."

"*Did* you attack him?" I asked.

Marnie looked away. "Yes. I did."

"So in Texas, him being an officer and a gentleman and you being partially responsible, they let him go."

Marnie shook her head at the memory. "The judge said that since he was going to be serving his country overseas and since he'd 'suffered enough,' all charges would be dropped."

"Okay," Ernie said. "So Freddy Ray is an asshole. So why are you here? Do you just want to start up again?"

"No, it's not about me. It's about Casey." She stared first at Ernie and then at me. "He says he hasn't been seeing her because he doesn't believe that she's really his daughter." She raised a finger and pointed it at Ernie's nose. "And before you ask, the answer is none of your business. Whether Casey is Freddy Ray's daughter or somebody else's doesn't make her any less precious to me."

Ernie sat down and let the silence grow for a while. Finally he raised both his hands in supplication and said, "Okay. I understand. You want to confront Freddy Ray and persuade him to do the right thing by his daughter. Okay, fine. But what do you want *us* to do about it?"

"I want you to be there when I talk to him."

"So you won't get hurt," I said.

"You got it," she replied. "And I want you to set up the meeting."

"Us?" Ernie asked.

She caressed his shoulder. "It would be so thoughtful of you."

Ernie and I looked at each other. A commotion was starting at the front of the club. The door had been opened and the troops were flooding in. Some of them wore cowboy hats along with their fatigue uniforms, a dispensation that had been specially granted—today only—by the post commander. They started hooting as soon as they saw the female musicians on the stage.

Marnie jumped up, ordering the curtains to be closed, and we, along with all the girls of the Country Western All Star Review, scurried back into the wings. Marnie pulled me aside.

"You're the only one who can help," she said. "Your friend, that Staff Sergeant Riley in Seoul, he helped me find out where Freddy Ray is stationed. It's Camp Henry, the place where we play tomorrow night. I just want you to find him for me so I can talk to him before the show."

Before I could answer, she hugged me and strode out on stage.

On her count, the Country Western All Star Review started up a hot number. The curtains were pulled open and the entire NCO Club ballroom, jam-packed with G.I.s, went mad with joy.

9

After midnight, the highway leading south toward Pusan seemed like the Land of the Dead. Nothing moves in Korea during the midnight-to-four curfew. Even down here, some 200 miles from the Demilitarized Zone, the ROK Army is worried about North Korean infiltrators; worried that they could come in by sea to blow up power plants and munitions factories and communications facilities. And the government isn't just suffering from delusional paranoid fantasies, either. Communist commandos have attacked before, in squads of up to three dozen men, and caused much death and suffering before they were stopped.

As we approached every major city, a heavily armed military roadblock awaited us. Ernie and I showed the grim-faced Korean soldiers our Criminal Investigation badges and our special twenty-four-hour vehicle dispatch—reserved for emergency military and government vehicles only—and were waved through.

The show at Camp Carroll had been a resounding success. Afterward, Ernie and I helped Mr. Shin load everything up and made sure that the girls of the Country Western All Star Review were safely bedded down in the transient billets of the bachelor officers' quarters. Then we'd jumped into the sedan and started back to Pusan.

Ernie was disgruntled—not so much at the lack of rest, but because we'd never had a chance to pop a cold one.

"Don't we get any time off?" he asked.

"During the show," I said, changing the subject, "I called Kill."

"And?"

"The KNPs have come up with a line on Weyworth."

"Good. Did they take him into custody?"

"Not yet. They're waiting for us."

"Why?"

"If he's the one, if he's the Blue Train rapist, they want to make sure that they don't jump their jurisdictional boundaries and pick up an American G.I. without proper cause. It could come back to haunt them. A technicality that could maybe provoke Eighth Army into asking for jurisdiction."

"Which would piss off the Korean people?"

"Understandably enough. Two Korean women have been attacked, one of them murdered. They want the perp tried in a Korean court, not by an American court-martial."

After the Korean War, for fourteen years, the Korean government had had no jurisdiction over American G.I.s.

It didn't matter if they'd robbed a Korean bank or stabbed the president of the country in broad daylight or wrenched the heart out of a statue of Confucius, the Korean legal system couldn't touch them. The most they could do was have the Korean police take them into custody and then, as soon as possible, turn them over to the American MPs. Regardless of the crime—whether it was murder, theft, rape, or embezzlement—American G.I.s always received a trial presided over by a panel of American Army officers. Never by Koreans. This grated on the Korean sense of fairness. Finally, in 1967, the US-ROK Status of Forces Agreement was promulgated and Korean courts were allowed, under specified conditions, to assume jurisdiction over 8th Army soldiers accused of a crime. However, there were still loopholes in the agreement, and often, in the interest of intergovernmental cooperation, jurisdiction was turned over to the Americans. But in a high-profile case like the Blue Train rapist, you could bet that the Korean National Police didn't want to take any chances of having a squabble over jurisdiction. They wanted Ernie and me to make the arrest and then, after the appropriate paperwork had been filled out, for 8th Army to turn jurisdiction over to them.

That's why Weyworth was currently under surveillance and why Inspector Kill wanted us to hightail it back to Pusan.

"Where do we meet him?" Ernie asked.

"At the police station. From there, he'll take us to Weyworth."

We slowed in front of the last military checkpoint entering the city of Pusan. Ernie rolled down his window.

The guard, a ROK Army sergeant holding an M-16 automatic rifle, barked at us and ordered us out of the vehicle.

"What the hell is this?" Ernie said. "We have our dispatch and, here it is, my identification." Ernie waved his badge. The biting beams of flashlights played across the old sedan, blinding us, so I could barely make out the six or seven soldiers surrounding us in the dark night. The sergeant again barked something in Korean, pointing at the ground in front of him, clearly demanding that Ernie step out of the car.

"Get bent, Charley," Ernie growled. "Here's my dispatch. Here's my badge. That's all you need and that's all you're going to get."

Ernie popped the idling sedan into drive. Immediately, a half dozen rifles were pointing directly at us.

"Easy, Ernie," I said, raising my hands. "Let's get out and see what this guy wants."

"Screw him," Ernie replied. But he reached forward and rammed the gearshift into park. He turned off the engine and placed both hands on the steering wheel. "What the hell is all this harassment about, anyway?"

"Probably just a routine check," I said. "Just play along. We'll be out of here in no time."

I stepped out of the passenger side of the car, crossed in front of the headlights, and handed the sergeant the clipboard containing our emergency dispatch. Like most standard forms printed by 8th Army, it was in English with a translation in small-type hangul lettering beneath each line. The sergeant glanced at the paperwork, handed it back to me, and then motioned again—this time with his rifle—for Ernie to get out of the sedan.

"*Bali!*" he said. Quickly.

Ernie glared at the man, cursed, and spit out the window. Then slowly, arrogantly, he unfolded himself out of the car.

The sergeant barked another order and three soldiers rushed forward, turned Ernie around, frisked him, and then shoved him facedown against the roof of the vehicle. The sergeant stepped close to Ernie and ordered the three soldiers to step away. When Ernie stood away from the sedan, straightening himself and adjusting his coat, the sergeant murmured something beneath his breath:

"*Keinom sikki*," the Korean version of son of a bitch.

Ernie swiveled, still holding his left arm high, and elbowed the sergeant across the face. Then Ernie raised his hands, grinning, as if he'd made a mistake. Nobody bought it. The sergeant shrieked and slammed the butt of his rifle into Ernie's stomach. I leaped forward, grabbed the sergeant around the neck, pulling him back toward me, but by then the other soldiers had closed in. I felt the hard slam of rifle butts against my ribs; hands grabbed me and I was jerked away. Reeling backward, I lost my balance and fell. Then, faster than you could say *keinom sikki* again, the business end of what seemed like a dozen rifle barrels were pointed right at my face. In supplication, I showed my open hands.

Ernie was still on the ground, still struggling.

Ernie and I sat on wooden stools with our hands cuffed behind our backs.

"Fine mess you've gotten us into," Ernie said.

"Me? *You're* the one who elbowed the sergeant of the guard."

"He had it coming."

"Maybe. At least it felt good watching you do it."

Ernie smirked.

For the half hour or so since we'd been sitting there, I'd been mulling over the incident. Why had that sergeant made us step out of the car, and why had he showed such animus toward Ernie? Usually the soldiers at the checkpoints are bored, grumpy, and grim, but I'd never encountered anything like this. This guy seemed to have it in for us. Personally. Outside, voices were raised in Korean. Arguing. Above the din, I recognized one of the voices. Inspector Kill.

The door slammed open.

His face was red; he was wearing a crumpled suit and his tie was loose, as if he'd been wearing the same clothes for days. Inspector Kill was outraged. He pointed at us, turned, and sputtered to the men behind him. I could pick up only part of what he said, but he was clearly incensed that we'd been arrested. The senior officer, an ROK major wearing dark-green fatigues, kept apologizing, half-bowing to Inspector Kill. Two soldiers rushed forward, passed keys between themselves, and unlocked our handcuffs. Ernie and I stood, rubbing our chafed wrists.

"Come," Mr. Kill said roughly.

We didn't need much encouragement. Following Kill, we paraded through the single-story cement-block building that was the ROK Army command post here north of the city of Pusan. A squad of uniformed KNPs waited for us out front. The door of a marked police car was opened.

Ernie and I climbed in the back. Kill sat in the front passenger seat. Sirens blared, and in seconds we were speeding toward downtown Pusan.

"I am sorry," Kill said in English. "There is much bad feeling in Pusan. About the Blue Train rapist. The military has been alerted and they know that the perpetrator is probably an American soldier. So in their minds, every soldier is a suspect."

"You think that's why we were arrested?"

"I'm sure of it. The sergeant who detained you told me himself that he had been carefully checking every foreigner he came across. And when he saw you two, out so late, it occurred to him that Ernie, Agent Bascom here, looked like a rapist."

I glanced at Ernie. "He does, a little."

Ernie flipped me a quick bird.

Inspector Kill shook his head. "Ignorant, to think that criminals can be spotted by their looks."

"Will he be in much trouble?"

"Yes. For the embarrassment he's brought to his superiors."

"No harm done," Ernie said, rubbing his back. "Except for a few bruises."

That was Ernie. He held a grudge for exactly five seconds. I was a little less forgiving. My head still pounded with a splitting headache, and my nose had been bruised again, more red and tender than it had ever been. Still, I had a job to do, and that ROK Army sergeant would probably be scrubbing latrines for the next six months.

"What happened to our sedan?" I asked.

"We'll have someone fetch it for you. "

"Where are we going now?"

"To Weyworth," Kill said. "For the moment, we have him surrounded."

Curfew had just ended. In the darkness, an occasional three-wheeled vehicle purred in from the countryside, a canvas-covered load of turnips or cabbage or garlic balanced on the bed of the truck, heading for the produce market. A man in a gray smock pushed a trash cart into a dark alley. Ambitious cab drivers were parked at the entrances to dimly lit tourist hotels, sitting with their arms crossed and snoring in the front seat, dreaming desperately of a fat fare. Old women, their heads covered with scarves, whisked debris from the front of their homes, brandishing short straw brooms.

The Five Star Yoguan was a four-story brick edifice with a long neon sign bolted to its side. The name was written vertically in hangul script and at the bottom was a half-circle with three wriggly lines rising from it, the symbol for hot baths.

"He's in room 307," Kill said. "I have two men on the roof and four men stationed on the stairwell halfway up from the second floor."

And another half dozen Korean National Policemen standing outside here with us. A drizzling mist from the ocean suffused the world with the odor of fish, a fleshy smell, reminding us that the sea was a living, breathing thing, an overpowering thing. We stood across the street from the yoguan, beneath a striped canvas awning in front of a small grocery store that was barred with an iron grating. Shivering.

"How'd you find him?" I asked.

"He registered under another name," Kill replied. "But the local constables had been ordered to check every foreigner in every hotel or yoguan in the area. Once we located him, we put him under surveillance. Last night, a Korean woman with a small child came to visit him. The constable stopped her after she left and she admitted that the man inside was Weyworth."

"The child was half-American?" I asked.

"Yes. A girl."

Jeannie's mother, I thought. Weyworth must've contacted her while he was in hiding.

"So we're all here," Ernie said. "Let's kick the freaking door in and get this over with."

Mr. Kill nodded. He barked commands to a couple of uniformed officers, and they scurried off around the edge of the building. We marched to the front of the yoguan. The double front doors were unlocked. Kill pushed through and we followed him into the darkness. Without taking off our shoes, we stepped up onto raised varnished flooring and then climbed a narrow stairwell, steps creaking angrily beneath us. Halfway up, we found four bored-looking uniformed cops. They straightened as Kill approached.

The hasp of a glassed-in case was broken. Inside, a neatly folded fire hose sat wedged between brackets and a sign above said *Pisang Yong*. Emergency use only. Other brackets sat empty.

"Where's the extinguisher?" I asked.

Kill shrugged. The exterior of this building was made of brick, but the interior was all wood. Fire safety is a big issue in Korea, especially with these old ondol buildings being heated by flaming charcoal briquettes.

Kill whispered something to the four cops and we continued up to the third floor. Down a vinyl-covered hallway, we found room number 307. The door was small—Ernie and I would have to crouch to get through—and there was one pair of shoes out front.

Ernie knelt and examined the inner labels.

"PX," he whispered to me. I nodded.

Kill raised his eyebrows and gestured toward the door, as if asking who wanted to go first. Ernie stepped in front of the door, braced himself, and then raised his foot and slammed it sole-first, with all his weight behind it, into the rickety wooden door. The door burst open. Like a cat, Kill darted into the room. Then me. Then Ernie.

The Republic of Korea, in the early seventies, did not have a drug problem. Marijuana, even hashish, was tolerated because the Koreans see those things as herbs, natural products of the earth, and not drugs. Besides, the hardworking and ambitious Korean populace wasn't interested in marijuana and hashish. The little that was grown in-country was almost exclusively sold outside military compounds to American G.I.s. Heroin, opium, cocaine—all the harder drugs—were absolutely prohibited by the Korean government. The penalty for trafficking in them was death; a penalty that, more than once, had been enforced. As such, no one but the extremely foolhardy ever tried to move any hard stuff into the Republic of Korea.

For Ernie, this was good. Like many G.I.s who'd served a

tour in Vietnam, he'd developed a drug habit. And after two tours, the habit had become an addiction. Being assigned to Korea, however, had saved him from that habit. Heroin wasn't available. Even if it had been, Ernie was heroically fighting off the urge to use the stuff, replacing it with a drug that was not only approved, but even encouraged, by the honchos of the 8th United States Army: alcohol. In the Class VI store on compound, a quart of Gilbey's gin could be purchased for ninety-nine cents, Johnnie Walker Red for less than four dollars. Regular-priced drinks in the NCO Club used to be fifteen cents for a can of beer, twenty-five cents for a highball. Both prices had recently been raised to thirty-five cents, causing an uproar among people like Staff Sergeant Riley and other aficionados of the distilled and brewed arts. At happy hour, however, which was held daily, the price of either a beer or a shot of liquor dropped to a dime. With these kind of prices, who could afford not to drink? Certainly not me, and *certainly* not Ernie. As long as I'd known him, Ernie had been completely over his heroin habit. Or at least that's how it had seemed until we burst into room 307 and found Specialist Four Nicholas Q. Weyworth spread-eagled on his sleeping mat on the warm ondol floor of the Five Star Yoguan.

Ernie sniffed the air. Later, he told me he could smell it.

Mr. Kill checked Weyworth's neck. Still a pulse. Still breathing.

Near Weyworth's sleeping mat, a red cylinder lay on the floor. Weyworth moaned. He seemed to be coming to. At least we wouldn't have to carry him out. I knelt to examine the cylinder, already knowing what it was: the fire extinguisher. Apparently, as stoned as Weyworth had been, he still maintained the presence of mind to want a fire extinguisher nearby. I was about to raise myself back to my feet when Ernie shouted.

"Drop!"

I did. Letting myself go completely, I collapsed face-down onto the floor. Behind me Weyworth wrestled with blankets, and just inches above my head something heavy whooshed through the air. With a jarring thud, it smashed into wood. Ernie and Kill leaped on Weyworth. He screamed. They struggled. I looked up and saw an ax, a short-handled firefighting ax, wedged into the wall just inches above where my head would've been. An ax that we later found fit perfectly into the empty brackets in the fire-extinguisher case. Savagely, Ernie punched Weyworth one, two, then three times. He lay still.

I rose to my feet, straightening myself out.

After Weyworth had been taken away, the Korean National Police inspector found recently used drug paraphernalia. The KNP lab confirmed that traces of Weyworth's blood were on the needle and smudges of the illicit drug were in the syringe. Specialist Four Nicholas Q. Weyworth—whatever else he had done or not done—was now, formally, toast.

Kill handled the interrogation. Ernie and I spent most of the day watching through a two-way mirror. A listless Weyworth admitted moving contraband for the Greek sailors, items highly prized in the world of Chinese medicine—antler horn from Siberian caribou, powder from the tusk of the African rhinoceros, and paws from the carcasses of the Asian tree bear—all items long since banned from use as legitimate herbal remedies.

Kill patiently unraveled the facts. The Greek sailors smuggled the items into the Port of Pusan. Weyworth, as an American G.I., was valuable to them because he could travel throughout the country without attracting suspicion. Also, the Greek sailors seldom had time to leave their ships. Weyworth's job was to transport the goods north to Seoul and deliver them to dealers there, who would in turn provide them to local Chinese herbalists. Weyworth brought the payment back and turned it over to the sailors. In addition to a share of the money, Weyworth accepted heroin as part of his wages. This was convenient for the Greek sailors because they visited ports where heroin was plentiful and cheap. A good deal all around. Everyone profited. Except for the endangered animals—and the sick people who bought this stuff thinking it would actually cure them.

By mid-afternoon, Weyworth was sober enough to stand in a lineup. Once he did, the woman who'd sold the purse to the Blue Train rapist and the cab driver who'd driven the rapist to the Shindae Tourist Hotel were brought in. Independently, they both confirmed what we'd already surmised: Specialist Four Nicholas Q. Weyworth was *not* the Blue Train rapist. Rape and heroin addiction are two vices that don't usually go together.

Ernie blew out his breath. "So, who else we got?"

I crossed my arms and leaned back as best I could on the straight-backed wooden chair. "Pruchert," I said.

"Pruchert?" Ernie asked. "He spent the last few days meditating in that cave."

"With who?"

"Huh?"

"With who? Who else was in that cave to keep an eye on him?"

Ernie thought about it. "Okay. So maybe he slipped out."

"Yeah. And maybe he walked down that mountain to that little village we saw down there, the one with that joint called the Chonhuang Teahouse."

"He could have," Ernie said cautiously.

"And from there, he could've caught a cab."

"A cab to where?"

"East Taegu or Pusan. A place where he could catch the Blue Train."

Ernie thought about it. "Awfully expensive."

"A cave's a good place to conserve your pay."

"And Pruchert's head was scratched," Ernie added. "A wicked slice."

"That it was."

"I figured when I saw it that it was from shaving his head."

"Could be. But we don't know exactly when he shaved his head."

Ernie thought about that too. "Was the rapist wearing a hat?

"Not that anybody's testified. But everyone has said that his hair was short, dark, giving the impression of being curly."

"A tight cap," Ernie said. "If they weren't paying attention, it might've seemed like short hair when they looked back on it."

"Maybe."

"So maybe we should talk to him again."

"Maybe we should."

Our sedan had been retrieved by Inspector Kill's minions. It was mid-morning now and Ernie and I were both completely exhausted. We told Inspector Kill that we were going to Hialeah Compound to gas up the sedan and maybe catch some shut-eye. Later, we'd interrogate another G.I. whom we had questions about.

"Between the first attack and the second," Kill told us, "the rapist waited less than a week. If he continues this pattern, we have two or three days to catch him, at the most."

We nodded. Rest didn't seem so important when he put it that way.

At the front gate of Hialeah Compound, a bored-looking MP opened the chain-link fence, rolling it back on its iron wheels. Before waving us through, he approached us.

"You Sueño? The CID guy?"

"Yeah."

"Norris wants to talk to you."

"Who?"

"Sergeant Norris. He's at the MP station. Says its important."

First, we topped off at the fuel point. Military training: always be ready to embark if an alert is called. Once the tank was full of mo-gas, we returned to the MP station. I found Norris in the briefing room, waiting to start his shift.

"Remember that merchant marine?" he said. "The one who was asking about you? The one who wanted to talk to you?"

"I remember," I said.

"I was down at the Port of Pusan earlier today and I checked. His ship is due in tonight. About two in the morning."

"You think he's on it?"

Norris shrugged. "Don't know. These guys move around a lot."

Still, he gave me the name of the sailor and the name of the ship. He was called Arkadus. The ship was the *Star of Tirana*.

Before I walked out, Norris said, "Watch yourself with these guys."

"Why?" I asked, turning. "Because they all carry knives?"

"Not just that. They play mind games. Like in chess. They always seem to be a few moves ahead of you."

"I've played a little chess myself."

"Maybe. But they play for keeps, these guys. It's all they have in life. The hustle. They either hustle or die. And if you try to stop them, you'd better get them before they get you."

I touched my forehead in a mock salute. Then I turned and walked out the door.

After some chow and some rest, Ernie and I made our way north. By the time we arrived at the Dochung Temple, it was already mid-afternoon. The monks were surprised to see us. The one who could speak English stepped in front of his brethren, a puzzled look on his face.

"Is Pruchert still in his cave?" I asked.

"Yes."

"We have to talk to him."

"It is very bad to disturb him during meditation. And twice in two days." The monk shook his head sadly.

"Show us. Please. It is very important."

The monk stared at us for a while and finally turned and strolled across the courtyard. We followed. At the side of the temple, the monk picked up an old-fashioned lantern made of green metal that I thought might be brass. He lit the wick, and when the light began to shine, he turned to Ernie and me and said, "Come."

Shadows crept up the sides of the mountain. When we passed near steep cliffs, I understood why the monk had brought the lantern. In some of these crevasses, it was already night. The pathway was narrow and well trod, and many of the rocks had been splashed with black-ink Chinese characters. I could read a few of them. They referred to "the path" and "eternal" and "the Buddha," although I couldn't read enough of them to decipher any complete sentences. The path continued to rise steeply, so steeply that we had to steady ourselves using the handholds that someone had thoughtfully provided. The monk moved quickly, like a mountain goat, but I soon realized that he was placing his feet in well-worn steps that he'd unconsciously memorized. Ernie and I started mimicking his every move, and our speed increased. We reached a plateau where dozens of small cave entrances were arrayed before us. Incense floated out of many of them, and in a few the dim glow of charcoal fires could be seen, sometimes illuminating a golden figurine. The monk found another path and continued up the side of the mountain. Here the trail branched off through thick brush in dozens of tributaries. Each one, apparently, had a cave, or a few caves, at the end. I wondered how the monk kept all this straight; but just as I was about to ask him, he stopped on a narrow rock shelf and pointed.

"In there," he said.

It was a four-foot-high opening that was just wide enough for a man to crawl through. The monk handed me the lantern and said, "Go." Then he swiveled on his leather sandals and quickly trotted back down the trail.

Ernie stepped forward and peered into the cave. "Nothing," he said. It was completely dark in there.

I stood next to him and breathed deeply. "No smell of incense."

"Maybe he ran out," Ernie said.

"After a few days, I suppose so."

"Must be cold as hell at night."

"I suppose so."

We stood in front of the cave. Stalling. Without admitting it to one another, we were both hoping that Pruchert would hear us and come out of the cave on his own. When he didn't, I looked around. The sun was going down quickly now and Chonhuang Mountain would soon be in total darkness.

"I'll go in first," I said.

"No," Ernie replied. "I'll go in first. You hold the lantern and stay right behind me."

"Okay.

He crouched and entered the darkness.

10

National Geographic sometimes runs articles about the mysteries of the underground world, the caves and rivers and lakes that human eyes have never seen. The photographs are beautiful and the caverns they depict breathtaking, but spelunking was not a pastime that I thought would ever appeal to me. Crawling through the moist dirt in this narrow tunnel, holding a flickering lantern in front of me, was anything but my idea of fun. After about ten yards, Ernie scrambled forward. We emerged into a tomblike cavern. I held the lantern aloft.

To our right, atop a stone shelf about four feet high, was an indentation large enough to hold a seated man. We climbed up on the shelf. I poked the lantern into the room-like space. Straw mats had been arranged carefully on the dirt floor, and above them a bronze effigy of the

Maitreya Buddha sat serenely on a stone pedestal. Sticks of burnt incense drooped out of a bronze holder. Ernie and I checked the rest of the chamber. There were no exits except the way we'd entered.

"The son of a biscuit took off," Ernie said.

"Wouldn't you?"

Ernie spit on the dirt floor. "I wouldn't come in here in the first place. Not unless I had to."

"Careful, Ernie. This is a holy place."

Ernie nodded toward the carved Buddha. "Sorry," he said.

As fast as we could, we crawled back out of the tunnel.

We pushed through the bead curtain covering the front door of the Chonhuang Teahouse.

"This is more like it," Ernie said. "Our kind of joint."

The problem was that they didn't want to let us in. A middle-aged man stood at the end of a short hallway, waving his palm at us negatively. "*Migun andei,*" he said. G.I.s not allowed.

"What'd he say?" Ernie asked me, incredulously staring down at the little man.

"He says American soldiers aren't allowed."

"Is he out of his freaking mind?"

Ernie reached out and shoved the man aside.

We paraded into the main room, which was mostly booths and a small serving counter, illuminated by the pink shaded light of table lamps. We wandered toward the back and used their bathroom to clean up. When we seated ourselves at a corner booth, we looked fairly presentable—we'd batted most of the dust off our trousers—and, better yet, there were two pretty hostesses waiting for us. Three or four of the other booths were occupied by middle-aged Korean gentlemen, all of them smoking and being served coffee or tea by attractive young ladies. The elderly man who'd tried to stop us from entering puttered around behind the serving counter, shooting us evil stares. The Korean customers didn't acknowledge our existence. The hostesses assigned to us, however, had no choice.

"Anyonghaseiyo," one of them said to me, bowing.

I acknowledged the greeting, and, after she asked me what we wanted to drink, I told her coffee for both of us. Out of a stainless-steel pot, she poured boiling water into two porcelain cups filled with Maxwell House instant. She stirred the concoction with a slender spoon and then offered sugar and cream. I took neither. Ernie took two heaping spoonfuls of granulated sugar. Neither of the hostesses spoke English, so I took the conversational lead.

"The Chonhuang Teahouse is very famous," I said.

"Famous?" The hostess seated next to me opened her eyes wide.

"A G.I. who I know, Robert Pruchert, told me about this place. He said the women who work here are very beautiful."

It wasn't such a long shot that Pruchert, after he made good his escape from the monastery, would stop here. This village, known as Chonhuang-ni, was by far the closest village to the temple. And the Chonhuang Teahouse was the only place in the tiny settlement that had a public toilet. The only place where somebody like Corporal

Robert Pruchert could clean up after a long walk, and the only place where he could buy a cup of coffee or something to eat before bargaining with a cab driver to drive him the hell out of here. Still, when I mentioned his name, both girls stared at me blankly. I persisted.

"He is studying at the Dochung Temple," I told them. "He shaved his head. He wants to become a Buddhist monk."

One of them smiled and placed both her slender hands in front of her mouth. "Oh," she said. "Bob-bi."

"Yes," I replied. "That's right. Bobby. Bobby Pruchert."

They exchanged words and then they both turned back to me and started chattering happily. Bobby had come in here more than once, always wearing his russet-colored Buddhist robes, which is why the owner, Mr. Roh, allowed him to come in, because Mr. Roh was devout and would never deny entry to a monk of the Dochung Temple.

"Why doesn't Mr. Roh usually allow G.I.s?" Ernie asked.

I translated the question. The girls almost cheerfully explained that in the past G.I.s passing through in convoys had occasionally stopped and used the latrine and made a mess. They'd ordered Oscar—the Korean-made sparkling burgundy—or brought in their own *soju* and gotten drunk and argued with the regular customers.

"Too much trouble," one of the girls said, summing up the entire American experience.

I turned the conversation back to Pruchert.

He came in here wearing his robes, the girls told me, but he always brought a bag slung over his shoulder. He'd go into the bathroom and change into civilian clothes, and then he was very polite and kind to the girls and he'd order a plate of pork fried rice; and when he was finished, the cab driver would come and take him away.

"*The* cab driver?" I asked.

"Yes," the girls replied. There was only one in town, the same man who even now was sitting outside in his hack.

"Where did Bobby go?" I asked.

The same place every time, one of the girls told me. They knew because Kwok the cab driver bragged about the large fare he was paid.

Ernie was leaning forward now, his coffee finished, catching much of what was being said.

"And where was that?" he asked in English.

I translated.

The girls answered in unison.

"Taegu," they told us. "Bobby always went to Taegu."

"Where in Taegu?" I asked.

At that, they shrugged their slender shoulders. We'd finished our coffee and exhausted the totality of their knowledge concerning Corporal Robert R. Pruchert. I slipped them a thousand-won note, thanked them, and left.

Kwok, the cab driver, made me bargain for his information.

"Business is not good," he told me in Korean. "Nobody takes a cab anymore. Rich man has his own car now. Not like before. G.I. no come no more. Maybe sometimes I carry pigs or chickens from one village to next. That's it."

"What about Pruchert?" I asked him. "Bobby Pruchert."

"The monk?"

I nodded.

"He all the time go same place."

That's when we haggled over a price, settling on four thousand won. I handed him the money.

"He go to Taegu."

"The train station?"

Kwok's eyes widened. "No. Never go train station."

"Then where?"

"*Mekju* house," he said. "G.I. mekju house." *Mekju* is beer.

"Where is this mekju house?" I asked.

"Outside G.I. compound."

There was more than one American compound in Taegu: Camp Henry, Camp Walker, and, equidistant between them, an aviation compound.

"Which one?" I asked.

Kwok scratched his head. "I don't know. I forget how you say."

"What district of Taegu is it in?"

That he knew. "*Namgu*," he said.

Namgu means the southern ward. With a map, I should be able to figure out which compound it was. But outside of both Camps Henry and Walker there were dozens of joints catering to G.I.s.

"What was the name of the mekju house?" I asked.

Again Kwok scratched his head, and when he was done with that he rubbed his chin. I handed him another thousand-won note. He grinned and stuffed it in his shirt pocket.

"*Migun Chonguk*," he said.

"Did it have an American name?"

"Maybe. But I couldn't read it."

It is common for nightclubs or chophouses catering to G.I.s to have two names; one in English, the other in Korean. Often, the two names have no relationship to one another. I didn't bother to thank Mr. Kwok. He'd been well compensated for his trouble. In fact, he'd been paid too much. Five thousand won was the equivalent of ten US dollars.

As we walked away, Ernie said, "He held you up."

"At least we know where Pruchert went."

"Maybe. Unless he's lying to us."

"He'd better not be."

"Why? What could you do to him?"

I didn't answer.

"You're not the type," Ernie said, "to come back and punch him in the nose."

We climbed in the sedan and Ernie started the engine. He'd been intrigued by his own question and wouldn't let it go. We pulled out on the two-lane highway and Ernie peeled off down the road, anxious to reach Taegu before we caught the brunt of the late-afternoon traffic.

"So if it turns out that this cab driver, Kwok, is lying to us, what are you going to do?"

"I'll tell Kill."

Ernie turned his attention back to the road, satisfied with my answer. "Right," he said. "That would do it."

What we both knew, without talking about it, was that if we told Inspector Kill that someone had information that might lead to the Blue Train rapist, and that person had lied to us, they'd be spending quite a few uncomfortable hours sweating it out in a Korean National Police interrogation room. Ernie and I wouldn't have to lift a finger.

Ernie was quiet for a moment, and then he said, "Who do you suppose is on this 'checklist'?"

We both knew that whoever it was might not have much time left to keep on breathing.

"So far," I said, "the only people who've been on the list have been two Korean women with children."

"On trains," Ernie added.

"Yes. Passengers on the Blue Train."

"So you think he'll stick with that?"

"Maybe not. The KNPs have increased their presence not only on the Blue Train but also on local lines with both uniformed officers and plainclothes. Whoever this guy is, he'll probably figure that out."

"So he'll branch out?"

"Maybe."

"To what?"

"Don't know," I replied. "It depends on what his obsessions are."

"Obsessions?"

"Yeah. Obsessions."

"That could be anything," he said.

"You're right. That's why the best bet is to catch him. Then he can tell us himself what his obsessions are."

"That should be fun listening to."

Ernie slowed at a railroad crossing but after checking that no train was coming, stepped on the gas again. We bounced across the tracks. On the far side, he said, "So, what was the name again of that mekju house?"

"Migun Chonguk."

"What the hell does that mean?"

"You don't know? Here, break it down. The first word is *migun*. What does that mean?"

Ernie thought about it a moment. "G.I.," he said.

"Right. Literally, 'American soldier.' And what does *chonguk* mean?"

Ernie thought about this one a little longer. Finally he gave up. "I've heard the word. It's just not coming to me right now."

"It means 'heaven,'" I told him. "Literally, 'heavenly country.'"

Ernie slammed the sedan in low gear, slowed for a truck ahead of us, and when the road was clear, he slid the automatic shift back into drive and sped around the slow-moving truck.

"I get it now," he said. "This signal site refugee, pretending to be a Buddhist monk, sneaks away from the monastery, stops in the Chonhuang Teahouse for a little refreshment and female companionship, and then he takes a cab ride all the way to G.I. heaven."

"That's about the size of it."

"Why did he go to all that trouble?" Ernie asked. "Why not just check out on leave from the Horang-ni signal site, catch a ride to Hialeah Compound, and then take the bus to Taegu?"

"Alibi," I said. "He was trying to establish one that might hold up."

Ernie nodded, thinking it over. "As if we're going to believe that he was meditating for ten days." Then he chuckled. "G.I. Heaven. This place, I've got to see."

* * *

It turned out that the district of Taegu that the cab driver, Kwok, told me about was the same district in which the U.S. Army's 19th Support Group headquarters at Camp Henry was located.

"We finally caught a break," Ernie said.

"What do you mean?"

"Camp Henry is where Marnie and the girls are playing tonight."

After finishing up their performances near the Demilitarized Zone, the Country Western All Stars had been systematically working their way south. Last night Waegwan, tonight Camp Henry.

The Korean countryside is beautiful this time of year, with trees covered in red and brown and yellow, distant mountains capped with white, and miles of rice paddies dotted with piled straw. But we were both tired of driving all over hell and gone, and sick of taking leaks on the side of the road, finding nothing to eat other than a bowl of hot broth from a roadside noodle stand.

Camp Henry was about three miles south of the East Taegu Train Station, the place where Pruchert might have bought a ticket and climbed aboard the Blue Train. Ernie drove slowly through town, following my directions as I studied our army-issue map. Old ladies hustled across streets with huge piles of pressed laundry atop their heads. Children in school uniforms marched across intersections in military-like formations, finally heading home after their long school day. Empty three-wheeled trucks made their way back to the countryside, and taxicabs with their top lights on cruised slowly by, searching for passengers heading home after the end of the workday.

Ernie rolled down the window. "Garlic," he said. "The whole city reeks of it."

"A lot of agriculture around here," I told him. "Pork bellies, rice, cabbage, garlic. It's what makes the world go round."

The front gate of Camp Henry was protected by a guard shack and a stern-looking American MP. We continued past the gate and then turned around, drove back past the gate again, and turned east across the railroad tracks. There were a few nightclubs we could see from the main road: the Princess Club, the Pussycat Lounge, the Half Moon Eatery. But most of the joints lurked back in the narrow pedestrian alleyways inaccessible by car.

When the G.I. village petered out, Ernie turned around and found a spot along the cement-block wall topped with concertina wire that marked the boundaries of Camp Henry. He pulled over and locked up the car.

We purposely didn't drive into Camp Henry proper. Not yet. The MP at the gate would check our emergency dispatch and our CID badges, and in about five seconds he'd be on the horn to the Camp Henry Provost Marshal. Other military law enforcement agencies track 8th Army CID agents more carefully than criminals, worried that we might file a negative report that could reflect poorly on their command. I didn't want the hassles. And I certainly didn't want any nosy MPs following us around the village.

We trotted across the main supply route and after half a block entered a narrow alley that housed the dark world of bars and brothels and business girls that lurks outside every army compound in Korea. The air was moist, from the flowers that stood in pots along the cobbled lanes and from the panfuls of water that were tossed by shopkeepers to discourage floating dust. Ernie strode confidently down the street.

"It's good to be back," he said.

From the windows above barrooms, feminine eyes stared out at us. Ernie spread his arms, wanting, it seems, to embrace the entire debauched alley and everyone in it.

We walked up and down three narrow roads and six alleys and a dozen byways but saw no sign that said "G.I. Heaven"—or, for that matter, "Migun Chonguk."

We stopped a couple of business girls on their way to the bathhouse. They both wore G.I. T-shirts without brassieres, and tight shorts enveloping their shapely posteriors; their straight black hair was tied up and clasped by stainless-steel clips. They balanced pans full of soap and washrags against slender hips. When I said, "Anyonghaseiyo," they giggled and stared at us boldly.

"I'm looking for a club," I told them in English. They seemed to understand, so I continued. "They tell me that its Korean name is Migun Chonguk."

"Migun Chonguk?" they both asked, brown eyes opening wide.

I nodded.

They looked at each other, looked back at me, and broke into laughter. In a few seconds, one of them regained her composure, waved her arm to indicate the entire area, and said, "*Da* migun chonguk." It's all G.I. heaven.

I stood there sheepishly, realizing that the cab driver back in Chonhuang-ni by the name of Kwok had been pulling my leg. Then I saw a sign behind the girls. It was a rectangular stripe of red paper pasted onto ancient brick. Slashed on it in black ink were the characters *mi* for beauty, *gun* for soldier, *chon* for sky, and *gook* for kingdom.

I pointed. The girls swiveled to look. Their expressions remained blank. With only sixth-grade educations—the mandatory minimum in Korea—they probably couldn't read the *hanmun*, Chinese characters. I walked over to the sign and pointed again and read it off for them. "Migun Chonguk." An arrow on the sign pointed down the darkest and narrowest walkway we'd seen yet.

"There?" one of the girls said, crinkling her nose.

They both snorted, turned, and walked away from us. Under her breath, I heard one of them say, "*Nabun nyon.*" Evil bitches.

Ernie strode over next to me. "They didn't seem too happy with the place."

"Disgusted would be a better word for it."

Ernie grinned. "We ain't there yet."

The entrance to the place known as Migun Chonguk, or G.I. Heaven, was a splintered wooden doorway at the end of a narrow pedestrian walkway lined with brick walls. In the center of the lane, filth flowed in an open sewer. Ernie and I hopped back and forth to either side of the path, finding precarious footholds on the moss-slimed rock.

"Stinks back here," Ernie said, trying not to inhale the stench of raw sewage and ammonia.

I tried the door. Locked. I pounded with my fist. We

listened. Nothing. I pounded again. Finally, the slap, slap, slap of plastic slippers. The door slithered open. A weathered woman's face peeked out. The mouth opened. It spoke.

"Whatsamatta you? Too early. Anybody sleep time."

"Too early?" Ernie said. "The sun'll go down in an hour or two."

He shoved the door open and crouched through the small opening. I followed. The courtyard was minuscule. Only enough room for a byonso made of rotted lumber, no bigger than a phone booth, and a half-dozen earthenware jars, each capable of holding about fifty pounds of cabbage kimchee.

The old woman closed the door behind us and slid a rusty bolt into place. She was less than five feet tall, hunched at the shoulders, her face marked with wrinkles and liver spots. Most of her teeth were missing.

"Anybody sleep time," she said again.

"*Mekju isso?*" I asked the woman. Do you have beer? After all, Kwok the cab driver had told us that Migun Chonguk was a G.I. mekju house.

The woman studied me and squinted her eyes. "Nighttime mekju have," she told me. "Now no have. Anybody sleep time."

Ernie wandered around the courtyard, peeking into the gap between the main hooch and the courtyard wall. He must not have found anything out of order, because he wandered over to the opposite side.

"G.I.," I told the old woman. "*Mori oopso.*" No hair. "*Odiso?*" Where is he?

She stared at me blankly. Out of my wallet, I pulled the photocopy I had made of Corporal Robert R. Pruchert's personnel records snapshot. The copy machine needed toner, so it was not a clear copy; but the old woman snatched the paper out of my hand and studied it carefully.

"He no have hair?" she said, pointing at the photo.

"No. All cut off," I said.

"Why?" She looked up at me quizzically.

"He want to be *deing deingi chung*," I said. A Buddhist monk ringing an alms bell.

"Deing deingi chung." She laughed. "How you know deing deingi chung?"

I shrugged and pointed at the picture. "You see that G.I. before?"

"Maybe," she said. "All G.I. same same. All the time Cheap Charley. All the time argue mama-san."

"How about the others?" I asked, pointing toward the hooch. "Do they know him?"

"*Jom kanman.*" Just a minute. "I checky checky."

Still clutching the photocopy in her gnarled hand, she slipped off her sandals and climbed up on the raised wooden floor. She padded down the hallway, wood slid on wood, and then a woman's voice erupted into moans of protest. Apparently, someone was waking up.

Ernie gave me the thumbs-up sign, slipped off his shoes, and stepped up onto the platform. In stocking feet, he tiptoed into the dark hooch. I had no reason to stand out here in this courtyard alone, so I took off my army-issue low quarters and followed.

Sliding wooden doors, made of latticework covered with oil paper, lined either side of the central hallway. Hazy sunlight oozed through the outside windows, blocked mostly by the taller buildings that surrounded us.

At the end of the hallway, one of the doorways had been slid open; Ernie stood near it, listening.

I stopped and waited.

The voices were arguing. All female. Despite the late-afternoon hour, someone was very angry at being awakened. Another woman started protesting shrilly. Behind me, blankets rustled and then another door slid open.

"*Weigurei?*" someone shouted. Why this way?

A lot of other voices were grumbling, and naked feet started to slap on vinyl-covered floors; one by one, doors on either side of the hallway slid open.

"*Wei-yo?*" one voice shouted. Why?

"*Sikkuro!*" someone else hollered. Shut up!

And then a gaggle of women surrounded us, many of them in cotton nightgowns, some in silk. They paraded past us, heading for the byonso, rubbing their eyes, coughing, cursing beneath their breath. Matches sizzled, cigarettes were lit, and the narrow hallway started to reek of cheap tobacco. Ernie and I stood in the hallway, towering over the small flock of femininity, realizing for the first time that not one of them was young. Every woman here was middle-aged or older. One or two of them must've had tuberculosis, to gauge by the coughing and spitting going on into porcelain pee pots.

One of the huskier women, wearing a red terry-cloth bathrobe, stopped in front of Ernie.

"What you do, G.I.?" she said. "Why you come see mama-san so early?"

Ernie shrugged. "I was in the neighborhood."

"Neighborhood? You likey this neighborhood?" She cackled and stalked off down the hallway.

After a few minutes, when the entire household was awake, pots and pans started to clang. Washrags and soap holders appeared, and the women vigorously scrubbed their faces and armpits, squatting in front of an outdoor faucet. When the ablutions were complete, the women returned briefly to their rooms, dried off, and changed into old housedresses and loose shifts.

The husky woman in a red robe was done first. She was wearing a green dress now, and she beckoned us toward the back, leading us into the largest room in the house, and told us to sit on flat cushions. Foot-high legs were unfolded and a five-foot-long mother-of-pearl table was placed in the center of the room. A brass pot of boiling water appeared, and women squatted near the edge of the table and stirred instant coffee or herbal concoctions into cups of boiling water. The husky woman, without asking, prepared us two cups of Maxim coffee crystals. She was about to shovel a heaping tablespoon of soluble creamer into mine when I stopped her.

"Just black," I said.

"Black?" she asked. "*Nomu jja.*" Too bitter.

Sensibly, Ernie tasted the coffee first and then accepted a half teaspoon of the creamer and two tablespoons of sugar.

Most of the condiments being pulled out of cupboards were PX-purchased. Sugar from Hawaii, seedless jam from Ohio, even a tin of cookies from Denmark. Placed in opposite corners of the room were a stereo set with Bose speakers and a small Zenith television.

When most of the women were gathered around the

table, sipping on various hot brews, I said, "*Yogi ei Migun Chonguk i-ei-yo?*" Is this G.I. Heaven?

At first all I saw were open mouths and wide eyes. Then the women started glancing at one another and then, simultaneously, they broke into laughter. The husky woman in the green dress, who seemed to be their leader, said, "Who teach you speaky Korean?"

"He taught me," I said, jabbing my thumb toward Ernie.

Ernie looked up from his coffee, in which he'd been totally absorbed.

"Him?" the husky woman said. Then she shook her head. "No. Not him. He dummy."

The other women murmured in agreement.

I grinned at Ernie. "You going to take that?"

He shrugged. "They know what I'm good at."

Indeed, they probably did. These women had already figured us out. As the conversation progressed, I became even more convinced of the accuracy of their observations.

The husky woman's name was Lucy. That's the only name she would admit to; she refused to give her Korean name.

"Long time ago," she said, "I stop using Korean name. My life as Korean over. Now I'm Lucy."

The other women nodded in assent. They were all of a similar age, the youngest were in their mid-forties, the oldest well above sixty. What were they doing together? Why did they all live here and not with their families? Why did they call this place Migun Chonguk? G.I. Heaven?

Of course, Ernie and I had known the answer almost from the moment we'd stepped inside the courtyard. Or at least we'd known part of the answer. This place was—or at least appeared to be—a brothel. But how did these women, whom most G.I.s would describe as old hags, survive when they were surrounded by a sea of desirable young business girls? That was the question. As we sat there talking with them, I believed I was starting to figure it out. They might have once been an active brothel, but they'd changed with the times, or changed because of necessity. Now they were the nerve center for black-marketing in this area. They offered the best deals both for the G.I.s who chose to sell their PX-bought goods directly and for the business girls who sold what their G.I. boyfriends gave them.

When my coffee was almost gone, another of the women refilled my cup. By now, ashtrays had been pulled out of hiding places and the little room was awash in cigarette smoke. Normally, I would've sought the relief of fresh air, but I was here to gather information and I suspected that the women of G.I. Heaven were guarding a wealth of information. The oldest of the women, the one who'd opened the door for us, was the housemaid and the cook. She spread out on the table the paper I'd given her with the picture of Corporal Pruchert. He'd still had hair then, when the picture was taken, but I didn't say anything more as they studied the sheet, passing it back and forth.

Finally, Lucy turned to me and said, "You CID."

"What makes you say that?" I asked.

"Anybody know," she replied. "Short haircut, wear coat and tie, come from Seoul. But you not worried about black market. You not bother us old ladies who only can live because of black market."

"That's not what we're here for," I said.

Lucy puffed on her cigarette, squinting behind the smoke as she studied the photo she held in liver-spotted fingers.

"What he do?" she asked.

"We're not sure yet," Ernie said. "Right now, we're just tracking his movements."

"Tracking?"

"We just want to see where he went."

"Oh."

"When was he here last?" I asked.

Lucy set the photo down and turned to face me. "We tell you, what you give Lucy? What you give my friends?"

"It's not what we'll *give* you," Ernie said, "it's what we *won't* give you. We won't pay attention to all this black-marketing and we won't give you a ride to the monkey house."

"What you know about monkey house?" Lucy said, suddenly angry. "Lucy long time ago go monkey house." She jabbed her thumb into her chest. "Lucy live. No die. Not like some people. That time Communist come. They tough. Not like KNP now. You send me monkey house? Huh! You *send* Lucy. Lucy not afraid."

Ernie glared at her but didn't say anything further.

Some of the other women started chattering about their experiences in the monkey house. None of them were strangers to doing time, but they hadn't done any time lately. Probably, with a successful black-market operation, the local police were being paid to look the other way. That would explain Lucy's bravado and her disdain for two CID agents from Seoul.

When they calmed down, I said, "People could get hurt, Lucy, if we don't find Pruchert. Innocent people."

She studied me once again, picking up her cigarette and puffing on it for a while, letting the silence grow.

"I know why you come," she said finally. "You come because of G.I. on Blue Train. G.I. who do bad things to Korean women."

"That's right, Lucy," I said. "I can't fool *you*, can I?"

She spoke rapidly in Korean, explaining to her fellow denizens of G.I. Heaven what we were here for.

"This G.I.," she said, finally. "G.I. on train, he hurt Korean women. Hurt them bad, *kurei*?" Right?

"Yes," I replied. "One of them was raped in front of her children. Another was raped and then murdered, also in front of her children."

Lucy repeated what I said. Some of the women looked sad, others showed no expression.

"We know about rape," Lucy said. "Anybody here know about rape." She pointed at the women surrounding the table, jabbing her forefinger at them one by one. "We all young during Korean War. G.I. come, Communist come, United Nations come, Chinese come. Anybody try find Korean woman. Any Korean woman run away. Sometimes hide. Most time can't hide. Why? Need food. Need water. Need medicine. Otherwise no can live. Our mama sick, daddy sick, baby sick, how we let them die?"

Lucy stared at me, expecting an answer. I had none.

"We do what we gotta do," she continued. "That time, who have most money? American G.I. So we go, learn speak American language. Learn about G.I., learn how to make money. Learn how to black-market. So G.I. hurt

Korean woman on Blue Train, we know. We know all about anything."

She waved her arm.

Some of the women nervously lit new cigarettes or poured themselves more hot water. One of them whispered, "*Aiyu, mali manta.*" You talk too much.

Lucy ignored the comment.

"So Lucy, will you help us find him, or not?"

She pointed at the wrinkled photocopy. "Pruchert, he not do."

"So you *do* know him?"

"We know."

"What makes you so sure he didn't do anything?"

"Lucy know."

"Maybe you should let us decide that," Ernie said.

Most women love Ernie and his irreverent attitude. For some reason, Lucy didn't.

"Okay," she said, "you decide. Hurry up, find out."

"Where is he, Lucy?" I asked. "When did you last see him?"

"Yesterday. He come do black market."

"What did he sell?"

"Wristwatch. Good one. G.I. only can buy one each year, so he sell good one."

Under the 8th Army ration-control system, only one each of certain expensive items can be purchased by any given G.I. during a one-year tour. Only one stereo set, only one television, and only one wristwatch. At the end of the year, before he's cleared to leave the country, the G.I. must either produce the item or produce a document showing he shipped it legally back to the States. There are ways around that, such as claiming the item was stolen, and some G.I.s are foolish enough to just sell the item on the black market and worry about justifying it later. They often get away with it because some units are not as diligent about checking on the rationed items as they should be.

"After he sold it, where did he go?"

"Same place he all the time go. You don't know?"

"No. I don't know. Tell me."

"He go casino. You know. Down in Pusan."

"He makes money selling on the black market, and then he takes that money and throws it away in a casino?"

"Lotta G.I. do."

"What casino did he go to?"

"In Pusan only one. Beautiful place. Haeundae Beach."

I'd heard of it, but I'd never been there. Maybe Pruchert went to the Haeundae Casino, and maybe he didn't. Maybe that's what he told Lucy. Maybe instead he took a cab over to the train station and hopped on the Blue Train.

"How do you know he went to the casino?" I asked.

"He all the time need money. All the time worried about honcho find out he black market. All the time worried honcho find out he go to casino."

Signal sites deal with a lot of top-secret traffic. People into various types of depravity, including compulsive gambling, are considered to be security risks and, as such, lose their clearances. The U.S. Army Signal Corps is a hothouse of pressure; a difficult job to perform and everyone watching everyone else. It figured that Pruchert would want to get away; and if he were black-marketing and gambling, he'd want to concoct a good cover story, such as meditating at a Buddhist monastery. Of course, he'd also need a good cover story if he were the Blue Train rapist.

I asked Lucy and the other women a few more questions, but it soon became obvious that if Ernie and I wanted to know more about Corporal Robert R. Pruchert, we'd have to find him ourselves.

We thanked the women and left. Lucy followed us to the front gate.

"Pruchert good boy," she told us. "*Dingy dingy* but good boy."

She whirled her forefinger around her right ear, indicating that Pruchert was dingy dingy. Nuts.

"So you don't think Pruchert is the Blue Train rapist?" I asked.

"No," Lucy said, crossing her arms. "He not."

"If you're so smart," Ernie said, "then tell us who is."

"I tell," Lucy replied. "Blue Train rapist bad man. Very bad man. But when anybody see any day, he look like good man. Lucy, any woman in G.I. Heaven, we all before trust good man. We all before tricked by good man. We all before, rape. Now, we anybody no trust."

We ducked out through the gate into the stinking pathway that ran in front of G.I. Heaven. Back on the pedestrian lane running through the bar district, Ernie shook himself like a golden retriever shaking off rain.

"Creepy," he said.

"It takes a lot to creep *you* out."

"That it does," he replied, "but G.I. Heaven managed."

* * *

We jogged across the main supply route. At the front gate of Camp Henry, the MP guard said, "Where in the hell you guys been?"

"What do you mean?"

"Last night in Waegwan, weren't you supposed to be guarding that USO show? The Country Western All Stars?"

Ernie stepped close to the MP. "What happened?"

The guy told us. Or at least he told us part of it. We ran to the Camp Henry Medical Dispensary.

11

Ernie pointed to the rubber tube sticking up the MP's nose.

"That must hurt," he said.

"Only when I yodel," the MP replied.

His name was Dorsett. He was the MP assigned last night to guard the Country Western All Stars after we'd left Waegwan. His hospital bed had been cranked up so he could watch the soap operas playing on AFKN. It was an open bay, and about a half dozen other G.I.s lounged in beds in various states of repose.

"So who popped you?" Ernie asked.

"That's what *I'd* like to know," he said.

Dorsett told the story. He'd been assigned to guard the rear of the Camp Carroll Female BOQ., bachelor officers' quarters. The Quonset hut assigned to the Country Western

All Stars was deserted except for them, and they each had their own room, but they had to share a communal bathroom. Through the high windows, Dorsett could hear the showers running.

"Did you let your imagination get the best of you?" Ernie asked.

"No way. I was plenty alert. Whoever hit me hid himself inside the closet that holds the water heaters. He must've been in there for over an hour, because that's how long we'd been there, even before the band finished their show. As I passed by, the door creaked open and before I could turn something hit me. I went down."

"Did you see anything?"

"Nothing. It happened too fast."

"What about your .45?"

"They found it later. In a trash can toward the front of the BOQ."

"What's the doc say?" Ernie asked.

"He says I'm a stupid butt for not checking inside the room that held the water heaters."

Marnie wasn't as excited to see Ernie this time. She seemed distracted and, for the first time since I'd known her, she was puffing away on a cigarette. As we strode up onto the stage of the Camp Henry NCO Club, the other girls greeted us. Cymbals clanged and the bass guitar plunked as Ernie sat down in front of Marnie and asked her what was wrong.

"Nothing's wrong," she said, turning her head, blowing out smoke.

"None of you were hurt last night, were you?"

"No. Nobody hurt. Scared shitless, but not hurt."

"Tell us what happened, Marnie," I said.

Marnie shook her head, making her stiff blonde locks rustle beneath the cowgirl hat. She sighed and started talking. "Shelly was taking a shower. The rest of us were in our rooms. I heard footsteps tromping down the central aisle, you know, man's footsteps, those big combat boots that the G.I.s wear, but I didn't think anything of it. I figured it was just the MP patrol or the base commander coming over to thank us or something like that. The footsteps went down the hallway, past my room toward the bathroom."

"The latrine," Ernie said.

"Whatever you call it. So I thought that was sort of weird, some man walking toward our bathroom, but before I could do anything about it, somebody screamed."

"Shelly?" I asked.

"None other. I threw on my robe and I was about to step out my door when I heard the same heavy footsteps coming back down the hallway, and I was looking for my shotgun and then I realized I'd left it back in Austin and suddenly I was afraid to open the door. Finally, when the footsteps subsided I ran to the bathroom and found Shelly. She was okay. She said some man had been there rummaging in her bag that was sitting on the bench in front of her shower stall."

"Did she see him?"

"Ask her."

By now, Shelly had joined us. She pulled over a stool and sat down. "I saw his back," she said. "He was wearing an army uniform, the same one everyone else wears around here."

"Fatigues," Ernie said.

"Yeah. But I didn't see his face. Only his back. He was Caucasian, I think, but even that I can't be sure of."

"But he could've been black," Marnie said.

Shelly shrugged. "Could've been. All I saw was his back and then I pulled the shower curtain shut and knelt down in the corner, trying to make myself small."

"But he left when you screamed?" I asked.

"Yes," Shelly replied. "In a hurry."

"Did he take anything?" Ernie asked.

Shelly rolled her eyes. "It's embarrassing."

Marnie spoke for her. "Damn, Shelly. It's only a bra and panties."

"Yeah, but they were *my* bra and panties."

"What color were they?" Ernie asked, deadpan.

Shelly rolled her eyes. "Red."

"Lace," Ernie asked, "or straight cotton?"

Shelly glared at him. "Lace," she said.

Ernie tipped an imaginary hat. "Thank you, ma'am," he said.

After Shelly left, Marnie inhaled deeply on her cigarette, held the smoke in her lungs for a while, and then blew the gray mist out in a steady stream. When it was gone, she seemed out of breath. Her voice came out weak.

"What she's not telling you is what happened *after* the guy ran out of the building."

"Tell us," I said.

"There's a phone in the hallway and the emergency number for the Military Police is painted on the wall, so I dialed it and a few minutes later the MPs showed up. They found that poor MP out back, still unconscious, and called an ambulance and took him away. They also found someone else outside. Someone in a jeep."

Marnie continued to puff on her cigarette.

Finally, Ernie said, "Freddy Ray."

"How'd you know?" Marnie asked.

"Just a guess. He knew you were playing at Camp Carroll. He hopped in a jeep and drove out there."

Marnie nodded.

"Did the MPs question him?" I asked.

"They questioned him."

"Did you have a chance to talk to him?"

Marnie shook her head. "No."

I finished her thought for her. "And some of the MPs thought that Freddy Ray might be the peeper, the guy who'd stolen Shelly's bra and panties."

"That's what they thought," she said.

"What do you think?" Ernie asked.

Marnie stubbed out her cigarette. "I don't know what to think."

She rose from her chair and strode over to her keyboard and plugged it in.

Camp Henry is a small compound, just five or six hundred yards wide in any direction. We walked the hundred or so yards from the NCO Club to the 19th Support Group headquarters. In the foyer, we read the signs and Ernie followed me down to the 19th Support Group Personnel Service Center (PSC). The door was locked. Ernie rattled it and then turned back to me. "It's six P.M. The duty day ends at five."

I went back to the entranceway and checked the sign. The Staff Duty Officer was in room 102. We went back down the hallway, turned left, and spotted a light on and a door open. We stepped inside.

The Duty Officer was a young man with curly brown hair. He sat behind a gray army-issue desk, his chair facing away from us, watching the Armed Forces Korea Network on a black-and-white portable television. He looked almost like a teenager relaxing on his mother's couch. When he heard us come in, he fumbled with the knob, turned off the set, and swiveled on the chair to face us. His rank was second lieutenant. His name tag said Timmons.

I showed him my badge.

"Lieutenant Timmons," I said, smiling. "Looks like you caught the duty tonight."

"Do I know you?" he asked.

"No. I'm Agent Sueño. And this is my partner, Agent Bascom. We're from the Seoul CID office."

"All the way down here?"

"All the way down here," I said.

Ernie took a seat on a padded gray vinyl chair. He usually let me handle bureaucratic transactions, as long as we got what we wanted.

"What can I do for you?" Timmons asked.

"What we're here about," I said, spreading my fingers, "is the security of the USO show."

"The Country Western All Stars," he said.

"The same. We're supposed to keep an eye on them, all five musicians, and we understand that there was a problem at Camp Carroll last night."

"So I heard."

"I want you to help us find Captain Freddy Ray Embry."

Timmons's face darkened. "The accusations they're making about him, they're not true. Captain Embry is one of our finest officers."

"I'm sure he is. Still, we have to talk to him. Where can we find him?"

"I'll get him on the horn right away."

Timmons reached for the phone. I stayed his hand.

"No. It's better if we talk to him in person."

"Where's he work?" Ernie asked.

"At the logistics supply depot. He keeps our eighteen-wheelers running up and down the spine of the Korean peninsula."

"He's off duty now," I said, "so where are his quarters?"

"I'm not sure." Timmons rose to his feet and walked across the room to a large metal cabinet bolted to the wall, fiddled with a combination lock, and finally pulled back the sliding doors. He searched until he found the right key, took it out, relocked the cabinet, and told us to follow him down the hallway. Timmons entered an office with a sign that said Officer Records. He switched on the light, unlocked a filing cabinet, and, after searching for a few minutes, found the personnel folder of Captain Frederick Raymond Embry. He pulled out the billeting assignment sheet and, as he did so, Ernie and I studied the black-and-white photo of Captain Embry.

Maybe I shouldn't have been surprised, but somehow I was. We all project our stereotypes onto people, and somehow I didn't expect a female country-western singer from Austin, Texas, to have been married to a black man.

And I hadn't expected a former Texas A&M cadet of the Reserve Officer Training Corps to be of African descent. Of course, the color barrier at Texas A&M had been broken years ago, but still most of the graduates during the sixties were white.

I studied Ernie's face. His expression didn't change. At least this went part of the way toward explaining Marnie's suggestion that the intruder very well could have been black.

Lieutenant Timmons jotted down Captain Embry's billeting assignment and handed me the slip of paper.

"Here you are," he said. "I'm sure Captain Embry will be happy to see his former wife."

"I'm sure he will," I replied.

I slipped the paper into my pocket and Ernie and I left the 19th Support Group Headquarters building. The Bachelor Officer Quarters were on the far side of the compound; still, the walk took us less than ten minutes.

"Timmons knew," Ernie said, "that Captain Embry had been married to one of the Country Western All Stars."

"G.I.s gossip," I said.

More than old ladies, I thought, but I left that unsaid.

When Ernie and I reached the BOQ area, we entered Building C. At the door to room C9, Ernie knocked. Nobody answered. Ernie pounded on the door again. Finally, the door creaked open. The room was dark.

Ernie said, "Embry? You in here?"

Nobody answered. Ernie repeated himself. Finally an exasperated voice said, "Who the hell is it?"

Ernie stepped inside.

I swept my hand along the wall, searching for the light switch. I found it and switched it on. Light blazed into the room, blinding me.

Someone shouted, "Turn that damn light off!"

I did. Ernie, meanwhile, had found a window and opened the shades. In the fading afternoon light, a man sat on the edge of an army-issue bunk, his face in his hands.

"Captain Embry?" I said.

"What the hell do you want?" he asked.

I told him. Then I started asking questions. Captain Embry denied having hit any MP last night and denied having entered the women's latrine. He vehemently denied stealing a red bra and panties.

"She wrote to me," he said. "Asked me to come see her when the show arrived. I did. I checked out a jeep last night, drove up to Waegwan. I was sitting outside their BOQ, trying to decide if I should really talk to her or if I should just let the past be the past."

He remained on the edge of his bunk, his head drooped, his big hands spread over square knees.

"Do you have the letter?" I asked.

He stared up at me, brown eyes luminously moist. Finally, he snorted. "Yeah. I have it. There. On the desk."

Ernie switched on a green-shaded desk lamp, rummaged through paperwork, and lifted a letter into the light and examined the envelope. When he was finished, he tossed it to me. By now the sun was just about down, but I had left the door open and there was enough illumination from the desk lamp and the fluorescent bulbs in the hallway to read. I scanned the letter quickly.

It was postmarked two days ago, in Seoul. Staff Sergeant Riley had evidently succumbed to Marnie's charms and located Captain Embry's address for her. The letter was formal in tone, not emotional, explaining when she'd be arriving in the Taegu area and under what circumstances, not inviting him to see her but not telling him to stay away either.

"Did you answer the letter?" I asked.

Embry shrugged. "No reason. By the time it got there, she would've been on the way down here."

"Did you see the MP on patrol around the building?"

"Yeah. I saw him. But I don't think he saw me. I was parked across the street next to a warehouse about twenty yards away. It was dark."

"Did you see anybody else there?"

"No. But I wasn't really watching. After they pulled up in the van and the girls went inside, I mainly just sat there smoking and thinking."

"Thinking about what?" Ernie asked.

"About whether or not I should really talk to her."

"Did you hear anything when the MP was attacked?"

"That was on the far side of the Quonset hut. I didn't hear anything."

"Did you see someone enter the front door?"

"Like I said, I wasn't really watching."

"But someone could've entered the front door?"

"They could've."

"How about the scream? Did you hear that?"

"I did. And then I looked up and somebody darted out of the door. The light was bad and he was moving fast so I couldn't make out much, but I was sure it was a G.I., a G.I. wearing fatigues."

"Where did he go?"

"He darted around the building. Out of sight."

"What'd you do then?"

"I sat there. I wasn't sure what to do. And then the MPs pulled up, siren blaring. I guess that sort of shook me out of my reverie. I climbed out of my jeep and walked forward and I was standing at the front door identifying myself to one of the MPs when Marnie came out."

"What'd she say to you?"

"Nothing. She just stared at me, with that old disapproving look, like I'd done something wrong."

"Had you?" Ernie asked.

"Get bent," Embry replied.

"Easy, Embry," I said.

"That's *Captain* Embry to you."

"Okay," I said. "Captain Embry. You still have a thing for Marnie. That's obvious."

Embry didn't reply.

I looked around the small room. "They tell me you have a good career going here. You're a respected officer in the 19th Support Group. The brass watches USO tours closely, Captain Embry. Don't screw things up. Don't interfere with Marnie or the show. Stay away from her. Stay away from the Country Western All Stars and you'll be all right."

"You have no authority to tell me to stay away from her."

"The hell we don't," Ernie replied. "One false move and we'll arrest you for stalking a USO civilian. And for being a Peeping Tom."

Embry rose to his feet. "Get the hell out of my room."

Atop a metal wall locker, Ernie spotted a cowboy hat.

He pulled it down and examined it, flipping back the inner lining. "Good brand," he said. "Handmade. Direct from Austin, Texas." Ernie tossed the cap in the air. Embry caught it on the fly. "Don't turn this little drama into *High Noon*," Ernie told him. "You're outgunned."

We walked out of the room.

As we walked back toward the NCO Club, Ernie asked me, "Why didn't you arrest him?"

"He seemed like a decent enough guy."

"But it had to be him. If we search his room, I bet we'd find that red bra and panties."

"Maybe. And maybe he's the one who's been stalking them since they arrived in-country."

"Yeah. Maybe we'd find everything there. Like the microphone and the cowboy boot, all that stuff."

"Maybe. Maybe not. But try to cop a search warrant from the Camp Henry Provost Marshal. Never happen."

Ernie knew I was right. The officer corps protects its own.

"But if something happens to Marnie?" he said finally.

"You'll just have to be more diligent in your protection," I told him.

Ernie thought about that. "Maybe I will," he said.

The Country Western All Star Review at the Camp Henry NCO Club that night was another resounding success. The G.I.s went nuts, as usual, even those who maybe weren't crazy about cowboy music but certainly appreciated the tight blue jeans and tight blouses the ladies wore—and the way they jiggled. Marnie seemed even more animated than she usually did, maybe because she thought her ex-husband might be in the audience. Even if he wasn't, he'd hear about the performance and, being human, he'd be jealous of all those G.I. eyeballs lingering over her voluptuous curves. Anyway, if she thought Captain Embry might show up, she was wrong, because Ernie and I stayed sober and patrolled the packed main ballroom and mostly empty backstage area at regular intervals.

There wasn't enough billeting space in the Camp Henry BOQ to house the Country Western All Stars, so the USO popped for rooms at the New Taegu Hotel downtown. After the show, while Mr. Shin and his crew were loading equipment in the vans, Ernie and I talked it over.

"We have to find Pruchert," I said.

"And I have to make sure Embry doesn't harass anybody," Ernie replied.

"Right. So I'll take the sedan and drive down to Haeundae Beach. You stay with the girls."

"Tough duty," Ernie replied. "I'll do my best."

"In the best traditions of the service."

During the show, Ernie and I had taken turns eating some decent chow in the NCO Club dining room, and the bowl of chili beans and the fried chicken with rice and gravy had made me feel more human. Still, I was exhausted. In the last few days, what with all the running around we'd done in the southern end of the Korean peninsula, I'd managed to catch only catnaps. I was afraid that my exhaustion might be more than I could handle while driving, so I asked the club manager if he had a spare thermos of coffee. I promised to bring the jug back once I was done with it. He complied. Thus fortified and provisioned,

I grabbed the keys from Ernie and set off south on the main supply route, heading toward Pusan.

If Pruchert was like most compulsive gamblers—and if he hadn't been lying to Lucy—he'd most likely still be in the Haeundae Casino. It's a twenty-four-hour operation, although they have to lock the doors during the midnight-to-four curfew—nobody in or out. Regardless of whether Pruchert was there, I resolved to report to Inspector Kill, and to 8th Army, as soon as I found the chance. They'd probably been wondering what we were up to, and—unlike Ernie—I was worried about aggravating them unduly.

Not that they deserved much consideration from us. After all, they'd assigned Ernie and me to two details—protecting the Country Western All Stars and finding the Blue Train rapist—both, in and of themselves, full-time jobs. And I was still worried about the rapist and his "corrective actions" and who else would be on his checklist. He'd strike again. Every moment brought us closer to his next attack.

With two jobs to do, I had no choice but to return to Pusan alone. Still, there was an advantage to being alone. Sergeant Norris, the Hialeah Compound MP, had given it to me. The merchant steamer known as the *Star of Tirana* was scheduled to pull into the Port of Pusan at 2 A.M. tonight. Aboard, according to Norris, was an East European sailor who'd been searching for me.

Why would a man I'd never heard of be looking for me? A man who came from a country in which I knew no one and where I'd never been?

As far-fetched as it sounded, I thought I knew the answer. Or, at least, I was afraid I did. If my hunch was right, I was in for a lot more sleepless nights.

If and when I met this man, I wanted to be alone. I certainly didn't want to involve Ernie, or anyone else, in something that might prove to be more dangerous than anything I'd encountered before.

12

For ten minutes I pounded on the big double door of the Haeundae Casino. Finally, I heard a voice shout from within, "*Nugu-syo?*" Who is it?

I held my badge up to a peephole and shouted back "*Kyongchal!*" Police!

There was a discussion behind the padded door, and it took another two or three minutes for the door to creak open. I pushed through, holding my badge in front of my face. In Korean, I said, "Where's the manager?"

A young man in black slacks, white shirt, and bow tie closed the door behind me. Next to him stood a dapper middle-aged Korean in a neatly pressed gray suit. He smiled benignly at me.

"I am the manager," he said in perfectly pronounced English. "My name is Han."

I held out my hand. He shook it.

"I'm Agent Sueño," I told him. "Eighth Army CID in Seoul. I'd appreciate it if you would not alert your customers or staff that I'm here."

"They know someone's here," he said, turning and staring into the carpeted expanse of the casino. "They heard the pounding. Of course, most of them are too entranced by the game to pay much attention."

Entranced? I had to ask. "Are you from the States?"

"Went to school there. The University of Nevada at Reno."

"Hotel and Casino Management?"

He nodded and smiled a mild smile.

This set my mind on a completely different tangent. Often, I ask people about their education. I was interested because I hoped, some day, to earn something higher than my GED. The G.I. Bill would still be available when I needed it, but so far I hadn't worked up the nerve to leave the Army. Suddenly, I realized I was exhausted, which is why my mind was wandering. I returned to the main purpose of my visit.

"Are there any Americans in there?"

"A couple."

"I'd like to observe them, if you don't mind, for a few minutes."

"Will you be making an arrest?"

"Possibly."

"If you do, we'd appreciate the greatest discretion. I'll call the guest over, offer him some refreshments in a side room, you can take it from there. And no violence, please."

"It won't come to that."

At least I hoped it wouldn't. I wasn't armed and I imagined Pruchert wasn't armed either, except maybe with a knife.

Standing beside empty blackjack tables, about ten yards away, were two burly Korean security guards. They wore dark suits and ties and were both taller and broader than most Koreans. They moved like wolves watching a herd. Calluses rose from their knuckles, developed from years of martial arts training.

I took a seat in a lounge area elevated slightly above the casino. Within seconds, a gorgeous waitress approached and I asked for a cup of hot coffee, no sugar. Two minutes later, she served me, bowed, and left me on my own. I sipped on the java gratefully, examining the players and the tables on the casino floor. I thought of the distance I'd covered today: from the holy interior of an ancient Buddhist cave, to the rolling rice paddies of Kyongsan Province, to the depravity of G.I. Heaven, and now to the plush interior of the Haeundae Casino, modeled on the best Monte Carlo had to offer. That's Korea for you, something for every taste.

Most of the tables were closed, green felt draped with leather dust covers. The late-night customers had been bullied into one pit, four blackjack tables in a circle, each table staffed by two female dealers wearing stylish red smocks. Behind them stood a bored Korean man in a dark suit, the pit boss. The customers were mostly Korean, a couple of people I figured for Japanese, and two Americans. One of the Americans was black. He stood behind a blackjack table, watching the action, not playing himself, kibitzing with the other American, who was, beyond any doubt, the man I was looking for: Corporal Robert R. Pruchert.

His head was shaved, and he was wearing a beige cap with a short brim. He also had on running shoes, khaki slacks, and a pullover long-sleeved shirt made of wool. He was standing with his arms crossed, studying the game and occasionally making comments to his American friend.

Mr. Han took a seat across from me.

"The two Americans," I said. "They've lost all their money."

"Sadly. That's why they can only stand and watch."

"Do many people do that?" I asked. "Stay in the casino even after they have nothing more to gamble with?"

"Only the worst. The average person leaves when they've lost what they came to lose. The worst gamblers lose everything, including money for cab fare home. So they linger, hoping one of their fellow gamblers will hand them a few chips so they can get back in the game."

"If they're that broke, wouldn't they use any money someone gives them to get home?"

"Not this type of person."

"And that American, the one in the wool shirt, is he that type?"

"The exemplar," Han said. "Periodically he comes in here with money, gambles until it's gone, and then stands and watches until he's ready to pass out on his feet."

"Then what does he do?"

Han shrugged. "Somehow, he leaves. Maybe he catches a ride with another gambler. I'm not really sure."

The pit boss in the center of the ring of blackjack tables motioned our way. Mr. Han rose to his feet and excused himself. A high roller was changing yen to won, in large amounts, and Han had to approve the transaction. I watched the men do their business, fanning stacks of crisp new bills onto the green felt, counting them, and then stacking chips in front of the impatient Japanese gambler.

I continued to drink my coffee, feeling the hot fluid suffuse my tired body with life. There was no hurry. I'd finish my coffee and then arrest him. Pruchert wasn't going anywhere. All the doors were locked and Manager Han and his burly security guards had moved in a little closer to the two Americans, anticipating trouble.

The waitress approached again and asked if I wanted a refill. I declined, but maybe I admired her legs a little too long because when I turned my attention back to the blackjack pit, Pruchert was gone.

I rose to my feet and strode over to Mr. Han, pulling him aside from the customers.

"The American," I whispered urgently. "The white one. Did you see where he went?"

Han shook his head, then snapped his fingers. The two burly security guards appeared next to him.

"The American," he told them in Korean. "Find him."

The two men hurried off.

"Probably," Han said, "he just went to the bathroom."

That's where I went first, but no Pruchert. The security guards searched the ladies' room and then the back rooms off the casino where drinks were poured and snacks prepared, including the employee break room.

"Where's the other exit out of here?" I asked Han.

"Only the back fire exit," he replied. "But he would've tripped the alarm."

We were standing in the center of the casino, our feet sinking into plush carpet, wondering where Pruchert could have disappeared to. I was about to question the other American he had been chatting with when a shrill whooping noise pierced the air.

"What's that?"

"The rear exit," Han said. "Someone opened it."

And then I was running.

Many people never really know exhaustion. They say they're tired and they work around the clock, but the truth is that they've never pushed themselves beyond the demands their minds and bodies make of them. I'm not saying they don't work hard. They do. But a nine-to-five job seldom demands as much from you as the military requires of its soldiers. One of the first things that the army subjects you to, once they have you trapped in basic training, is sleep deprivation. You're seldom in bed before midnight and you're up in the morning, like clockwork, at zero five hundred hours. Sometimes, during special exercises, they don't let you sleep at all.

While undergoing this trial, you realize that sleep deprivation is one of the most painful parts of your training; it also starts to dawn on you that your judgment has clouded. Making the wrong decision, even in a situation that would normally be clear-cut, becomes a distinct possibility.

I ran out the back door of the Haeundae Casino.

The alley was modern—broad and covered in blacktop—not like the vile lanes in G.I. villages. Truck deliveries were made here. A four-foot-high cement loading platform loomed off to my left. I paused because I saw no shadows fleeing, nor did I hear any footsteps pounding on pavement. If I turned right, I'd be running toward civilization: tourist hotels, boutiques, fancy eateries; all along the main road that circles the bay and caters to the people who flock to Haeundae Beach, especially during the summer months. But now, during the midnight-to-four curfew in early autumn, there'd be no refuge there. All shops would be closed and there'd be no cabs to whisk you away to safety. The cement sidewalks would only make it easier to be spotted by the curfew police. If I turned left, I'd be heading toward the sea. Toward darkness. Toward the sound of breakers. Toward ships. Toward chaos. That's where Pruchert would go.

I ran left, into the night.

Soon I hit the pedestrian walkway that arced along the curve of the shoreline, twenty yards in from the beach. I paused and studied dark waters. By starlight I spotted the vague shadows of ships bobbing in the center of the Port of Pusan; to my right were the high-rise buildings that lined the port. Along the sand, I saw nothing. No revelers. No families traipsing timidly up to the edge of the water. No vacationers toting travel bags to the shuttered bathhouse that squatted a quarter mile to my right. And then I saw movement, off to my left along the edge of the water, just a flicker in the glinting moonlight. Without thinking about it, I ran. First across the sand, lifting my feet high; then across a spongy running surface, sand moistened and solidified by the sea, picking up speed.

As the shadowy figure ahead of me angled away, I realized that it was a thin man with long legs and limbs. A man who from this distance—about two hundred yards behind—appeared in every respect to be Corporal Robert R. Pruchert.

"Halt!" I shouted, inanely. I had no pistol to back up my command.

Where was he going? What lay to the northeast on the far edge of Haeundae Beach? Rice paddies? Shipyards? I had no idea, and my guess was that neither did Pruchert. He'd panicked when he saw me, then he'd hidden; finally he'd sneaked out the back of the casino and run. Where, he couldn't be sure.

I was catching my stride now, settling in for the distance. He was too far ahead for me to sprint and catch up. With no end to this beach in sight, this pursuit was becoming an endurance contest. Pruchert was panicked, running hard, not pacing himself. If I kept close, controlled my breathing, and settled into a good pace for a two-mile run, I'd probably catch up with him eventually. Once he collapsed.

Every soldier in the United States Army is required to take a physical training test every year. The test includes push-ups, sit-ups, and a two-mile run. I take pride in my scores. I'd yet to max the test but I'd come close. My training regimen consisted mainly of doing push-ups and sit-ups first thing in the morning and then jogging, as time permitted, around the Yongsan South Post gymnasium.

I hadn't jogged for a few days, not since the Blue Train rapist investigation began, but my body hadn't forgotten what to do. Slowly, across the wet sand, I was gaining on Pruchert. And then, without warning, he veered sharply to his left.

As I came closer, I saw what he was heading toward: a low line of shacks. Some sort of shops for the crowds that jammed Haeundae Beach during the daytime. Pruchert was running right toward the center of the shops, and in the dim light I watched as he approached the shops as if he were going to ram into one of them headfirst—and then he disappeared.

I blinked, straining to see what had happened.

As I plowed through sand, a gap appeared in the center of the line of shops. A passageway, dark now, and covered so that not even moonlight entered. Where did it lead? Either to the other side or, maybe, into a courtyard. When I reached the passageway, I slowed to a trot. No movement. No sign of Pruchert. Walking quickly, I entered the dark passage. After a few steps, I was blind, realizing that I'd made a mistake. I groped forward, holding my hands out, expecting at any moment to step into a pit lined on the bottom with *punji* sticks. Instead, I reached the inner courtyard I had imagined. Some of the shops were covered with wooden doors or metal shutters, but a few still had dim blue lights on within, behind polished glass. I stepped close to one of the windows. Two yellow eyes and a row of teeth darted toward me. I jerked back. Then I realized what it was.

A fish tank.

Live fish. It figured. These were not shops, but seafood eateries. I read the signs in cursive hangul: hot noodles, fresh seafood, raw squid, spiced octopus. Everything the discerning gourmand could desire. The fish seemed to sense my presence; tail fins waggled, jaws gaped open and then clamped shut, tentacles raised themselves in squiggly greeting.

I trotted to the far side of the courtyard. Another passageway. I ran through it, quicker this time, figuring Pruchert had already emerged on the other side and would be a half mile up the beach by now. As I hurried, I was reckless about where I stepped and ran into a straight-back chair that had been left in the center of the passageway. I was alert enough not to fall, although I banged my shins pretty hard, and I managed to catch myself on the back of the chair as I kept moving and to toss it off to the side where no one else would run into it.

As I did so, something moved out of the shadows. I caught a glimpse of him just before he hit me. Corporal Robert R. Pruchert. It was a good left and caught me moving into it, and I staggered. Then I was hit again and, for a few seconds anyway, that's all I remembered.

When I came to, I was kneeling on all fours. I looked up, slowly becoming aware of where I was and what was around me. There was no sign of Pruchert. I stood unsteadily, took a step forward and then another. I breathed deeply, the sharp tang of fish and salt entering my lungs. Soon I was running away from the conclave of seafood restaurants; by the time my head cleared, I had reached the pathway that paralleled the beach. The moon hung no higher in the sky, so I knew I hadn't been out long, only stunned, and now I had a good view down the beach for about a mile. No sign of Pruchert. Once he thought he had me off his tail, he would've headed toward civilization, maybe tried to hide until curfew was over and then find a cab. Where to hide? Near a tourist hotel, where there'd be plenty of taxis waiting outside at four A.M.

I ran back toward the casino.

About a hundred yards off to my right, in the old town section, someone darted into a dark alley. I barely caught a glimpse, but my impression was that this was someone taller and heavier than Pruchert. That didn't make sense at this time of the morning in this part of the world. Near the alley, cobbled lanes wound sinuously between tile-roofed homes. I slowed to a walk, listening. No running footsteps. All was quiet in this sleepy neighborhood at this early hour. I entered the alley.

It ran about twenty yards, curving to the left out of sight, lined on either side by the backs of brick-walled homes. Finally it opened into an unkempt rose garden surrounding an open-sided pagoda. A fat bronze kitchen god smiled out at me. In a stand in front of the pagoda, incense glowed. I passed the kitchen god with his fragrant environs and entered another alley emanating like the spoke of a wheel from the round garden. It was a clear pathway running downhill toward the tourist hotels. About twenty yards away, beneath a tiled overhang, two men were standing. As I approached, they emerged from the shadows.

Pruchert, Corporal Robert R.; and, next to him, the somewhat taller black G.I., the one Pruchert had been talking to in the casino. Both of them were holding bricks in their hands.

I could've turned around. In fact, I seriously considered it. I was exhausted, my head throbbed with an exploding headache, my nose still hurt, and I was still perspiring from the long run down the beach. However, whatever decision I was going to make had to be made immediately. I made it.

Striding forward, I didn't slow my pace. Everything in my face and my demeanor was meant to convey that I was here to kick some serious ass. Although in my current depleted condition I didn't believe I could take these two guys, I had to give the impression that there wasn't the slightest bit of doubt in my mind that I could turn them both into pulverized hamburger without even working up a sweat. As I strode forward, I reached in my jacket pocket and pulled out my badge. I held it up, pointing it at them like a shield.

"*You!*" I shouted. "You with the brick in your hand," addressing the tall black man. "You are not in trouble yet, but if you continue on this course you soon will be. Do you understand me?"

I stared into his eyes, waiting for him to nod assent. He did.

"Now drop the brick," I said, "and step aside." Although he hesitated, I pretended I hadn't noticed. "I'm Agent Sueño, badge number 7432, of the Criminal Investigation Division, Eighth United States Army. Any interference in this enforcement action will be considered a criminal offense. Is that understood?"

Neither man dropped his brick. Neither man stepped back.

I strode toward Pruchert, completely ignoring the other man with the brick, and shoved Pruchert on his shoulder. He stared at me dumbly. I ordered him to turn around. He did. Then I slipped my badge into my pocket and started frisking him. He hadn't yet dropped the brick. The man behind me held his ground.

I frisked Pruchert as if it were the most routine operation in the world. As I did so, I slapped the brick out of his hand. It clattered to the ground.

I cuffed him. At any moment, I expected to feel something heavy and solid landing on the back of my head. Nothing happened. When Pruchert was securely hand-cuffed, I turned and stared at the other G.I.

"What's your name?" I said.

"Bollington," he replied.

"Rank?"

"E-4."

"What unit?"

At this he balked. He looked away and said, "I don't want to get into any trouble behind this."

"So far," I said, "you haven't done anything to get in trouble for."

I squinted at him, waiting. He glanced away from me and then looked back. He told me his unit, which, frankly, I wasn't paying any attention to. All my attention was riveted on his right hand, the hand that held the brick.

"Let me see some ID," I said.

Bollington's long fingers loosened and the brick fell to the ground.

Before Pruchert and I were halfway back to the casino, I saw a red light flashing. And then another. Police vehicles, on the edge of town where the high-rise buildings of the Haeundae Beach area started. A blue KNP patrol car sat nearby.

Pruchert and I walked up to the MP sergeant. He turned, and I realized that I knew him. Sergeant Norris.

"Sueño," he said. "I thought you were in Taegu."

"I was, earlier today."

"We received a report about a disturbance at the Hae-undae Casino involving Americans."

I shoved Pruchert toward him. "Here's your disturbance."

Norris handed Pruchert off to his partner, who frisked him again and shoved him into the backseat of the jeep.

"You'll want to turn him over to the KNPs," I said.

"Why?"

I explained.

Norris whistled. "The Blue Train rapist. Good collar for you."

Pruchert leaned forward in the backseat of the jeep. "What?" he shouted in a reedy voice. "What's this about rape?"

"Shut the hell up," Norris said.

The other MP shoved Pruchert back against the seat.

We held a quick conference with the KNPs, with me doing the translating. We finally arranged for Norris and his partner to drive Pruchert over to the Pusan KNP Station. I rode with the KNPs. My stomach felt queasy, from the fried chicken and gravy I'd eaten earlier in the evening, from exhaustion, from the stress of the collar. I didn't want to start interrogating Pruchert yet and somehow screw things up.

Besides, I trusted Inspector Kill.

He'd been notified and was on his way to the station.

* * *

The case against Pruchert was based strictly on the fact that he'd had the means and the opportunity to commit the murder. The means, simply because he was bigger and stronger than the women who'd been raped, although we hadn't found the murder weapon yet. The opportunity, because he'd been away from his post of duty during the times the crimes had been committed. Furthermore, he'd taken elaborate precautions to cover his tracks; to make it seem as if he were studying Buddhism in a remote monastery when in reality he was black-marketing in the slums of Taegu and using that money to feed his gambling habit. Did he have another habit? A habit of rape?

Both of the victims had been robbed, their purses rifled for whatever bills were available. Certainly Pruchert was well known in the Haeundae Casino. Was he also well known in the Walker Hill Casino in Seoul, closer to where the first rape had been committed? That was something Inspector Kill would be checking out.

The interrogation lasted for two hours, and Pruchert was smart enough to stick to a simple story. If his gambling habit—and his black-marketing habit—were uncovered, he'd lose his top secret clearance. Without that, he'd no longer be able to work on the highly classified signal equipment at Horang-ni Signal Site. Pruchert wasn't rich, he had nobody at home backing him up, and he needed his job in the army. He was good at what he did on that job, and he fully expected to make warrant officer some day if he stuck with it. Therefore he'd taken elaborate precautions to keep his extracurricular activities secret. In the army, with so many men living together in close confines, everyone knows everyone else's business—and this is especially true at a remote signal site. So Pruchert came up with a cover story. He was studying Buddhism, and was so devout that he actually was giving serious consideration to becoming a monk. The teachers at the Doc-hung Temple didn't take on novices who they didn't think were serious. On the other hand, they were a trusting lot. When Pruchert told them that he wanted to meditate on his own, alone in a small cave, they gave him the privacy they thought he needed. He had betrayed that trust and told Inspector Kill now that he regretted having done it.

"I had to get away," he told Kill. "Don't you see? Everyone was watching me."

"Why do you gamble?" Kill asked.

"I don't like to gamble," Pruchert responded.

"Then why do you do it?"

"I did it once. Some buddies took me over. They thought it was fun. I didn't. I lost all my money, everything I had in the bank." He leaned forward and grabbed the cuff of Inspector Kill's coat. "Don't you see? It took me years to save it, years of hard work. I had to get my money back."

The compulsive gambler's famous last words: I have to get my money back.

Kill told Pruchert about the Blue Train, accusing him of traveling north toward Seoul, committing the rape, and leaving the train near Anyang. Pruchert vehemently denied it. Kill continued, claiming that when Pruchert returned from Seoul and arrived at the Pusan Station, he followed Mrs. Hyon Mi-sook to the Shindae Tourist Hotel and, while her two children cowered in the bathroom, he raped her; and when she resisted, he stabbed her to death.

Again Pruchert denied it. "The only time I'm ever on the Blue Train," he claimed, "is when I travel from Taegu to Pusan, after I've black-marketed with Lucy."

Lucy. The woman who was the leader of Migun Chonguk, G.I. Heaven.

After the interrogation, Inspector Kill had Pruchert locked in a cell, alone, to ponder his fate. He told Ernie and me that he was going to contact the Walker Hill Casino with a description of Pruchert to see if he was a regular there and, if so, when he'd last been there to gamble. Casinos in Korea keep records of the exchange of foreign currency to won, the Korean currency. These records are required by the government. If we were lucky, they might have Pruchert's name in those records.

For my part, I promised to spend the morning back on Hialeah Compound checking Pruchert's ration-control records, to see if we could get a handle on how much he'd been black-marketing and from where he'd made the purchases. Inspector Kill dispatched a patrol car to pick up the vendor who'd sold the rapist the purse in front of the Pusan train station and the cab driver who'd driven him to the Shindae Hotel. Once they were brought in, they'd see if the two witnesses could identify him.

I thanked Inspector Kill and told him I was returning to Hialeah Compound. Once more he insisted that I travel in one of his police sedans. I told him that I had my own wheels this time, although actually I could use a ride to the Haeundae Casino to retrieve the army sedan.

He consented and, after being dropped off near the vehicle, I made my way through the early-morning Pusan traffic, heading toward Hialeah Compound.

In the sedan, on my way to Hialeah, I thought about my latest conversation with Sergeant Norris. After we'd delivered Corporal Pruchert safe and sound to the Pusan Police Station, Norris had pulled me aside and said, "I talked to him again."

"Who?"

"That sailor. The one who wants to talk to Sway-no."

"What'd he say?"

"He wants you to meet him. The safest place is along the docks, at the end of Pier Seven. There's a chophouse there that East European sailors sometimes use. He doesn't want to meet you there. 'Too many eyes,' he said. But behind the chophouse about twenty yards, there's an overlook along the water."

"When?"

"Twenty-three hundred hours, any evening. He'll be there waiting every night."

"He sounds serious."

"He is."

"Have you told anyone else about this?"

"No one," Norris replied. "Not even my partner. There's something about the guy. He's nervous, worried. I think it could be something important."

"Any idea what?"

"He wouldn't spill. He only wants to talk to you."

"How long will he be in port?"

"Until Thursday."

That gave me four nights. "Okay," I said. "Thanks."

Before I walked away, Sergeant Norris grabbed me by the elbow. "He said for you to come alone, but I think you should take some backup with you."

"That might scare him off."

Norris thought about it. "At least be armed," he said finally.

"You're suspicious of this guy," I said.

Norris frowned. "Not of him so much, but of the people he might be dealing with."

"Like who?"

"I wish I knew. He hasn't told me anything. He only wants to talk to you. It just seems odd, though."

"What does?"

"That he knows you by name."

Norris was right. That did seem odd.

The Hialeah Compound Data Processing Center said they'd work on gathering Pruchert's ration-control records for me and I could pick them up that afternoon. At the MP station, I called Riley.

"Where the hell have you been?" Riley screamed.

I held the phone away from my ear. "Chasing criminals," I said. "What the hell do you think?"

"Do you consider your partner, Bascom, to be one of those criminals?"

"What are you talking about?"

"Taegu. Camp Henry. At oh two hundred hours this morning. MP report sitting on the Provost Marshal's desk this morning. Looks like your buddy Ernie punched out a captain in the United States Army."

"Embry?"

"Aha! I knew you'd know what I was talking about. There was a fight at the . . ." Riley rustled through some paperwork. ". . . the New Taegu Tourist Hotel in downtown Taegu. The KNPs were called, along with the MPs, and then a medical unit ambulance from the compound. It looks like Captain Frederick Raymond Embry was roughed up royally. He's in the dispensary on Camp Henry right now."

"How badly was he hurt?"

Riley looked at the paperwork again. "He'll live. A few stitches. And maybe his nose will be a little twisted."

"How about Ernie?"

"Scratches and bruises. Nothing serious. He was treated and released to the tender mercies of the Camp Henry MP station."

"They have him locked up?"

"What else? You can't go beating up officers for no good reason."

"No good reason? Captain Embry was stalking one of the women in the band, Marnie Orville. Ernie was assigned to protect her. We even have reason to believe that Embry might've been the one who attacked that MP."

As usual, instead of rewarding us for doing a tough job, 8th Army was berating us for doing what they'd told us to do.

"Marnie?" Riley asked. "She's in the report here too."

"And *you're* the one," I said, "who helped her locate Freddy Ray Embry, so she could contact him and get this shit started."

Riley ignored me. "Let me see," he said, shuffling through more paperwork. "Yeah, here it is. Marnie Orville says that Agent Ernie Bascom attacked Captain Frederick Raymond Embry without provocation."

"'Without provocation'? I'm on my way." I slammed the phone down.

By the time I'd made the two-hour drive to Taegu, I was so tired that I was starting to hallucinate. Still, I made my way to the MP station, parked the green army sedan in the gravel lot, and walked inside and asked the desk sergeant about Ernie.

"No one's allowed to talk to him," the desk sergeant told me.

"By God, I will," I said. "I didn't drive all the way up here for nothing."

"I don't give a damn how far you drove. Nobody talks to him."

"By whose orders?"

"Major Squireward."

"Where's his office?"

"You don't have a need to know."

I was about fed up with everybody's attitude around here. I grabbed the desk sergeant by the collar of his fatigues and hauled him part way over the counter.

"You get Agent Bascom out here, and you get him out here now! You got that?"

The desk sergeant clawed at my arms, and I kept pulling. Soon he was on top of the counter, kicking with his combat boots. He rolled off of the counter and hit the wood-paneled floor with a thud. By then, other MPs had run in from the back rooms. One of them grabbed me, and I swiveled and punched him. Then nightsticks came out. A couple of them swung, and I dodged and grabbed more green material. I felt myself falling, and a huge pile fell on top of me. Somehow, someone clamped handcuffs on one wrist; two men held the other wrist steady as the second cuff was clamped shut.

They dragged me into a back room.

It was another twenty minutes before I stopped cursing. And kicking the bottom of the door with my foot, smashing the hell out of my toe.

13

The best way to pass the time in a jail cell—as I've learned from my two or three sojourns therein—is to sleep. Due to my state of extreme exhaustion, sleep was something I had no trouble doing. Actually, I wasn't locked up in a jail cell, but rather in an interrogation room with no windows and a doorknob that turned freely but wouldn't unlock. In the center of the room was a scarred wooden army-issue field table and two dented gray metal folding chairs. I pushed the chairs together, both facing the wall, and did my best to lie down on the impromptu bed. It was dreadfully uncomfortable, but my exhaustion was so complete that within seconds I was dead to the world.

A door slammed open and jerked me awake.

"On your feet!" someone shouted.

I staggered upright.

"The position of attention!" the same voice shouted.

I realized who it was; the same desk sergeant whom I'd jerked across the counter. It figured that he'd be a little cross.

When I was in a reasonable approximation of the position of attention—my back straight, my feet together, my hands at my sides, thumbs aligned with the seams of my trousers—the desk sergeant opened the door and an officer wearing his dress green uniform strode in. His name tag said Squireward, the gold maple leaf on his shoulder indicated his rank as major, and I already knew that he was the Provost Marshal of Camp Henry and of the 19th Support Group.

Major Squireward stopped in front of me and examined me like a hawk would a particularly distasteful rodent. Finally he said, "What have you got to say for yourself, Sueño?"

"About what, sir?"

"About pulling Sergeant Copwood across the counter."

Sergeant Copwood leaned his weight from one foot to the other. "He didn't pull me *all* the way across the counter, sir."

"Shut up, Copwood." Squireward continued to glare at me. "So what is it, Sueño? What's your excuse?"

"No excuse, sir."

"Then you admit you were in the wrong."

I shrugged. "I have the right to remain silent, sir, like anyone else."

Squireward's narrow face seemed to suck in on itself, and his brown eyes flashed behind the hooked nose.

"We'll see about that," he said. "We'll see if you can

retain the right to remain silent. I'm not standing for that type of behavior in my area of operations, Sueño. Do you understand? I'm pushing this thing all the way up to Eighth Army. You think you're smart now, coming down here from Seoul and throwing your weight around, but we'll see who laughs last."

I didn't respond. I knew better. Most members of the US Army officer corps, when they're angry, want desperately to deliver their tongue-lashings. If they're allowed to do that, given time, they'll calm down; once they come to their senses, any attempt they make at punishment will be less severe. Not that I thought Major Squireward could do much to me, but there's no sense in tempting fate.

"I've already demanded," he said, "that you and your partner, that guy Bascom, be removed physically from Camp Henry and all Nineteenth Support Group subordinate units. I want you out of here, and I want you out of here now. You got that?"

I nodded. "Got it, sir."

"Good. And to that end, Seoul has sent down a babysitter for you. I'm signing both you and that Bascom character over to him, and he'll escort you out of Taegu. Is *that* understood?"

"Understood, sir."

Major Squireward glared at me again, this time for a long moment. Finally, he said, "It had *better* be understood, Sueño. It had better be. And it should also be understood that your investigation of the Blue Train rapist failed miserably."

"How's that, sir?"

"Talk to your KNP buddy down there. What's his name? Inspector Kill. He'll tell you."

With that, Major Squireward pivoted on his highly polished low quarters and marched out of the interrogation room.

The "babysitter" who signed for Ernie and me was Staff Sergeant Riley. After we walked out of the front door of the Camp Henry MP station, Ernie said, "How the hell did you get down here so fast?"

"Chopper," Riley replied. "The Provost Marshal has a case of the big ass."

"That's news?" Ernie asked.

"For starters," Riley said, "you punched out Captain Freddy Ray Embry and put him in the aid station; and you, Sueño, roughed up the desk sergeant at the Camp Henry MP station."

"Allegedly," I said, "on both counts."

"'Allegedly,' my ass," Riley replied.

"Why is it," Ernie asked, "that Eighth Army is always willing to believe the worst about us?"

"Because you *deserve* to have the worst believed about you," Riley replied.

Ernie climbed in the driver's seat of the old green sedan, pulled out his keys, and turned on the ignition. It started right up. Riley sat in back. I rode shotgun. On the way out the gate, Ernie waved to the MPs. They frowned back at him, hands on the grips of their .45s.

"Where to?" Ernie asked.

"Pusan," Riley replied. "We turn this vehicle in, and then I'm to escort you both back to Seoul."

"Belay that," I said.

"What? There's no *belaying* shit. I'm under orders to return you two assholes to Seoul."

"First," I said, "we talk to Inspector Kill."

"The hell you will," Riley replied.

"The hell I won't," I said.

Inspector Kill shook his head sadly and pushed a sheaf of pulp across his metal desk. "No good," he said.

I was sitting in the Pusan Central Police Station. Riley and Ernie were waiting for me in the sedan, partly because in the middle of the day, in downtown Pusan, Ernie couldn't find a parking spot, and partly because Ernie was playing the role of mental health nurse while Riley fumed and turned red and cursed about being under orders to escort us back to Seoul. "Immediately if not sooner" was the way he put it.

"You brought in the witnesses," I told Kill.

He nodded. "Separately. Both the woman who sold the purse in front of the train station and the cab driver who transported the Blue Train rapist to the Shindae Hotel. Both witnesses took their time, they studied the man, but in the end they both said the same thing. It's not him."

"But they don't see many foreigners," I said. "We all look alike to them. Maybe they're mistaken."

Kill shook his head. "The old lady in front of the train station sees plenty of foreigners; they shop there for souvenirs. And the driver works the Texas Street area. He probably has almost as many foreign passengers as he has Korean. They both took their time. We emphasized to them how important this was." Kill fondled the black-and-white photo of Corporal Robert R. Pruchert. "It's not him. He's not the Blue Train rapist."

Finally I accepted what he was telling me. Then my self-questioning began. What had I done wrong? Where had my investigative procedures failed? There are only so many American G.I.s at the compounds in Taejon, Waeg-wan, Taegu, and Pusan, totaling only in the hundreds, and they're watched closely; passes and leave requests are monitored by their superiors. They don't just run up and down the spine of Korea on the Blue Train willy-nilly.

Most crimes committed by American G.I.s in Korea are solved easily. G.I.s aren't criminal masterminds and they don't cover their tracks well. Often, it seems that many of them actually *want* to be caught. Maybe they're tired of the slogging routine of military life. Maybe they're tired of living in a country where they don't understand the language and can't read the signs, where they don't understand the customs and everything seems to be done backward. When Koreans wave a hand they usually mean "come here," not "good-bye." When they say "yes," they are often trying not to embarrass the person who's doing the asking, and what they really mean is "no." For Americans, who are used to revering youth and beauty, it seems odd that in Korea the young and the beautiful are expected to prostrate themselves in front of the old and the ugly. So G.I.s commit crimes out of rage and frustration, or just out of a desire to leave "frozen Chosun" and go home. That's what I thought the Blue Train rapist case was. A guy acting out his resentments. A guy waiting to get caught.

Apparently, I was wrong.

The disappointment must've shown in my face. Kill leaned forward and slipped the photograph into a folder. "We'll catch the right man," he said. "You'll see."

I told him about Ernie and me being ordered back to Seoul.

Kill's face hardened. "Eighth Army promised us your services until this case was solved."

"I know. But my partner was involved in an argument with a superior officer. They're very angry about that."

"The people of Korea," Kill said, "are very angry about the Blue Train rapist."

He walked me out of his office and down the long corridor. "I will contact my superiors," he said. "They will contact yours. Don't leave Pusan until you've heard from me."

I promised I wouldn't.

In the foyer, just in front of the arched entranceway to the Pusan Police Station, a small group of people waited. Two were old grandparents wearing traditional Korean hanbok, supporting themselves on canes; another was a middle-aged man in a natty blue suit. With them were three children, a boy and two girls. The blue-suited man's eyes widened when he spotted Inspector Kill. He stepped forward and bowed. The man wore glasses; he had a square face with high cheekbones, and I could see that his eyes were deeply lined in red. The children cowered next to their grandparents.

"This," Mr. Kill told me, "is Mr. Ju, the husband of Hyon Mi-sook."

In Korea, a wife doesn't adopt her husband's family name but keeps the name she was born with. This then was the husband of the woman who'd been brutally raped and then murdered in the Shindae Hotel. The children staring at me in wide-eyed horror had huddled in the bathtub while their mother had been humiliated, stabbed, and partially dismembered.

Without thinking, I held out my hand.

Mr. Ju recoiled from it. He stepped back, waving his palm negatively. "*Andei.*" No good. He launched into a vituperative spiel, some of which I couldn't understand but, unfortunately, much of which I could. He said the American government must certainly know who had murdered his wife because soldiers are controlled and all their time accounted for, and therefore we Americans must be protecting the man who tore apart his family. He accused me of trying to block the investigation, trying to stall for time, hoping Koreans would forget about the outrage. He vowed *he* would never forget. He would continue to demand that we give up the killer even if it meant that Korea finally stood up for its rights and forced every last miscreant American G.I. to leave the country.

By now he was screaming, pointing his finger at me. The children were crying, burying their faces in the folds of their grandparents' silk garments. A few uniformed cops loitered nearby, not sure what to do. Inspector Kill stepped toward Mr. Ju and held up two open palms.

Involuntarily I retreated from Mr. Ju's assault, wanting to say it wasn't true, we weren't hiding anyone, but afraid of what he was saying; afraid of the truth of what he was saying. In each unit of the United States Army—especially while stationed overseas—we live cheek by jowl, both on duty and off. We know all about one another, often more than we *want* to know. If someone was leaving his unit, leaving his place of work, leaving his bunk in the barracks, and traveling around the country raping and murdering women, somebody who lived or worked with him would know of his strange behavior, or at least have strong suspicions. As of yet, no one had contacted 8th Army law enforcement. Not one tip. Partly that was because the story hadn't appeared in the *Pacific Stars and Stripes* and therefore hadn't risen above the level of rumor. But Riley confirmed to us that no tips had come in to the 8th Army CID office or the 8th Army MP station or any MP station in the entire country.

Was Mr. Ju right? Was 8th Army covering something up?

It had happened before. The Army protects its own. That's not just an observation, it's a motto that many soldiers—if not most—live by.

I stepped away from the screaming man, away from the crying children, away from Inspector Kill, who was trying to calm down the hysterical civilian. With a knot in my gut as big as a winter cabbage, I shoved my way out of the Pusan Police Station and stumbled down the stone steps. Ernie was in the sedan waiting for me, engine idling.

When I climbed in the front passenger seat, Riley said, "What the hell happened to you?"

My only response was "Drive."

Ernie slipped the car in gear, stepped on the gas, and roared his way through the midday Pusan traffic.

After a few minutes, I started to calm down. The roads had widened now and were filled with fewer cars but, so far, no one had said a word. Even Riley was keeping his big trap shut. To fill the silence, Ernie started to explain what had happened between him and Captain Freddy Ray Embry.

"The USO popped for some really nice rooms in downtown Taegu," Ernie told us. "Marnie and I were on the sixth floor—"

"What's this 'Marnie and I'?" Riley growled.

"Just what I said," Ernie repeated. "'Marnie and I.' We were staying in room 607, up on the sixth floor."

"You're supposed to be guarding those broads," Riley said. "Not cohabitating with 'em."

Ernie shrugged. "So, anyway, it was just before the midnight curfew hit and suddenly there's this pounding on the door. For a minute I thought it was the bed because Marnie was screaming at the time and thrashing around a bit—she's a big girl—but finally I realized that somebody was at the door. I tried to get up, but Marnie wouldn't let me go until finally I broke her grip and slipped on my jockey shorts. When I opened the door, there's this big ugly G.I. screaming at me, wanting to know what I was doing with his Marnie."

"She was really thrashing around that much?" Riley asked.

"Like I said, she's a big girl. It was Freddy Ray at the door, raising all kinds of hell, so naturally I told him to get bent. He tried to barge into the room, and I shoved him back, and then he came at me again, and next thing I know we're wrestling in the hallway, knocking shit over, and finally I break free and pop him with a couple of good lefts. By now, heads were poking out of doors, most of them the other girls from the Country Western All Stars, but a few Korean faces. Freddy Ray and I bounced around for a while, trading punches, but neither one of us getting the best of the other until finally, from out of the emergency stairwell, about a dozen Korean National Police wearing helmets and riot gear storm into the hallway. After a little more pushing and shoving, they take us both into custody. By now, Marnie's wearing a see-through pink nightgown and she's out in the hallway screaming at the cops to let Freddy Ray go. They can't believe it. A half-naked American woman, taller than most of them, and they don't know whether to use their batons on her or punch her out or what. And she wrestles with them and knocks a couple of the KNPs down, but finally they form a moving wall and shove her back into the room and shut the door."

"She was naked," Riley asked, "in her see-through nightgown?"

"Yeah," Ernie replied, eyeing Riley. "Try to remain calm."

"What happened then?"

"They handcuffed me and took me downstairs and threw me in a police van in the back along with Freddy Ray Embry and drove us over to the monkey house."

"Did you and Freddy Ray get into it again?"

"What were we going to do? Butt heads? Our hands were cuffed behind our backs. He cussed me out and I gave him what-for, but mainly I was thinking about how freaking cold I was."

"Was Freddy Ray hurt bad?"

"Hell, no. I think he cut himself on one of those flower

vases on a stand. A lot of blood, and when the MPs arrived he was complaining like I was Jack the Ripper, but if it took even a half-dozen stitches I'd be surprised."

"It took eight," Riley replied.

"See?" Ernie said.

"Did he accuse you of having a knife?"

"He told the MPs he 'wasn't sure' whether I had a knife. I'm sitting there in my jockey shorts and where am I going to hide a knife?"

They both stopped chattering when we pulled up to the big concertina-wire-covered front gate of Hialeah Compound. An MP stepped forward and examined our dispatch.

"There's an order for you to leave the compound," the MP said.

"We have to get our stuff at billeting," Ernie replied.

The MP handed us our dispatch back and returned to the guard shack. After making a phone call, he returned.

"They say okay. But they want you to turn in the sedan at the motor pool while you're at it."

We didn't respond.

The big gate was rolled back on squeaking wheels and we drove slowly onto Hialeah Compound.

In the morning, Ernie and I rose early and left Riley sleeping it off in billeting. We ate chow at the Hialeah Compound PX snack bar and then made our way to the MP station. I wanted to see a map.

They had a big one nailed to the wall of the MP briefing room. Almost six feet high with thumb-sized red tacks implanted at every compound, signal site, and supply depot in the 19th Support Group area, which included every army installation south of Seoul. Ernie pointed to a blue tack.

"K-2," he said.

The Air Force base on the outskirts of Taegu. The only other blue tacks were the ones at Kunsan and Osan, both farther north.

"Our man could be a zoomie," Ernie said.

"Maybe," I said. "But Private Runnels, our only witness who's actually spoken to the guy, thought he was Army."

There's a certain terminology that G.I.s use that's different from the Air Force, the way they refer to unit designations and ranks and things like the BX, base exchange, rather than the PX, post exchange.

"He could've been wrong," Ernie said. "Or our man could've been purposely trying to mislead him."

"You're right. I'll have Riley make phone calls today up to Osan's main personnel office, compile us a list."

"Give him something to do, so maybe he'll stay sober."

"For a while, anyway. Still, I don't think this guy is Air Force. He boarded the train in Pusan, according to Runnels. That would've been a long way to travel just to throw us off the track. And the way he climbed those barbed-wire fences in Anyang: this is a guy who's used to accomplishing the physical."

"Not as brainy as the zoomies."

"Not that he's stupid. It's just that he throws his athletic ability in your face."

"A guy like that doesn't usually join the Air Force," Ernie agreed.

"So what *does* he join?"

"The Marines," Ernie replied.

Other than a small contingent at the embassy, there were no US Marines stationed in Korea.

"And if not the Marines?" I asked.

"The Special Forces."

We looked at each other, and then we both returned to the map.

It was off the edge of the main part of the map, in its own little square: an oval-shaped island—about 50 miles south of mainland Korea and 175 miles southwest of Pusan—with a mountain smack-dab in the middle. Cheju-do. The Island of Cheju. We studied the map for a moment. Hallasan was the name of the mountain, a still-smoking volcano. At the base of the mountain was a small red pin. A training area. Run by a contingent of the United States Army Special Forces, more commonly known as the Green Berets.

Marnie stepped out from behind her electric keyboard, grabbed a G.I. from the front row, and started shimmying in her tight blue jeans and even tighter cowgirl blouse. A heartfelt somebody-done-somebody-wrong song was being belted out by the Country Western All Star Review behind her. The G.I.s of Hialeah Compound howled their mad delight.

I shouted in Ernie's ear, "She's letting loose tonight!"

He nodded his head, grinning from some sort of inner satisfaction.

Riley was still grumbling, complaining that we should've left for Seoul by now, but drowned his anxiety by jolting down a shot of bar bourbon followed by sips from a cold can of Falstaff.

We were in the Hialeah Compound NCO Club. Instead of turning in the sedan at the motor pool like the MPs wanted us to, we'd returned to billeting, where I'd spent the rest of the morning and half the afternoon sleeping. When I awoke I'd taken a long shower, shaved, and then climbed into my last clean set of clothes. Riley kept complaining all the while that we were supposed to check out of billeting, turn in the sedan, and return to Seoul ASAP. Both Ernie and I told him to shove it, and he grew increasingly worried until I told him finally that the orders would be changed.

"How the hell do you know that?"

"I know," I replied.

He squinted his eyes, studying me. "It's that Mr. Kill, isn't it? He's going to pull some strings."

I didn't answer.

"Look, Sueño," Riley said. "You can get over on the honchos of Eighth Army sometimes. But when you do, they never forget. They make a record of it and that record is never washed clean. When this case is over and when Mr. Kill is no longer around to protect your low-ranking butt, your ass will be theirs."

I shrugged.

Riley found some coffee down in the billeting office, and a deck of cards, and he'd spent the rest of the afternoon playing solitaire and getting himself wired on caffeine, waiting for the bar at the NCO Club to open.

The song finally ended and Marnie took a bow, to wild applause. The G.I. she'd been dancing with returned to his seat, reluctantly, and Marnie told the crowd that the

Country Western All Stars would be back after a short break. The curtain closed; somewhere someone turned on a sound system, the music coming out a lot quieter than the raucous sounds that had just been blaring from the speakers and amps of the live band.

"Did you check with the MPs?" Ernie asked.

"Screw them. If they haven't sent somebody to find us and escort us off-compound, it's because they've received word from Seoul to leave us alone."

Riley was talking to a group of G.I.s at the table next to us, bragging about how tough it had been in Nam during "the big one," as he called it. They were egging him on and laughing at him because he was so drunk.

"You gonna stay here?" I asked Ernie.

"Where else do I have to go?"

"Nowhere. I'm going downtown."

"To meet Kill?"

"Something like that."

Ernie studied me. "What are you up to, Sueño?"

"Nothing. I'm not sure yet. I'll let you know when I do."

"You'll need backup."

"Not on this one." I didn't want to get him involved in something I didn't yet understand myself.

"Is it a girl?"

"Never mind, Ernie."

"When will you be back?"

"What are you? My mother?"

"It's not like you to run off without telling me what you're up to."

"It's probably nothing. Don't worry, I'll be back before curfew."

I glanced at Riley. He was aware that the G.I.s were laughing at him, but this only made him more aggressive in his storytelling. He was tall enough at five nine or ten, but so skinny from never consuming anything other than whiskey and coffee that he weighed only about 125 pounds. Still, he had a habit of acting like the toughest guy in two towns, especially after a couple of cold ones.

"Keep an eye on Riley," I told Ernie.

"After three or four more shots of bourbon," Ernie replied, "I'll carry him back to billeting and tuck him in bed."

I left the Hialeah NCO Club, made my way to the front gate, and flashed my CID badge at the pedestrian exit. The MP didn't bat an eye. This confirmed to me that Mr. Kill had been true to his word and Ernie and I had been taken off Major Squireward's escort-out-of-the-area list. I walked through the narrow wooden passageway and emerged into the Pusan night.

Salt-laced mist washed the air. Moist streets glistened from the glare of neon. A cab cruised by. I waved him down, the back door popped open, and I climbed in.

The cab driver said nothing. Probably because he didn't speak English and didn't expect me to understand Korean. He turned his head and waited for my instruction.

"Texas," I said finally.

He nodded. An automatic spring popped the door shut and he shoved the little Hyundai sedan into gear.

The chophouse had a Korean name only, no English translation, written in black letters slashed across splintered wood: *Huang Hei Banjom*. Eatery of the Yellow Sea.

Technically we weren't on the Yellow Sea. The Port of Pusan is located at the southeastern corner of the Korean peninsula where the Yellow Sea and the Eastern Sea converge. This can be confusing because the Eastern Sea, as the Koreans call it, is known as the Sea of Japan to the rest of the world. Koreans, however, don't like to give unwarranted credit to the country that brutally occupied them for thirty-five years.

I stood across from the entrance to Pier Number 7, hidden in the shadows beneath a stack of wooden crates, studying the people who entered and departed the Eatery of the Yellow Sea. There were few Koreans, and the ones who did enter probably worked there. The main clientele was composed of Caucasian men. But not G.I.s. Their hair wasn't cut short, they weren't wearing neatly pressed PX blue jeans, and they didn't sport nylon jackets with dragons embroidered on the back. These were men who looked as if they'd walked out of another century. Their hair was long and unkempt, and some of them had several days' stubble on their faces. Their pants were loose, unpressed, hanging over scruffy brown leather brogans that in some cases looked as if they were about to fall off. Even from my distance of some twenty yards, their peacoats looked sopped through with the drizzle that washed across the pier in airborne waves from the sea.

Exotic foreign ports, sailors living a carefree life, none of that applied here at the Eatery of the Yellow Sea. This was a place for working men; poor working men at that, featuring hot noodles and fried rice and bottles of cheap rice liquor, soju, that would get you drunk and let you forget about today until the inevitable tomorrow. Greeks didn't hang out here. They had their own places, somewhat classier than this joint. The Eatery of the Yellow Sea was for poor foreign sailors clinging to the bottom rung of the maritime ladder.

Occasionally I heard laughter from inside. Men's voices in a language I didn't understand. Through fogged windows I spotted a portly Korean woman with a bandanna tied across her hair serving the foreign sailors, not saying anything to them that I could see. No beautiful young women wearing hot pants and halter tops here. These sailors couldn't afford the fare.

They looked harmless enough. Poor working men searching for a warm meal, a shot of fiery liquor, a respite from their dreary life of labor on an indifferent sea.

I waited until there was no one entering or leaving, and then I strolled past the Eatery of the Yellow Sea, stepped onto Pier Number 7, and followed creaking wooden planks that led into the darkness. Finally, I reached an overlook above the sloshing waters of the Port of Pusan. I stood next to a thick wooden piling, allowing the shadow to make my silhouette less distinct. I shoved my hands in my pockets and inhaled deeply of the cold night air. Occasionally a seagull dove toward the water and then gracefully lifted skyward. Clouds covered a silvery moon, sometimes parting to reveal its beauty. I stared up, wondering at the magnificence of the world in which we lived, and at its horrors.

I waited.

14

I stood alone on the walkway at the edge of Pier Number 7 for well over an hour. At half past eleven, I was certain that whoever had promised to be there must've been pulling Sergeant Norris's leg. Sailors wandered in and out of the Eatery of the Yellow Sea, but no one turned down this dark pathway that ran along the edge of the bay.

When he did appear, he seemed to emerge from the shadows. He must've seen me, but he walked right past. Then, without turning his head, he said in English, "Follow me."

I did, at about six paces. The wood-planked pathway turned slightly, until we were out of the glow of the single floodlight in front of the Eatery of the Yellow Sea. He stopped and turned, keeping both hands in the pockets of his thick jacket.

"You're Sway-no," he said.

"Sueño," I replied, correcting his pronunciation.

"Ah." He nodded. "Spanish."

"I'm an American."

"Yes. So I was told."

His accent was difficult to place. Eastern Europe, I supposed, but that was more from a process of deduction than from any analysis of the sounds. Which country this guy was from, I couldn't say. He was five or six inches shorter than me, maybe five eight or five nine, and he must've weighed close to 180; sturdy, with a low center of gravity. His face was mostly hidden in shadow, but, from what I'd seen when he walked past me, it was nondescript: brown hair, brown eyes, thick eyebrows, and a prominent nose rounded at the end. He seemed fairly young, not yet forty, but his cheeks sagged like an old man's jowls.

"What's your name?" I asked.

"That's not important."

"Okay. It's not important. So, what do you want?"

"Nothing," he replied. "I am only doing a favor for someone. I am relaying a message."

"And there's no money in it for you?"

He shrugged. "Maybe some."

"What's the message?"

"First, I must make sure that you are Sueño."

"How do you want to do that?"

"I need to see your identification."

"Okay. But that could be faked."

"Yes. But that first."

I pulled my badge up and held it out, twisting it toward moonlight. He stepped forward, squinted his eyes, and read, making no move to pull his hands out of his pockets. Finally, he stepped backward. I slipped my badge back into the inner pocket of my coat.

"Now what?"

"I ask you a question."

"What question?"

He paused for a moment and then said, "In a snowstorm in Itaewon, we left one place and found refuge in another. What are the two places?"

I stopped for a moment, stunned by the question. I knew what he meant, but I was so shocked by the implications that for the moment I was unable to allow the full import to sink in. Thoughts flashed around in my brain like a pinball looking for a home.

The sailor could see that I'd been thrown off balance.

"Well?" he asked.

I cleared my throat. "Just a moment. Let me think." And then I told him. "We left the home of Auntie Mee and then we found refuge in a yoguan, a Korean inn."

"Very good," he replied. "You passed the test. I'm convinced that you are truly Sueño."

Then he pulled his right hand out of his pocket. A piece of thick paper—vellum or parchment, really—about the size of a playing card cut in half, wavered in the evening breeze. "Here," he said. "For you."

I took it out of his hands.

"What is it?"

He gestured toward the fragment. "Read."

With both hands I held it up to my nose and twisted it to catch as much light as possible. Chinese characters. Only a few. What appeared to be a name and a date designation. Not dates like we use them, but characters for numbers and the formal designation of an imperial reign.

"Take that," the sailor told me, "to someone who knows about these things. Let them help you determine its value. Then come back with money, however much you think my information is worth, and I will tell you how to obtain the full manuscript."

"There's more?" I asked.

"Much more."

If this guy was a dealer in antiquities, I wouldn't be interested in doing business with him. Not just because what he was doing was probably illegal but, more importantly, because I was in a different line of work. I'm a cop, not a hustler. But the question he'd asked me, the question about a stormy night in Itaewon, changed everything.

"When will I meet you?" I asked.

"We will be traveling to Tsushima for a few days and then we'll return here. One week from today. We'll only be in port three days. I'll be here every night. If you bring someone with you or try to follow me, the deal will be off."

I nodded.

The man left me with the fragment and started to walk away.

"Wait," I said. He paused and stared at me. "The night in Itaewon. How do you know about that?"

He pointed to the fragment in my hand. "The owner of the manuscript, the one who entrusted it to me, she told me to find you and to trust no one but you."

"You've seen her?"

"Yes."

"Where?"

"Where do you think?"

He glanced toward the north, stared at me for a moment, and then shoved his hands deeper into his pockets and stalked away.

The next day, before catching the ferry from Pusan to Cheju, I decided to check in at the Pusan Police Station. The uniformed Korean policeman in the hallway told me that Inspector Kill was busy. I told him it was important and stepped past him. An office at the end of the passageway had been temporarily assigned to Inspector Kill for the duration of the Blue Train rapist investigation. When I opened the door, Inspector Kill's back was to me and he was leaning over the safe behind his desk, fiddling with the locking mechanism. Apparently, he was changing the combination. He stopped what he was doing, sat up straight, and turned to look at me.

The fragment the mysterious sailor had given me was made of a brittle but very thick fibrous material. I held it in my open palm, touching only the wax paper the sailor had wrapped it in. I dropped it on the center of Inspector Kill's desk.

"*Igot muoya?*" he said in Korean, startled by something that he immediately recognized as being valuable.

"You're a calligrapher," I told him. "You know about Chinese characters and about ancient styles of writing. Maybe you can tell me what this is."

Kill closed the door of the safe, turned back to his desk, and studied the fragment. After a few seconds, he looked up at me. "Where did you find this?"

"It's a long story. First, what does it mean?" I pointed. "This character means something about a king and there's a lot of numbers, so I thought maybe it was a date."

Inspector Kill looked at me with increased interest. "You've studied hanmun." Chinese characters.

"A little."

He was impressed. Koreans revere education. Since the end of the Korean War, their schools and universities have been churning out mathematicians and scientists at an increasingly rapid rate. But despite this emphasis on modern knowledge, Koreans are still most in awe of the traditional forms of education, a curriculum that has been taught since the days of Confucius: Chinese characters, calligraphy, the ancient texts known as the Four Books and the Five Classics. These are thought of, even today, as the only true education. That a foreigner, especially an American G.I., would know how to read and write even a few Chinese characters never failed to impress.

Inspector Kill turned back to the fragment. He reached in the desk, rummaged around for a while, finally pulling out a magnifying glass, and laid it on the table. Then he searched in another drawer and came out with a pair of gloves made of fine white cloth. He slipped them on. Gingerly, using a pair of silver chopsticks, he turned the fragment this way and that, examining it under the magnifying glass. As he studied, he spoke.

"Korea made the first paper," he said. "Not from the skin of animals—that had been done since time immemorial—but from bamboo, ground with a pestle, and then mixed with lime and the leaves of a birch tree. Finally the pulp was stretched on a screen to dry." He switched on a green lamp. "Here, look at the grain in this paper. Even now, you can see tiny chunks of wood."

With the chopsticks, he pointed to a dark splotch.

"So this paper is very old," he said. "Probably made during the early part of the Chosun Dynasty, before modern paper was introduced. And you're right about the date. It's indicating the reign of King Sejong Daewang."

Even I'd heard of Sejong Daewang, Great King Sejong. A statue of him presided over the entrance to Doksoo Palace in Seoul, and his stern visage stared out from every freshly minted hundred-won coin. He was credited with having devised the hangul alphabetic script, freeing Korea from the Chinese writing system, and with other innovations that seem modern to us today, such as keeping track of national rainfall, distributing loans to farmers from the royal treasury, and even devising an early version of the seismograph, to measure the intensity of earthquakes.

"Is that it?" I asked. "Is that all this fragment has on it, the date?"

"Maybe not."

Deftly employing the chopsticks, Inspector Kill pried one sheaf of the parchment loose from the other. Like a flower opening to sunlight, it unfolded into a fragment almost as large as a full page of typing paper.

More characters. Smaller handwriting shoved together in the "grass" style—that is, written quickly, like cursive handwriting, making it more difficult for a novice like me to read. Inspector Kill used the magnifying glass and leaned closer.

"Whoever wrote this," he said, "used a horsehair brush and expensive ink."

"You can tell just by looking at it?"

"That's my initial guess. We can have a more thorough analysis done in the lab."

"You've worked on ancient texts before."

"A few times," he replied. "There are plenty of antiques and heirlooms and manuscripts hidden around Seoul and the rest of Korea. Sometimes they're stolen. Sometimes they're involved in crimes in other ways."

"Like people squabbling over an inheritance."

"Like that," he said. "So if the paper was expensive and the writing brush made of horsehair, the most expensive of the time, and the ink of highest quality, chances are that whoever wrote this was a highly educated man."

Inspector Kill said "man" because in those days women were seldom allowed the opportunity to become literate.

"Can you decipher what it says?" I asked.

"A little."

Kill followed the writing, gliding the glass slowly above the rows of tightly scripted text. Three or four paragraphs' worth, all in all, were jammed into a small space.

Finally, Inspector Kill leaned back, as if shocked by something.

"What is it?" I asked.

"Who gave you this?"

"I told you it's a long story."

He lay down the magnifying glass and looked at me directly. "It's a story," he said, "that some very important people will soon become very interested in."

"Why? What's this all about?"

Then he told me. As he spoke, I pulled over a straight-backed chair and sat down.

According to Inspector Kill, this fragment was part of a narrative concerning the chase for a man, some sort of "wild man," who had been considered dangerous by the authorities at the time—sometime during the reign of King Sejong, approximately 1418 to 1450. This "wild man" was extremely strong and resourceful and managed to elude men on horseback by entering a network of caves in the Kwangju Mountains near Mount Osong. Upon entering the caves, the officials discovered a network of tunnels that took them much farther than they ever imagined. So far south, in fact, that they emerged in an area near Mount Daesong, located on a plateau between the Imjin River to the west and the tributaries leading to the Han River valley to the east. What apparently follows in the remainder of the manuscript, according to Kill, would be a detailed guide to those underground caverns, a guide that without the help of the "wild man" would've taken years to compile, if it had been possible at all.

"To drop into these caverns," Inspector Kill said, "would be suicide if you didn't know that there was a route out. And know how to find that route."

"Okay," I said. "This stuff is of great interest to spelunkers," I said, "but what good is it to us today?"

"What?" Kill asked.

"Spelunkers," I repeated. "People who crawl through caves."

"For fun?"

I nodded. "For fun."

Inspector Kill shook his head, unable to imagine such a thing being fun. He rose to his feet. "I'll show you why this information could be valuable."

We walked over to a map of Korea tacked to his wall. He pointed, still wearing his white gloves.

"Here," he said, "are the Kwangju Mountains." He pointed to a range that slashed across the center of the Korean peninsula. "According to that fragment, the wild man dropped into the caves here, near Mount Osong, and led his pursuers through a maze of caverns and underground rivers that took them three days to traverse. Eventually they emerged here." Kill pointed again. "Somewhere near Mount Daesong."

I studied the two points, my mouth falling open. "Oh," I said.

"Now you see the value of this information?"

I nodded.

"The rest of the manuscript," Kill continued, "could be of vital national interest. One side, where these men entered the caves, is in North Korea; the other side, where they emerged, is in South Korea."

"The remainder of the manuscript," I said, almost speaking to myself, "shows the way beneath the DMZ."

The Korean Demilitarized Zone is the most heavily fortified demarcation line in the world: 700,000 Communist soldiers in the north; 450,000 ROK soldiers in the south. Not to mention a division of 30,000 American soldiers sitting smack-dab in the middle.

"So maybe now," Inspector Kill said, slipping off his gloves, "you'll tell me where you found this fragment."

"Maybe I will," I said. But for some reason I hesitated.

"Okay," Kill said. "You think about it. I'll lock this fragment in the safe." He did. Then we started discussing the Blue Train rapist.

* * *

Ernie puked over the railing.

When his guts were empty he stood and looked at me, bleary-eyed. "How long does this goddamn boat ride take?"

"Eleven hours. Another two hours left," I said.

"Two hours?" Ernie groaned.

Before we left Hialeah Compound, I'd checked with Specialist Holder at Headquarters Company about the personnel assigned to the Special Forces Training Facility, Mount Halla.

"I have no data on them," he told me. "The Green Berets run their own show. They don't want rear-echelon pukes like us mucking around with their personnel records."

"Do you have any idea how many trainers are assigned?"

"No idea. All I know is that combat units from up north in the 2nd Division area are flown out of the DMZ all the way down south to Cheju Island for specialized training. Rappelling. Mountaineering. Commando tactics. Things like that. How many Special Forces troops are assigned there at any given time, I don't know."

"Who's the commander?"

Holder thumbed through a stack of computer printouts. "Some guy with about half his jaw blown off. Weird-looking character. Looks like a puppet made by Señor Wences. But mean. Don't ever mention his jaw. Here it is." Holder pointed to a name. "Laurel, Ambrose Q., Lieutenant Colonel. Not exactly a name you'd associate with someone so tough."

"How'd he lose his jaw?" Ernie asked.

"Vietnam," Holder replied. "Training Montagnards or something like that."

It wasn't much information, but it was a start.

We returned to billeting, woke up Riley, and gave him the chore of contacting the Air Force and compiling a list of zoomies who were on pass or leave or official travel on the days of the two assaults on the Blue Train.

"Can do," Riley said, without complaint, sitting upright on the edge of his bunk, holding his head, trying to clear his mind. He was a blowhard and a drunk, but in the final analysis Staff Sergeant Riley was one hell of a soldier. He'd complete the mission, no matter how miserable he felt. I told him where we were going.

"Cheju-do?" he said. "This is no time for a vacation."

As the most southerly spot in the Republic, Cheju Island was known for its warm weather and balmy beaches, a Korean version of Hawaii.

"This is no vacation," I said. "We're going to check out the Special Forces."

"Those guys? You think one of them might be the Blue Train rapist?"

"Could be. We won't know until we check."

"They'll eat you for lunch."

"We'll see about that," Ernie replied.

We left Riley sitting on the edge of his bunk, growling, spitting up, preparing to become human again.

The ferry that ran from the Port of Pusan to Cheju Island was huge. It was said that it could hold three hundred passengers. There were only about two dozen of us aboard on this trip, though, maybe because it was the last ferry to depart in the evening. Ernie and I were the only foreigners. The other passengers kept to themselves, mainly because they were couples, recently married. Cheju Island had become the traditional place for a honeymoon in Korea.

Ernie stared at the happy couples. "What are they grinning about?"

"They just got married, Ernie."

"That's a reason to be happy?"

I slapped him on the shoulder. "You'll cheer up when we hit shore."

Ernie's eyes spun, and he leaned over the railing and threw up again.

The ferry disembarked at a pier about a half mile from Cheju-si, the city of Cheju. In the early morning sunlight, Ernie and I carried our overnight bags and stood in line at a covered awning waiting for a taxi. When it was our turn, I leaned in the passenger-side window and spoke Korean to the driver.

"The American compound on the side of Mount Halla, do you know where it is?"

He nodded.

"How much?"

"*Meto-ro dobel*," he said. Double meter because it was outside of his authorized area of operations. That's the way cabs are regulated in Korea. If they transport a fare outside of their designated area, they aren't allowed to bring a fare back. Therefore, the passenger must pay double. Ernie always balked at this arrangement, figuring they'd pick up an illegal fare on the way back anyway. Still, it seemed fair to me. We climbed in.

I asked the driver if there were yoguans in the area of the compound and he said there were. We sped along the edge of Cheju City and we were almost immediately thrust into a lush green countryside. Rice paddies stretched all around us and ran up the sides of hills, leading in a terraced parade up toward the huge mountain that loomed off to our left. Ernie peered out the window.

"It's smoking up there."

"Mount Halla's a live volcano," I said.

"Oh, great. First I get seasick; now I get splashed with molten lava."

The road was a narrow two-lane highway. Three-wheeled trucks and other cabs and ROK Army military jeeps sped past us. After about a mile, we veered toward the sea and the driver pointed toward a rocky promontory.

"*Haenyo*," he said.

I rolled the window down to see better.

"Haenyo," Ernie repeated. "What's that?"

"There, Ernie," I said, pointing. "Those little black dots in the water. See that?"

"Yeah. I see 'em. So what?"

"That's them. The haenyo. The women of the sea. They dive for things."

Ernie raised himself to get a better look. "You mean like they dive for pearls?"

"Not too many pearls left, I don't think. They dive for food. Sea anemones and octopus and seaweed and stuff like that."

"They make a living doing that?"

"Yes. It's like fishing. See those floats nearby? Those are the game bags where they keep their catch."

Ernie glanced at me. "How do you know so much about the haenyo?"

"I read about them. At the Eighth Army library."

Ernie plopped back into his seat, staring at me in disgust. "You would." To Ernie, reading was something that was done on an as-needed basis only, when you were desperate for information.

The cab turned off the main road and started bouncing over a dirt track. We climbed steadily up Mount Halla. The road turned back on itself, reversed course again, and suddenly we popped into a tunnel hewn out of solid granite. The tunnel ran about a hundred yards, then emerged onto a shelf overlooking a plateau. We turned and turned again, finally crossing a ridge and looking down upon a valley with a mountain stream. On the far edge of the stream, across a short wooden bridge, was a gate covered by an arch that said Mount Halla Training Facility, and in smaller letters, United States Army Special Forces, Cheju Contingent. The buildings were Quonset huts painted puke green, the roads between them covered with neatly raked gravel, broad enough for a squad of soldiers to march through. Closer to us sat a village of about thirty buildings. The ones on the edge were farmhouses covered with thatched straw. Closer in to the main road that ran across the bridge were a few two-story buildings.

"A G.I. village," Ernie said. "I'd recognize it anywhere."

A sign said Nokko-ri. Nokko village. The cab driver drove through the narrow roads and took us to the one yoguan in town. He waited patiently as I counted out his fare. Faces peeped out of windows, slender fingers parted beaded curtains. Ernie climbed out of the cab, stretched, and gazed around, tucking his shirt in his pants, chomping on ginseng gum.

We were something new to the people of Nokko-ri; G.I.s arriving on their own, in a fancy city taxicab, not in a military formation.

Ernie studied the unlit neon signs of two bars: the Sea Dragon Nightclub and the Volcano Bar.

"I think I'm going to like it here," he said.

The owner of the Nokko-ri Yoguan was delighted to see Ernie and me and told me, in Korean, that she could order food in, or even a hostess if we wanted one. I thanked her but told her we didn't need any of that right now. What we did do was rent a room, dump our overnight bags, and head back out toward the main gate of the Mount Halla Training Facility.

There were no MPs at the front gate, only surly Korean contract security guards. As soon as they saw our CID badges, they picked up the phone and called their superiors.

Ernie and I waited. After twenty minutes, Ernie was becoming increasingly antsy. "Who do these guys think they are," he asked, "keeping us waiting like this?"

"Look at this place," I told him. The facility was like the Special Forces' own little fiefdom. Instead of a moat, a wooden bridge across a narrow stream. Instead of stone walls, chain-link fences. Instead of a castle, Quonset huts. "Way out here, whoever the commander is probably isn't used to interference. When some honcho comes down to visit or an Eighth Army inspection team shows up, that

Colonel Laurel gets plenty of warning. They're not used to two CID agents dropping in unannounced."

"Well, they better open the gate pretty soon," Ernie replied, "or I'll kick the damn thing in."

After another five minutes of waiting, Ernie made good on his pledge. He kicked the wooden pedestrian gate.

15

An American staff sergeant in tailored green fatigues stood before us, his fists pressed against his hips, a pistol belt wrapped around his narrow waist. His jump boots gleamed with black polish, and a floppy green beret sat snugly atop his head. He was a muscular man, built low to the ground, making it seem impossible for anyone—or anything—to knock him over. He grinned at us.

"Welcome," he said, "to the greatest training facility in the world."

His name tag said Warnocki. I showed him my badge and told him why we were here, explained that we wanted access to the unit morning reports, the daily count of personnel strength.

"You suspect one of *us*?" he asked, jamming a thick

thumb into the center of his chest. "You think a Green Beret could be the Blue Train rapist?"

"We suspect *everybody*," Ernie said, "until they're cleared."

Warnocki's grin grew even broader. "Man, I'm going to enjoy seeing you explain that to Colonel Laurel."

"How about the morning reports?" I asked.

"No way is this staff sergeant going to give you access to Official Use Only information."

"We have an open writ," I told him, "backed up by the Provost Marshal of the Eighth United States Army."

"Well, la-dee-da."

"You could come up on charges, Warnocki, for obstructing an official investigation."

He shrugged his heavy shoulders. "You'll have to talk to Colonel Laurel about all that. If he tells me to die, I die. If he tells me to show you the morning report, I show you the morning report."

"Okay, then," Ernie said. "If that's the way you want it. Let's talk to him."

"You know how to swim?" When neither Ernie nor I answered, Warnocki continued, "That's where he is right now. Swimming. Or, more exactly, diving. With the haenyo."

Ernie and I glanced at each other.

"That's right," Warnocki said. "Between training cycles, that's how he relaxes."

"Fine," I said. "Take us to him."

"Now?"

"Now."

Warnocki shrugged again. "Okay," he said. "Your funeral. Follow me."

We followed him out of the guard shack and onto the main compound, across the broad expanse of gravel where three poles stood bearing the flags of the United States, the Republic of Korea, and the United Nations. Beyond that were half a dozen Quonset huts.

"No cycle in right now," Warnocki said. "An artillery unit from the Second Division is supposed to be flying in tomorrow. We have a week to take them through rappelling, mountaineering, commando intercept, interrogation resistance, and patrol tactics, and, if we have time, a little waterborne survival training."

"That's where the diving comes in?"

"Colonel Laurel's an expert at it." Warnocki grinned again. "Without equipment."

"Where's the rest of the cadre?" I asked.

"In the motor pool," Warnocki replied. "Pulling maintenance on our vehicles."

"Don't you have Koreans to do that?"

"Yeah. But somebody has to supervise."

"How many other Special Forces personnel do you have here?"

Warnocki grinned again. "You'll have to talk to Colonel Laurel about that."

Three jeeps sat at the edge of the motor pool, along with an army puke-green bus and a two-and-a-half-ton truck. No other American personnel—or Koreans, for that matter—were visible.

Warnocki hopped into the nearest jeep and said, "All aboard."

I sat in the passenger seat, Ernie in back. Warnocki started the engine and spun around in a U-turn, and soon we were heading out the back gate of the Mount Halla Training Facility; a listless Korean security guard pushed it open for us, and then we were barreling downhill on dirt roads, too fast for comfort.

Unconcerned, Ernie gazed at the craggy peaks in the distance and the ocean glimmering blue in glimpses below. I turned in my seat and looked back. Above the training facility, a communications tower teetered on the edge of a precipice; beyond that, wisps of smoke rose steadily out of the caldera of the volcano known as Mount Halla. I breathed deeply of the fresh sea air, thinking of the mystery man who'd brought an ancient fragment from so far away, thinking of the woman who'd been murdered, thinking of her crying children. Thinking of what the Blue Train rapist had next on his checklist.

Before we'd left Hialeah Compound, Marnie Orville had complained because Ernie wouldn't be seeing her that evening.

"But you're the one who got Ernie in trouble," I told her. "You didn't tell the truth about what happened between him and Freddy Ray Embry in Taegu. You said Ernie started it."

"But that wasn't my fault," she whined. "I had to protect Freddy Ray."

"*Protect* him?"

"If he gets kicked out of the Army," she continued, "how is he going to pay his child support?"

"Marnie," I said, staring directly into her pale blue eyes, "when we first met you, you said that Freddy Ray *wasn't* paying his child support."

"That was just a little white lie."

"A little white lie? The Army takes these things seriously."

"I just wanted to find him so I could tell him that he ought to take his responsibilities as a father more seriously. Casey misses him, and she keeps asking me why her daddy never comes to see her."

"You caused all this trouble just for that?"

"Yes," she snapped. "Just for that. My daughter is important to me."

I had said the wrong thing and now she was indignant. Still, I soldiered on.

"When he showed up at your BOQ at Camp Carroll in Waegwan," I said, "you suspected Freddy Ray of being the peeper, didn't you?"

Marnie crossed her arms. "I'm not sure."

"That's why you sent him away without talking to him," I continued. "It suddenly dawned on you that maybe he was the one following you from compound to compound, the one stealing small items. Isn't that what you thought, Marnie?"

"You're the detective," she snapped. "Why don't you find out?"

"Maybe I will," I said, "once I have a little time."

Marnie snorted. "We're not important enough."

There wasn't much point continuing to talk to her. Instead, I said good-bye, then said good-bye to the other ladies of the Country Western All Stars and told them I hoped we'd be back from Cheju Island soon enough to catch their act again. Shelly, the lead guitar player, stepped forward and hugged me. Then she leaned away, smiling, and squeezed my hand.

Marnie followed me outside, where the others couldn't hear. "I don't think Freddy Ray's the peeper. I did, but I don't anymore," she said.

I turned. "Why not?"

"Because of what he did last night in Taegu. He came for me. He didn't sneak up or peep through a window, he knocked on the door like a man."

"And punched out Ernie."

Marnie shrugged and turned and walked back into the Quonset hut.

Lieutenant Colonel Ambrose Q. Laurel looked spindly in his head-to-toe black wet suit, a tremendous contrast to the burly Warnocki. About a dozen women sat on rocks on the beach, the hoods of their wet suits pulled back, revealing suntanned faces and moist black hair. The sea was blue close in, then gray, fading into a solid wall of mist about a hundred yards offshore. Most of the women were working on equipment—netting, flotation devices, sturdy-looking wooden-handled knives—and while they worked, they smiled at us, amused to have so much G.I. company.

"You dive with these ladies?" I asked Colonel Laurel.

"That's right," he said, staring directly at me, his gnarled face without expression.

He was not a tall man, five six or five seven, and he

couldn't have weighed more than 140 pounds. His grim expression was partly caused by the awkwardness of his situation. The full-length photo I'd seen in his personnel folder showed him standing proudly in his dress green uniform, shoulders thrust back, chest dripping with medals. But what wasn't hidden, neither in his photos nor in this personal encounter, was the savage wound to his chin. Much of the jawbone had been blown off. It was partially reconstructed now, but still protruded only slightly below his mouth, an oddly shaped mass, not the pugnacious square jaw that a military man covets. He shoved his misshapen face out at me, and at Ernie, as if he were ready to fight.

"We're here to check your morning reports, sir," I said, "for the last two or three weeks, however far back we have to go. We'd like to know who in your unit was on leave, temporary duty, or who has otherwise left Cheju Island and traveled to the mainland."

"Why?" he asked.

I told him.

"None of my men," he said slowly, enunciating every word, "would ever be involved in such a thing as a rape or a murder."

Then he stood silent, daring us to speak. I dared.

"Nevertheless, we have to check. It's our duty."

Something told me that long, involved explanations were not going to work with this man. Get right to the point. Stand your ground. Ernie stood at my side, unmoving. The haenyo sensed the tension between us, and the clinking of equipment grew more sporadic.

Colonel Laurel's intelligent blue eyes held mine. Was

he wavering? I couldn't be sure. The thin lines of his lips were unreadable. Finally, he spoke.

"The men in my unit have no need of rape. Women flock to Green Berets."

"Yes, sir. I'm sure that's true. Still, we'd appreciate it if you'd give Sergeant Warnocki here permission to show us the records."

Colonel Laurel stared at us for what seemed like a long time. The only sound was the gentle washing of waves on the beach, the occasional swish of thread through netting, and the steady cawing of sea birds. Finally, Colonel Laurel spoke.

"You think you can come to Cheju Island and just decide that you're going to poke your noses into the personal records of the brave men of the Special Forces?" He didn't wait for an answer. "You think I'm some nervous career officer who falls apart at the sight of a couple of CID badges? You think you frighten me? You think that prissy-ass, no-combat-experience Provost Marshal up there at Eighth Army scares me?"

Colonel Laurel paused. Ernie took the opportunity to roll his eyes and stare up at the sky, clicking his gum loudly. Laurel turned his attention to him.

"Am I boring you?" he asked. "You think I'm just being difficult? You think that if you dial up some chief of staff back in Seoul that I'm going to roll over and allow you access to the movements of my men?" Laurel stepped toward Ernie, his arms akimbo, an enraged rubberized scarecrow.

"I think, sir," Ernie replied, keeping his voice steady, "that I know what they used to say in Nam: the Special Forces take all the glory while the grunts do all the dying."

For the first time, Warnocki stopped grinning. He stepped closer to Ernie, as if to take him down from behind. I moved closer to Warnocki. By now, Ernie and Colonel Laurel were nose to nose, glaring at one another. Ernie's nose was about half a foot higher. The haenyo sat immobile.

"You get anywhere *near* my unit morning reports," Colonel Laurel told Ernie, "or anywhere near my *compound*, and I will personally plant my army-issue combat boot up your rear-echelon ass."

"Why wait, *Colonel*?" Ernie replied. "You can try it now."

With a motion that was too fast for me to stop, Warnocki grabbed Ernie's left wrist and, in some deft twisting motion, rotated the forearm upward. Involuntarily, Ernie bent forward at the waist. Without thinking, I hopped forward and slammed Warnocki with a straight left to the side of his head. The tough man staggered, didn't go down, but released his grip on Ernie.

Ernie swiveled on Warnocki, raising his right fist when Colonel Laurel shouted, "At ease!"

The sound was so loud, and so jarring, that all of us— me, Ernie, and Warnocki—froze in mid-motion.

"Assume the position of attention," Colonel Laurel commanded.

We did.

Laurel walked up to Ernie and stood there for a long time, letting the strength of his authority seep into our overheated minds.

"You will *not*," he said finally, "under any circumstances, have any more conversations or associations with any of the men in my unit. And you will *not*, under any circumstances, access the records of my unit's personnel strength or of my men's comings and goings. Not unless," he added, "I release the information myself. Is that understood?"

Ernie nodded.

"Is that *understood*?" Laurel shouted.

"Yes, sir."

"Warnocki," Laurel said, spinning away, "take the jeep back to the compound."

Warnocki nodded, grabbed his beret, which had fallen into the sand, replaced it on his almost-bald head, saluted Colonel Laurel, and trotted off toward the jeep. On the way, he grinned at me broadly. It wasn't a friendly grin. More like being laughed at by a skull.

After Warnocki disappeared, Colonel Laurel turned back to us.

"If you mess with my men again," he told Ernie and then me, "I won't stop him next time."

"*Stop* him?" I said. "You were about to lose one muscle-bound staff sergeant."

Laurel stared at me, his face once again unreadable, looking very much like a sinister puppet. Without saying anything further, he turned and marched across wet sand. The haenyo stood as he approached.

Together, the rubber-clad troupe of females followed Colonel Laurel to a boat with an outboard motor. All of them climbed aboard except for two sturdy women who shoved the boat out toward the breakers, turned it around, and then pulled themselves aboard. Laurel jerked on a hemp lanyard and the engine of the old boat coughed to life. He and the women bounced over the waves and then, after about fifty yards, faded into the mist.

Ernie dusted sand off his trousers.

"'About to lose one muscle-bound staff sergeant,'" he mimicked. "Man, Sueño. That doesn't sound like you."

"Women have been raped," I said, "in front of children. One of them brutally murdered, in front of children. To me, all this macho posturing is less than nothing."

Ernie watched as I climbed the sand dunes and marched toward the two-lane highway that paralleled the beach. Then, as if remembering something, he hurried and caught up with me.

"What do you mean, we can't *force* Colonel Laurel to show us his morning report?" I asked. "What kind of nonsense is that? He's a military man, isn't he? He takes orders like anyone else."

I sat on the front edge of the ondol floor of the living room of the woman who owned the Nokko-ri Yoguan. Her family lived just behind the reception counter. She kept a bright red phone on a knitted yellow pad and charged me five hundred won for the call to Hialeah Compound in Pusan.

"They're stovepiped," Riley told me, his voice coming in scratchy over the line. "They don't take orders from Eighth Army. Only from Special Operations Command in the Pentagon."

"So we have the Provost Marshal contact Special Ops," I told him. "Tell them to order Colonel Laurel to let us see his morning reports."

"That'll take time," Riley replied. "The Special Forces always stalls. First the Pentagon weenies will contact Colonel Laurel, and then they'll wait to hear back from him, and then they'll have a conference, and finally, after typing everything up in triplicate, they'll respond to Eighth Army."

"We don't have time," I shouted. "The Blue Train rapist could strike again at any moment."

Riley didn't answer. He wasn't wasting his breath. He was just giving me time to let it sink in: the military bureaucracy moves at its own pace, and no one, with the possible exception of a four-star general, can hurry it up.

"Okay," I said. "I'll find another way."

"Be careful with those guys," Riley said. "I wouldn't want my two favorite investigators to come up missing."

"What do you mean?"

"There's a volcano up there, isn't there? They could drop you in."

"Thanks for the encouragement."

"Don't mention it."

I hung up on him.

It had only taken a half hour for Ernie and me to hitch-hike our way back from the beach. People were curious about two American G.I.s in civvies standing alone on a lonely road. A three-wheeled truck loaded with garlic pulled over and gave us a ride all the way to the intersection that led to Nokko-ri. From there, we caught a ride with a Korean contract trucker carrying a load of heating fuel up to the Mount Halla Training Facility. He let us off right in front of the Nokko-ri Yoguan. In both cases I offered the drivers money, but in both cases they smiled and waved it off. Once you get away from the hustlers who congregate outside the gates of military compounds, Koreans are generous to a fault.

There was a chophouse just twenty yards in front of

the main gate, and in English they advertised *ohmu* rice and *yakimandu* and *ramian* noodles. Ernie and I sat at one of the rickety wooden tables, and the old woman who ran the place approached, wearing a white apron and a white bandanna wrapped tightly around gray hair.

"When do the G.I.s start coming out of the compound, Mama-san?" Ernie asked.

"Maybe five o'clock," she replied. "After cannon go boom and flag come down." She thought about that and added, "Tonight *skoshi* G.I., tomorrow *taaksan*."

Only a few G.I.s tonight. Tomorrow plenty. The merchants in Nokko-ri were well attuned to the comings and goings of Colonel Laurel's training cycles.

We both ordered ramian and split a plate of the yakimandu fried dumplings. Ernie was about to add a liter of cold OB beer to his order when I stopped him.

"We have work to do," I said.

"Work? Like what?"

"Like finding somebody who knows what's going on inside the Mount Halla Training Facility."

"They're all Green Berets," Ernie said. "They're not going to tell us nothing."

"I'm not talking about Green Berets," I said. "Somebody else."

"There ain't nobody else."

"Yes, there is."

I pointed through the dirt-smudged window of the Nokko-ri Chophouse. Ernie followed my finger and gazed up the side of Mount Halla.

"Smoke coming out of the volcano," he said. "So what?"

"Off to the right a bit," I replied.

Then he spotted it. A communications beacon. And next to that, a squat building.

"That's American?" he asked.

"Must be," I replied. "How else is Colonel Laurel going to stay in touch with the honchos at Eighth Army?"

"I don't think he gives a shit about the honchos at Eighth Army."

The old woman brought two steaming bowls of ramian noodles, and then she slid the yakimandu between us. Ernie stared at the fare sourly.

"Where's the kimchee?" he asked.

"You likey?"

"I likey."

The woman smiled and in short order delivered one plate each of pickled cabbage and pickled cucumber and a bowl of water kimchee. As she set them on the table, the sharp tang of vegetables fermented in brine bit into my nostrils.

Ernie smiled and ordered a Seven Stars Cider. I stuck with the barley tea.

The cab driver wound around one sharp bend after another. The road was narrow, just wide enough for one vehicle. There were only a couple of bypass areas where a vehicle could move off to the side to make way for another.

"What happened to the jillions of dollars Eighth Army spends improving roads?" Ernie asked.

"I guess they spent it elsewhere. Must not expect many visitors up here."

The cab driver's name was Mr. Won. He had been introduced to us by the woman who owned the Nokko-ri Yoguan. I think he was her brother-in-law or something. Mr. Won leaned forward, both hands gripping the steering wheel, concentrating on his driving, ignoring us completely. Ernie sat in the front passenger seat. I sat in back. Below were rock-strewn valleys with little vegetation. Every now and then, I glanced back and saw the Mount Halla Training Facility and the village of Nokko-ri, growing ever smaller as we moved higher up the mountain. In the distance, the sea stirred placidly.

Finally, we rounded one more switchback turn, straightened out along the edge of the mountain, and there, on a plateau-like ledge, sat the squat green building I'd seen from the comfortable environs of the Nokko-ri Chophouse. Spiraling straight up was the metal edifice of the red-and-white communications tower.

Mr. Won stopped the car and immediately turned off the engine. His shoulders slumped forward and for a moment he bowed his head to fists still clenched on top of the steering wheel.

"*Yogi kidariyo?*" I said to him. You'll wait here?

He nodded. As we'd agreed, he'd receive the bulk of his money once we were returned safely to the Nokko-ri Yoguan.

The small communications compound was surrounded by a high chain-link fence topped with concertina wire. It was all rusted out as if it hadn't been replaced in years. A sign hung near the single gate in the fence: *Chulip Kumji*. And below that: Authorized Personnel Only.

Ernie strode up to the gate, studied it for a moment,

and then pressed a buzzer. There was a rusty speaker next to the buzzer, but we heard no response. He pushed the buzzer again, and then again.

Finally a voice erupted from the speaker. "Yeah?"

"Who's this?" Ernie asked.

"Vance."

The voice sounded sleepy, as if we'd just woken him up.

"What's your rank, Vance?" Ernie asked.

"Spec Four."

He was waking up now and becoming a little nervous.

"My name is Agent Bascom. I'm from the Eighth Army CID in Seoul. My partner here is Agent Sueño. We want you to open the gate so we can talk to you."

"CID?"

A slight sense of panic now.

"Yes. But we're not here about the black market. We just need some information."

"I'm not allowed to open the gate when I'm alone."

"Alone? How many people are stationed up here?"

"Supposed to be three. A lieutenant, an NCO, and me, a technician. But we haven't had a lieutenant since I been here."

"How long is that?"

"Six months."

"And where's the sergeant?"

"Parkwood?"

"Yeah. Parkwood."

"He's on a supply run."

"When do you expect him back?"

"Don't know."

"You don't know?"

There was a hesitation. "Sometimes he stops in the ville."

Ernie slipped his badge out of the inner pocket of his coat and held it over his head. "Specialist Vance, from where you're at, can you see my badge?"

There was a pause. "Yeah."

"I'm going to ask my partner to show his badge too."

I held mine over my head.

"Do you see them both?" Ernie asked.

"Yeah."

"Open the gate, Vance."

"But I was told . . . "

"What you were told doesn't matter," Ernie said. "We have a warrant, we've traveled all the way from Seoul, and it's important."

There was a long pause. Finally, the gate buzzed. Ernie pushed it open.

The place was a dump. What you'd expect from two lonely bachelors living alone. There was a small reception area and then a large air-conditioned room filled with metal units as big as refrigerators, covered with buzzing lights and wires. A number of work consoles blinked at us and beeped. Beyond were a storage room piled high with crates of army C rations and a kitchen jammed with dirty dishes. In the largest room, piles of dirty laundry were draped atop army-issue bunks, unshined shoes, and combat boots. One cowboy boot poked its toe out from beneath green blankets spread in sweat-matted disarray.

"No houseboy up here?" Ernie said.

"I wish," Vance replied.

Specialist Vance was a smallish man, with a slouch to

his shoulders and a hangdog expression enhanced by—or maybe caused by—drooping jowls. His skin was clear and his dark brown hair had not a hint of gray, but somehow he carried himself with the aura of a person who, at a very young age, had already been defeated by the world.

"Get down to the ville much?" Ernie asked.

"Only when we have a reason to drive the truck down there. Parkwood usually goes."

"He's the ranking man."

Vance nodded. "There's supposed to be at least two of us here at all times, but without a lieutenant that's impossible. So sometimes, like now, it's down to just me."

A bell on one of the consoles started to ring.

"Excuse me," Vance said.

He sat down at a keyboard and tapped on a few buttons until a printer came to life and started rat-tat-tatting on a sheet of paper. As it rolled off the printer, I read it. Military acronyms. Routine stuff, about deadlines for supply reorders.

"This isn't for you," I said.

For the first time, Vance looked up at me. "Naw. We get a lot of stuff that's on general distribution to all units in Eighth Army. We send it down to the training facility anyway in case they have a need to know. Some of the traffic, on those machines over there, is strictly for relay. You know, microwave stuff that we pass on to the next commo site north of Pusan."

"Horang-ni?"

"Yeah. Horang-ni. How'd you know?"

I shrugged. "And they relay it on up to the line to Seoul?"

"Right."

Ernie strolled around the work area, staring at somebody's short-timer calendar. A naked lady was half covered with red ink. He turned away from the calendar and as he did so his shoulder brushed against a half-dozen clipboards hanging on a nail. Four of them clattered to the ground. Onionskin papers scattered across the tiled floor, and Ernie stooped to pick them up.

"What are these?" he asked.

Specialist Vance helped him pick up the reports, reorganized them, and put the clipboards back on their nail, one by one. "IG results," he said.

"The Eighth Army Inspector General stopped here?"

"Naw. Just the Long Lines Battalion IG."

Ernie gazed around the cluttered work area. "Whoever he was, he must've ripped you guys two new ones."

"Yeah," Vance said. "It's been a mess with no lieutenant and me doing most of the work. You know, all the routine stuff like maintenance reports, microwave alignments, checking telecom circuits. I do most of it."

"But not enough," Ernie said.

"No, we flunked the IG. They're even threatening to bar Parkwood from reenlistment."

Ernie peeked inside a couple of filing cabinets. "Don't you have any booze around here?"

"Naw. We used to. But neither Parkwood nor I drink."

"But there used to be someone who drank?"

"An old sergeant, before Parkwood arrived. That's all he did."

"My kind of guy," Ernie said.

"So you relay traffic down to the training facility," I said.

"That's one of our main jobs," Vance replied.

"Do they relay stuff up here?"

"Of course. And then we send it on."

"Like their morning report?"

"Yeah. We send it over to Sasebo in Japan."

"Not up to Eighth Army?"

"No. The training facility's under a separate command."

"Do you keep records here of that morning report?"

"No. I read it every day, though. Sort of gives me an idea of whether or not the ville's going to be crowded."

"Like when all the SF guys are on duty, they must have a training cycle in."

"You got it. And those Second Division guys go nuts down in Nokko-ri. Drive the prices sky-high."

"I thought you said you don't go down to the ville often," Ernie said, but he smiled as he said it.

Vance flushed red. "Only sometimes."

"I don't blame you for going to the ville," I told him. "I'd go down there as often as I could if I worked in a remote place like this."

Vance nodded but didn't reply. I continued.

"So Sergeant Parkwood probably won't be back until tomorrow morning, right? Not if he's smart."

"Maybe," Vance said.

Ernie cut in. "Don't worry so much, Vance. We're not here about all that. We just want to know who in the last two or three weeks has been on TDY or in-country leave from the Mount Halla Training Facility."

"That's all?"

"That's all," Ernie replied. "After we get that, we'll leave you alone."

"I don't mind the company. Honest. It gets sort of lonely up here."

"I can imagine. So tell us about the Green Berets at the Mount Halla Training Facility."

"One guy's due back tomorrow," Vance said. "He went back to the States on a thirty-day mid-tour leave."

"Who's that?"

"Munoz. I think he's Puerto Rican. At least that's what his travel orders said, that he was going there, to Puerto Rico I mean."

I jotted the name down in my notebook.

"Nobody else has been gone," Vance said. "Except for maybe if they took the regular chopper run to Pusan on the weekend. But even that's unlikely. There's only nine Green Berets stationed there, not counting Colonel Laurel. And he insists on a CQ every night, so they pull a lot of duty."

CQ. Charge of Quarters.

"They're a strack unit," Ernie said.

"Right," Vance said admiringly. "Straight-arrow military."

"So to the best of your knowledge," I said, "only one guy has been gone from the Mount Halla Training Facility in the last few weeks."

"As best as I can tell," Vance replied.

"How about their ration-control cards?" I asked.

"Their what?"

"The ration cards. You know, like at the PX when your ration-control plate is anviled when you buy something like liquor or beer. They have a PX, don't they?"

"A small one."

"So somebody has to deliver their ration cards."

"Yeah. I forgot about that. Sergeant Amos runs it up to Seoul every week."

"What's his full name?"

"Walker R. Amos, Sergeant First Class."

I jotted the name down. "Why him? Why is he the only one to run it up every week?"

"Something about his profile," Vance replied. "He's older than the other guys. Can't do all the physical training they do."

"So Colonel Laurel makes him escort the ration cards up to Seoul each week. Sort of demeaning, isn't it?"

Vance shrugged.

"So he takes the weekly chopper to Pusan. From there does he take the train?"

"I guess," Vance replied. "I never heard of anybody traveling up to Seoul any other way. Unless they take one of the training flights that come in."

"There's an airport?"

"Yeah. The ROK Army has one."

"Can you think of anyone else who's left the compound recently?"

"No. That's it. Not unless you count Colonel Laurel."

"When did he leave?"

"Last week. I don't remember the exact day. There was some sort of commander's call in Seoul."

When Ernie and I climbed back into the cab, I studied the ranks and names I had jotted down. The first was Munoz, a buck sergeant. That meant he was relatively young; maybe he'd gone back to visit his family in Puerto

Rico. Lifers don't travel that much. Once you've spent a decade or two in the army, your family tends to forget about you and you tend to forget about them. The second man, the one who'd delivered the ration cards to Seoul, was a sergeant first class, which meant he'd been around a while. The full name was Walker R. Amos. Could he be black? If so, and if it could be proven that Munoz had gone to Puerto Rico, I could eliminate both men and I'd be back to square one. I asked Specialist Vance, but he'd never met either man personally. But something told me that SFC Walker R. Amos would be white. Something told me we were close to the Blue Train rapist. Very close.

Mr. Won was even more petrified driving down Mount Halla than he had been while driving up. I didn't like the way he kept jamming on the brakes, pressing the pedal almost to the floorboard. Ernie finally said something.

"When was the last time you put in new brake pads, *Ajjosi*?"

I shushed him. The man didn't understand anyway. Best to let him concentrate on his driving and hope for the best. I actually thought of telling Mr. Won to stop so we could get out and walk the three or four miles downhill back to Nokko-ri, but I didn't think he could stop this old cab now if he wanted to.

Ernie spotted it first. He pointed.

"Look!"

A puke-green quarter-ton truck, army-issue, chugging up the incline.

"Must be Parkwood," I said, "coming back from his supply run."

"There's a bypass," Ernie said, "closer to him than to us."

"I hope he has the sense to use it," I replied.

Mr. Won didn't understand a word we were saying. He stared in terror at the winding road ahead, jamming on the brakes, both hands knuckled white atop the steering wheel.

I reached over and honked the horn.

If the man driving the truck below heard it, he gave no indication.

16

When I was growing up in East L.A., freeways blossomed everywhere. The Santa Ana, the San Bernardino, the Pomona, the Harbor, the Long Beach, all were being renovated or widened or extended or planned or laid down. Overweight politicians in stiff business suits were constantly cutting ribbons. It was as if by paving the entire planet and drawing lane-change lines to the end of the earth, we'd finally find happiness. That was one of the reasons I'd been so smitten by Korea when I first arrived. Sure, there were roads and cars and trucks—and a new four-lane freeway was being built to run between Seoul and Pusan—but still, there were plenty of places for people to actually walk. Muddy lanes, dirt roads, cobblestoned pathways, tree-lined avenues, streets with shops pressed up against one another—occasionally you'd even spot

wooden carts pulled by oxen, a man leading the snort-
ing beast, a woman and small children huddled together
on wooden planks. Not all human movement had been
turned over to the internal combustion engine. Even the
Blue Train seemed more human to me than driving on an
eight-lane freeway.

Every day of my youth in the Los Angeles Basin, my
lungs had been involuntarily filled with smog. Now, on a
remote volcano on the edge of Asia, it looked as if I were
finally going to meet the fate of so many of my compatri-
ots. I was finally going to become a statistic in a head-on
collision.

"The asshole didn't stop at the bypass!" Ernie shouted.

Mr. Won had both feet pressed on the brake pedal, but
it wasn't doing much good. The momentum of the cab was
now carrying us downhill at about fifty miles per hour.
Around the sharp curves, he was barely maintaining control, drifting toward the left edge of the lane, and the G.I.
driver of the truck below seemed to have no idea that he
was only a few seconds from impact.

I reached forward across Mr. Won and once again
sounded the horn. Beyond a boulder, the truck loomed
into view. We went screaming around a curve.

I crouched behind the front seat, covering my head.
As I did so, Mr. Won screamed. He veered to the extreme
left, trying to avoid a head-on with the truck. The wheels
spun on gravel and the cab started tipping to the left. Out
of the side window, I glanced down into the abyss. The
wheels still had traction and we were moving forward—
but two or three more inches to the left and we'd plum-
met to our deaths. I glanced forward just in time to see

the quarter-ton truck barreling toward us. Ernie cursed, grabbed the steering wheel, and shoved it hard to the right. Won let go of the wheel and covered his eyes. Green iron grating flashed in front of me and then something slammed into the rear of the cab. We spun, three, four, five times; and finally, with a jarring thump, came to a shuddering halt in the ditch on the right side of the road.

I sat up. Dust rose around us in an enveloping cloud.

"You all right?" I asked.

"All right," Ernie replied. He reached for Mr. Won. "How about you, Baba Louie?"

Won uncovered his eyes, looked around, and started to moan. Ernie and I both climbed out of the cab and pulled him out of the driver's-side door. We laid him on the edge of the road, searching as we did so for wounds. He didn't have any.

"He's just shaken up," Ernie said.

"He deserves it," I replied, "for having such lousy brakes."

On the road above us, the quarter-ton truck continued to churn its way up Mount Halla, oblivious, apparently, to our plight below.

The back of the cab was smashed in.

"You think it'll still run?" I asked Ernie.

"Won't know until we try. Give me a shove."

He climbed into the driver's seat, started the engine, and thrust the shift into a low gear. On three, he stepped on the gas and I stood behind the cab, pushing it forward. After rocking it three times, the back wheels caught and it climbed out of the ditch. Deftly, Ernie turned the cab around. I helped Mr. Won to his feet, led him to the cab, opened the door, and allowed him to lie down on the back seat. I sat up front with Ernie.

Using the lowest gear possible, bumping against earthen berms when possible, Ernie churned slowly down Mount Halla.

"Shopping?" Ernie asked, incredulous.

"Yeah," I replied. "We have to go shopping."

The cannon fired at the Mount Halla Training Facility and the retreat bugle sounded. Up and down the main drag of Nokko-ri, lights were beginning to switch on. In front of the Sea Dragon Nightclub, a red and gold serpent sparkled to life, a lewd tongue flicking out flames.

"It's time for a wet," Ernie said. "We've done enough work for today. Nearly got ourselves killed, and now you want to go *shopping*?"

"On the black market."

"I don't care what freaking market it is, I'm gonna get a cold one."

"Where?"

Ernie pointed across the street from the Sea Dragon to the Volcano Bar.

"Okay. I'll meet you there in a half hour or so."

Ernie shrugged, thrust his hands in his pockets, and stalked off across the street. He gets like this sometimes, pissed that he doesn't have an eight-to-five job—especially when happy hour hits.

The woman who ran the Nokko-ri Yoguan told me where to go. Down the street behind a fruit stand in the open-air Nokko-ri Market, everything was on display:

web gear, ponchos, rubber overshoes, steel pots, ammo pouches, metal space heaters, canvas tent halves with poles. About the only type of military equipment you couldn't buy there was weaponry.

I rummaged through the parkas and the heavy over-coats and the gloves and the fur-flapped headgear and the insignia and the badges until I found what I wanted. One set for Ernie. One set for me.

Ernie was drunk.

It wasn't like him to get blasted so early, but the reason was clear. Next to his frothing brown bottle of OB beer sat a thick glass tumbler, half full of a clear brown liquid. I watched him raise it to his lips, where it was—once again—emptied.

"*Yoboseiyo*," Ernie called to the young man behind the bar. "Yogi," he said, pointing to the empty glass. Dutifully, the young man grabbed a quart of booze from behind the bar, scurried over, and refilled Ernie's glass. The bottle was labeled Christian Brothers Brandy. What was actually in the bottle was another story; once the import tax is paid and a bottle is revenue-stamped, it is refilled and reused—sometimes for years.

I sat on the bar stool next to Ernie and ordered a beer. He swiveled his head slowly and stared at me.

"You finish your *shopping*?"

"Yeah," I said, taking the proffered beer and slapping some money on the bar.

"Find any *bargains*?" he asked.

I didn't bother to answer. Ernie was in a surly mood,

and I thought I knew why. This was the first time in a while that we'd been away from Marnie Orville and the Country Western All Stars. Maybe he was thinking about her. Maybe he was thinking of her close proximity to her ex, Freddy Ray Embry. Whatever Ernie was thinking, I knew better than to ask. Instead, I surveyed the club.

There was a rock band tuning up, hipless young men with straight hair just covering their ears. Business girls filtered in, chattering about their hairdos and their clothes and occasionally mentioning the American unit that was scheduled to arrive tomorrow. Ernie and I were an anomaly here. Most of the tables were filled with young Korean couples who thought it daring to enter G.I. nightclubs. After the band tortured a couple of numbers, Ernie and I wandered across the street to the Sea Dragon Nightclub. It was quieter there, and darker. Round cocktail tables were lit dimly by lamps covered with red shades. On stage, velvet curtains were drawn shut. Business girls sat alone or in pairs. The bar was empty. We filled it. As if on cue, somebody started up a sound system; some American vocal group singing about the sea.

Instead of a young man behind the bar, a tall Korean woman was wearing a white tuxedo shirt with cummerbund, bow tie, and high collar. Almond eyes shaded in purple stared at us quizzically. Somehow, in the opulence of this joint, beer didn't seem appropriate. I ordered bourbon on the rocks. Ernie had the same. Within an hour, the joint was packed with young Korean people, well dressed and trendy. Too trendy. I felt as out of place as a tarantula in a kimchee jar. Once again, we were about to leave when a familiar face appeared in the seat next to us.

Warnocki.

He was still wearing his fatigues, and his green beret was still cocked to the side of his round head. He smiled. Without asking, the slender barkeep brought him a beer. With narrow fingers she poured it for him into a glass, white foam bubbling up to the edge. Warnocki laid money down, thanked her, and delicately took a sip. When he set the glass down, he turned to me and said, "You almost bought it on the mountain."

"You heard about that?"

"Colonel Laurel makes it his business to hear about everything."

"Has he decided to cooperate yet," Ernie asked, "and show us the morning report? Lives are at stake."

Warnocki's smile didn't change. "Your request has already hit Special Ops. They're taking it under advisement."

I swiveled on my bar stool and stared Warnocki right in the eye. "So, what do you think, Warnocki? Do you think the Blue Train rapist could be one of your Green Berets?"

"Sure," he replied, still smiling. "And if it is, you'd better hope you never catch him."

The flesh on his face didn't move, but somehow his grin grew even larger.

Ernie stood up. Warnocki leaned back on his bar stool, holding up both hands in mock surrender. Then he grabbed his glass, downed it in two huge gulps, wiped his mouth and, still grinning, slid off his bar stool and sauntered carelessly away, cocking his beret a little farther to the side as he pushed through the padded double doors of the Sea Dragon Nightclub.

Early the next morning, we took a cab away from Nokko-ri and headed toward the ocean. When I told the driver to let us off at the intersection of the main coastal highway, he seemed astonished.

"*Wei-yo?*" he asked. Why?

There was nothing in any direction except the sandy coastline and rice paddies.

"Don't worry," I told him and paid him what I owed him.

After he drove away, Ernie turned to me and said, "What are we doing way the hell out here?"

"Waiting for a bus," I said.

"*What* bus?"

"The one that is bringing Bravo Battery, Second of the Seventeenth Field Artillery, from the Cheju Airport to the Mount Halla Training Facility."

Last night I had persuaded the owner of the Nokko-ri Yoguan to do a little ironing for me. In the morning, the two uniforms I had purchased on the black market were waiting for us, patches sewn on, boots shined, brass belt buckles polished. Ernie put his on, grumbling, but finally acquiesced to what he referred to as one of my "crazy plans." Then we'd taken the cab out to this intersection to wait. After twenty minutes, three green army buses rolled up. I waved down the first one. The Korean driver stared out at me, smiling. I climbed aboard, Ernie right behind me.

We were wearing pressed fatigue uniforms and matching fatigue caps, and also black leather armbands that said: Cadre, Mount Halla Training Facility. To clinch the illusion, I had stuck a pencil behind my ear and carried a clipboard. The world always welcomes a man with a clipboard.

"Welcome to Mount Halla," I shouted to the men in the bus and then turned around and told the driver to move out. Nobody questioned us. They figured we were just some sort of advance party escorting them to the compound. Ernie and I found a spot in the back of the bus and sat down. Within ten minutes, the convoy of three buses had stopped at the big chain-link main gate of the Mount Halla Training Facility. The dispatches were checked and, once everything was found to be in order, a Korean guard swung the gate open.

When the buses reached the edge of the central parade field, they stopped. Special Forces trainers wearing blue helmet liners stood outside, shouting.

"*Move!* I want every swinging dick off that bus and standing in formation. Now! All I want to see is assholes and elbows. Let's go!"

Within seconds the men had filed off the bus and were standing in formation in the center of the parade field. Before the last G.I. stepped off the bus, Ernie and I crouched behind seats in the back. The driver, thinking the bus was empty, closed the door and slowly started to turn the vehicle around. Before he reached the main gate, I stood up and hurried forward.

"Let us off here, Ajjosi," I said.

He was startled, but years of aberrant G.I. behavior had prepared him for anything. He stopped the bus and opened the door, and Ernie and I hopped off. We left our armbands on the bus, but I kept my clipboard. After the bus pulled away, we slipped into the shadow of a Quonset hut.

"Where to?" Ernie asked.

I glanced at my clipboard. "Munoz, Sergeant E-five, and Amos, Walker R., SFC. Those are the two guys we have to talk to."

"So how do we find them?"

"Moolah the hell out of me." And then I spotted street signs on a pole. White arrows pointed in four directions. One of them said S-3 Training. We followed it and soon found a Quonset hut marked Mount Halla Training Command. In the distance, angry voices shouted and, in unison, dozens of boots pounded on dirt. As best I could tell, the G.I.s were being divided up into smaller groups and marched to the various training stations, rappelling or commando tactics or whatever other edifying courses Colonel Laurel had cooked up for them.

We tried the front door. Locked.

"They're all out there with the troops," Ernie said.

"You check on that side," I said. "I'll meet you out back."

Ernie nodded and trotted around the corner.

What we were looking for was an open window, a door, anything so we could gain access. Before I reached the rear, Ernie was already whistling. The back door of the Quonset hut was also locked, but one of the windows was filled with an air-conditioning unit. It wasn't turned on, and there was enough space between the metal casing and the windowsill to reach inside the building.

"Let me have that clipboard," Ernie said.

I handed it to him and Ernie used the metal clip to pry a rusty nail that held the overhead sliding window in place. Once the nail started to budge, he pulled on it with his fingers and, after much twisting and rotating, it popped free. I performed a similar operation on the other side of the window and we slid it upward, giving us about two feet of open space above the air conditioner.

I knelt down and Ernie stepped up on my back. As he slid his upper torso above the air conditioner, I braced him and pushed on the bottom of his boots.

"Whoa!" he said. "Not so fast."

After groping in the dark room, he finally found a handhold atop a filing cabinet and pulled himself inside. About thirty seconds later, he'd opened the back door. It was dark inside, so I turned on the lights.

"Someone will see," he said.

"They're busy," I replied. "Besides, if I find what I'm looking for, this shouldn't take long."

In fact, it didn't take long at all. Military men love wall charts, the bigger and gaudier the better. This one was marked Schedule of Assignments. The name of every Special Forces trainer was listed on the left, including Staff Sergeant Warnocki and even Lieutenant Colonel Laurel. Warnocki, apparently, was the rappelling expert, and Colonel Laurel taught every class concerning diving. Sergeant Munoz, the man Specialist Vance had told us about, was indeed blocked out on leave for the past four weeks, having returned to duty yesterday, Friday. It would be easy enough to find out for sure if he'd actually traveled to Puerto Rico, but for the moment I would assume he had. Sergeant First Class Walker R. Amos, the man who carried the ration-control cards to Seoul, wasn't blocked out at all on the chart. His specialty was apparently Survival, Escape and Evasion.

"That can come in handy on a train," Ernie said.

On the opposite wall, we found a map of the compound. The mock prisoner-of-war camp was clearly marked.

Ernie and I did our best to mingle with the trainees. They stood in a loose formation inside the main gate of the "Volcano POW Camp." It was nothing more than a few wooden shacks surrounded by concertina wire. We didn't see anyone there other than trainees.

"Where are the Green Berets?" I asked one of the G.I. trainees.

"Inside the biggest shack," he said. "They're taking us in there two at a time."

"For what?"

"Hell if I know. But none of the guys who've gone in so far have come out."

Ernie and I stepped away to talk about it. Neither one of us was armed.

"You have your handcuffs?" I asked.

"I'd feel naked without 'em," Ernie replied, patting the small of his back.

"So we have to take him down quick and clean, before any of his buddies have time to react."

"Okay. So, how do we do that?"

"Pretend we're a couple of trainees, to put him off guard."

We stepped toward the front of the formation. Nobody complained. None of the G.I.s were anxious to go in first anyway. In about five minutes, two men stepped out of the shack. They were probably Special Forces trainers, but you couldn't tell by their uniforms. They were wearing the dark green-and-red epaulette combat gear of the Warsaw Pact. One of the men was white, the other black. They pointed at Ernie and me and said, "Move it."

Ernie and I trotted forward.

"On the ground!" one of them shouted.

We both dropped to the low crawl position and then they started kicking us—not hard, but firmly enough to get us moving. Eating dust, we crawled into the shack. So far, we couldn't be sure how many trainers there were or which one was SFC Amos. On their mock Communist uniforms, they didn't wear name tags. Ernie and I continued to play along. The shack was dark, illuminated by only one yellow light.

"All right," one of our captors said. "If you're dumb enough to be captured and locked up by the enemy, then you're going to be treated like the complete idiots you are. And often, the only means of escape is through tunneling. Like rats."

One of the captors kicked me. "You know how to dig holes?"

I shook my head.

He kicked me again. "Speak up!"

"*No!*" I shouted.

"I didn't think so. So we've already dug a hole for you. Check under that bunk over there. You have ten seconds to find it."

Ernie and I crawled forward and beneath a rickety wooden bunk there was flooring made of the same splintery planks. Ernie clawed at them and within seconds managed to pull one of the planks up. I pulled another and soon we had revealed a dark pit that dropped into the ground.

Behind us, automatic fire. Blanks, I knew, but the sound reverberated like thunder and the air filled with acrid smoke.

"Beat it!" one of the captors shouted. "Get out! Through the tunnel!"

Ernie slid down first. I followed.

It was completely dark down here and so narrow that my shoulders dragged against dirt. The air was tight. Occasionally Ernie's boots kicked mud back into my face.

What were we doing down here? We should've arrested those guys up in the shack, but if they resisted we probably wouldn't have been able to take them both down. Besides, we weren't even sure yet which one was Sergeant Amos. If it was the black guy, I was toast. I was betting it was the white guy. He was about the right height and he was certainly strong enough to overpower the women and make his escape over the high fences at Anyang. But so far, because of his cap, I hadn't even seen the color of his hair.

Also, his nose wasn't big enough to justify the huge proboscises that had been drawn in the witness sketches. Besides, there were probably other trainers at the end of this tunnel.

The tunnel seemed endless. I remembered that the shack was sitting alone, far from any obvious place to come back up to the surface. We kept crawling.

How sure was I that this guy, Sergeant First Class Walker R. Amos, was actually the Blue Train rapist? Fairly sure. We'd meticulously eliminated every other American G.I. who could have been on the two trains involved. If this Amos guy had carte blanche to take the ration-control cards to Seoul, he'd be able to travel on the Blue Train pretty much at will. I had to assume that he could be dangerous. Very dangerous.

The tunnel closed in on me. Was it getting narrower,

or was it just my imagination? No, it was definitely narrower. I had to pull my shoulder in and constrict my chest, making it more difficult to breathe. For a second, I considered turning around, until I realized that was impossible. I had to go forward wherever it led, which maybe was the point of this training.

Finally, Ernie's boots kicked back strongly and then I realized that his body was twisting upward. Ahead of him light glimmered. Then he was gone. I breathed fresh air, and strong hands were pulling me up to freedom. I inhaled deeply, enjoying the rich oxygen, my eyes squinting at the bright lights of the fluorescent bulbs overhead. We were in some sort of aid station. One G.I. lay on a cot, a blue-smocked medic hovering about him. A much larger group of G.I.s sat at two picnic tables pushed together, munching on crackers and sipping cool drinks and staring back at us, smirking.

Amidst this calm scene, Ernie was wrestling with someone.

The man went down on the floor with a thump and others started shouting, and then we had all gathered around the two wrestling men. Ernie sprang to his feet, triumphant.

"Got him," he said.

The man lying on the ground, his eyes wide, was Caucasian, about six feet tall, and his hands were trussed firmly behind his back. The name tag on his field jacket said Amos. Medics started to shove Ernie, but I jumped in front of them and pulled out my badge.

"CID," I said. "Back off. Or you'll be interfering with an arrest."

"Arrest?"

Everyone was incredulous.

Ernie pulled the handcuffed man to his feet.

"Good to meet you at last," I said.

"Meet me? We've never met before."

"But I know of you," I said. "I've been studying your movements on the Blue Train."

Then the light of understanding entered the man's eyes. "You mean this," he said, looking down at his field jacket. "The name tag."

Ernie kept a tight hold on his arm.

"You think I'm Amos," he said finally.

We waited.

"This isn't my field jacket. It's cold in here so I just borrowed it from Sergeant Amos. He left it here when he changed into the Warsaw Pact uniform."

"He's one of the two guys at the other end of the tunnel?" I asked.

"Right. But *he* couldn't have done anything to be arrested for. He's a fine man."

"Never mind that," Ernie said. "Which one is he? The white one or the black one?"

"The black one," the guy said. "He's the preacher who conducts our nondenominational services every Sunday."

Colonel Laurel was livid. But I was pretty angry too. So was Ernie. Neither one of us really cared about whether we got court-martialed for insubordination, and we let him have it.

"The Blue Train rapist could strike again at any moment," I shouted. "More women could be hurt. More children scarred for life. But instead, all you can think about is the insult to your integrity. I need to know where everyone has been for every minute of the last few weeks. Once I know that, I either find the Blue Train rapist or I eliminate all of your men and we go on our way."

Colonel Laurel's mangled jaw was clamped shut. His eyes shot blue lasers of hatred. After word spread about what we'd done, training had halted and a gaggle of Green Berets, led by Sergeant Warnocki, had escorted us to Colonel Laurel's Quonset hut.

"Damn you!" he shouted. He paced around his office, in front of the flags of the United States, the Republic of Korea, and the United Nations. For a moment, I thought he was going to smack us. Instead, he stopped pacing and spoke.

"All right, then. You have one hour. Warnocki! Escort these men to the orderly room. Let them examine the morning report, leave records, temporary duty orders, anything that will allow them to trace the whereabouts of the members of this command. But no classified material. Understood?"

"Understood, sir."

Warnocki jammed his thumb toward the door.

Ernie and I saluted Colonel Laurel. He didn't bother to respond.

It took me twenty minutes to gather all the information I needed. Warnocki slouched in a vinyl chair. Ernie gazed at me quizzically but I didn't want to tell him what I'd found. Not yet, not in front of Warnocki.

"Let's go," I said.

As we walked out the door, Warnocki followed.

"Aren't you going to report to the Colonel?" he asked.

"Later. Where will he be this afternoon?"

"Out with the haenyo. Teaching diving techniques."

"They have scuba gear?" Ernie asked.

"Naw. He teaches 'natural' techniques. How to hold your breath, how to gradually increase the depth of your dives, how to use the currents to your advantage, stuff like that. The way the haenyo do it."

Ernie and I returned to the Nokko-ri Yoguan and changed out of our muddy clothes.

The truth of the matter was that I was devastated. All of my theories had been shattered. Sergeant First Class Amos couldn't be the Blue Train rapist, because all the eyewitness reports had agreed that the culprit was a white man. Amos was black. Since he was such a frequent rider of the Blue Train, I did briefly interview him and ask if he'd noticed anything suspicious. Although he'd heard about the attacks, he'd noticed nothing unusual himself. On the day the Blue Train to Seoul had stopped to allow the funeral procession of the late First Lady to pass, he'd been on an earlier train.

Once we changed back into our civvies, Ernie said, "Now what?"

I didn't know. We walked out of the yoguan and I stared up at the sky. From the peak of Mount Halla, a wisp of smoke trailed lazily up into the endless blue. I thought of the commo site, and flunking an IG inspection, how seriously the army takes those things. Then I remembered something Vance had said, and suddenly I knew.

"What?" Ernie asked.

When I didn't answer, he asked again, more insistent this time. "What?"

"Come on," I said, "let's find a cab."

We were three quarters of the way up the mountain, with the same cab driver, Mr. Won, still driving his unrepaired cab and more nervous than ever. He'd made us pay triple fare instead of double. Ernie pointed. "There!"

Won pulled off at the next bypass. The three of us climbed out to get a better look. Zigzagging down the mountain, we could see him from a mile off. The quarter-ton truck from the communications site.

"That must be him," I said. "Let's roll the cab out here to block his way."

Ernie jumped in the driver's seat and Mr. Won screamed at us to stop. Oblivious, Ernie started the engine, shoved it into gear, and drove the cab across the road so as to block the way of the oncoming truck.

"He'll have to come wide around that curve," Ernie said. "If he doesn't slam on his brakes, he'll barrel right into the cab."

Keeping the keys so the protesting Mr. Won couldn't move his vehicle, Ernie and I trotted up the road and hid behind some rocks next to the spot where we figured the truck would have to come to a stop. Or at least slow down.

Up above, the engine roared louder.

17

The quarter-ton truck rounded the last corner and the driver's head, small in the distance, was square and dark, almost-black hair cut very short: Ronald T. Parkwood, the ranking NCO and the only other man besides Vance stationed at the Mount Halla commo site. When he saw the taxicab blocking half the road, a moment of surprise suffused his features, but then hairy forearms took over, jerking the steering wheel to the right, rolling the quarter-ton into a skid. Expertly, he twisted the steering wheel back to the left, turning into the skid, straightening out the truck and slamming, with a horrific crash, into the rear of the little Hyundai sedan. Behind me, Mr. Won groaned.

Ernie and I erupted from our hiding places and sprinted toward the truck, but Parkwood was still in control, rolling forward, shifting gears, finally gunning the engine and making the wheels spin. Laughing, he sped off down the road. An arm reached out of the left cab window, raised in the air, flipping us the bird.

"Dammit!" Ernie shouted.

He jumped into the driver's side of the cab and tried to start the engine. It only whined in protest; no matter how hard he tried, it wouldn't turn over.

"Specialist Vance," I said. "He's still up there. And there's a phone. We can call. Come on."

Ernie and I started up the mountain, running when we could, leaning forward and striding when the incline became too steep. Reluctantly, Mr. Won followed.

We'd chased the Blue Train rapist from Seoul, down the Korean peninsula to its southernmost tip, and then beyond, to this island deep in the heart of the cold Yellow Sea. Now we were truly as far south as it was possible to go and still fall under the purview of the United States Forces Korea. The gate in the chain-link fence surrounding the Mount Halla Communications Center squeaked on its hinges.

"He left it open," Ernie said, perspiration pouring off his forehead.

"Apparently," I replied, "he doesn't plan on coming back."

The door to the main building had been propped open with an old combat boot.

"He wanted us to enter," Ernie said.

I nodded.

Behind us, Mr. Won, the cab driver, stood nervously outside the gate, wringing his hands, still staring back down the mountain toward his damaged cab. On the way up, he'd harangued me about how he was a poor man and he couldn't afford to have the cab repaired—if, in fact, it even *could* be repaired. I told him to contact the 8th Army Claims Office. He might have to hire an attorney but eventually, they'd make good his loss, not only for repair of the cab but also for lost wages. That's what I told him. Whether that would come to pass, I couldn't guarantee.

Unconsciously, Ernie touched the inner pocket of his jacket. Nothing was there. No .45. But I didn't think we'd need one. The Blue Train rapist was long gone. What I had to do was find a telephone, contact the Korean National Police, and make sure that Sergeant Ronald T. Parkwood didn't get off the Island of Cheju.

The communications room was shattered. Metal boxes had huge dents in them, keyboards and control panels had been smashed, wires—some of them still sparking—stuck out in every direction. Clipboards with maintenance checklists on them had been smashed in two.

"Christ," Ernie said. "He must've taken a sledgehammer to this stuff."

I checked the phones. Dead. So much for calling ahead to the KNPs.

"Where's Vance?" I said.

Ernie hurried toward the back room. I followed. The living quarters had been similarly smashed. Glassware, metal utensils, pots and pans, chunks of roast beef, and sprays of broccoli were splattered everywhere. An expensive stereo set with microphone lay on its side atop a smashed electric guitar. The single cowboy boot I'd seen before lay beneath a pile of dirty clothes that, incongruously, included a red lace bra.

"Somebody threw a tantrum," Ernie said.

"Vance!" I shouted. "You in here?"

When no one answered, Ernie and I tiptoed through the mess until we reached the small outdoor exercise area. That's when we saw him. His arms were tied behind him with a sturdy rope. Somehow, Parkwood had managed to hang him over the pull-up bar, about eight feet off the ground. His knees had been hooked over the bar and then his ankles tied by electric cords securely to his thighs.

"God," Ernie said. "Must've hurt like a bastard."

Still, that much torture wasn't enough for Sergeant Ronald T. Parkwood. He'd then tied a twenty-five-pound barbell to an electric circuit wire and attached the other end of the wire in a loop around Specialist Vance's neck. Slowly, Vance had been strangled to death.

I could've saved him if I'd managed to put it together earlier. On the Blue Train, Runnels the courier had said that the rapist was making his first checkmark on a list of corrective actions. Here at the Mount Halla commo site, Specialist Vance told me they'd failed their IG inspection. The list of deficiencies hanging on clipboards was massive and had to be corrected. If they weren't corrected—and corrected in a timely fashion—Parkwood would be denied reenlistment.

To civilians, especially civilians with gainful employment, that may not sound like much. But if you have little or no education, and you've been trained by the army to do a job that only the military has a need for, and you only have a few more years until you reach your twenty-year retirement, a bar from reenlistment can seem like death. Parkwood had a choice: correct the long list of deficiencies from the IG inspection, or get out of the army. He decided to get out. But before he left, he set about, for some reason known only to himself, to correct his *own* list of deficiencies in his life, and in so doing he'd murdered innocent people and destroyed the lives of those who had loved them.

A red tongue lolled out of Vance's open mouth. His upside-down face was purple, wearing an expression as if screaming in horror. Ernie found a butcher knife among the jumbled kitchen utensils and was about to cut Vance down when Mr. Won pushed through the open door behind us.

I swiveled in time to see his face: wide-eyed with terror. Then he turned, grabbed his stomach, and barfed up what must've been his breakfast: a half-pound of partially digested cabbage kimchee, a little rice.

Ernie managed to get the cab rolling. Not started, but rolling. When it began gliding downhill, gradually picking up speed, he tried the ignition again. This time it turned over. Still, he kept it in low because the brakes, by now, were totally worthless. I sat up front next to Ernie. A pale-looking Mr. Won sat in back.

We screeched around corners, taking a couple of them on two wheels. When the road leveled even temporarily, Ernie slowed as much as he could, bouncing the side of the cab against boulders, scraping the bumper against bushes, purposely running the tires through mud or thick gravel. Each time Ernie completed such a maneuver, Mr. Won looked as if he was going to be sick again.

Finally, we made it in one piece to the base of the mountain and a few minutes later we pulled up in front of the main gate of the Mount Halla Training Facility. When we hopped out of the cab, Mr. Won held on to my sleeve, a pleading look on his face. I reached in my wallet and handed him one of my business cards; when that wasn't enough, I pulled the small wad of military payment certificates out of the wallet and handed them to him. About forty bucks.

He held the money with both hands, staring at it forlornly.

"The Eighth Army Claims Office," I said, patting him on the shoulder.

And then I was off.

Ernie was already arguing with the gate guards; shoving one of them, one of them shoving back. After about two minutes of that, Staff Sergeant Warnocki appeared. He listened to our story, scratching his nearly bald head beneath his beret.

Finally, he asked, "So, where did this guy go?"

"That's what we don't know," I replied. "But I have to call the KNPs to make sure that they don't let him off the island."

"Okay," he said. "Come on."

The three of us trotted over to the orderly room. There I placed an AUTOVON call to Pusan. Inspector Kill picked up immediately. I explained what I knew. He reassured me that he would contact the Korean National Police on Cheju and this man known as Sergeant Ronald T. Parkwood would never leave the island.

I hung up the phone.

"So, did anybody see a quarter-ton truck around here?"

Warnocki shook his head. Then he said, "Wait a minute. This guy, Parkwood, he works at the commo site, right?"

Ernie and I both nodded.

"Works out a lot," he continued. "Sort of buff, for a rear-echelon puke."

"That's him," I replied.

"He was into diving." Ernie and I both stared at him blankly. Warnocki continued. "Between cycles, Colonel Laurel gives water survival courses to anybody who's interested, using the techniques he's learned from the haenyo."

"Did you go?" Ernie asked.

"Of course. All the SF personnel did. He's our commander."

"And Parkwood went too?"

"Yeah. Held back, though. Didn't mingle with the rest of us."

"So if you were trying to get off this island," Ernie asked, "and you figured that even if you managed to get on the ferry, you'd probably be picked up by the time you landed in Pusan, where would you go?"

"I'd steal a chopper," Warnocki said.

"And if that wasn't available?"

"A boat."

We started to run, but Warnocki shouted for us to wait. He reached in his pocket and pulled out a set of keys. Inside a padlocked filing cabinet, he lifted out a pistol belt with a holster and strapped a .45 automatic pistol around his waist. Outside, he slid back the bolt to make sure a round was chambered. The three of us climbed in Warnocki's jeep.

* * *

"Something's wrong," Warnocki said.

The three of us were lying on a sand dune, looking down on the boulder-strewn beach next to the ancient wooden quay where the haenyo launch their craft. Lieutenant Colonel Ambrose Q. Laurel was sitting on a flat rock with his back to us, staring out to sea. Two haenyo, clad in full-body wet suits, were working listlessly on repairing nets.

"Why do you say that?" I asked.

"Colonel Laurel never sits still: he's always on the go. And he wouldn't ignore the haenyo like that. He has great respect for them."

Behind us, boots crunched on sand.

I turned to look to see who it was, but by then Warnocki was rolling down the sand dune like a mad dervish. As he rolled, he reached in his holster and somehow pulled out the .45. He raised it and a shot rang out. I blinked in surprise and struggled to stand up. Ernie was already on his feet, hands held to his side, strangely immobile.

And then I realized why he was immobile.

The death end of an M-16 semiautomatic rifle was pointing right at him.

Sergeant Ronald T. Parkwood held the rifle, pointing it directly at us as he climbed the sand dune. His face was unshaven, his eyes squinting in rage, glaring at us over a nose that wasn't as huge as portrayed in the witnesses' sketches, but pretty good-sized anyway.

"Drag him up here," Parkwood shouted.

And then I realized what he meant. Warnocki sat on the far side of the dune, clutching his right thigh, cursing, trying to stop the bleeding. His .45 lay a few feet from him in the sand.

"If you try for it," Parkwood told Warnocki, "you'll be dead." Then he turned to us. "Now drag him up and get him down to the beach!"

Ernie and I did what we'd been told. Once we were on the far side of the dune, Warnocki was able to hop, with our help, down the ten yards to the beach. The haenyo had stopped working, and were staring at Parkwood. Colonel Laurel stood up.

"You've shot one of my men!" he roared.

"Shut the hell up!" Parkwood replied. "Any more mouth and I'll shoot you. And these haenyo while I'm at it."

Colonel Laurel clamped his mangled jaw shut.

"In the boat," Parkwood said. "Everybody."

We walked toward the pier.

"Leave him here," Parkwood said, pointing the rifle at Warnocki, "on the beach where I can see him."

We sat Staff Sergeant Warnocki down on moist sand.

"Now everybody, up on the quay. Into the boat. And don't launch until I give the order."

It was a fairly large boat, with no sail, only two oars on either side. Seating planks crossed it with enough space for about ten people, about the size of a normal fishing party of haenyo. There was an outboard motor at the stern. Colonel Laurel sat farthest forward, then the two haenyo, and finally me and Ernie.

Warnocki stared after us angrily. With that leg, even if he managed to crawl back to the jeep, he wouldn't get far. He was losing blood at such a rate that he'd probably pass out soon. Still, Parkwood wasn't taking any chances. Just as the rest of us sat down in the boat, Parkwood, still on the beach, aimed the M-16 rifle at Warnocki and fired.

Warnocki scrambled backward like a crab. The first round missed. The second came closer, grazing Warnocki, I think, on the shoulder. But by then, Warnocki was at the top of another sand dune and rolled down to safety on the other side.

Colonel Laurel had risen to his feet and started moving toward Parkwood. Parkwood swiveled the rifle, pointed it at Laurel, and growled, "Sit down!"

Colonel Laurel sat.

The haenyo stared at the bottom of the boat, as if in complete defeat.

Parkwood braced himself against a wooden stanchion and took a bead on Warnocki's jeep parked on the edge of the highway some quarter-mile distant. He fired a single round, apparently hitting the radiator because a puff of steam rose into the cold blue sky.

Satisfied, Parkwood sloshed through shallow water and climbed in the boat, sitting with his back to the outboard motor, grinning at us. Keeping the rifle in his lap, he jerked on the lanyard and the engine started up. He unhooked a line and putt-putted the boat away from the quay. After crossing a few small swells, we were at sea, heading I wasn't sure where.

At first we all just stared at one another and at the still-smoking rifle in Parkwood's lap. As the ocean rose and fell, it seemed to calm us, and the hopelessness of the situation started to sink in. We were being taken out to sea by a madman, by the Blue Train rapist, by a man who'd already proven his disregard for human life. As long as he held that rifle, we were defenseless against him. And as we floated on this cold, dreary sea, there was no help in sight.

About a mile out, still in sight of the coastline, Parkwood ordered the haenyo off the boat.

Colonel Laurel protested. "We're too far out," he said. "They'll never make it."

"Bull," Parkwood replied. "These women can swim for miles."

The haenyo apparently agreed with him. They glanced back at Colonel Laurel, as if in apology. He nodded back, granting them permission. After all, on Cheju Island women are the breadwinners—or seafood winners, if you will—and these women had families to support. As sleekly as a pair of seals, the two women rolled off the edge of the boat and started paddling their way toward shore. Once they were about a hundred yards away, they stopped and stared back, as if saying good-bye. Then they turned toward shore and started seriously stroking toward home.

Parkwood ordered Ernie and me farther toward the front of the boat. Now the three of us were on one end, Parkwood on the other. He kept his finger in the trigger housing of the M-16, the barrel lying loosely on his lap. With the other hand he steered the boat away from Cheju Island.

"Where are we going, Parkwood?" I asked.

"Shut the fuck up."

I shut up.

After a few minutes of glaring at the endless sea, he spoke again, this time directing his comment to Ernie.

"So, how's Marnie?" he asked.

"Marnie?" Ernie was as surprised as I was.

"You know who I'm talking about," Parkwood replied. "Is she still screwing Freddy Ray?"

The original complaints by the Country Western All Stars regarding various missing items—a microphone, a pair of panties, and finally a single cowboy boot—we had assumed were the results of carelessness or the booty of the occasional souvenir-hunting thief. They had seen a pattern in it; Ernie and I hadn't. Now I realized that those were precisely the items that I'd seen earlier in the living quarters at the commo site atop Mount Halla, all jumbled in with a ton of other items, but there nevertheless. Most recently I'd also seen a red lace bra and panties. Originally, I'd written it off to G.I. bravado. There's not a barracks in the US Army where a set of female panties isn't prominently displayed somewhere, as a trophy of conquest.

"How long have you been stalking the Country Western All Stars?" I asked.

Parkwood grinned at me. "Ever since I saw the USO flyer in our weekly distribution. I haven't missed a performance. Except for maybe the one tonight." He grinned more broadly.

"Where are they playing tonight?" I asked.

"I thought you two were supposed to be watching them. At least I know Ernie here was staying as close to Marnie as he possibly could."

It's a crawly type of feeling to know that someone has been watching you, especially when we were the ones who were supposed to be providing security. But Parkwood was a nondescript kind of G.I.—a little under six feet tall, not heavy, not skinny, Caucasian with brown eyes and brown hair; probably the most prevalent description possible in the United States Army. All he had to do was sit quietly and he'd blend into any crowd. We'd never see him. And we never had.

The only thing unusual about him was his nose, round-tipped and slightly longer than normal.

"Did you pay Vance," I asked, "to cover for you while you traveled around the country?"

"Hell, no. I wouldn't pay that wimp nothing. He did what I told him and he was glad to do it."

"Glad?" Ernie asked.

"Yeah, glad. So I wouldn't beat the shit out of him."

Parkwood guffawed at this, finding himself enormously funny.

Behind me, molars ground in the remnants of Colonel Laurel's jaw. He wanted to try something, but it would be suicide and he knew it. Still, our odds might not get better, no matter how the scenario played out. Was Parkwood just going to force Ernie and me off the boat, so we could die out here, without wet suits, in the middle of the cold Yellow Sea? Or would he shoot us first? I decided to ask.

"Why did you bring us along, Parkwood? Why not just waste us back on the beach?"

Ernie flinched. Parkwood noticed it and grinned.

"Good thinking," he told me. "Why not just waste you? I thought of that. But there's always somebody who puts two and two together, and the ROK Navy patrols these waters like crazy, so I figured I'd better take a little insurance with me."

"We're hostages," Ernie said.

"You're just now figuring that out?"

I wanted to ask him about the rapes, but I decided not

to ask directly. Parkwood was a guy who liked clever conversation, at least when he was the one holding an M-16.

"Those fences," I said, "at the Anyang Railroad Station must've been quite a climb."

"Not when you're in good shape." He took his hand off the rudder and stared at his palm. "I did cut myself, though."

The boat swerved against the choppy sea. Quickly, Parkwood grabbed the rudder again and steered the little boat toward the north, or at least what I thought was the north. By now, we were out of sight of Cheju Island. How could Parkwood be so confident that he was heading in the right direction? Probably just counting on blind luck. Most people don't realize that the Republic of Korea, besides the main land mass of the Korean peninsula, is composed of about 5,000 islands, Cheju being merely the largest among many. The Koreans are an ancient seafaring people. If Parkwood kept steering us in the general direction of north, he'd hit something eventually.

The air was growing increasingly frigid, and the steady sea spray battering my face and body didn't help much. Ernie, so angry he could hardly talk, was turning blue. After more than an hour, Parkwood spotted something ahead of us.

"There it is," he said. " Chujagun Island. We pass through the channel there and then it's only a couple of more hours to the mainland."

Parkwood was heading directly to the mainland, rather than traveling the much longer northeasterly route to Pusan.

"You've traveled by boat before?" I asked.

"Beats the ferry."

Which is one of the reasons why we never saw his name on the Pusan-to-Cheju manifests.

"How'd you know," I asked, "that day in Anyang, that the Blue Train was going to stop to let another train pass?"

"I didn't," he said. "I knew about the assassination, but I had no idea when the funeral train would come by."

"So how did you plan to escape once you arrived at the Seoul Station?"

He shrugged. "Just winged it."

"You have a lot of confidence in your abilities," Ernie said.

"I've been at this a long time," he said.

"'At this'?"

"Yeah. Since I was a kid."

Parkwood told us about his first train ride. It was back in the early fifties: '54 or '55, he thought, although he was too young at the time to be sure. Back then, the Super Chief of the Santa Fe Railroad was still a major mode of transportation to and from the West Coast.

"We boarded the train at Union Station in Los Angeles," Parkwood told us. "Me, my mom, and my younger sister. The three of us, all dressed up like people did in those days. Me wearing a little suit with short pants and a bow tie, my sister with a new dress and a straw hat with a red ribbon on it. My mom, of course, looked like a blonde version of Barbara Stanwyck with a tight black skirt and net stockings and a tight vest to show off her figure. She even wore a pillbox hat with a half-veil on it, all the rage in those days."

"Other than the clothes," I said, "she looked like Marnie."

"Oh, a pop psychologist." He gazed out at sea and then back at me. "I guess she did, a little. We were quite a trio, and my mom said my dad hadn't seen us off because he was busy working, but we all knew the truth. They'd fought, he'd left, and, for what seemed a long time to me at the time, he hadn't been back. Other guys started showing up in our apartment. 'Uncles,' my mom called them. And then we boarded the train to go back east, to her parents' house in Denver."

Colonel Laurel turned his head as discreetly as he could, using his peripheral vision to scan the horizon.

"At each stop," Parkwood continued, "my mom would tell us to wait and she'd get off the train to buy some Life Savers, and some cigarettes for herself. My sister and I were very well behaved compared to other kids: we didn't complain and whine, and we didn't make noise when the lights were lowered at night and people pushed their seats back to get some sleep. But I did worry when my mother left the train. I worried that she'd have to wait in line too long, that a cashier would be slow in making change. I worried that she might not return to the train in time. But she always did, just before the conductor yelled, 'All Aboard!' and the train pulled out of the station. The stops were mostly desert stations made of adobe and brick, with Indian women in bowler hats and blankets squatting in front of handmade pottery."

Ernie interrupted. "Can you get to the point, Parkwood, while we're still young?"

Parkwood grinned. "While I'm holding the rifle," he said, "you have to listen."

Ernie grunted.

Parkwood continued. "Finally, we reached the Rocky Mountains. At night, rain squalls and thunder and lightning reached out from jagged peaks like hands trying to grab us. And always the clickety-clack of the train's metal wheels.

"I'm not sure exactly where it was," Parkwood continued. "Somewhere before we reached Raton Pass, I remember that. My mom told us to wait and be good and she handed me a half-eaten roll of Life Savers. This time she didn't say why she was getting off. She just did. I waited. So did my sister, although she was younger and therefore less concerned. Finally, I heard the conductor yell, 'All aboard!' I stared at the door, the door my mother usually returned through, but she didn't appear. The engines started and then the train began to roll.

"I considered getting out of my seat to look for her, to tell the conductor to stop, but I did neither. My mother had told me repeatedly not to get out of my seat, and I always listened to her. She was my goddess and I worshiped her. I always did as she ordered."

Parkwood gave a half laugh and looked around, as if just remembering that he was floating in the middle of the Yellow Sea.

"She never returned, of course," he said. "My sister and I rode on, alone, wondering what to do, until a nice young man in a neatly pressed suit and a snap-brim hat sat down in the seat my mother had left. He talked to us. Nicely. I told him that my mother hadn't gotten back on at the last stop. He nodded kindly and told me that she would almost surely catch up with us, maybe at the next stop, maybe at our destination, but there was nothing to worry about. I felt so grateful to him for saying that.

"My sister had to go to the bathroom. She'd been waiting for my mom to return because Mom always told her not to go by herself. The nice young man offered to take her. Together, they walked off hand in hand. They were gone a long time."

Parkwood stared at us.

"It all seems obvious now, doesn't it? A woman who's lost her husband no longer wants the responsibility of raising two brats, so she takes off. A man riding on a train sees an opportunity and takes advantage of it and gets himself a little four-year-old stuff in the rolling bathroom of a train."

Ernie stared at Parkwood with unalloyed disgust.

"So you've had a tough time, Parkwood. Welcome to the club. But that doesn't justify the rape of two women, the murder of one, and certainly not the torture and murder of a fellow soldier, Specialist Vance."

Parkwood grinned at him, happy at being the center of attention. Ernie decided to pop his bubble.

"Later, the nice-looking man on the Super Chief took you into the bathroom too, didn't he, Parkwood?"

Parkwood's fist tightened around the trigger housing. "No! He didn't!"

"Sure he did," Ernie said. "That's why you added Vance to your 'checklist.' Probably reminded you of him. You probably don't even have a sister. And when the dapper young man took you into the men's room, you sort of liked it. You liked the stink and the degradation of it, and the rough sex. Maybe you liked it a little too much."

The sea was choppier now. We were entering an isthmus about a half mile in width between two islands. Parkwood raised the rifle; but instead of pointing it at Ernie, he pointed it at me.

"You keep it up," Parkwood told Ernie, "and I'll add *him* to my checklist. I'll force him off the boat. You can watch him drown."

Ernie shrugged. "He's a good swimmer."

"Not with a bullet in his thigh, he's not."

Colonel Laurel seemed to have spotted something. I wasn't sure what, but I expected him to make a move. I braced myself.

"Parkwood!" Laurel shouted. "You put that goddamn weapon down. Now! And quit pointing it at your fellow soldiers."

Parkwood gazed at him curiously. "Are you serious?"

The colonel's mangled jaw tightened. He sat up as straight as he could in the rocking boat. "You're damn right, I'm serious. You've done enough damage." He started to rise. "Now give me that goddamn weapon!"

With his right hand, Parkwood kept the rifle pointed straight ahead, his left hand steering the outboard motor. He continued to stare at Colonel Laurel, flabbergasted at his temerity to demand, in this little boat, that the M-16 rifle be turned over to him. Colonel Laurel rose to his full height.

Behind Parkwood, and all around the boat, black orbs rose out of the water. Startled, Parkwood turned to see what they were, and as he did so, I leaped toward him. Ernie yelled, and before Parkwood could turn and re-aim the weapon, we were on him. Scratching, clawing, in a frantic lust to turn the barrel of the M-16 away from us and up toward the sky. Ernie hit the rifle, and it pointed into the sea. I plowed into Parkwood's chest just as the rifle fired. He reeled backward, letting go of the outboard motor, which immediately sputtered and died. Somehow he kept his balance and shoved me back slightly, but there was no stopping me. I bulled forward. Parkwood tilted backward and, with me following, we both fell into the sea.

The cold sucked every ounce of breath out of my lungs. I was underwater. I couldn't breathe. Above, in the murky green, the boat rolled slowly by and all around me black silhouettes glided by. Seals, I thought. Or sharks.

And then one of them bit me.

18

Actually, it wasn't a bite. Rather, it was a strong hand that pulled me to the surface.

Sputtering, coughing, gazing around me in the cold sea, I was disoriented and it took a while for anything to come into focus. A half-dozen black figures floated nearby. Then I realized who they were. The haenyo. Somehow they'd anticipated Parkwood's path and set up an ambush in this narrow strait. There were many clans of haenyo through-out these islands, not all on Cheju, and it seemed they communicated well. Someone shouted. Colonel Laurel. He was in the water too, swimming madly, and then I realized what he was angry about. The boat was floating away. In the melee, the boat had almost been capsized. Parkwood had fallen off, the M-16 rifle with him, but he'd managed to climb back aboard. I raised myself as high as

I could in the choppy waves but could only see the back of someone hunched over the outboard motor. In a few seconds, the engine sputtered and then roared and finally started to pull away until it disappeared into the mist.

The haenyo motioned for me to start swimming for shore. I did. But I stopped every few yards to survey who was left in our little school of swimmers. Laurel shouted, "Your partner, he's not here!"

"Where is he?"

"He's still in the boat. I think he hit his head on the bulkhead. Hard."

"Christ," I said. "How about the M-16?"

"The bottom of the ocean," Laurel said.

"We have to get to a phone," I said.

"That we do," Colonel Laurel agreed.

I turned and started swimming toward land. I was swimming against the current. It was difficult. One of the haenyo came up beside me and motioned for me to aim farther to the left. In twenty minutes, Colonel Laurel and I and half a dozen women of the sea were climbing up a sea-soaked ladder to the dry, splintery planks of a fisherman's landing.

The boat was found late that evening, about 2 A.M., on an island called Shinji-do, some thirty miles north of the straits where the haenyo had rescued Colonel Laurel and me. According to the local KNPs, no trace of Parkwood had been discovered. Ernie, however, had been found. Alive. He'd been transferred to a medical clinic and from

there a ROK Navy chopper had flown him to Hialeah
Compound in Pusan.

I learned all this through a phone conversation with
Inspector Kill. He was coordinating the all-points bulletin the Korean National Police had put out for Sergeant
Ronald T. Parkwood. From the landing point of the little
craft on Shinji-do, it was a short walk to a main highway;
from there, it was thought Parkwood had waved down a
local cab and caught a ride to the Shinji Bus Station. A
ticket seller there remembered trying to communicate
with a hairy-fisted foreigner who wanted to buy a ticket
to Pusan. Of course, she couldn't sell him a direct ticket to
Pusan. He had to buy a ticket north to Kuangju first, and
from there he'd be able to catch the eastbound express that
left every twenty minutes for Pusan. The foreigner hadn't
understood all this but hadn't made a fuss, because the
bus to Kuangju had been about to leave and apparently
he'd been in a hurry. His change, the ticket seller said, was
thirty won—about five cents—and he didn't bother to wait
for it, just grabbed his ticket and left. The young woman
was afraid that the police were there about the thirty won
but relieved when she discovered they weren't.

"Anyway," she told the KNPs, "foreigners are always
trouble."

The KNPs were still trying to locate the bus driver and
the stewardess on the Shinji-to-Kuangju express, but so
far they hadn't found them. Kill doubted they'd have much
to say, but it was a base he had to cover. Police in Kuangju
were at the bus station now, interviewing ticket sellers and
others who might've spotted Parkwood. There are no US

military bases in that part of Korea, so chances were that an American would be remembered.

"How about the bus station in Pusan?" I asked.

"We have some good men there," Inspector Kill assured me. "Also at the train station."

"Good. I should be in Pusan before sunrise."

Colonel Laurel, with the help of the haenyo, had already hired a car.

When I walked into his ward in the Hialeah Compound Dispensary, Ernie was sitting up in his hospital bed.

"Did you see the jaws on that nurse?" he asked.

"Jaws?"

"Hips. I'm tired of skinny Korean girls."

I poured myself some water from a jug sitting on Ernie's nightstand. "Not all Korean girls are skinny."

"Show me a fat one."

I decided to change the subject. "You ready to get back to work?"

"Yeah." Ernie threw back the covers and kicked his legs off the edge of the bed. "Where are my shoes?"

"Over there. In the closet."

Ernie padded barefoot across the room, stripped off his hospital gown, and started putting on his clothes.

"I don't remember nothing," Ernie said, "from when you jumped at Parkwood until I woke up with the KNPs shining a flashlight in my eyes. I was still in that boat, on a beach somewhere."

"Shinji Island."

"Wherever. They helped me into the backseat of their

patrol car and later, from the roof of their police station, I was airlifted back here."

"You didn't hear Parkwood say anything?"

"No. He was gone when I came to."

I sipped on the water. Ernie finished tying his shoelaces.

"He could've killed you," I said.

"Yeah. Good for me he didn't."

"But why not?"

"Why not? You think maybe he should have?"

"He's killed two people that we know of so far. Mrs. Hyon and Specialist Vance."

"Maybe I'm not his type." Ernie slipped on his jacket, checking to make sure that his CID badge was still in the inner coat pocket.

"Maybe he's through with killing."

"Don't count on it," Ernie said.

As we walked out of the clinic, nobody tried to stop us. The front door opened automatically to a late morning of swirling ocean mist.

"Maybe we should check out some weapons," Ernie said, "from the MP arms room."

"Maybe we should," I said.

Riley was in his room at Hialeah Billeting, drunk again.

"Where you guys been?" he growled.

"Goofing off," I said.

He nodded his head knowingly. "I thought so. The Provost Marshal is pissed that you took this guy, Parkwood, into custody and then you let him go."

"Actually, we never had him in custody."

"That's even worse. If you're alleging that he's the Blue Train rapist, they want him interrogated to see if it's true or not."

"It's true," I replied. "Eighth Army is just looking for a way to weasel out of this."

"They're not trying to weasel out of nothing. They want him in custody and they want him interrogated and they want it to happen now."

Riley's eyes rolled and his head lolled on his neck. He reached across the footlocker and grabbed a bottle of Old Overwart and poured himself a shot glass full of amber fluid. Sticking out his thin lips, he sipped carefully.

"What happened to the Country Western All Stars?" I asked.

"You just missed them. They left for Seoul about an hour ago, including Casey."

"Casey?"

"Yeah. Marnie's daughter."

"She's here in Korea?"

"Yeah. Marnie didn't want to tell you, but she told me." Riley thrust his thumb toward the center of his narrow chest. "They're not supposed to bring relatives on USO tours. No. They're not supposed to. But Marnie paid for an airplane ticket for her mom and Casey. They stayed in that hotel in Seoul, keeping out of the way, hiding from the USO honchos and Eighth Army and everybody, and then when she found Freddy Ray, she had Casey sent down here."

"Her mom was here in Korea too?"

"Yeah. The whole time."

"But now she's stayed behind in Seoul?"

"Yeah. She has emphysema and can't get around too well."

Ernie had purchased two beers out of the vending machine down the hall, one for him and one for me, and he was listening as he popped them open.

"That damn Marnie," Ernie said. "Always full of surprises."

"That's her," Riley replied.

"She confided in you, did she?" Ernie asked.

"Damn right. She knows a good man when she sees one." Riley took another swig of his bourbon.

"So Casey was sent down here," I said, "and she and Marnie and Freddy Ray had a family reunion. Is that what happened?"

"Exactly. A family reunion that turned into a brawl."

"So they didn't get along," Ernie said.

"No," Riley replied. "Thanks to you."

"They argued about me?"

"What else?"

"So the Country Western All Stars are in the van now, heading back to Seoul. How long ago did they leave?"

"About an hour. But they're not all in the van."

"What do you mean?"

"I mean Freddy Ray had to return to his unit. And Casey gets carsick easy. So Marnie and her are taking the train back."

"The train? You mean the Blue Train?"

"What else? The one that left Pusan Station ten minutes ago."

"Marnie and Casey are alone?" I asked. "The others are in the van? Driving?"

Riley looked peeved. "What did I just say?"

Ernie and I looked at each other. Without discussing it, we put down our beers.

As we walked down the hallway, Riley shouted after us, "Hey! Where're you guys going?"

Inspector Kill met us at the Pusan Train Station.

The young KNP detective there, Mr. Ho, read from his notebook and gave us a complete rundown of what he'd observed. A tall blonde woman with a small child had boarded the Blue Train about ten minutes before its departure. There were five other foreigners, none of whom matched the description of Parkwood. However, Mr. Ho admitted, Parkwood's description matched a lot of Caucasian males and could have been easily altered, by something as simple as wearing eyeglasses, for instance.

I checked with the Pusan Rail Train Office, and the G.I. who worked behind the counter handed me the manifest. Parkwood wasn't on it, but he could've been using a stolen ID. I described him to the clerk. The guy shrugged. He didn't look at his customers much. He hated them, he told me, after doing this job for almost a year, and didn't bother looking at them.

"They're always whining about their seating or about how long they have to wait for their ticket or something else that nobody can do anything about. Besides, I'm a short-timer," he said. "Too short to care."

Under normal circumstances, Ernie might've slapped the guy. As it was, we didn't have time. Inspector Kill had already arranged for a helicopter to fly us north. On the drive to the airfield, he said, "Parkwood could board that train at the East Taegu station or even up in Taejon."

"Yes," I replied. "He's had enough time to get up there from Kuangju. But he wouldn't know that Marnie is on the train."

Ernie pulled a photograph out of his pocket and showed it to us. It was of a blondish woman in her early to mid-thirties, wearing a tight skirt, a tight vest, and a pill-box hat with a half-veil. Next to her stood a young boy in shorts and bow tie and jacket and, on the other side, tugging on the hem of her skirt, a little girl in a flowery dress with curly brown hair sticking out from beneath a straw bonnet with a long ribbon.

"Where'd you get this?" I asked Ernie.

"At the bottom of Parkwood's wall locker, up at the Mount Halla commo site. I guess he dropped it there when he was packing."

"Why didn't you tell me about it?"

Ernie shrugged. "At the time, it didn't seem so important. Besides, I had other things on my mind."

"This must be his mom," I said, showing the photo to Inspector Kill. "And him and his sister, the one who was abused on the train when they were children."

I repeated the story Parkwood had told us to Inspector Kill. His face looked grim.

"Marnie Orville," he said, pointing at Parkwood's mother, "does she look like this woman?"

"A little," I said. "Both tall, both blonde."

"And both traveling with children," Ernie added.

* * *

Once we were in the air, the chopper pilot flew low, following the track of the Blue Line. Mr. Kill was tense. He didn't like flying and avoided it whenever possible. Eventually we caught up with the train, moving past Kyongju, the ancient capital city of the Silla Dynasty.

Inspector Kill ordered the pilot to take us to the East Taegu station, the next stop on the Blue Train's itinerary, with all due haste. He had a plan. I listened. Ernie and I would board the train in Taegu. Alone. The Korean National Police, meanwhile, would not try to board the train in Taegu because they had not yet mustered their forces and Inspector Kill was worried that a haphazard operation might scare Parkwood away. He was a resourceful criminal, according to Kill, and at the first hint of police gathering, he would flee. How long it would take us to find him then was anybody's guess; but while we searched for him, he could cause a lot of damage.

"We have to assume," Kill told us, "that Parkwood will try for Marnie Orville, and if he does, we have to catch him today, while he's still panicked and on the run. There can be no mistakes."

So the plan was for me and Ernie to board the Blue Train in Taegu, keep a low profile while the train was rolling, and then, as we approached the next stop, Taejon, to search every compartment for Parkwood. Meanwhile, Inspector Kill would be waiting for us at Taejon, with an emergency team ready to surround the train and respond to any unforeseen contingencies.

"Are you armed?" he asked.

I showed him my .45.

Inspector Kill nodded approvingly.

Of the four stops along the route of the Blue Train—Pusan, East Taegu, Taejon, and finally Seoul—East Taegu is the most bustling, second only to the Seoul Station itself. It's a large station, monumental in its concrete dimensions. As the Blue Train huffed and chugged its way into the station, four or five dozen people stood on the loading platform, holding tickets, waiting to board. None of them was Parkwood.

Ernie and I waited under a dark awning. Steam blew out of the sides of the Blue Train and it finally came to a halt.

"Did you see Marnie?" Ernie asked.

"Not yet. The windows are all fogged."

"She has to be in there."

A few dozen people filed off of the Blue Train. As soon as they had pushed their way onto the platform, the new passengers holding tickets started to board. Ernie and I waited until the last minute—when the Blue Train started to roll forward—to sprint to the train and hop on. We took a seat in the last car, one arranged for us by Inspector Kill. At first we did nothing, just stared ahead at the sea of black-haired Koreans in front of us.

The uniformed conductor came by and punched holes in our tickets. The stewardess smiled as she walked by but didn't make eye contact. A vendor came by with a tray strapped around narrow shoulders, selling dried cuttlefish and ginseng gum and tins of imported guava juice.

Ernie fidgeted in his seat. I closed my eyes and tried to breathe deeply.

* * *

I felt bad about the rape of Mrs. Oh Myong-ja, the first victim, and worse yet about the rape and murder of Mrs. Hyon Mi-sook, especially considering that her children were forced to huddle in the bathtub while she was systematically humiliated and then sliced to death. But those were crimes that I had no personal hand in, crimes that would have been impossible for me to prevent. The murder that bothered me most was the murder of Specialist Vance, the young technician who worked at the Mount Halla Communications Center.

"We shouldn't have left him there alone," I told Ernie.

"Bull," Ernie replied. "At the time, we had no way of knowing Parkwood was the killer."

"Sure we did."

"How?"

I explained it to him. First the stalker of the Country Western All Stars. We hadn't taken the musicians' complaints particularly seriously, assuming they were random acts. But what had disappeared was a microphone, a pair of the bass player's underwear, and finally a lone cowboy boot. All three of those things were among the piled-up junk in the G.I. living quarters on Mount Halla.

"That could've been coincidence," Ernie replied. "And anyway, how were you going to pick them out?"

"And the checklists," I continued. "When you work at a remote signal site, your life centers around checklists: maintenance checklists, communications checklists, electronics checklists. That's all you do, hour after hour. Day after day."

"Parkwood had checklists on the brain, you're saying," Ernie said.

"And he was about to be barred from reenlistment for lousy performance on an IG inspection," I said. "He knew things had been going wrong for too long there at the Mount Halla commo site. He'd never correct it all."

The third reason I should have known was by Vance's demeanor. He was frightened, covering up the unscheduled absences of his partner even though he himself claimed never to go to the ville.

And finally, Parkwood had tried to run us off the road.

"Maybe he's just a bad driver," Ernie replied. "There's plenty of them around."

To Ernie, whatever happened, happened. No sense stewing about it. No sense blaming ourselves.

A half hour north of Taegu, rice paddies started to give way to woodland. The Blue Train was rising into the Sobaik Mountains. Once we reached the summit, we'd be on our way down into the broad valley that held the city of Taejon. It was then, during our descent, that Inspector Kill had instructed us to begin our search. That way, by the time the train pulled into the Taejon Station, Parkwood—if he was aboard—would be in a panic. He'd flee from the train, right into the arms of the waiting Korean National Police.

Inspector Kill's plan, however, didn't take into account the possibility that if Parkwood was on this train, he might harm someone—particularly Marnie—before we *reached* Taejon. Ernie and I felt that we couldn't wait any longer. We started our search.

For the moment, we didn't check the rear baggage compartment. We wanted to check the people in their seats first. Ernie waited at the end of each passenger car, ready to provide cover, while I walked down the center aisle, slowly working my way forward. I took my time, making sure that Parkwood wasn't lying in between two seats or hadn't ducked down to avoid us.

Was he carrying a weapon? I doubted it. Not firearms, at least. In Korea, there's no such thing as a convenient gun shop to stop in and pick yourself up a Saturday night special. If Parkwood were armed, it would be with a knife or a club or a straight razor. Still, since Parkwood not only kept himself in good shape but had also proven himself to be ruthless, we had to be careful.

The Korean passengers stared up at me curiously as I passed. Some of the men frowned. Occasionally, a woman smiled. For the most part, I was glanced at and then ignored.

In the third car forward from the rear, there were a few American passengers. Some of them were reading, some of them trying to catch some shut-eye. None of them was Parkwood. One was a private first class wearing his khaki uniform, munching on the contents of a can of potato sticks. A brown leather briefcase was handcuffed to his wrist. I sat down.

"You the courier?"

He nodded to me, mouth open, lips still moist with flakes of pulverized potato. His name tag said Arguello.

"*De donde eres?*" I asked him. Where you from?

He told me. Someplace in Texas.

I described Parkwood to him. He said he hadn't seen anyone like that.

"Were you watching?" I asked.

He shook his head warily. "No. This is a pretty boring job. I just read." He glanced at a stack of comic books.

"Okay, partner," I said, rising to my feet. "Don't overdo the potato sticks."

Ernie and I continued to search the train.

We worked our way through the three rear passenger cars until we reached the dining car. I found the head cook and explained the situation to him; he claimed he'd seen no American man who matched the description I gave him. By now, the conductor had gotten wind of what we were up to, and he joined us. I showed him my badge and explained why we were here. He nodded gravely. They'd already been notified by the KNPs that two American detectives would be on the train.

I asked him if he'd seen anyone who matched Parkwood's description. He said he couldn't be sure. There were a number of Americans scattered throughout the train, and he really hadn't paid much attention. The only Americans who were attracting attention were the tall blonde and the small girl sitting up front in passenger car number two.

"When did you last see them?" I asked in Korean.

"Only five minutes ago," he replied.

"Are they all right?"

"Fine. Except the little girl doesn't like guava juice."

"Can't blame her for that," Ernie said, understanding what the conductor said.

* * *

We continued to search the train. The bathrooms were located at the end of each car, near the door that led to the open-air walkway. We checked each one. If it was occupied, we lingered until it was vacated, just to make sure that Parkwood wasn't hiding inside. After all, he'd used a Blue Train bathroom as the venue for his first outrage.

There was no doubt now that we'd passed the summit of the Sobaik Mountains. The train was visibly tilted downward, and at times it swerved to the right and to the left as it navigated treacherous terrain. Rain spattered the windows.

Oh, great, I thought. Just what we need. Another complication.

Finally, we entered Marnie's car. She and Casey were easy to spot. A patch of blonde and a wisp of brown in the midst of monotonous rows of straight black hair. When we reached her row, I knelt and said hello. Casey's brown locks were puffed into a curly bouffant. She stared at me with bright, amber-tinted eyes.

"I'll be damned," Marnie said. "What are you doing here?"

I tipped an imaginary cowboy hat. "Just providing service, ma'am."

"You think I can't take care of myself?"

"I *know* you can take care of yourself. But the Eighth Army honchos think you're just a helpless flower of the prairie."

"'Flower of the prairie.' I like that. Make a good country song."

She twisted in her seat. Ernie, standing in the back, grinned and waved at her.

"Oh God," Marnie said, rubbing her temples.

"Who's that, Mommy?" Casey asked.

"Never mind, honey. You boys aren't going to be hanging around us, are you?"

"No. We're just walking through the train, doing our routine security check. And when we get to Seoul, we have to escort you to the hotel."

"Like hell."

"Eighth Army will provide a sedan."

"With a driver?"

"The best."

Marnie Orville didn't like risking her life in a speeding tin-can taxicab any more than anyone else did.

"In that case," she said, smiling, "I accept."

"If you need anything, you just whistle," I said.

Marnie pointed her forefinger at me as if it were a pistol and winked. "You got it."

I waved good-bye to Casey. She waved back.

Ernie and I finished checking the passenger cars. No sign of Parkwood. Up ahead, a locked metal door was marked *Chulip Kumji*. No Admittance. Even on this side, the big engines vibrated.

"Parkwood's not on the train," Ernie said.

"Maybe not," I said. "But we haven't checked everywhere."

"Not up here," Ernie said.

I stared at the locked metal door. "No. And we still need to look at the rear storage compartment. And behind that, there's a caboose."

"That's for the crew, isn't it? Their break room."

"Maybe so. I'm not sure. Let's find out."

We marched steadily back down the aisles, smiling at Marnie and Casey as we passed. On the way, we policed up the conductor and told him what we wanted. He accompanied us to the rear of the train.

The rain was coming down harder now, and on either side of us rice paddies had started to appear, along with the occasional tile-roofed farmhouse. Taejon wouldn't be far now.

The conductor led us to the storage compartment. As we entered, two older men in blue smocked uniforms stood to their feet. They were skinny men but wiry, and the conductor spoke to them respectfully, asking if there'd been any foreigners back here during this run. They shook their heads but were cooperative when Ernie and I asked to search the car anyway. Packages and crates were stacked neatly on rows of wooden shelving. Ernie and I checked under and behind them. Nothing. We asked to be shown the caboose. It was empty except for some communications equipment and what the conductor told me was an emergency generator, to be used if the train were ever stranded in a snowy mountain pass and had to create its own electricity. Again, there was no sign of Parkwood. Just to be sure, Ernie stepped out on the rear platform. Once there, he stared at the track behind us, raised both arms in the air, and said, "My friends and fellow Americans!"

"What the hell are you doing, Ernie?"

"Harry Truman started this way, didn't he?"

"Come on. Let's check on Marnie."

Before we reached the dining car, we heard screams. Female screams. Then we were running, and the high-pitched woman's voice became more distinct. I recognized it immediately.

Marnie Orville.

19

"**S**he's gone!" Marnie screamed when we reached her car. "Casey's gone!"

I checked the seat. Marnie was right. No sign of her daughter Casey.

"Calm down," I said. "Tell me what happened."

People were standing, kneeling on their seats or milling in the aisles, keeping a respectful distance from the tall, blonde, hysterical woman.

"I went to the bathroom," Marnie said. "Just for a minute. I tried to take Casey with me, but she refused. Said it was too stinky. She can be stubborn when she wants to be, and I didn't want her to make a scene. So I left her here and told her not to budge an inch from that seat."

And then Marnie was crying, her words indecipherable now. I should have warned her that Parkwood might be on the train, but at the time I hadn't wanted to alarm her. A mistake. But too late now.

I turned to the Korean passengers staring at us. "Did anyone see anything?" I asked in Korean. "Did you see where the little girl went?"

People looked at one another. One woman finally spoke up.

"I think she got out of her seat and went that way." She pointed toward the front of the train.

"No!" another passenger said vehemently. "She went *that* way," she insisted, pointing toward the rear. "I thought she was going to join her mother."

"Yes." Many people nodded, agreeing with the second woman, maybe because she was older.

I grabbed Marnie by her shoulders. "Look at me. Was this the first time you'd gone to the bathroom without her?"

Marnie looked away.

"Don't be ashamed. I need facts."

"No," she said. "Casey hated those bathrooms. She didn't like squatting down over the little toilet in the floor and she didn't like the fact that they were always out of toilet paper. She wouldn't go unless she was about to pee in her pants."

"So she'd been left alone before at some time during this train ride?"

Marnie nodded meekly. Then her body shuddered as if she had suddenly remembered something. She straightened her back and knocked my hands off her shoulders.

"Why are you interrogating me? Accusing me of not being a good mother? You should be searching for Casey. Search, goddamn you! Search!"

I hadn't been accusing her of being a poor mother, but this wasn't the time to argue.

"Ernie, you go to the front," I said. "I'll go to the back."

Ernie nodded.

I started off toward the rear. Without being asked, the conductor followed me.

By now the train was slowing and we were pulling into Taejon Station. I had already reached the rear. No sign of Casey. We'd checked every bathroom along the way and burst into the baggage compartment and searched once again. I'd even checked the wooden crates, pulling on them quickly, to see if they could be pried open. No luck. The caboose and the back platform were similarly empty.

I turned and ran back toward the front. Crossing from one car to another, I bumped into Ernie.

"Nothing up front," he said.

"Nor back here. Let's check on Marnie."

We ran down the aisles. The brakes of the big engine were catching now and steam hissed out of the sides of the train. Passengers stood, locating their bags in the overhead compartments.

"Did you check the overheads?"

"Yes. She's not there, unless somebody stuffed her into a freaking suitcase."

"Even that we'll have to check," I said.

Inspector Kill and maybe a couple of squads of KNPs would be waiting for us on the platform. I turned to the conductor. "We'll have to check all luggage," I said in haste and in a state of near panic. Just then, the train jerked and the brakes hissed louder than ever.

We entered Marnie's car. I sprinted forward. When I stopped, Ernie bumped into me. We both stared at an empty seat. I turned to the people around me.

"Where is she?" I asked.

In reply, I received a lot of blank looks. I repeated the question in Korean.

People shook their heads. They hadn't been watching her. An elderly man stepped forward.

"I'm not sure where she went," he told me. "But I noticed after you left that she searched in her daughter's traveling bag. She pulled out a piece of paper, like a note, and unfolded it and read it. It was pink paper with a drawing on it for children. Shortly after that, she picked up her bag and left."

The train shuddered to a halt. People started filing toward the doors. I wiped steam off the window and stared outside. No sign of the KNPs. Inspector Kill was probably farther back, keeping his men hidden, waiting for Parkwood to make a move. And then I saw her, carrying an overnight bag slung over her shoulder. Her head was down, and she moved through the crowd quickly.

"There she is!" I shouted.

Ernie peered out the window. "She's alone."

We ran toward the front of the car. A man in grease-stained overalls was hurrying down the aisle toward us. He shouted at the conductor. We stopped. Apparently he was one of the engineers who worked up front.

"We heard about the missing child," he said to the

conductor, speaking rapid Korean. "I'm not sure what it means, but I thought I would tell you. When one of our young assistants came out back, just after we left Taegu, a foreigner slipped in with us up there. He smiled and acted very friendly and used sign language to indicate that he was interested in the engines and how we conducted our business. Occasionally people come up there and if they don't cause too much trouble we let them watch. And also, he was a foreigner, and who knew how he'd react if we told him to leave. Maybe it was a mistake, but we let him stay."

The conductor nodded. I wanted to tell the engineer to get to the point but knew that my interruption would only slow things down. The engineer continued.

"He stayed up there with us the entire ride. Finally, he came out, back here, and when he returned he pounded on the door and we let him back in. This time, he had a foreign girl with him and he acted like he wanted to show her the engine and the controls and such, but she seemed frightened and just stared at the ground. He laughed and tried to coax her into having fun, but she would have none of it. Finally, just before we pulled into Taejon, he opened the door, peeked outside, and then pulled the girl out with him, almost running."

"Where did he go?" I asked.

"Onto the platform. After that, who knows?"

Outside, there was no sign of Marnie. And no sign of Parkwood, and no sign of Casey.

I went to the train station's KNP office and asked for

Inspector Kill; but instead of helping me contact him as I expected, the officers on duty acted strangely reluctant.

"What's wrong?" I asked in Korean. "Inspector Kill said he'd be here, waiting, with police officers to help us."

"He will be along," one of them said.

More entreaties yielded no further information.

Ernie and I walked toward the center of the open lobby of the huge domed station. "What's going on?" Ernie asked. "It's almost as if they're trying to help *him*."

"Yeah. Parkwood with Casey in tow would've been easy to spot. Even by a rookie cop. They should've collared him before he took ten steps off the train."

"How the hell did he pull it off?" Ernie asked.

"Parkwood suspected that we, or somebody, would be on the train searching for him. After he made it from Kuangju to Taegu, he bought a ticket; and shortly after boarding the train, he bullied his way into the engineer's compartment."

Americans have a strange power in Korea. People know that we helped them during the war, and they know that their self-defense and economic growth are dependent on American wealth and American military might, so they treat us with great tolerance. G.I.s are like 300-pound gorillas that wander into genteel front parlors. Everyone knows that the burly primate won't cause too much trouble as long as he's fed bananas, kept well diapered, and allowed to do whatever the hell he wants to do.

"So Parkwood waited up front until the train had almost reached Taejon," Ernie said. "Then he came out, snatched Casey, and left a note of some kind for Marnie."

"Right. While we were searching the train, she read the

note, and it probably told her to meet him someplace and come alone."

Ernie looked around. "So why in hell isn't Inspector Kill here?"

Just as he said that, a squad of uniformed KNPs entered the front door of the station. Ahead of them, wearing a suit and a long brown raincoat, strode Inspector Gil Kwon-up.

Ernie crossed his arms and glared sullenly at Kill.

"Sorry I'm late, gentlemen," Inspector Kill said when he reached us, but, strangely enough, he was smiling.

"Parkwood took off," I told him, "with the little girl Casey and Marnie Orville, the mother, following. We don't know where they are."

"Why are you late?" Ernie asked.

"Unforeseen circumstances," Kill said.

Ernie studied him. "So why are you so happy?"

"Because," he said, "the stewardess on the Blue Train is a very observant and astute young woman."

"What do you mean?"

"She found this, she gave it to the conductor, and the conductor gave it to one of our representatives." Between his thumb and his forefinger, Kill was holding a folded piece of pink paper. "And now," Kill said ceremoniously, "I present it to you."

Ernie snatched the note out of his hand, unfolded it, read it, and handed it to me.

A fat-cheeked kitten smiled out of one corner. The note was scribbled in English: "Come alone. Casey's with me. Bathhouse number three on the Gapcheon River."

I handed the note back to Kill. "Where's that?"

"A resort area, north of the city."

"Do you have transportation?"

"Waiting," he said, waving his arm toward the front of the station. "At your service."

We hurried out of the station to a row of blue police vans.

The rain had let up a bit, just a heavy mist now, but the banks of the Gapcheon River were completely deserted. During the summer, refugees from the city of Taejon spend the day basking in the sun and frolicking in the cool waters of the rapidly flowing stream. A few miles north, the Gapcheon joins the much larger Geum River, which eventually makes its way to the Yellow Sea. The beach is long and flat with a gravel-like sand, and the water is choppy and fast-flowing but relatively shallow. A bather has to wade at least a hundred yards offshore until the water reaches six feet in depth.

Bathhouses are popular in Korean resort areas. The idea is to swim in the river or the lake and then take a hot shower and a steam bath and, if you can afford it, enjoy a full-body massage. Also, there are places to change your clothes and rent swimsuits if you didn't bring one with you. It was in one of these establishments that Parkwood had set up his rendezvous.

Our convoy of a half-dozen police vehicles pulled up along the deserted road that paralleled the river, parked, and stopped. We stared at bathhouse number three. No movement. It appeared to be deserted.

Ernie started to get out of the car. Inspector Kill told him to stay.

"Why?" Ernie asked. "What are we waiting for?"

"For Parkwood to come out," Inspector Kill replied.

"Come out? Marnie could be in there. He could be hurting her."

Inspector Kill didn't answer him. He just sat quietly in the front passenger seat. Ernie looked at me.

"I don't know about you guys, but I'm going in there."

Ernie climbed out of the car. I climbed out with him.

Reluctantly, Mr. Kill got out of the car too. All the uniformed KNPs stayed in their vehicles, awaiting Mr. Kill's orders.

Calmly, Mr. Kill took off his raincoat. He folded it and set it on the seat inside the sedan. Then he took off his jacket and undid his tie. Finally, he slipped off his shoes.

Ernie stared at him, dumbfounded.

"You gonna take a swim?"

"If I have to," Kill replied. "When you flush Parkwood out, please send him in my direction."

Ernie squinted at Kill, trying to understand his strange behavior, but finally gave up. He turned and started marching across the thick gravel. I followed. Footsteps crunched as we approached bathhouse number three. On this side, there were no windows: the entranceway faced the river. Ernie unholstered his .45. With his free hand, he pointed for me to take the left side of the building; he would take the right. We met out front.

Quietly, Ernie trotted up the wooden steps. He tried the door. Locked.

Behind us, the Gapcheon River rolled serenely as it had rolled for centuries. Crows cawed and swooped low. Ernie leaned back, raised his right foot, and kicked the door in.

The interior was dark. Wood planks squeaked beneath our feet. The bathhouse smelled of incense but also of some herb I couldn't quite place. Laurel leaves, maybe, like the ancient Greeks used in their baths. One dim bulb shone at the end of the hallway. Doors lined either side. As we passed, we opened them and checked each small cubicle: a body-length table, a work bench, and empty towel racks. No Marnie. No Cascy. No Parkwood.

Finally, we reached the end of the hall. A door was open to a much larger room, tiled for showers. Spigots stuck out of cement walls. Casey was squatting, partially hidden, next to some wooden shelving narrow enough to hold slippers. I crouched next to her. She appeared to be all right physically, but her hands and her head rested on her knees. She wouldn't look up. Marnie sat alone on the far side of the room. Her blouse and her blue jeans were ripped all to hell. She was doing her best to put them back on, but various parts kept slipping off her voluptuous body. Finally, she gave up and, almost naked, threw the clothing to the floor.

"Don't look at me like that!" she screamed. Ernie and I stared at her. "I did it because I had to, to save my daughter."

I nodded slowly. Ernie's .45 was out. He wasn't staring at Marnie anymore, or even at Casey. He scanned the room, moving from side to side, sliding back plastic curtains in the private stalls.

"Yes," Marnie screeched, answering a question we hadn't asked. "Casey was watching. He wouldn't let her leave the room."

"Where is he?" I asked.

Marnie stared at me as if she didn't know who I was talking about.

"Where is Parkwood?" I repeated.

"That's his name?" she said softly.

Clearly, Marnie Orville was still in shock. After the fright of having her daughter kidnapped, of being raped in a tile shower room, who could blame her?

I asked again, softly, "Where did he go, Marnie?"

Casey raised her little arm. "He went that way," she said.

Her finger pointed to the right. Ernie hurried over and at the end of the row of private showers found a door that was hidden from view. He shoved it open. It led down a short hallway.

"Don't leave us!" Marnie shrieked.

Ernie glanced back at me, as if to ask, "Are you staying?"

I nodded.

He took off into the darkness.

I did my best to help Marnie cover herself, ripping down one of the shower curtains as an overgarment. Casey soon made her way to her mom, and the two began hugging each other. Casey was crying and Marnie was crying. I was glad to see the tears: it meant she was coming back to herself.

I asked if they felt well enough to follow me, and they both nodded. With me in the lead, we entered the dark hallway Ernie had gone down. After about ten paces, it led down a wooden stairwell that twisted back on itself. The basement was dark, but a yellow light shone at the far side.

"I don't want to go in there," Marnie said. "Let's go back."

"Come on, Mommy," Casey said. "Ernie's all alone."

Somehow she'd picked up his name. I patted her on the head. Marnie nodded her consent and we crossed the dark cellar. Halfway through, Marnie screamed. I turned and saw a long tail scurrying off behind wooden crates.

"Mommy," Casey said. "It's only a mouse."

A rat, to be exact, but I didn't correct her. When we reached the far door, I peered into the yellow-lit room. It was storage: giant beach umbrellas, inflatable rafts, boxes filled with rubber flippers. I took a few steps inside. Marnie and Casey followed. One of the boxes fell, dumping a gaggle of squiggling things onto the ground. I leaped back. Marnie screamed. Casey leaned down and picked one up.

"They're only goggles," she said, holding one up to the light.

I felt foolish, but there was no time for embarrassment.

On the far side of the storage room, a door let out into another room streaming with sunlight. A service counter. In front of that, a small foyer and then plate-glass windows. Printed on the windows were the words in hangul:

Bathhouse Number Three, Rentals. Stupidly, I was proud that I could read the sign backward.

But when we stepped around the counter, I lost my sense of pride. I heard a shout outside. And then a gunshot.

Ernie stood on the river side of bathhouse number three, his .45 held straight out in front of him, taking aim on a man running toward the beach.

"Halt!" Ernie shouted.

When the man didn't stop, Ernie fired off another shot. The round flew ineffectually into the far bank.

"He's out of range, Ernie," I said.

"I know that."

He holstered his pistol and was about to take off in pursuit when engines behind us roared to life. In seconds, a fleet of blue KNP sedans went flying across the gravelly sand, heading toward the Gapcheon River.

"They're cutting him off," Ernie said.

Marnie and Casey stood behind us. The rain had started again, and drops pattered against the plastic curtain that Marnie held over herself and Casey.

We watched as the sedans sped across the sand like a phalanx of hounds, spinning around on the slick surface some fifty yards in front of Parkwood. He stopped, turned, and started running back toward us.

Slowly, regally, Mr. Kill strode barefoot across the beach. When he was about ten yards away from us, he pointed and said, "Take the women back to that car. There's a female officer there."

A smart-looking woman, wearing the neat blouse,

skirt, and cap of the Korean National Police, stood at attention next to a sedan. Marnie didn't need any more encouragement than that. She grabbed Casey and, keeping the shower curtain wrapped tightly around her, the two of them almost ran toward the road.

Kill sauntered casually toward the flowing water. Parkwood was heading right at him. Something was in Parkwood's hand.

"What is it?" Ernie asked. Then he answered his own question. "A straight razor."

Suddenly, I was worried for Kill's safety. "Is he armed?"

"I don't think so," Ernie replied.

The two men were closing on one another. Clearly, the intent of the officers driving the sedans had been to drive Parkwood back to Inspector Kill. Their plan was working. Parkwood had run out of options. He had nowhere to go. But as he approached, it was clear from the perspiration pouring from his forehead and the clenched look of his face and the way he gripped the straight razor in his right fist that this was a man who wouldn't go down without a fight.

I started toward Inspector Kill.

From out of nowhere, two blue-uniformed KNPs stepped in front of me. One of them held out his palm. "Inspector Kill," the man said in English, "wishes to interrogate the suspect on his own."

"The man has a straight razor," I said, pointing.

Their faces remained impassive. "We know that," one of them said.

"What are you?" Ernie asked. "The Bobbsey Twins? Parkwood's going to cut Inspector Kill's spleen out."

Ernie stepped forward. With a deft move, one of the

officers punched him in the stomach. Ernie grabbed his gut and bent over. I shoved the officer. The two men stepped back.

"You didn't have to do that!" I shouted.

Two more officers joined them. The four men stood between Ernie and me and the sea, resolutely. Ernie and I could fight them, sure; but even if we gained the upper hand, we'd never reach Kill in time. Whatever would happen between Parkwood and Inspector Kill was about to happen. No one would interfere.

I turned to Ernie. "You okay?"

"Okay. You think that little turd could hurt *me*?"

If the KNP knew what the word "turd" meant, his face didn't show it.

Parkwood was now just a few feet from Inspector Kill.

Taekwondo, literally the path of kicking and punching, is a national passion in Korea. Korea's practitioners of martial arts are some of the most accomplished in the world. Still, martial arts aren't magic. A desperate man with a dangerous weapon is not something to be taken lightly. The correct response, when confronted with a man as desperate as Parkwood, is to take him down with overwhelming force. If you can't do that, if it is either you or him, you have to kill him immediately, using whatever method possible, whether it be a shotgun blast to the face or a vicious knife-thrust to the throat. To take him on man to man, in the spirit of martial fairness, is not only piss-poor police work, it is ludicrous. But, apparently, that is exactly what Inspector Kill planned to do.

When they closed, Parkwood was wary. He knew this was too good to be true. He suspected Kill was going to try some trick. He swiped the straight razor at Kill's face a couple of times, but Kill barely moved back at all, only an inch or two, just enough to avoid the blade. Parkwood glanced around, seeing us standing in front of bathhouse number three, the KNPs staying back either on the road or next to their sedans. The situation was clear to everyone: Kill was offering to take him on, one on one.

As if the satisfaction of the moment had finally settled in, Parkwood smiled. He knew he wasn't going to get away, but he could at least take a cop down with him—a Korean cop at that. He slashed again at Inspector Kill. More viciously this time. Kill backed away and backed away and backed away again. Parkwood thrust forward a little faster each time. Just as the repetitive movements were attaining a rhythm of their own, Kill sidestepped, moved in, and kicked the back of Parkwood's knee, forcing him to stumble to the ground.

I expected Kill to attack then and knock Parkwood unconscious, to finish this thing. But he didn't. Ernie stood in rapt attention, as did all the cops on the beach. I was uncomfortable. Everybody else seemed to be enjoying themselves immensely.

Parkwood leaped to his feet, angry. He came at Kill with the blade swinging back and forth, cautious now, not going to be fooled again by the sudden sidestep. Kill backed away, circling. It became apparent that Kill was leading Parkwood where he wanted him to go. They stumbled into the shallow waters of the river and then back out again. Parkwood was wet now, more angry than ever, rapidly becoming exhausted. As if realizing he was being played for the fool, he stopped. Above the roar of the surf, I thought I heard him growl at Inspector Kill: "Come on." He waved the blade toward his own body, as if inviting Kill to come and get it.

Kill did. He darted forward, like a mongoose tempting a cobra.

The blade flashed out but missed again. Kill darted in and then out, again and again. Parkwood kept missing but refused to chase, a smart move on his part. Within seconds, realizing that his gambit to get Parkwood to follow again wasn't working, Kill stepped in so close to the blade that I held my breath. Even Ernie gasped.

The blade flashed out, slicing into Inspector Kill's shoulder. Surprised, Parkwood stared after him. Kill gazed down. Crimson blood rushed out along the slice in his white shirt. Angry, Kill approached again but backed up more quickly this time. Parkwood was smiling now, enjoying the flush of this victory. He started to follow. Again, Kill led him into the water, back out of the water, the blade missing his body by only fractions of an inch, but Parkwood was committed now. His strength was leaving him; even in the misting rain, the perspiration poured freely off his forehead, and his arms and legs seemed to be getting heavy. That's when Inspector Kill struck. Like a sudden flash of lightning in a dark night, he stood his ground when Parkwood came at him and plowed a right fist into Parkwood's charging forehead.

Parkwood staggered. Kill backed up, allowing him room to fall, but Parkwood didn't go down. He regained his footing and leaped at Kill, the blade slashing in front of him. Instead of backing up out of reach, Kill raised his left foot and slammed it into Parkwood's face. They fell into the water, Kill on top, pummeling Parkwood—and then suddenly Parkwood was on top.

Involuntarily, all the KNPs took two steps forward. Then one of them shouted for everyone to maintain their positions. They did as they were told.

Parkwood bent over Kill, apparently with both hands wrapped around Inspector Kill's neck, but I couldn't be sure because Inspector Kill was fully underwater. And then suddenly, Parkwood leaped up as if he'd been electrocuted. When we saw the reason why, Ernie grunted. The sole of Kill's foot had kicked straight up, ramming into Parkwood's groin, lifting him into the air. Kill exploded out of the water now, his face a mask of rage. He leaped on Parkwood.

Suddenly, I knew what would happen. I knew what this was all about. I knew why Inspector Kill was called the best homicide investigator in Korea. I knew now that he not only solved the cases he'd been assigned to, but he also brought them to trial and brought them to judgment and brought them to execution. Like a Confucian scholar of old, a sage schooled in the Four Books and the Five Classics, that was his right. His right to be judge, jury, and executioner. His right as a *chunja*, a superior man.

I ran forward, shoving the two KNPs out of my way, shouting.

"Don't! Don't do it! Halt!"

I fumbled inside my jacket for my .45, but the holster kept rising up with the pistol, not setting it free.

Mr. Kill leaned over Parkwood now, holding the larger

man's head underwater, the muscles on Kill's forearms bulging with the strain. He didn't hear me. He didn't hear anything.

Finally, I freed the .45 and fired a round into the air.

Kill looked up. Awareness entered his eyes. He looked down at his hands, as if realizing for the first time that they were underwater, as if realizing for the first time that they were clutching Parkwood's throat. Quickly, he rose to his feet and stepped backward, away from Parkwood.

Parkwood didn't move.

I shoved the .45 back in my holster and splashed into the river. When I reached Parkwood, I shoved Kill out of the way and leaned down and pulled Parkwood's heavy body toward shore. Ernie helped me. We finally laid him out on the moist sand, and I bent down and cleared his air passage while Ernie loosened his belt and pants. Then Ernie shoved down on his stomach. We turned him over and tried to get as much water out of his lungs as we could, but within seconds we had him flat on his back again and I breathed air into his mouth. His chest rose. I did this three times, and then Ernie pumped his stomach again and I breathed into his lungs three times more.

We did this for a long time.

The rain stopped.

Finally, red-tinted toenails stood in front of me. I looked up. It was Marnie Orville, the plastic shower curtain still wrapped around her shoulders.

"He's dead, George," she said. "Stop now. Stop, please."
She was crying.

I looked down at Parkwood. Marnie was right. He was dead now. And he'd been dead for a long time.

20

Marnie Orville and Captain Freddy Ray Embry got back together.

After he heard what had happened, Freddy Ray rushed up to Seoul and told Marnie that he was sorry for all the things he'd done and he asked for another chance. For Casey's sake, she told us, Marnie forgave him. They were remarried in a military chapel at Camp Henry with a bunch of Freddy Ray's fellow officers wearing their dress blue uniforms and holding silver swords crossed overhead as the happy couple emerged from the chapel.

Casey was the flower girl.

Ernie studied the marriage photos and grinned. "I done good."

"You done *good*?" I said. "You almost broke up their marriage forever."

Ernie's grin broadened. "You really don't understand women, do you, Sueño? If it hadn't been for me, Marnie never could've made Freddy Ray jealous and Casey would've had to grow up without her daddy."

We were in the CID admin office. Staff Sergeant Riley was ignoring us, shuffling through the small mountain of paperwork that had built up while he was gone. I decided not to push it. If Ernie was happy with what he'd done, then let him be happy.

Miss Kim, meanwhile, had stopped typing on her hangul typewriter and stared at Ernie in utter astonishment.

The 8th Army honchos were also happy with what we'd done. For once. The Blue Train rapist had indeed turned out to be an American G.I.; but by the time that was fully revealed to the Korean public, the guy was already dead, and dead at the hands of a man, Inspector Gil Kwon-up, who was now a bigger national hero than ever. Of course, the official line was that Parkwood had been killed inadvertently while resisting arrest—and, in a way, that was true. If the guy had just given up and hadn't insisted on waving that straight razor around, he'd still be with us today.

I wrote a letter to Specialist Vance's mother, telling her what a wonderful man he'd been and telling her that even though I'd only worked with him briefly, he'd proven himself to be a courageous soldier and he'd died fighting.

Back on that beach on Cheju Island, Staff Sergeant Warnocki had tied a tourniquet around his own leg and dragged himself to the main road, where a Good Samaritan picked him up and rushed him to the nearest medical clinic. He fully recovered from his wounds and was now back training troops on the slopes of Mount Halla.

When he made his occasional appearance at the 8th Army officers' club, Lieutenant Colonel Ambrose Q. Laurel was asked about the case, but the word was that he was reluctant to talk about our adventure at sea. He was ashamed that Parkwood had gotten away with as much as he did, right under the noses of his Special Forces troops. And maybe he was also ashamed that we'd had to be saved by the haenyo.

The Country Western All Stars returned to the States. I had intended to ask Shelly out for coffee, but, after returning from Taejon, I was so busy that somehow I never got the chance.

21

Maybe it was what I'd seen on the banks of the Gapcheon River that made me change my mind about the fragment I'd given to Inspector Kill. Within twenty-four hours of leaving Taejon, I had already wrangled a chopper flight back to Hialeah Compound. I took a cab to the Pusan Police Station, and when I walked down the long hallway, nobody challenged me. The door to Inspector Kill's temporary office was open. I entered and shut the door behind me. The safe was locked. It was an old safe, big and black, made in Germany, probably thirty or forty years old. A survivor of the Korean War and of World War II.

I knelt in front of the safe and twisted the knob.

I'm not a safecracker, but I do know something about human psychology. And I know something about Koreans. Even the best of them is superstitious. On that day when Inspector Kill was changing the combination to his safe, I had barged in on him. After I left, he must've continued with what he was doing. What combination would he choose? Something easy to remember, certainly. I changed the letters of my name to their corresponding numbers in the English alphabet: 19 for S, 21 for U, and so on. On the fourth number, the safe clicked open.

I pulled the fragment out, stuck it in my pocket, and relocked the safe.

Life was just starting to return to normal—mainly to busting Korean dependent housewives for selling instant coffee on the black market—and I wanted a second opinion as to what the fragment was all about.

I asked Mrs. Pei, my Korean-language teacher, to refer me to someone who could help me understand more about it. She called a man who had once been a professor of hers, and he consented to talk to me. It was a dark night when I found his address high on a hill in the Sodaemun district of Seoul. A maid let me into a rosebush-covered courtyard, and then I was ushered into a sitting room furnished with Victorian artifacts.

Professor Lim was an elderly man wearing silk hanbok with a wistful smile and only a few strands of silver hair left on a liver-spotted skull. I explained as much as I could about what the merchant marine had told me, and then I handed him the fragment. As he fondled the ancient document, he held his breath. He slipped on reading glasses, consulted an old volume in a small library in an adjacent room, and finally, after mumbling to himself for a long while, looked up at me.

"You gave this to the authorities?"

"Briefly. Then I took it back from them."

He told me that this fragment was part of an ancient manuscript long rumored to exist but often discounted by certain scholars as a myth. "Its value," he told me, "cannot be calculated."

That part, I already knew.

The following weekend, I hopped on the free army bus to Munsan. From there, I took a cab to the fishing village of Heiyop-ni. They didn't see many foreigners here, but no one followed me as I climbed a winding path to the top of a hill. The grounds were spotted with ancient burial mounds. Beneath a small clump of elms, I sat on yellow grass and stared out into the mouth of the Imjin River.

There were a few rocky islands in the distance; and beyond those, in the mist, loomed the Communist dictatorship of North Korea. A woman I'd known, Doctor Yong In-ja, had gone that way, voluntarily, to escape charges of murder here in the South. I'd let her go, ignoring my duty as a law enforcement officer, rationalizing my actions by convincing myself that she didn't fall under my jurisdiction. I didn't regret having let her escape. My only regret was that I hadn't gone with her.

Now, apparently, she was trying to contact me. That's what the fragment had been about. She was in possession of a valuable manuscript, and she was willing to make a deal to turn it over to the South. Her price, apparently, would be to attain her freedom. Help in escaping from North Korea.

How I'd go about bargaining for that help, I didn't yet know.

The next morning, Riley was already in the office when I brought in two cups of coffee from the snack bar and plopped them on his desk.

"One's for you," I said.

"You win the Irish Sweepstakes?"

"No. I just felt generous."

Riley lifted the plastic lid, sipped on the hot java, and then said, "Were you in the safe earlier this morning?"

"No," I replied. "I just got here."

"Somebody was. They moved my receipt book."

I stood up. "Is the safe still open?"

"Yeah."

I walked over to the safe, swung back the heavy door, and looked inside. It was gone.

"I had a sealed envelope in here," I said, "marked Sueño. Did you take it out?"

"Not me," Riley said.

I sat back in front of his desk and drank my hot coffee. Before half of it was gone, I knew what had happened. Inspector Kill. He'd wanted the fragment back, he'd figured I was the one who took it, and now, somehow, he'd managed to get it back in his possession. I should never have showed it to him in the first place, but that was back when I trusted him.

What I would do next, I wasn't sure. Doctor Yong In-ja was a shrimp between warring whales. Somehow, the shrimp had to be saved.

Continue reading for a preview of the next
Sergeant George Sueño novel

THE JOY
BRIGADE

1

Yellow floodlights loomed out of thick fog. Atop the rickety wooden dock, soldiers paced.

"Red-star jokers," Mergim told me, squinting into the mist-laden night. "They inspect ship. After that everything okay. Maybe."

I leaned on a taut steel cable, gripping it tightly. The sea rumbled below: dark, listless, reeking of slimy death. We were five miles inside the Taedong River estuary in the Democratic People's Republic of Korea, or DPRK, better known as North Korea.

Mergim scratched his unshaven face, searching my eyes for signs of panic. Apparently, he found them. "Don't worry," he said, slapping me on the back. "I come here many times. Still alive." As if to demonstrate, he pinched the loose skin on the back of his hand. "You be okay." Then he turned back to the dock. "Maybe."

My name is George Sueño. I'm an agent for the Eighth United States Army Criminal Investigation Division in Seoul, South Korea. But now I was standing on the deck of an Albanian merchant freighter, a ship called the *Star of Tirana*. I was clad in unwashed woolen work pants, staring into the vast predawn darkness of communist North Korea, wondering if this entire operation had already been exposed and, more importantly, if I'd be tortured to death by those pacing red devils.

Mergim had briefed me on what would happen once we docked, and he was telling me again in an attempt to calm me. It wasn't working. My fear of North Koreans, "the enemy," ran too deep.

Concerned, Mergim reached into his dirty wool jacket and pulled out a green vial. He popped the cap. Grease-stained fingers held up a blue pill. "You want?"

I shook my head. If I were to survive, I would need my wits about me. I turned and stared at the dock, and the demons pacing upon it, willing myself to be calm. When a foghorn sounded, I nearly leapt off the edge of the boat.

"You okay?" Mergim asked, eyeing me.

"Okay," I said. The deck of the old merchant ship rolled slightly, or at least I thought it did.

"I go work," Mergim said. "You stay." He patted me on the shoulder. "Take deep breath. Don't think too much."

He turned and his soggy leather boots pounded down the iron-planked walkway.

When he was gone, I reached inside my crinkled canvas peacoat, making sure that my phony Peruvian passport was still folded into my inner pocket. I breathed deeply, willing myself toward calmness. The tart aroma of garlic wafted on the air. This country was definitely Korea, but a different Korea than I'd known.

My job here was clear. Once we were on dry land in this port city known as Nampo, I had to somehow make my way to the Nampo Southern Section People's Grain Warehouse. From weeks of studying aerial surveillance, I knew exactly where it was. The problem would be managing to evade our North Korean minders and slip away unseen from the area set aside for foreign merchant marines. Once I reached the grain warehouse—if I ever did—I'd be escorted elsewhere by a contact who would be waiting for me, a former soldier who went by the name of Hero Kang. That's all I knew about him. That and a password. If he betrayed me—or if Mergim betrayed me—I'd be lost in a world of pain. The North Koreans had tortured Americans before, most notably the crew of the USS *Pueblo*, a U.S. reconnaissance vessel captured on the high seas. The sailors had been beaten, hanged by their thumbs, left naked in their cells, and subjected to weeks of brutal interrogation. Those who survived the ordeal were released from captivity less than five years ago. The others were returned in coffins.

We docked with a thud. Sailors tossed thick ropes from the deck and dockhands scurried below to secure them. After a gangplank was lowered, uniformed men scrambled aboard—two squads, I figured—all of them armed with AK-47s.

The skipper of our little boat, Captain Skander, was already standing on deck. He had a long gray beard and a protruding belly, but in the glare of the overhead flood-lights he held himself like an admiral, shoulders thrust back. In my few days aboard, I'd developed loyalty for this ship and crew despite myself. The crew was mostly Alba-nians, and a smattering of other nationalities. I was proud that Captain Skander seemed so courageous amid this sea of swarming Korean Communists. Although I knew that Albanians were technically Communists themselves, these Albanians didn't seem like Communists. They seemed like workingmen on the sea—hustlers, all corrupt certainly, but okay guys.

North Koreans in brown uniforms and round helmets secured the deck, motioning for the crew to step back. We did. Finally, an officer climbed aboard. He was older than the other Koreans and had gold piping along the red epaulets lining his shoulder. He stepped toward Captain Skander and they conversed quietly. In English, I thought, because I caught a few words: ". . . inspection . . . contra-band . . . manifest . . ."

For most of the trip I'd been clueless about the chat-ter surrounding me because the main language spoken aboard was Albanian. In Kuala Lumpur, where I'd been sent by military intelligence to wait while they arranged my passage, three sailors from the *Star of Tirana* became unexpectedly sick only hours after they docked. Desper-ate for a strong back to help below with cargo, they'd hired me. I'd been aboard ship now for almost a month. We'd worked our way north along the Pacific coast of Asia, first to Hanoi, then Hong Kong, then Shanghai, and finally across the Yellow Sea to Nampo.

According to my passport, I was José Aracadio Medin,

an experienced cargo handler who'd been stranded in Kuala Lumpur after the owners of his previous ship had gone bankrupt. In fact, what I knew about working on the sea could fit into a tin teacup, but Mergim had been well paid to watch out for me and show me what to do—paid an additional stipend on the side, not by his ostensible employer but by someone who was in the employ of either the South Korean government or the United States government. Which one, I knew better than to ask.

All of this had been arranged. I never could have set it up myself.

The North Korean officer barked a command. The entire crew, along with Captain Skander, was herded into the forecastle. Then the armed North Koreans started a systematic search of the ship. The sailors grumbled, complaining because they'd been rousted out of their racks so quickly that they hadn't brought either cigarettes or matches. Despite their bellyaching, no one dared confront the armed boarding party. The captain sat down on an impromptu stool of wound hemp rope, looking resigned. It took the better part of two hours for the Koreans to complete their search. When they were done, Captain Skander was called across the deck to report to the North Korean officer.

As they talked, the Korean officer lit up a cigarette and held it with the tips of his fingers. He gazed into the still-dark sky. Apparently, accusations were made. Captain Skander waved his arms as he spoke. The North Korean officer didn't even bother to look at him.

Mergim, squatting beside me, tensed.

I wanted to ask what the problem was but resisted

the temptation because I didn't want to draw attention to myself. On this entire voyage I'd been as low-key as possible, making no friends among the crew except for Mergim. Mergim was in my work group, by design, and while on the job I mainly mimicked what he was doing. I wasn't sure if Captain Skander was privy to our charade. I hoped not. The fewer who knew that an American soldier was aboard this freighter, the better.

As the North Korean officer and Captain Skander argued, I regained my composure. This was beginning to look suspiciously like a shakedown. Maybe the North Korean customs officer and Captain Skander would haggle, a price would be settled upon and paid, and everyone would go about their business. That's what I thought back then. As I learned more about the DPRK, I would come to realize that nothing is ever simple.

Finally, the two men came to some sort of resolution. Captain Skander returned scowling.

Two armed Koreans emerged from below deck holding plastic packages wrapped in gauze tape. They set the packages on the deck. When their commander nodded, one of them pulled a knife from his belt and sliced open the first package. He held a pinch of the brownish powder up to the light. The commander asked where he'd found it, and the soldier replied. Other than the Koreans themselves, I was probably the only man on deck who understood them. They'd found it in one of the sailors' sea bags. The package was slashed with Chinese characters. When the beam from a flashlight passed across the thick ink, I was able to read them. *Antler horn*. A highly prized aphrodisiac used in Chinese medicine. But, like all personal business transactions, selling it was illegal in North Korea. The powdered horn of the Siberian caribou could be legitimately obtained only as a gift from the Great Leader.

One of the Albanians was called forward. I recognized him. A slender youth with a scraggly red beard named Zarkos.

The North Korean officer barked at him in English, "Is this yours?"

Zarkos stood dumbfounded, not understanding.

Captain Skander stepped forward to translate. Once he understood, Zarkos stroked his beard nervously and shook his head. Then he launched into a long tirade I didn't understand, the gist of which, according to Mergim, was that the powder wasn't his and he didn't know how it had landed in his sea bag. The North Korean officer was unimpressed. He said something softly to his men, and two of them stepped forward and rammed the butts of their rifles into the young man's back. He shrieked in pain. The men around me surged forward, but the business ends of half-a-dozen AK-47s immediately trained on them. The sailors backed off. Zarkos struggled briefly but was overcome by a Korean, who deftly knotted his arms behind his back. With the help of two more members of the boarding party, they shoved Zarkos toward the gangplank.

Captain Skander roared in protest, but the North Korean officer ignored him.

After Zarkos had been hauled ashore, the Korean officer, puffing serenely on his cigarette, stepped in front of the sailors. "My name is Commander Koh," he said in Korean. A young Korean soldier translated. "Welcome to paradise!"

The Albanian sailors shifted their weight, hunched their shoulders, and glanced surreptitiously at one another. None of them laughed, a tribute to their long experience of living under Communist regime.

"Our country is paradise," Commander Koh continued, "because our Great Leader, the shining light of our people, hero of the Korean War, and fearless general of our invincible forces, provides us with all our wants and needs. You are fortunate to be here, in this land of plenty, even if it is for only these few short days." Commander Koh paused, took a last drag on his cigarette, and flicked it overboard. "Your ship has passed inspection. All except the man who's been taken ashore. He will be competently dealt with. The rest of you will be guests of our Great Leader tonight in the People's Hall of International Friendship. Due to the open heart and generous spirit of our Great Leader, entertainment will be provided."

Below us, Zarkos had somehow broken free from his captors. He struggled toward the gangplank, but his dash for freedom was cut short by an alert soldier's swift kick to the groin. Zarkos curled into a ball, rolling on the deck and moaning in pain. His body convulsed and he vomited onto the splintered planks.

"The entertainment begins at eighteen hundred hours," Commander Koh continued, ignoring the performance below. "You will not be late." Then he turned away, adding, *"Kutna."* Finished. The entire armed boarding party retreated down the gangplank.

Captain Skander stared helplessly as Zarkos was dragged away. When the groaning sailor disappeared from view, the captain turned and spoke to the men in a somber tone.

Later, Mergim explained that Captain Skander believed that the bastard North Koreans only wanted money. It was routine with them. The North Koreans would negotiate a deal with the Albanian shipping cooperative and the contract would be signed, but all along the North Koreans would consider the price too low and make plans to extort more money to bring the contract up to a level they thought appropriate. Captain Skander assured the crew that the shipping cooperative would come up with the money and Zarkos would be freed and back aboard before the *Star of Tirana* left Nampo.

Grumbling, the sailors returned to their duties.

Mergim agreed with Captain Skander's analysis. For one thing, the powder that the North Koreans called antler horn was too finely ground to be a natural product from Siberian caribou. "Customers want chunks," Mergim explained, "to see what they're buying. Then they grind it down themselves. That stuff in those packages is some other kind of powder, not real antler horn." Then Mergim added, "The red-star jokers want to show us who's boss. Every time I come here, they push sailors. Push too hard sometimes."

After he left, I stood at the railing alone, holding my hands in front of me to make sure the quivering had stopped. Then I went below to help with the cargo.

"She's a hot number," Mergim said, leering.

There was only one woman in the People's Hall of International Friendship who was less than geriatric, and most of the sailors were watching her each and every movement. She was a slightly portly young woman, probably in her mid- to late-twenties, with thick legs and sturdy hips. Ample breasts were pressed tightly beneath a high-necked red cotton dress and a full-length white apron, her straight black hair held in place by a matching bandanna.

I'd already noticed that the other Korean workers called her Pei. Food Worker Pei. I hadn't let on that I understood, of course. To have done so would have brought attention to myself that could have proven more than just embarrassing. It could have proven fatal.

The other workers in the People's Hall were either frail older men who scurried about in the back galley or grandmotherly types who wore the same uniform as Food Worker Pei but didn't fill them out nearly as voluptuously. We'd all been at sea a long time and none of us could take our eyes off her.

"She wears rubber gloves," Mergim told me.

"Huh?" I sipped on my hot barley tea and set it down. "Rubber gloves? What do you mean?"

"She's not wearing them now," he said.

We watched as Food Worker Pei slid a platter of stainless-steel soup bowls onto the center of a round table of Albanian sailors. Showing complete egalitarianism, the sailors were required to pick up their own bowls, along with the spoons and the wooden chopsticks and the plates piled high with brown rice. Once the platter was empty, Pei hoisted it back up, swiveled, and sashayed back to the kitchen.

"Later," Mergim continued, "when the old women are cleaning up, then she wait in front hallway."

"Waits for what?"

Mergim grinned. "For rubber glove treatment." In short strokes, he pumped his fist up and down.

My eyes widened. "You're serious."

"Of course, I'm serious." Mergim puffed on his cigarette, looking slightly offended.

I glanced at the armed men guarding the three exits. "What about the guards?"

"They smoke outside. Don't look. Probably they get money too."

The People's Hall of International Friendship was not like the fleshpots of the Orient one reads about. It was fenced in, about a hundred square yards, with an outside patio that could be used in good weather and a large dining hall where most of the sailors ate their evening meals while in port. There was no menu. Whatever was served was served, take it or leave it. The menu du jour was a dish I recognized from my years in the South, *kom-tang*. Sliced beef with onion and egg in a hot broth. No pork—the Koreans had assured us that no pig product would be used since they knew that most of the Albanian sailors were Muslims. Not that the Communist governments of either country approved of religion, but the sailors were paying for their meals, cash on the barrelhead. The strapped North Korean government, meanwhile, was greedy for money they could exchange on international markets, so they complied with the Albanian sailors' bourgeois requirements.

During my briefings in Seoul, I'd been told about the corruption among the staff of the People's Hall of International Friendship. I'd even been told that some of the bolder foreign sailors had smuggled in contraband and then paid staff members to lead them to illicit dealers who operated near the port. The North Korean authorities almost certainly knew about these things but turned a blind eye, probably because much of the profit ended up in their pockets. It was a safe bet that Commander Koh, the customs officer in charge of the Port of Nampo, kept the lion's share of the money earned not only from smuggling but also from Food Worker Pei, with her voluptuous figure and her rubber glove.

After the dinner plates had been removed, the half-dozen older women brought out glass bottles, about the size of American pop bottles, filled with a clear fluid. They plopped three bottles in the center of each table. The label said *Red Star Soju*, in both Korean and English. Immediately, the sailors started squabbling over the bottles. The Korean women shook their heads in disgust. The custom is to pour for your comrades first and then one of your comrades pours for you. Mergim, who'd been here before, offered to pour some of the clear rice liquor into my tin cup. I refused. I'd stick with barley tea.

"You don't want to get drunk?" he asked.

I nodded toward Food Worker Pei. She stood in the foyer, flirting with one of the guards.

"Ah, that first." Mergim tapped the side of his head. "Smart."

The Albanian sailors were tossing back huge shots of the fierce rice liquor, and some of them had already called for more. Once they laid Hong Kong dollars on the table, the old women delivered.

A shrill voice erupted from ancient speakers. Static screeched but the voice kept on, unperturbed, extolling the glories of the Great Leader and the paradise that was the Democratic People's Republic of Korea. The strident message was delivered first in Korean, then in English. None of the Albanian sailors paid any attention; they were more interested in guzzling soju. But then the voice stopped and strains of martial music erupted out of the old speakers like an ancient brass band. A side door opened and a troupe of men and women wearing the brown-wool, high-necked uniforms of the Korean People's Army marched in. The men wore round caps lidded like ancient jars, the women soft caps with short brims, both emblazoned with huge red stars. They goose-stepped toward the front of the hall, swinging their fists as they marched. Soon they were posing before us, raising the red-star flag of North Korea, singing, striking new poses, and finally engaging in something that could loosely be called a dance. It was more like a series of poses that they switched to on cue, creating a tableaux that illustrated events narrated by the lyrics. When one song stopped, another started without pause. As best I could gather, they were telling the tale of the Korean people's epic struggle against colonial forces—the Japanese, who had occupied Korea from 1910 to 1945; and then, to hear the North Koreans tell it, the United States from 1945 onward, in the southern portion of the country. The twentieth century had been a constant struggle for them, a series of tribulations they saw as ongoing.

The sailors glanced occasionally at the entertainment but mostly ignored it. The men in the troupe were all baby-faced and slender, their movements nothing less than effeminate. The women were strong, determined, and assertive, and their cheeks glowed crimson when they belted out tunes praising the Great Leader. Since they were fully clothed in heavy wool uniforms, including thick tunics, long skirts, and black combat boots, the sailors didn't have much to look at.

It was an hour before the performers took a break, promising to be back for more. Finally, the scratchy speakers subsided into silence.

"I want to go back to Hong Kong," Mergim said, slugging down another shot of soju.

I'd noticed some movement in the front hallway. "I'll be back," I told him, then stood up and strode past drunken and arguing Albanian sailors.

The truth was that I didn't plan to return at all, not if I could help it. I hoped Mergim would be all right. He'd been a good friend to me, and even though he'd been well paid for his efforts, I'd grown fond of him and respected the tough life he'd led. My handlers in Seoul had assured me that the Communist Albanian government would look after him. I prayed they had been telling the truth.

The guard talking to Food Worker Pei noticed my approach and turned and sauntered away. Without looking at me, she stepped into a hallway that led toward the back of the building.

I followed.

It was dark back there, but I saw her a few yards ahead, moonlight filtering though a smoke-smudged window. She was slipping something on over her right hand, something that creaked and flapped like thick rubber. Not supple like the synthetic materials made in the West. More like a flipper.

Stephanie Barron
(Jane Austen's England)
*Jane and the Twelve Days
of Christmas*
Jane and the Waterloo Map

F.H. Batacan
(Philippines)
Smaller and Smaller Circles

Quentin Bates
(Iceland)
Frozen Assets
Cold Comfort
Chilled to the Bone

James R. Benn
(World War II Europe)
Billy Boyle
The First Wave
Blood Alone
Evil for Evil
Rag & Bone
A Mortal Terror
Death's Door
A Blind Goddess
The Rest Is Silence
The White Ghost
Blue Madonna

Cara Black
(Paris, France)
Murder in the Marais
Murder in Belleville
Murder in the Sentier
Murder in the Bastille
Murder in Clichy
Murder in Montmartre
Murder on the Ile Saint-Louis
Murder in the Rue de Paradis
Murder in the Latin Quarter
Murder in the Palais Royal
Murder in Passy
Murder at the Lanterne Rouge
Murder Below Montparnasse
Murder in Pigalle
Murder on the Champ de Mars
Murder on the Quai

Lisa Brackmann
(China)
Rock Paper Tiger
Hour of the Rat
Dragon Day

(Mexico)
Getaway

Go-Between

Henry Chang
(Chinatown)
Chinatown Beat
Year of the Dog
Red Jade
Death Money

Barbara Cleverly
(England)
The Last Kashmiri Rose
Strange Images of Death
The Blood Royal
Not My Blood
A Spider in the Cup
Enter Pale Death
Diana's Altar

Gary Corby
(Ancient Greece)
The Pericles Commission
The Ionia Sanction
Sacred Games
The Marathon Conspiracy
Death Ex Machina
The Singer from Memphis

Colin Cotterill
(Laos)
The Coroner's Lunch
Thirty-Three Teeth
Disco for the Departed
Anarchy and Old Dogs
Curse of the Pogo Stick
The Merry Misogynist
Love Songs from a Shallow Grave
Slash and Burn
The Woman Who Wouldn't Die
The Six and a Half Deadly Sins
I Shot the Buddha

Garry Disher
(Australia)
The Dragon Man
Kittyhawk Down
Snapshot
Chain of Evidence
Blood Moon
Wyatt
Whispering Death
Port Vila Blues
Fallout
Hell to Pay

David Downing
(World War II Germany)
Zoo Station
Silesian Station
Stettin Station
Potsdam Station
Lehrter Station
Masaryk Station

David Downing cont.
(World War I)
Jack of Spies
One Man's Flag

Leighton Gage
(Brazil)
Blood of the Wicked
Buried Strangers
Dying Gasp
Every Bitter Thing
A Vine in the Blood
Perfect Hatred
The Ways of Evil Men

Timothy Hallinan
(Thailand)
The Fear Artist
For the Dead
The Hot Countries

(Los Angeles)
Crashed
Little Elvises
The Fame Thief
Herbie's Game
King Maybe
Fields Where They Lay

Mette Ivie Harrison
(Mormon Utah)
The Bishop's Wife
His Right Hand
For Time and All Eternities

Mick Herron
(England)
Down Cemetery Road
The Last Voice You Hear
Reconstruction
Smoke and Whispers
Why We Die
Slow Horses
Dead Lions
Nobody Walks
Real Tigers

**Lene Kaaberbøl &
Agnete Friis**
(Denmark)
The Boy in the Suitcase
Invisible Murder
Death of a Nightingale
The Considerate Killer

Heda Margolius Kovály
(1950s Prague)
Innocence

Martin Limón
(South Korea)
Jade Lady Burning
Slicky Boys